RESORT TO MURDER

TP FIELDEN

ONE PLACE. MANY STORIES

HQ
An imprint of HarperCollins*Publishers* Ltd
1 London Bridge Street
London SE1 9GF

This paperback edition 2018

1

First published in Great Britain by
HQ, an imprint of HarperCollins*Publishers* Ltd 2018

ISBN: : 978-0-00-819375-1

MIX
Paper from
responsible sources
FSC™ C007454

This book is produced from independently certified FSC™ paper
to ensure responsible forest management.

For more information visit: www.harpercollins.co.uk/green

Printed and bound in Great Britain by
CPI Group (UK) Ltd, Croydon, CR0 4YY

'Peak comfort read has been achieved'
Red

'This is a fabulously satisfying addition to the
canon of vintage crime. No wonder the author has
already been signed up to produce more adventures
starring the indefatigable Miss Dimont'
Daily Express

'Unashamedly cosy, with gentle humour and a pleasingly
eccentric amateur sleuth, this solid old-fashioned whodunit
is the first in what promises to be an entertaining series'
The Guardian

'Highly amusing'
Evening Standard

'TP Fielden is a fabulous new voice and his dignified, clever
heroine is a compelling new character. This delicious adventure
is the first of a series and I can't wait for the next one'
Wendy Holden, *Daily Mail*

'A golden age mystery'
Sunday Express

'Tremendous fun'
The Independent

'One of the best in the genre'
The Sun

TP Fielden is a biographer, broadcaster and journalist. *Resort to Murder* is the second in the Miss Dimont Mystery series.

For Laurel Wilson
Voyager, forager

ONE

Pale aquamarine and milky like the waters of Venice, the sea moved slowly inland. The shoreline at Todhempstead welcomed the advance reluctantly, giving up its golden sands inch by inch, unwilling to concede a single yard of the most beautiful beach.

The body lay some way distant from the incoming tide, but sooner or later it would have to be moved.

For the moment, though, it lay there, surrounded by a frozen tableau – a small group of people immobilised by what lay at their feet. Death changes behaviour patterns, imposes a protocol of its own.

She was young, she was blonde, and she may have been pretty but for the hideous open wound that claimed half her face. Her dress was glamorous in an inexpensive sort of way, arranged around her decorously enough. It was still dry, a sure indicator it had not been here too long.

Frank Topham looked down with some discomfort. The long shallow beach had at its furthest end a high embankment, surely too far away for the victim to have fallen from and landed here. The injuries which claimed her life were too severe – that much was evident – for her to have walked or crawled to her final resting place, yet there were no footprints around the body apart from those made sparingly by the small group of eyewitnesses.

Nor was there any blood.

These contradictions jarred Inspector Topham's usually tranquil state of mind, but were swept aside for the moment as he looked down on the wretched girl.

'Twenty, I should say,' he murmured to the two faceless acolytes standing at his shoulder.

'No shoes,' said one.

'No handbag,' replied Topham.

The other lit a cigarette and looked up at the sky. He didn't seem terribly interested.

Whatever passed next between these custodians of the peace was drowned by the arrival of the up train from Exbridge, a billowing, grunting triumph of the steam engineer's art, slowing as it made its long approach into Todhempstead Spa station.

'Better get her away,' Topham said to the police doctor. The man on his knees looked over his shoulder at the advancing waves and nodded.

'No evidence,' said Topham wretchedly. 'No clues. We're moving the body and there's no clues.'

Taking his cue, the second man moved vaguely away and came back. 'Tizer bottle.'

'Is the label wet?' asked Topham without even looking at it.

'Yer.'

'Chuck it,' snapped the inspector. 'No use to us.'

He moved swiftly off to the slipway where the car was parked, not wanting the men to see his face. There had been too many deaths back in the War, but wasn't that why he had fought? So there wouldn't be any more? It was a man's job to die, not a woman's.

For a moment he turned to look back at the scene below. The dead body claimed his focus, but, beyond, it was as if nobody cared that the world had lost a soul this morning. In the distance two sand-yachts raced each other across the broad beach, and overhead an ancient biplane trailed a long banner flapping from its tail. Smith's Crisps, according to its message, gave you a wholesome happy holiday.

Far in the distance he could see a solitary female figure, dressed in rainbow colours, standing perfectly still and looking out to sea as if what it had to offer was somehow more interesting than a dead body. It was as if nobody cared.

Inspector Topham got in the car and pulled out on to the empty road. He reached Todhempstead Spa station in a matter of minutes, but already the Riviera Express was pulling out, heading on towards Exeter at a slow roll – huffing, grinding, thumping, clanging. He could get it stopped at Newton Abbot to check if there was evidence on the front buffers of contact with human flesh from the downward journey, to quiz the train guard and the driver. But they'd all be back again this afternoon on the return trip, and he doubted, given the distance of the body from the railway embankment, that this was a rail fatality. Though, with death, you could never be sure about anything.

As he drove back to the Sands, his eyes lifted for a moment from the road ahead. It was already mid-June and the lanes running parallel to the beach were bursting with joy at summer's arrival. Though the bluebells and primroses had retreated, the hedgerows were noisy with young blackbirds testing their beautiful voices, while, beneath, newly arrived wild roses and cow parsley reached out, begging to be noticed.

How, asked the policeman, could anyone wish a young girl dead at this season, when hope is in the air and the breeze is scented with promise? His years in the desert, those arid wastes of death, might be long behind but still they cast their shadow. He drove down the slipway on to the beach, got slowly out, and nodded to his men.

'Body away,' said one.

'Come on then.'

Topham removed his hat and got back in the car. His square head, doughty and in its own way distinguished, grazed the ceiling because of his ramrod-straight back. Despite the rising heat he still wore the raincoat he'd donned in the early morning when he got the call. He'd been too distracted by what he'd seen to take it off.

Too honest a man, too upright, perhaps too regimented in his thinking to see life the way criminals do, Frank Topham was both the very best of British policing and, some might argue, the worst. There was a dead woman on the beach, but if it was murder – if – the culprit might never be caught. No clues, no arrest.

No hope of an arrest.

The car approached Temple Regis, the prettiest town in the whole of Devon, and, as the inspector drove up Cable Street and over Tuppenny Row, his eyes took solace in the elegant terrace of Regency cottages whose pink brickwork blushed in the summer sunshine. Further down the hill he could hear the clanking arrival of the 10.30 from Paddington, its sooty steamy clouds shooting upwards from Regis Junction station. Life was carrying on as if nothing had happened.

Topham entered the police station at his regulation quick-march. The front office was empty apart from the desk sergeant.

'Frank.'

'Bert.'

'Anything for the book?' The sergeant had his pen poised.

Topham hesitated. 'Accidental. Woman on T'emstead Beach.'

The other man gazed shrewdly at him. 'You sure? Accidental?'

Topham returned his gaze evenly. 'Accidental.' He tried to make it sound as though he believed it.

'Only I got a reporter in the interview room. Saying murder.'

'Reporter?' barked Topham nastily. 'Saying murder? Not – not that Miss Dimont?'

'Nah,' said Sergeant Gull. 'This 'un's new. A kid.'

Topham's features turned to granite at the mention of the press. Though Temple Regis boasted only one newspaper, it somehow managed to cause a disproportionate amount of grief to those police officers seeking to uphold the law. Questions, questions – always questions, whether it was a cycling without lights case or that unpleasant business with the curate of St Cuthbert's. As for Miss Dimont . . .

To Frank Topham's mind – and in the opinion of many other Temple Regents too – the local rag was there to report the facts, not to ask questions. So often the stories they printed showed a side to the town which did little to enhance its reputation. What good did it do to make headlines out of the goings-on the Magistrates' Court? Or ask questions about poorly paid council officials who enjoyed elaborate and expensive holidays?

And how they got on to things so quickly, he never knew. What was this reporter doing asking questions about a murder? It was only a couple of hours ago he himself had clapped eyes on the corpse – how had word spread so fast?

'So,' said Sergeant Gull, picking up his pencil and scratching his ear with it, 'the book, Frank. Murder or accidental?'

'Like I said,' snarled his superior officer, and strode into the interview room.

*

You can be the greatest reporter in the world but you are no reporter at all if people don't tell you things. A dead body on the beach is all very well but if you're out shopping, how are you supposed to know?

In fact Miss Judy Dimont, ferocious defender of free speech, champion of the truth and the thorn in the side of poor Inspector Topham, hardly looked like Temple Regis' ace newspaperwoman this afternoon. As she ordered a pound of apples in the Home and Colonial Stores in Fore Street she might easily be mistaken for a librarian on her tea break: the sensible shoes, the well-worn raincoat and the raffia handbag made it clear that here was a no-nonsense, serious person who had just enough time to stock up on the essentials before heading home to a good book.

'One and sixpence, thank you, miss.'

The reporter reached for her purse, smiled up at the young shop assistant, and suddenly she looked anything but ordinary. Her wonderfully erratic corkscrew hair fell back from her face and her sage-grey eyes peeped over the top of her spectacles, which had slithered down her convex nose. The smile itself was joyous and radiant – the sort of smile that offers hope and comfort in a troubled world.

'Tea?'

'Not today thank you, Victor.' She didn't like to say she preferred to buy her tea at Lipton's round the corner. 'I think I'll just quickly go over and get some fish.'

'Ah yes.' The assistant nodded knowledgeably. 'Mulligatawny.'

This was how it was in Temple Regis. People knew the name of your cat and would ask after his health. They knew you bought your tea at Lipton's and only gently tried to persuade you to purchase their own brand. They delivered the groceries by bicycle to your door and left a little extra gift in the cardboard box knowing the pleasure it would bring.

'I tried that ginger marmalade,' said Miss Dimont, with perfect timing. 'Delicious! In fact it's all gone. May I buy some if you have any left?'

The assistant in his long white apron hastened away and, as she wandered over to the marble-topped fish counter, she marvelled again at the interlocking cogwheels which made up Temple Regis' small population. Over by the coffee counter the odd little lady from the hairdresser's was deep in conversation with the secretary of the Mothers' Union in that old toque hat she always wore, winter and summer. Both were looking out of the window at a pair of dray horses from Gardner's brewery, their brasses glinting in the late sunlight as they plodded massively by.

They'd all meet again at the Church Fete on Saturday, bringing fresh news of their doings to share and deliberate upon. While the rest of Britain struggled with its post-war identity crisis – move forward to the brave new world? Or go back to the comfortable past? – life in Devon's prettiest town found its stability in the little things of here and now.

'Do you have any cods' heads? If not, some coley? And a kipper for me, please,' just in case anybody should think she was reduced to making fish soup for herself, delicious though that would be!

It had been a perplexing day, and the circular rhythms of the Home and Colonial had a way of putting everything back in perspective. The Magistrates' Court, the one fixed point in her week which always guaranteed to provide a selection of golden nuggets for the front page of the *Riviera Express*, had failed her – and badly. Quite a lot of time today had been taken up with the elaborate appointment of a new Chairman of the Bench, and that had been followed by a dreary case involving the manager of the Midland Bank and a missing cheque.

It shouldn't have come to court – everyone has the occasional lapse! – and under the previous chairman the case would have been thrown out. But the Hon. Mrs Marchbank was no longer with us, her recent misdeeds having taken her to a greater judge, and in her place was the pettifogging Colonel de Saumarez, distinguished enough in his tweed suit but lacking in grey matter.

'Anything else, miss?'

'That's all, thank you.'

'Put on your account?'

'Yes please.'

'Young Walter will have it round to your door first thing.'

'I'll take the fish with me, if I may.'

The world is a terrible place, thought Miss Dimont, as she emerged into the early evening sunlight, what with the Atom Bomb and the Suez Crisis, but not here. She waved to Lovely Mary, the proprietress of the Signal Box Café, who was coming out of Lipton's with a wide smile on her lips – how aptly she was named!

'All well, Judy?'

'Couldn't be better, Mary. Early start tomorrow though, off before dawn. A life on the ocean wave, tra-la!"

'See you soon, then, dear. Safe journey, wherever you'm goin'.'

Miss Dimont walked down to the seafront for one last look at the waves. After the kipper, she would sit with Mulligatawny on her lap and think about the bank manager and the missing cheque. It had been a long day in court and she needed a quiet moment to think how best the story could be written up.

*

Things were less tranquil back at her place of work, the *Riviera Express*.

'What about this murder?' roared John Ross, the red-faced chief sub-editor. It was the end of the day, the traditional time for losing his temper. He stalked down the office to the reporters' desks. 'Who's on it? What's happening?'

Betty Featherstone clacked smartly over from the picture desk in her high heels. She was looking particularly radiant today though the hair bleach hadn't worked quite so well this time, and her choice of lipstick was, as usual, at odds with the shade of her home-made dress. The way she carried a notebook, though, had a certain attraction to the older man.

Betty was the *Express*'s number two reporter though you wouldn't know that if you read the paper – her name appeared over more stories, and in larger print, than Judy Dimont's ever did, but that was less to do with her journalistic skills than with the fact that the editor liked the way she did what she was told.

You could never say that about Miss Dimont.

'Who's covering the murder?' demanded Ross heatedly.

'The new boy,' sighed Betty.

The way she said it carried a wealth of meaning in an office that was accustomed to the constant stream of new talent washing through its revolving doors – in, and then out again. Either they were so good they were snapped up by livelier papers, or else they were useless and posted to a district office, never to be seen again.

'Another rookie?' snapped Ross, the venom in his voice sufficient to quell a native uprising. 'When did *he* arrive?'

'This morning,' said Betty. She'd yet to try out her charms on the newcomer, but as ever she was willing to give it a try – he looked rather sweet, though of course those nasty photographers would be calling her a cradle-snatcher again.

'Where's your Townswomen's Guild story?' growled Ross, for Betty was not his cup of tea and her bouncy figure left him unmoved.

'Here you are,' she trilled, handing over three half-sheets of copy paper bearing all the hallmarks of an afternoon's attention to the nail-varnish bottle.

'A stimulating talk was given by Miss A. de Mauny at Temple Regis TWG on Tuesday,' it began, one might almost say deliberately masking the joys ahead.

'Titled Lady Rhondda and the Six Point Group it gave a fascinating account of the post-war women's movement, taking in the . . .'

She could see Ross's eyes glaze over as he read on. In truth, she'd found it difficult herself to stay awake during the earnest but dense peroration by the town's only clock-mender. There weren't too many jokes in her talk.

'For . . . pity's . . . sake . . .' groaned Ross, a man ever-hungry for sensation. 'We're short on space this week. The Six Point Group? Naaaah!'

'Husbands of TWG members advertise extensively in this newspaper,' said Betty, primly parroting the words of her editor when she'd protested at having to attend the dreary event.

'I'll have to cut it.'

'Do what you like,' said Betty. Her mind was already on the evening ahead. A drink perhaps with that new reporter, the start of something new?

And maybe, this time, it could be for ever?

TWO

Miss Dimont sat in the public bar of the Old Jawbones, a beaker of rum on the stool in front of her, surrounded by a group of men – bulky, muscular, unshaven and with the occasional missing tooth – who roared their approval as she raised the glass to her lips and drank.

It was 10 o'clock in the morning.

This scene of depravity had an explanation but not one that could ever find the approval of her editor, the fastidious Rudyard Rhys. A stickler for decorum among his staff, he would shudder at the thought of his chief reporter behaving in so abandoned a fashion. In a filthy old fishermen's pub! At ten o'clock in the morning!

Miss Dimont didn't care. She shot a waspish remark at her fellow-drinkers and they burst once more into laughter. One more swig of rum and then, picking up her notebook, she moved slowly and almost steadily towards the door.

'Whoops-a-daisy, Miss Dimmum!'

'Don't you fall down now, Miss Dimmalum!'

'And doan fergit y'r turbot!'

The Jawbones was unused to entertaining female company at this hour, reserving its best seats for the men who filled their nets quickly and sneaked back into harbour for a quick one before breakfast. But there she was, a beauty in a haphazard sort of way, with her grey eyes, convex nose, beautiful smile and unmanageable corkscrew curls. The fishermen liked what they saw.

Miss Dimont emerged onto the street and took a deep breath of the fishy, salty air. Across the quay lay the rusty beaten-up old fishing vessel which had so recently put her life in peril. The memory made her sit down quite sharply.

'Awright, missus?' A handsome old seadog in faded blue overalls and battered cap came over and settled himself next to her.

His countenance was like a road map, all lines and detours, and his hands were ingrained with dirt. But he had charm – not like those men she encountered when she arrived before dawn to join the *Lass O'Doune*. She thought she'd never met such a band of brigands, strangers to the scrubbing brush and razor alike, unfamiliar with the finer points of etiquette.

By the end of her treacherous journey, though, they had acquired other attributes – they had become handsome. They had become warm, and kind. And they were undoubtedly heroes.

But it had not started well. 'We were tol' to expect a reporter,' said the captain, Cran Conybeer, eyeing her with disfavour in the predawn darkness.

'I *am* a reporter,' snapped Miss Dimont, pushing her spectacles up her rain-spattered nose and standing ever so slightly up on her toes.

Captain Conybeer wasn't listening. 'We don't 'ave *wimmin* aboard,' he said firmly. 'Send a reporter an' we'll take 'un out.'

Miss Dimont had experienced worse rebuffs. 'You've just won the Small Trawler of the Year Award,' she said, her words almost lost by the screeching of the davits as they hauled the nets up. 'You're the first Devon crew ever to win it. My newspaper has reserved two whole pages to celebrate your courage and skill, to tell Temple Regis how brilliant you are and – just as important,

I'd have thought – to let your competitors know how much better you are at the job than they are.'

This last point hit home, but even so the captain remained reluctant.

'Yers but . . .'

'The article has to be written by the end of the day if it's to get into next week's newspaper. It's 4.30 in the morning and there is no other reporter available to come with you on this trip.'

'We doan allow *wimmin*.'

Miss Dimont slowly pushed back her hair and looked up into the captain's wrinkled eyes, sparkling in the gas lamp which illuminated the ship's bridge.

'Perhaps this will help,' she added quietly. 'I was an officer in the Royal Navy – the Wrens, you would call it. I served my country and I served the sea.'

This last bit was not strictly accurate but it was enough for the wavering Conybeer.

'Come on then, overalls on, we'm late as 'tis.'

And so, before the dawn light rose, the *Lass O'Doune* set out down the estuary and straight into a force nine gale – unseasonable in June, but that is the sea. The next four hours were a terrifying combination of chaos and noise, of unforgiving waves crashing across the decks and the ocean rampageously seeking the lives of those who sought to draw nourishment from it. Clad, pointlessly, in hooded oilskins – the sea had a way of finding its way underneath the stoutest protection within minutes – the men fought nature valiantly as they reeled in the nets and deposited their wriggling silvery spoils on the deck.

Fearless under fire, thought Miss Dimont, as she clung uncertainly to a rail inside the bridge – like soldiers in battle. Then, shouting to the captain, she weaved her way towards the deck so she could experience at first hand what his men had to do to make their living.

With a lifeline attached to her waist, she stepped out into the roaring, rushing hell and hauled on the nets alongside the other men. The job was not difficult, she discovered, it just required nerve and strength.

Arranged as a special demonstration for the press, the voyage out into the ocean lasted a mere three hours, though to Miss Dimont it seemed like four days. No wonder she'd found herself in the snug of the Old Jawbones with a jigger of rum in front of her!

And now, the battle done, she sat outside on a bench taking in the sun while Old Jacky shared his thoughts with her.

'Just goin' on me 'olidays,' he was saying.

'Oh,' said Miss Dimont, rallying. 'Anywhere nice?'

'Down 'oo Spain,' said Jacky. 'See if I can get some deckhand work.'

'You mean – you fish all year, then when you go on holiday . . . you *fish*?'

The wrinkled old sailor smiled at her and shifted his cap.

''Bout right.'

Just then Cran Conybeer came out of the Jawbones and saw his most recent crew member marooned on her bench.

'Lan'lubber,' he said, laughing. 'You carn walk, can you?'

'Of course I can,' said Miss Dimont in her peppery voice, rising unsteadily to her feet.

'You come along a me,' said the captain, hoisting Miss Dimont up gently and putting his arm through hers. 'You come along a me, I'll make sure you're safe.'

*

At the landward end of the pier at Temple Regis stood the Pavilion Theatre, a crumbling structure with precious little life left in it whichever way you looked at it. If there was one thing

14

the town cried out for it was a cultural centre where visitors could congregate at the end of an exhausting day's holidaymaking to be entertained and where locals, too, could pick up some crumbs of artistic comfort at the bookends of the season. This was not it.

For years the Pavilion had been run – first successfully, then gradually less so – by Raymond Cattermole, a former actor. Occasionally, a star from London would descend for a short season in support of their old friend, but Cattermole's home-grown fare was proving less appetising as the years went by. He looked for comfort to his current squeeze, Geraldine Phipps, and sometimes beyond – for after a lifetime of ups and downs on the stage the old Gaiety Girl would rather have a glass of gin than a spot of pillow talk. And so, after a particularly disastrous performance of his one-man show *My West End Life*, the actor-manager came to the conclusion there was no point in sharing his genius with the oafs in the one-and-thruppennies, and for some days now his doors had been shut.

This afternoon, however, a side door creaked open a crack and from within came a rasping but cultured voice.

'Come in, dear. Mind the rubbish.'

The young man mooched down the long corridor towards the large back room which, though lacking home comforts, had at least the consolation of a bottle of Plymouth gin.

Mrs Phipps, who had commandeered the only glass, swilled out a mug under the cold tap and placed it before her guest. 'Pour away to your heart's content. He left a crate of it behind.'

Her guest made himself a cup of tea.

'So tell me again, dear, what are they called?'

'Danny Trouble. And The Urge.'

The ancient Mrs Phipps blenched. 'Are you sure?' She lit a Navy Cut and her hands shook slightly as she did so.

'They're cool,' said her grandson. 'Just what's needed in a dead-and-alive hole like this.'

'You know,' said Mrs Phipps sourly – the gin had not yet mellowed the edges – 'I learned what entertainment was more than half a century ago, but from what you tell me these young men are far from entertaining, just rude. I've seen their sort on TV – no finesse, no culture, no style. They may look sweet onstage in their matching suits and their shiny guitars but from the way they curl their lips and waggle about I'd say they neither seek the adulation of their audience, nor do they even try to charm them.'

'That's the point!' exclaimed Gavin Armstrong. 'It's the love-'em-and-leave-'em principle. The girls adore it.'

Mrs Phipps took refuge in the gin.

'You should see them – they're positively electric! Onstage it's like November the Fifth and the 1812 Overture all rolled into one.'

'There's another thing,' said Mrs Phipps sharply, 'the electricity. They all have these electric guitars, don't they? That must use up an awful lot of juice. What I need to do here now Ray's hopped it is get costs down and . . .'

'What you need is The Urge, Granny.'

'What I *need*, Gavin,' continued Mrs Phipps, who in her time had experienced more urges than her grandson could possibly imagine, 'what I need to do is keep this theatre open – and to do that I've got to find an act which is cheap and a guaranteed box-office success. Not something that's going to eat up the profits with sky-high electric bills and frighten the locals away at the same time.'

'They won't need all those spotlights you've got. They don't need a stage set. They don't need make-up – though one or two could do to cover up their spots, I'll admit – and the last thing they need is people ushering the punters into their seats. In fact the fans'd probably tear out the seats if they did.'

'Disgusting,' spat Mrs Phipps, pouring herself another. 'Nothing but louts and Teddy boys. Don't you see what people want on a nice night out? They want glamour, they want to be carried away on wings of song.'

'No they don't, Gran. These days what they want is deafening noise.'

Mrs Phipps shuddered. 'To think we fought our way through two wars to end up like this,' she said. 'Once upon a time and not so long ago, gentlemen would wait at the stage door of the Adelphi with a gardenia, a bottle of perfume and a taxi waiting to whisk me off to supper at the Café Royal.'

'Darling thing,' sighed Gavin, 'the days of the Gaiety Girl are long gone. The war's been over for an age, and there's a whole new generation that wants something different, something original. Danny Trouble and The Urge are it.'

'They're noisy and uncouth,' said Mrs Phipps, who had no idea whether they were or not.

'They're definitely that all right,' said Gavin, with pride.

'But what will the townsfolk say? The council? The press?'

'Ah,' said Gavin, a wily smile on his lips, 'you can't fail with the press. They'll have to write about them, one way or the other. That's guaranteed! Either it'll be "Disgrace to Temple Regis" or else "Britain's Top Beat Group Come to Town", and hopefully both. The theatre will be full. Every night.'

'No,' said Mrs Phipps, exhaling a hefty cloud of nicotine, 'no, Gavin. It really won't do.'

'It's the new religion!'

'Then you're a poor missionary, and I am no convert,' said Mrs Phipps, absently peering into her glass.

'Look,' said Gavin, 'we both have an opportunity here, Granny. Raymond's scarpered and you don't know when or if he'll be back . . .'

'Oh, he'll be back,' said Mrs Phipps, 'he can't live without me.'

'You didn't say that last time he ran off with Suki Raffray.'

'Don't mention that Jezebel's name!' screeched Mrs Phipps. It had been an ugly business.

'You don't know when or if he'll be back,' repeated Gavin, seizing his moment. 'The theatre has to open for the new season next week – what are you planning to put on? I've got Danny and the lads on a contract until the end of the year, but that's all. They've just had their first Number One and pretty soon some manager will come along who knows what they're doing, and that'll be curtains for me.

'Bringing them down here, they'll be the first beat group ever to do a summer residency in a British seaside resort. That'll give them headlines, it'll give Temple Regis headlines, and people will come flocking to this . . .' he paused, searching sarcastically for the word '. . . er, *delightful* town.'

'Plus,' he added ingratiatingly. 'you can pay them less than you paid Alma Cogan last year. They'd have a regular income, and I'd get paid.'

Mrs Phipps looked across at her grandson and shook her head. 'You father had such hopes for you, Gavin. The Brigade . . . maybe the Foreign Office afterwards . . .' She sighed. 'But since you ask, what I had in mind was Sidney Torch and his Light Orchestra. I know Sidney, and he'd come down here for me in an instant, I feel sure of that. They have *such* beguiling music, darling, just the sort of thing to attract the traditional holidaymaker. He came down here once before, years ago, and you know, they even got up in the aisles and danced!'

'With Danny Trouble they'll never sit down,' said Gavin tartly. 'What this place desperately needs is something for the younger crowd.

'You know, Granny' he went on, 'this is 1959 – people don't want to dance cheek to cheek any more, they want rock and roll!'

'I suppose you may be right,' conceded his grandmother, who was becoming alarmed at the prospect of having to confess to Temple Regis that the Pavilion Theatre would remain dark through the summer season. 'We do need something new. People got fed up with Arthur doing his *West End Life* – that's why he ran away, you know. They got up and started catcalling.'

'It wasn't Suki Raffray, then? Why he ran away?'

'IT WAS NOT SUKI RAFFRAY!' shouted Mrs Phipps. 'Don't mention that name again!'

'Then you agree, Granny? That Danny and the boys can come for the six-week season?'

'What else can I do?' said Mrs Phipps, shaking her head so hard her fine silvery hair escaped its pinnings. 'I have no alternative.'

'You won't regret it, Gran.'

Mrs Phipps shuddered as she reached again for Plymouth's most famous export.

'I feel as though someone just walked over my grave,' she said.

THREE

The atmosphere in the editor's office at the *Riviera Express* was as it always was – dusty – but the moment the newspaper's chief reporter walked in it got dustier.

Judy Dimont was everything an editor could wish for – a brilliant mind, a dazzling shorthand note and charm enough to entice whole flocks from the trees. Yet, as Rudyard Rhys raised his eyes from the task in hand, a particularly recalcitrant briar pipe, he could see none of this. Before him stood a striking woman of indeterminate age dressed vaguely in a macintosh with its belt pulled tight at the waist, and with a waft of corkscrew curls slipping joyously from the restraints of a silk scarf. A faint scent of rum entered the room with her.

'Got the fishermen,' said Judy Dimont, a trifle dreamily. 'What extraordinary men they are! Why, do you know . . .'

'Rr . . . rrrr,' growled her editor, whether by way of approval or dissent it was hard to tell, but enough to douse Miss Dimont's tribute to those in peril on the sea.

Rhys returned to his pipe. 'There was a murder while you were out on your jolly boating trip,' he said, a nasty edge to his voice. 'As my chief reporter I should have liked you there.'

'There was a force nine out beyond the headland,' said Miss

Dimont, not a little proud of her early morning exploits. 'Rather difficult to spot a murder from there. Anyway, who . . .'

'Had to send *him*,' said Rhys, nodding towards a corner of the room. A young man half rose from his seat and, with a slight smile, gently inclined his head. In a second the chief reporter had it summed up – wet-behind-the-ears recruit, probably the son of a friend of the managing director, going to be useless, a dead weight, another failed experiment in attracting the nation's young talent into local journalism.

Miss Dimont was not without prejudice but in general she was kind. She did not feel kind this morning.

'Well then, let *him* write it up,' she said, eyeing not without prejudice the item which hung round his neck and which looked suspiciously like an old school tie. 'I've got this feature to write and then, if it's OK with you, Mr Rhys, I'm going home. I was up at three this morning to catch the tide.'

For a man who once had worn Royal Navy uniform himself, Rhys showed a surprising lack of interest over the vicissitudes of the ocean. 'Give him a hand,' he ordered, and dismissed them both with the swish of a damp page-proof.

Pushing up the spectacles which adorned her glorious nose, Miss Dimont stepped, with an audible sigh, out into the corridor. The last thing she wanted – another trainee reporter dumped on her!

'Have you found yourself a desk?' she inquired shortly, not even bothering to look over her shoulder as she strode into the newsroom.

'They . . . they told me to sit opposite you,' said the young man. 'The other lady, er . . .'

'Betty.'

'Yes, Betty's . . . um . . . I think she's . . . er, not quite sure. I think she's been sent elsewhere.' The words seemed hesitant but he appeared pretty self-assured. 'Newbury something.'

'Newton Abbot?' she said.

'That's about the size of it,' said the young man. 'She didn't seem too happy.'

This did not please Miss Dimont one bit. Betty Featherstone was effectively her number two and, though uninspired, was a useful reporter who did her share of filling the copious news pages which made up the weekly digest of events in Devon's prettiest town. Having her dispatched to the district office was a blow. It would increase the chief reporter's workload and, at the same time, require her to shepherd this innocent lamb through his first weeks on the paper until he got the hang of it.

Or disappeared.

The young man sat down opposite her. 'Erm, we haven't been introduced. Valentine is the name.'

'Judy Dimont, Mr Valentine. Welcome to the *Riviera Express*.' The words didn't have quite the cheery ring they might, but then she was not used to rum for breakfast. She felt tired and wanted to go home to Mulligatawny.

'Er, Valentine's the first name,' the boy said.

'Surname?'

'Waterford.'

'Well, *that'll* look pretty as a front-page byline,' she said, not entirely kindly. 'Raise the tone a bit.'

'I was thinking of shortening it to Ford. It's a bit of a mouthful,' he said apologetically.

'Well, you won't need to do anything with it if you don't write up your murder,' said Miss Dimont crisply. 'No story, no byline. You *do* know what a byline is?'

'Window dressing,' said Waterford. 'For the reporter, it's compensation for not being paid properly. A bun to the starving bear.'

His words caused Miss Dimont to look at him again. Could, for once, the management have recruited some young cannon fodder who actually had a few brains?

'Makes the page look nice, makes the reading public think they know who wrote the story,' he went on, smiling. 'A byline makes everybody happy.'

Good Lord, thought Miss Dimont, her head clearing rapidly. He's what, twenty-two? Obviously just finished National Service. How come he knows so much about journalism?

'How come you seem to know so much about . . .'

'Uncle in the business,' said Valentine, looking with unease at the large Remington Standard typewriter in front of him. He carefully folded a sheet of copy paper into the machine, took out a brand-new notebook and started to tap. Very slowly.

Obviously he does not need my help, thought Miss Dimont, and set about her own preparations to bring to life the world of Cran Conybeer and his lion-hearted friends.

Just then Betty Featherstone wafted by, attracted by the mop of tousled hair atop Valentine Waterford's handsome young head. Despite her marching orders she was evidently in no hurry to catch the bus to Newton Abbot.

It was a sight to behold when Miss Dimont got to work. She hunched over her Quiet-Riter and the words just flowed from her flying fingers. Her corkscrew hair wobbled from side to side, her right hand turned the pages of the notebook while the left continued to tap away, and her lovely features sometimes pinched into an unattractive scowl when she found herself momentarily lost for a word or phrase. But as the paper in her typewriter smoothly ratcheted up, line by line, the story of the extraordinary events of her pre-dawn foray in the English Channel came gracefully to life.

'. . . single?' Betty was saying, adjusting the broad belt which held in her billowing skirt – how lovely he looked with his slim figure, borrowed suit and polished shoes! She was not one to waste time on irrelevancies.

'Been in the Army,' said the young man, 'not much time for

all that.' It was clear to Miss Dimont, though not to Betty, that this was not the moment to turn on her headlights.

'Can I help?' Judy interrupted, nodding Betty away.

'Matter of nomenclature,' said Valentine.

'What's the difficulty?'

'It's supposed to be a murder. But it's an accidental death. Though it *could* be a murder,' he said. He went on to explain his arrival at Temple Regis Police Station, his briefing by the ever-garrulous Sergeant Gull (murder) followed by a second briefing by the taciturn Topham (accidental).

'Which do I call it? Murder? Or accidental?'

'Well, just wait a minute now,' said Miss Dimont, suddenly very interested. 'Who is it who's supposed to have been murdered?' She had, after all, some experience in such matters.

'Young lady, possibly early twenties. Bad head injuries, found in the middle of a big wide beach.'

This sounded very odd.

'Mystery death,' ordered Miss Dimont crisply. 'If even the police can't find the word for it, then it's a mystery. Tell me more.'

Waterford described the discovery of the body, details kindly supplied by Sergeant Gull. Then he reported the deliberate down-playing by Inspector Topham: 'Rather angry about it he was, actually. Reminded me of my sergeant-major.'

'He *was* a sergeant-major.'

'That would explain it.'

'When's the inquest?'

'Inquest?'

He's rather sweet, thought Miss Dimont, but he knows nothing. 'Anything unusual about a death,' she explained, 'there's a post-mortem. The coroner opens a public investigation into the circs.'

'Excellent. There's a lot to learn, isn't there? And my journalism training course doesn't start until I've been here three months.'

So you're going to be a dead weight until then, thought Miss Dimont. 'You know how to make a cup of tea?'

'Er, yes.'

'Jolly good,' she said briskly. The boy wonder took the hint and slid away.

Miss Dimont paused for a moment to consider what she'd just been told. Though she made little of it, she was no stranger to death; and since her arrival in Temple Regis she'd figured significantly in the detection of a number of serious crimes. Within recent memory there was the case of Mrs Marchbank, the magistrate, who had managed to do away with her cousin in the most ingenious fashion. The fact that the police couldn't make up their minds whether this new case was murder or accidental set the alarm bells ringing, but first she must finish the job in hand.

It took less than an hour to turn out six hundred words on the *Lass O'Doune*'s battles against nature, her triumphant victory in bringing food to the mouths of the nation, and the safe return from tumultuous seas. Miss Dimont made no mention of her own part in hauling in the rough and seething nets, her drenching by the ocean deep, the souvenir piece of turbot which she and Mulligatawny would share tonight – she did not believe in writing about herself.

Betty had no such qualms: she was always ready to illustrate her stories with a photograph or two of her digging a hole, baking a cake, riding a bicycle or anything else the photographer demanded. Actually she had one of those faces which looked nicer in photographs than in real life, and her editor often took advantage of her thirst for self-publicity. By comparison Judy Dimont was disinclined to make a display of herself: her elusive beauty was more difficult to capture, though Terry Eagleton, the chief photographer, had taken some gorgeous portraits of her only recently.

While she'd been finishing the fishermen piece, Valentine

Waterford was having his copy rewritten by the chief sub-editor. He returned to discover Miss Dimont's tea cold and untouched.

'Perhaps a cup of coffee instead?' he asked anxiously. 'I'll get the hang of it, I expect.'

'Well,' said Miss Dimont, 'you better had. We all take turns to make the tea and,' she added pointedly, 'some people round here are quite fussy.'

'I've decided on Ford,' he replied, looking again as all young reporters do at his first story in print, and marvelling. 'It fits into a column better.'

'Good idea. Now come and tell me more about this dead body.'

*

The drab, bare hall behind St Margaret's Church had never seen anything like it. Where normally baize-topped card tables were laid out for the Mothers' Union weekly whist drive there were racks of clothes and a number of long mirrors. The hooks containing the choir's cassocks and surplices had been cleared, in their place a selection of skimpy bathing costumes. Hat boxes littered the floor, the smell of face powder filled the air, and a number of young ladies in various states of undress could be seen bad-temperedly foraging for clothing, hairpins and inspiration.

'Season gets earlier and earlier,' said one grumpily. 'Ain't going down well with my Fred.'

'Lend us your Mum rolette, dear.'

'Certimly not. That's personal.'

'Oh go on, Molly, I always pong otherwise. Nerves, you know.'

'Shouldn't have nerves, the length of time you've been at this malarkey.'

They'd all been at it too long, if truth be told. But fame is a drug, and the acquisition of fame just as addictive. You had to look – and smell – your best at all times.

Molly Churchstow was looking a little long in the tooth today. Her life had become a triumph of hope over experience, for the longed-for crown which came with the title *Queen of the English Riviera* continued to elude her. But she remained determined: so determined, in fact, that her Fred had given up hope of ever marrying her, for the rules clearly stated that a beauty pageant contestant must be single. Even the merest glimpse of an engagement ring meant she would be jettisoned in the early rounds, once the maximum publicity of her enforced departure had been squeezed out of the local newspapers. Beauty queens must forever be single and available to their adoring public!

Molly hoped to be this year's Riviera queen, having previously triumphed in the hotly-contested title fights for Miss Dawlish, Miss Teignmouth, and Miss Dartmouth, but it had been a long struggle with diminishing rewards. It would unkind to suggest that over the years she'd become a prisoner of her ambition – for Molly had a bee in her bonnet about being loved, being admired, and becoming famous.

Most of the girls in the grey-painted hall had a similar tale to tell. Each had tasted the mixed blessing of being a beauty queen: you got your photograph in the paper, people stopped you in the street for your autograph, you got a better class of boyfriend, usually with a car, and your love life was destined always to be a disaster.

But oh the thrill! The parades with mounted police, the brass bands, the motorcades through the town! The popping flashbulbs and your name in the papers!

'Oh Lord, my corns,' said Eve Berry, and sat down heavily. 'How long are Hannaford's giving you off? Or are you havin' to do overtime to make up for the days off?'

'Stocktaking in the basement with that lecher Mr French. It's never very pleasant. You?'

Molly did not reply to this but hissed back, 'Watch out, here comes The Slug.'

Looking not unlike like his nickname, Cyril Normandy elbowed his way through a dozen girls, his heavy feet crushing girdles, make-up bags, lipsticks and anything else which had fallen to the floor in the melee. Another man of his age and girth might dream and dream of sharing a room so filled with temptation, but not Normandy. Greed was etched into every line on his fat face and he looked neither to left nor right.

'Stuff something into that top, Dartmouth,' he said roughly to Molly. 'You're flat as a pancake.'

Molly was used to this.

'As for you Exmouth,' he said, referring to Eve's title – he never used Christian names – 'those shoes!'

'You'll have to let me have some on tick,' said Eve, unsurprised by this attack on her battered high heels. 'Can't afford a new pair.'

The fat man looked at her meanly. 'Borrow some,' he snapped. 'And get a move on, you're due out there in two minutes.'

Altogether twenty-one girls were entered in this eliminating heat. Up for grabs was not only the Riviera queen title, but also the chance to go through to the next round of Miss Great Britain. And, after that, Miss World! Here in the church hall in Temple Regis there was a lot at stake, even if most of the girls were experienced enough to predict the outcome.

Normandy moved away towards the door, blowing a whistle as he went. The prettiest girls in Devon – those at least who were prepared to take part in this fanciful charade – lined up by the door, giving each other the once-over. They were uniformly clad in one-piece bathing suits, high heels, lacquered hair and bearing a cardboard badge on their right wrist signifying their competition number. Their elbows were as sharp as their mutual appraisals.

The Slug launched into his usual pre-pageant routine like a football manager before the match.

'Just remember,' he barked, 'smile. You're all walking advertisements for Devon so smile, damn you!

'You're all about to become famous. And rich. Watch your lip when you're interviewed, keep smiling, and don't fall over. There's expenses forms on the table in the corner you can fill in afterwards.'

'That's a laugh,' whispered Eve to Molly bitterly, thinking about the shoes.

'"*Smile*",' parrotted Molly, but she did not suit the action to the word.

Normandy was adjusting his bow tie and smoothing his hair prior to sailing forth into the sunshine. His fussy self-important entrance into the Lido would cause the gathered crowds to cease their chatter and crane their necks. This was part of the joy of seaside life, the beauty pageant – an opportunity to sit in the sun and make catty comments about the size of the contestants' feet.

'I hadn't expected this on my first day,' said Valentine Waterford. 'A murder *and* a beauty competition.'

'Don't get too excited,' said Judy, putting on dark glasses with a dash of imperiousness. The bench they were sitting on was extremely hard. 'And move over, you're sitting on my dress.'

The young man edged apologetically away. 'Look, it's good of you to come,' he said, 'I rather expected to have to fend for myself.'

'I wanted to go out to Todhempstead Beach. Just to take a look at where they found the girl.'

'Wasn't anything to see,' said Valentine. 'I drove out there after talking to the Inspector.' His account faltered as the bathing belles made their entrance to a round of wild applause; Eve Berry wobbled slightly in her borrowed heels but managed to avert disaster. 'By the time I got there it was all over, bit of a waste of time.' He was betting with himself who would win.

'That's where you're wrong,' snipped Miss Dimont. 'If you're going to be a journalist you must learn to use your eyes.' Why was she behaving like this? Rude, short, when really he was very charming. It must be the girls.

'Empty beach, almost nobody there,' he replied. 'Only a couple of markers where presumably they found the body, but the tide was in and so you couldn't see the sand. What else *was* there to see?'

Miss Dimont considered this.

'Your story, the one you wrote this morning, said "mystery death"' she said. 'If you're going to be a reporter and you're going to write about mysteries, don't you think it's part of your job to try to get to the bottom of them?'

'I see what you're getting at,' replied Valentine, 'in a way. But surely that's the police's job? We just sit back and report what they find, don't we, and if they mess it up we tell the public how useless they are?'

He certainly *has* got a relative in the business, thought Miss Dimont. A lazy one.

'Tell me, Valentine, who's your uncle, the one who's in newspapers?'

'Gilbert Drury.'

'Oh,' said Miss Dimont, wrinkling her nose. 'The gossip columnist. That makes sense.'

'Well,' said Valentine, beating a hasty retreat, 'not really my uncle. More married to a cousin of my mother's.'

A wave of applause drowned Miss Dimont's reply as the contestants for the title of Queen of the English Riviera 1959 were introduced one by one.

The master of ceremonies introduced his menagerie. 'Ladies and gentlemen,' he boomed into the microphone, 'you do us a very great honour in being here today to help select our next queen from this wondrous array of Devon's beauty.'

Something in his tone implied however that he, Cyril Normandy, was the one conferring the honour, not the paying public. The hot June sunlight was gradually melting the Brylcreem which held down his thinning hair and at the same time it highlighted the dandruff sprinkled across the shoulders of his navy blazer.

'As you know, it has fallen to Temple Regis to host these important finals this year, and let me remind you, ladies and gentlemen, the winner of today's crown will go on to compete in Miss Great Britain in the autumn. So this is a huge stepping stone for one of these fine young ladies, on their way to fame and fortune, and, ladies and gentlemen, it will be you who is to be responsible for their future happiness!

'Just take a very close look at all these gorgeous girls, because, ladies and gentlemen, it is *your* vote that counts!'

'Are you taking notes?' said Miss Dimont crisply from behind the dark glasses.

'I, er . . .'

'You'll find it an enormous help as you go along to have a pencil and notebook about your person. Sort of aide-memoire,' she added with more than a hint of acid. 'For when you're back at the office searching your memory for people's names. You'll find they come in handy.' Maybe the hot sun was reacting badly to the lost sleep and the early-morning rum, not to mention the force nine. This was not like Miss Dimont!

The well-padded MC had a microphone in his hand now and was interviewing the girls by the pool's edge, apparently astonished by the wisdom of their answers. But while he debriefed them on how proud they were to be an ambassador for Britain's most-favoured county, about their ambitions to do well for themselves and the world, and, most importantly, what a thrill it was to support the town whose sash they had the honour to wear, they were thinking of the free cosmetics and underwear, the trips to London, the boys they might yet meet, and how their feet hurt.

'Don't seem to have the full complement,' puzzled Valentine, looking down the flimsy programme.

'What was going on back at the police station,' pondered Miss Dimont, ignoring this and returning to her earlier theme, 'about whether it was murder or misadventure?'

'One missing. Erm, what?'

'Inspector Topham.'

'He was definite it was accidental.'

'Something has to account for the fact that Sergeant Gull told you it was murder. I've never known him wrong.'

'But the Inspector outranks him. It was the Inspector who went out to view the scene. So it must be the inspector who's right.'

'Never that simple in Temple Regis,' murmured Miss Dimont, thinking of Dr Rudkin, the coroner, and how he always liked to sweep things under the carpet. 'No, for the word to have got back to the sergeant that it could be murder must mean that's what the first call back to the station said.'

'But why were the body markers so far away from the railway embankment?' Valentine was suddenly more interested in this conversation than he was in the girls who were parading up and down the pool edge. 'She couldn't have fallen, or been pushed, that far away from the railway line.'

'There you have it—' Miss Dimont smiled and, lifting her dark glasses, turned to face the trainee reporter '—in a nutshell. A mystery death. Needs looking into, wouldn't you say?'

Valentine Waterford smiled back. He had no idea what a time he was in for.

FOUR

Perched high on the cliffs at the tip of the estuary, Ransome's Retreat boasted the most beautiful gardens in the west of England, its terraces tumbling over the rocks into apparent infinity and its borders filled with a dazzling year-round display.

Palm trees wafted. Magnolias, a century old, lined the paths between terraces and from the branches above hung heavy Angel's Trumpets. The glasshouses were filled with ripening peaches and pineapples, and the newly shaved lawns gave off a honeyed scent which made visitors feel they had arrived at the gates of Eden.

'Some more tea, Mr Larsson?'

'I'm exhausted.'

'No more visitors today, sir,' the manservant said soothingly. 'All gone now.'

'Just too tiring,' complained the old man. 'Debilitating. And such a bore.'

The world-famous inventor of Larsson's Life Rejuvenator looked as if he could use a touch of his own medicine. Though the contraption had made him a rich man, keeping it before the public eye these days sapped his energy. His hand fluttered slightly as he reached for the teacup.

There was a time, before the War, when his factory could not make enough of them. The little leather-covered boxes containing a complex electrical device had been shipped all over the world. Larsson's clients included royalty, film stars, cabinet ministers, and a wide range of society figures, especially ladies of a certain age. It was guaranteed to put a spring back in everyone's step.

Post-war, however, when most people felt lucky just to be alive, there seemed to be less of a thirst to have one's life rejuvenated – maybe just waking up and finding one was breathing was enough. And certainly, in these straitened times, even the rich were finding better things to do with their money.

'No more phone calls, Lamb,' he said. 'I'm going to take a nap.'

Bengt Larsson – Ben to that small circle who called themselves his friends – was rich. Very. But his estate in Argentina bled money, the Cote d'Azur mansion similarly, and his two private airplanes – one in Deauville, one in Devon – cost a packet to keep going. Fame is a furnace which needs constant stoking.

Fame can also be a fickle friend: left half-hidden among the pillows on the terrace bench the great man had just vacated was a crumpled copy of the *Daily Herald* the dutiful Lamb had tried his best to hide at breakfast. Larsson's face, still handsome after all these years, stared out from a page whose headline screamed:

THE LARSSON LEGACY:
DEATH, DEPRESSION, DEGRADATION
– this is what you can expect
when you buy his famous Rejuvenator

This morning the *Daily Herald* exposes the truth behind the world-famous Larsson Life Rejuvenator, which has made its Swedish-born inventor one of the country's richest men. An investigation by this newspaper proves beyond all doubt that Bengt Larsson's promises that your

life will be healthier, longer and livelier by the use of his machine are false. The inventor, who started his career in a chemist's shop in Hull, has made repeated promises about the efficacy of the Rejuvenator. It has been endorsed by actors, radio stars and other famous figures, but a laboratory trial conducted by the (turn to p.5)

From the sun-dappled lawns blackbirds collected their worms and flew up into the eucalyptus trees to nourish their young, oblivious to the crisis unfolding beneath. The manservant Lamb collected the tea things and moved indoors out of the hot sun. Calm, of a sort, descended.

In the garden room Pernilla Larsson was writing a letter. Or, more exactly, not writing a letter. This latest press attack on her husband was not only bad for business, it unsettled life at Ransome's Retreat. And though as the inventor's fourth wife, she had brought a new stability to his restless life, Larsson was an unpredictable man given to violent mood swings and she could never be sure where things would go with him. It made concentrating very difficult.

'Lamb.'

'Yes, madam?'

'Have you given my husband his sedative?'

'In the second cup, madam.' Mistress and servant looked steadily at each other.

'Ask Gus to come in.'

'Very well, m'm.'

Just then an array of ancient clocks positioned across the ground floor of the ancient house raggedly signalled their agreement that it was four o'clock, and a confident-looking young man entered with a sheaf of papers in his hand.

'What worries me,' he said, 'is not the *Herald*. It's those idiots at the *Doctors' Medical Journal*. They're determined to get him.'

'They've always hated him. Ever since he published *A New Electronic Theory of Life*.'

'Quacks,' uttered Gus Wetherby with a sneer. 'Just because they've got medical qualifications they think they know everything. There are people on that journal who are out to get him, no matter what. Medics! Wouldn't surprise me if they weren't behind this latest press attack.'

Pernilla Larsson took off her glasses and looked at her son. 'There are a lot of people,' she said slowly, 'who might be behind this latest attack. People have turned against Ben, they really have.'

'Not altogether – we still have the daily visitors. The pilgrims to the shrine.'

'I wish he hadn't started that movement. It's an embarrassment in the present circumstances – it was supposed to be about health and vitality, but they turned it into a religion! It's one thing to say your invention can extend human life, quite another to allow people to believe there's something mystical attached to it.'

'They're nuts. They think his book is the Bible.'

Wetherby picked up a biscuit off the tea tray. 'That was all before the War,' he went on. 'People looking for something that couldn't be found. Hoping to contact loved ones, trying to make sense of that lost generation after the First War. People who didn't believe in spiritualism and Ouija boards and all that junk, but were looking for something . . .'

'That couldn't be found,' said Pernilla, completing his sentence. The two often thought as one, it was uncanny.

'So where are we?' she said, collecting her thoughts. 'Are the specifications right?'

'I had them checked. We can go ahead.'

'There's just the matter of convincing Ben.'

The conspirators paused. 'Look,' said Gus, 'even Ben knows

the game's up. Once upon a time people believed the Rejuvenator really did what it's supposed to do but . . .'

'You know he won't accept criticism,' warned Pernilla. 'And he can't accept the idea of change.'

'That's the problem, he's a one-trick pony. All that publicity at the beginning – "Hope for the Aged – Electricity to Make Old Folk Young" – that kind of thing, it went to his head. And all he'd invented was a dolled-up and very expensive box of tricks, something that you plugged yourself into when you felt low which delivered a weak electric current and made you think you felt better.'

'Don't be disloyal!' snapped Pernilla, though her response seemed automatic rather than anything else. 'HE believed in it, THEY believed in it, therefore we must believe in it too.' She paused for a moment, pulled in two directions. 'Though I must confess the letters which are rolling in these days – people don't *want* to believe any more. They want their money back.'

'He shouldn't have charged so much.'

Pernilla looked around the long, low room, its walls dotted with Impressionist paintings. 'It bought all this,' she reminded him quietly.

'It can be done again,' said Gus forcefully. 'Now that we've found the formula for a Rejuvenator which really *does* work.'

Pernilla nodded. 'All those old men,' she sighed. 'All wanting to be young again. All thinking, with the Rejuvenator I can have a younger model.'

Gus raised an eyebrow and smiled. Didn't his mother become the fourth Mrs Larsson for precisely that reason?

'Oh yes!' she said, catching his meaning. Her cigarette holder described an elegant parabola as she laughed, her salt-and-pepper hair glowed, and her jewellery flashed in the sunlight. She looked expensive.

'We still have to find a way to kill the kind of publicity we're getting in the press,' said Gus. 'Have to announce the new model. Different name, fresh start.'

He warmed to his theme. 'Got to stop those attack dogs at the *Medical Journal*. It would make sense for us to tell them, look, the Rejuvenator is a thing of the past, a creature of its time, whatever they want to hear – stopping short, of course, of saying that it never actually worked.'

Wetherby broke his biscuit in half but left its tumbling crumbs to disappear into the folds of the sofa while he thought. 'We say it's a new idea with a new inventor – me. Push Ben back into the shadows. For heaven's sake, he's eighty. Time to take a back seat!'

'It's been his whole life.'

'Let him enjoy what's left of it. Look,' said Wetherby, standing up, 'this is possibly the most idyllic place anywhere in the world – this house, these gardens, this climate. Back seat!'

'He won't agree.'

'He'll *have* to agree,' said Gus Wetherby harshly, 'or we're all dead.'

*

The sun made its slow descent behind the Temple Regis skyline, gilding the rooftops, casting long black shadows across the greensward towards the broad open sands.

'There are five hundred stars,' sighed Athene Madrigale, the famous astrologer, looking upwards, 'all competing with each other for my attention.'

Her companion did not take much notice of this. Athene often spoke like that.

'I have been listening to the waves shuffling the stones. I have been watching the moon pulling the waves. Can you hear?'

There was a pause.

'A shame about the dead girl,' said Judy Dimont slowly. 'Horrible, really.'

Athene nodded. They understood each other's preoccupations.

Night was Athene's daytime. It allowed her the space to clear her mind for the impossible task of telling Temple Regents what lay ahead in their lives. Her column in the *Riviera Express* was the most important part of the newspaper, foretelling events in readers' lives with startling accuracy:

Pisces: an event of great joy is about to occur – to you, or your loved ones.

Sagittarius: look around and see new things today! They are glorious!

Cancer: never forget how kind a friend can be to you. Do the same for them and you will be rewarded threefold!

People read her column and felt better. Those very few who had been privileged to actually meet Athene were struck by her special radiance, and it was only a fool who dismissed her outpourings as ingenuous nonsense.

Tonight, she was wearing a lemon top, pink skirt and purple trousers. The plimsolls on her feet were quite worn and of differing hues, but one of them matched perfectly the blue paper rose she wore in the bun on the back of her head. In the half-light the overall effect was strangely soothing.

'I can't believe it was an accident,' said Miss Dimont. They had walked over to a bench on the promenade and sat to watch the last golden light slowly disappear from the horizon.

'The girl?' asked Athene.

'Yes, the girl.'

'I was there,' said Athene. 'On the beach.'

'Todhempstead Sands?'

'Yes.'

'Good Lord, why didn't you say sooner, Athene? This could be murder, you know.'

Athene turned her head slowly to her companion. 'She didn't die there.'

Miss Dimont, the veteran of many a similar inquiry, was bemused. How could Athene Madrigale be witness to a murder – or an accidental death, whichever it was – and not tell anyone?

'Why . . . ?' she started.

'I was counting the clouds, dear. It's very difficult – have you ever tried? Altostratus, cumulonimbus, dear sweet cirrus – I was too busy to really see what happened.'

'But . . .'

'I only noticed when those policemen came down onto the beach. Then I saw the girl's body.'

'So how could you know whether she died there or not?'

'The clouds told me.'

Miss Dimont kicked her raffia bag in frustration. On the one hand she had an eyewitness, on the other she did not. Then again, most things Athene said turned out to be true – but if this was a murder, if the girl *had* died on or near the beach, as evidence it was valueless.

For the time being, at least.

'I'm going back to the office,' said Judy. 'Coming?' Home and Mulligatawny were going to have to wait tonight.

'Have to think carefully about my column,' said Athene. 'I'll make you some of my special tea if you're still there later.'

Miss Dimont walked over to the kerbside where Herbert, her faithful moped, stood expectantly awaiting their next expedition. At the kick of a pedal, he sprang cheerfully into action and together they made their way back up the promenade towards the *Riviera Express*.

Though during the day the newspaper office was like a ship's engine room, a positive maelstrom of movement and drama, by the time dusk fell the place was usually empty – as if news only happened during the day! She walked up the long corridor to the newsroom, past the mousetraps laid down to capture nocturnal visitors, but as she approached she could hear the slow, almost ghostly, tapping of a typewriter.

She pushed open the door and looked down the long office to her desk. Seated with his back to her was the new boy, Valentine whatsisname. He appeared to be writing something up, and was taking his time about it.

Miss Dimont was not pleased. She wanted the place to herself.

'Hello, Valentine,' she said, not entirely kindly. 'Don't you have a home to go to?'

The young man swung round and delivered a rueful smile. 'Actually there was a bit of a palaver over accom,' he replied. 'They parked me in the oddest place – a bed and breakfast done up to look like a castle, only the inside walls of the house were painted like the outside of the castle. Not *quite* the home from home.'

From this light mockery might be deduced the young Waterford once actually lived in a castle. He'd been quite evasive about where he came from.

'They all go there,' said Judy. 'Usually last longer than you before making a bolt for it.'

'Actually there's a cottage belonging to the family. Thought it better to go there. Bedlington.'

Miss Dimont looked over his shoulder at the paper in Valentine's typewriter. 'So what are you writing now?'

'I was given a word of advice by Mr Ross,' he said, nodding amiably towards the old Scotsman. 'He said the first thing you should do when you join a newspaper is write your own obituary.'

'Are you thinking of dying any time soon, Valentine?'

'You never know.'

'How old are you?'

'Twenty-three soon.'

Miss Dimont sat down at her desk. It had been her intention to write a Comment piece about the award-winning fishermen – brave, hardy men bringing lustre to Temple Regis along with their rich daily harvest – but it was getting late and she'd had an early start. Her return to the office was more a delaying tactic because by now she was exhausted – and the thought of kick-starting Herbert, who could be obstructive if left waiting too long in the dark, suddenly drained her of the will to go home.

'How are you getting on?' she asked, more out of good manners than with any real interest.

'It's difficult. School, army, one day on the newspaper. Not a lot to write about. Then I thought, well, I could add a bit about my family background so I started doing that. But then it seemed rather boastful so I . . .'

Miss Dimont's eyes travelled down to the wicker bin by Valentine's ankle and saw that he must have been at his task for some time – it was overflowing with rejected copy paper, scrumpled and torn and trodden on. This young man is *very* keen, she observed.

'What is there of interest about your, er, the Waterfords?' she asked.

'Well, rather ancient. Been around a long time, quite a few of us. None of them journalists.'

'Except your uncle.'

'Mmm. Wish I'd never mentioned him. I can see he's not popular down here. In London, of course . . .'

'People down here don't often go to Mayfair,' said Judy, quite sharply. 'Your uncle Gilbert never seems to leave it if you believe what he writes in his column.'

'I shan't be following in his footsteps.'

'I'm going home,' she said. 'Don't take all night with the

obituary. It's helpful if you set yourself a deadline and then stick to it. Look,' she said, pointing at the great newsroom clock, 'it's 8.30. Give yourself until 9.30.'

The young man ran his hands despairingly through his wavy blond hair. He was going to be a handful to train up, she could see.

On the other hand, he really was quite pleasant to look at.

FIVE

'Morning, Mr Rhys.' It was nine o'clock and the sun's rays were already unbearably hot through the newsroom windows. The journey into town atop the trusty Herbert, hair blowing in the breeze, had been sheer joy for Miss Dimont, but indoors the atmosphere seemed suddenly oppressive.

'I said, good morning, Mr Rhys.'

'Rr...rrr.' The editor did not even have a briar pipe to argue with this morning; instead the point of contention had apparently been the *Daily Herald* on the telephone.

'Come in, Miss Dim.'

He *would* call her that, and really there was no need – especially on such a fine day, so full of promise.

'Please don't.'

'Miss Dim*ont*. What are you doing this morning?'

'In court,' said his chief reporter. 'Do you want me to take along Mr, er, Ford?'

'Ford? Who's Ford?'

'The new recruit. Wants to shorten his name for byline purposes.'

'There'll be no bylines round here,' snorted the editor, 'until he starts pulling in some stories. Anyway that's not what I wanted to talk to you about.'

Uninvited, Miss Dimont sat down opposite her employer. There was, after all, a time when he'd stood before *her* desk while she sat and issued instructions, but that had been long ago. It was one of life's ironies that the War had a way of changing things for the better and the peace, for the worse. Life was peculiar that way.

'Ben Larsson,' said the editor. 'You saw the piece in the national press yesterday.'

'Well deserved. The man's a mountebank,' said Miss Dimont firmly. 'A fraud. I thought they treated him with kid gloves, considering.'

'He is – without doubt Miss Dim*ont*, without a shadow of a doubt – the most famous resident of Temple Regis,' hissed the editor. 'While he remains at Ransome's Retreat we treat him with the respect that position demands.'

Miss Dimont laughed aloud. 'Oh yes!' she hooted, 'just think of the number of complaints we've had in the past couple of years about the Rejuvenator – how it claims to do everything, and manages to do nothing! How people have been diddled out of their money. That's quite apart from all those sad souls who make their pilgrimage to the Retreat because they believe Larsson is somehow skippering the advance party of the Second Coming. They make Temple Regis a laughing stock.'

'That's not the point.' If Rhys sought a quiet life, sheltered from controversy, he really had chosen the wrong profession, thought Miss Dimont. 'I don't want anything about Larsson in the paper, d'you understand, and if the *Daily Herald* calls again asking for more details, as they did just now, just say we are not at home to sensationalism.'

'It was a perfectly legitimate story. They did an investigation and it proved beyond all doubt that . . .'

'I *know* what the paper did,' snapped Rhys. 'I can read, Miss Dim! I just don't want that rubbish in my pages so I called you in here – because you can stir up trouble, once you get going – to tell you to leave this one alone. No stories about Larsson in the paper, and no help to Fleet Street.'

'They'll come down here anyway and camp in your office, like they always do when there's a big story.'

Her words hit home. When in the past the national press had paid a call, they invariably left the good people of Temple Regis thinking what a weak and flabby offering they had for a weekly newspaper – even if it did have Athene Madrigale as its star columnist. Rhys hated the Fleet Street pressmen with their trilby hats and big coats and lingering cologne and expense accounts taking up the desks in his newsroom, a privilege he could not deny them if he were still to call himself a newspaperman. They came like cuckoos to the nest, sucking up the nourishment, making a nuisance, and destroying the sense of calm and harmony Mr Rhys tried hard to maintain throughout the year. He really *should* have chosen another job, but there it was; a failed novelist doesn't have that many career choices.

The windows in his office were wide open and you could hear the swooping seagulls mocking him outside.

'Stay away from the Retreat and get on with what you're supposed to be doing,' warned the editor. 'Hear me?'

'This murder,' Judy said, artfully changing tack. 'The girl on the beach.'

'Rr . . . rrrr. Accident, the police are saying. Don't go mucking about in things. You know what people will say.'

Indeed Miss Dimont did know. On the one hand the townsfolk lapped up anything a bit unusual in their weekly newspaper, and a murder certainly made a nice change, on the other, the city fathers hated it: bad for business. If Temple Regis was to maintain its claim to being the handsomest resort in Devon, the last thing they wanted was holidaymakers thinking they might trip over a body or two on the beach. Rudyard Rhys unequivocally sided with this position.

Miss Dimont sat back and said nothing more. To a large extent Rhys had to rely on what he was given, editorially, by his staff – and if his chief reporter came up with something newsworthy, it would inevitably find its way into the paper. Newspapers are like that: they don't want you doing things but when you do them, they're grateful.

Only they never say so.

'However,' said Rhys, for he felt he had to show initiative as a leader, 'this piece of Betty's, about the woman and the Six Point Group.'

'Yes, Mr Rhys?'

'I think we can do better than that. Go and see this Miss de Mauny. For heaven's sake, how many women do you know who fix clocks for a living?'

'None,' said Miss Dimont frostily. *For heaven's sake*, a nice article on clock-mending when you could have a murder? And a national scandal about old Ben Larsson as well? Had he lost all sense?

Valentine was waiting when she got back to her desk. 'I'm with you again today,' he said shyly. 'Hope you don't mind.'

'Magistrates' court,' said Judy, as if it were a punishment. 'That'll mean a *notebook*. And a *pencil*. How's your shorthand?' She knew he didn't have any.

'Erm, well . . .'

'I'd get some classes if I were you. Lovely Mary will help you out.'

'Lovely . . . ?'

'Runs the Signal Box Café. Used to be secretary on her father's dairy farm.' They walked out of the office together. 'How went the obituary?'

'I discover I have led a fascinating life. I hadn't realised quite what a remarkable chap I am. And my death, such a loss to Temple Regis. *"The town mourned at the sudden departure . . ."*.'

'You didn't finish it?'

'I was there till midnight. Whichever way I wrote it, it looked wrong. You start a sentence and by the time you get to the other end you've forgotten why you started it that way. So you undo it and start again. You put the front at the back and the back at the front. That seems to work. Then you realise that actually the story starts in the third paragraph, so you tear out the first two and are happily tapping along when you realise that paras one and two have some bearing on the new first paragraph and without the nourishment they provide to the narrative, you're sunk.

'So then you amalgamate all three paragraphs into one – you've got all the story there now. But then there's nothing left to say. You're supposed to write three hundred words and it's all been said in a fraction of that.'

Well, clearly he has some linguistic ability, thought Miss Dimont, if no discernible writing talent.

'But there's another way of looking at it,' went on Valentine, striding manfully forward towards the courthouse, blond hair flapping in the warm breeze. 'I discovered that at about 11.15. You start with the family history and, as you know . . . '

'Ancient family. Lots of them. None in journalism except for the one we don't mention.' Miss Dimont's recall, and sharp gift for precis, were second to none.

'It was no good. When I wrote about them I realised nobody cares about your folks. Not sure I do myself. So after about half an hour I chucked that away and started again. Suddenly it all started to come together. I realised what had to be said, and I said it. D'you want to take a look?' He delved into his jacket pocket and pulled out a crumpled twist of copy paper.

'No thanks,' said Judy briskly. 'I'll read it when you're dead.'

*

48

The gloomy cathedral-like room which dispensed what passed for justice in Temple Regis looked even drearier this morning. It was probably the joyous June light piercing through the unwashed stained-glass windows that did it.

The Magistrates' Clerk, Mr Thurlestone, was his usual distant self. He resented the sparkling fabric Miss Dimont wove from the mundane and plodding proceedings over which he presided – almost as if it were another world she was describing!

Furthermore, the things she chose to write about! A complicated two-day fraud case, through which the Clerk had to guide his somnolent magistrates before telling them what their opinion was of the accused, what should be said to him in summing up, and what his sentence should be – uphill work indeed for Mr Thurlestone – was dismissed in a paragraph or two.

On the other hand, the matter of the curate cycling without lights! Miss Dimont had made banner headlines out of that, yet all it had been was a minor transgression rewarded with a five-shilling fine. But oh, the fuss she made about it! It made a mockery of the justice handed down by his court.

Miss Dimont indicated to her junior reporter where he should sit, and wandered over to the Clerk's bench to collect the charge sheet. It was handed over with Thurlestone's customary disdain.

'The point about being here,' Miss Dimont said, returning to the reporters' bench, 'is not to be overawed by the weight of the law – that's what Mr Thurlestone and the magistrates expect from you. And that is precisely what you are not going to give them.

'They're just as full of foible and weakness as the people they sit in judgement on. They may never have done a wrong thing in their life, but that doesn't make them right.'

Valentine nervously fished out his notebook. It was clear he had mislaid his pencil.

'The only thing that's right is the law,' Judy went on, lowering her voice to a whisper as proceedings commenced. 'And that's why we're here, to watch out on behalf of the public. Make sure it's administered correctly. And report back.' She handed the young man a spare pencil she'd fished from her corkscrew curls.

The young reporter had yet to discover there was what might be termed 'previous' between his senior and the Clerk. Thurlestone quite often allowed the hangers and floggers who sat behind him on the bench to overprescribe the medication. Some of them had a taste for sweeping all miscreants into jail, especially the knicker snatchers and sheep molesters, and sometimes he felt powerless to resist their lust for retribution. Miss Dimont often had to remind the town, in the Comment page, of their frailty.

Not this morning, though.

'Oh, look!' she exclaimed with delight, 'what have we here?' She had been reading the charge sheet.

'Call Mrs Phyllis Bickington.'

A small woman of startling beauty stepped into the dock to confirm her name and to swear that, by God, she would indeed tell the truth.

'Phyllis Ada Bickington, you are charged with assault on your uncle, also described as your husband, Adam Porrit Bickington. How do you plead?'

'Not guilty.'

'Sit down.'

The events in the Bickingtons' turbulent domestic life were slowly laid bare. Miss Dimont lay down her pen and watched as Valentine struggled to keep up with what was turning into a ripsnorter of a case. Reuben Bickington had fallen in love with his brother's daughter, and secretly married her though there was an age gap of nearly thirty years between them. All three lived on a farm hidden in a valley some five miles from Temple Regis, a place where no tourist ever went, and precious few locals dared either.

As the story slowly unravelled, Valentine's eyebrows crept up his forehead. The court was told that in the Bickington valley, such marriages were not uncommon – 'though they do stop short at allowing brother and sister,' whispered Judy. 'Mostly.'

That there was a culture gap between uncle and niece – she had been to school, he had not – became evident early in the proceedings. Certainly there had been disagreements over his unusual treatment of farm animals. But the case ground to a halt when it emerged that Phyllis was covering up for her father, her husband's brother, who had come round to their cottage and delivered a fraternal thrashing over an aspect of the couple's personal life which was not allowed to be mentioned verbally but had to be written down.

This did not please Colonel de Saumarez, the Chairman of the Bench, who was itching to deliver a homily on arcane vices in rural communities before sending the woman away for a well-deserved spell in the cooler. Instead, after consulting Mr Thurlestone, he was obliged to let Mrs Bickington walk free without, he added through gritted teeth, a stain on her character.

'Poor thing,' said Miss Dimont as she was led away, 'she can only be seventeen.'

'Doesn't seem possible,' said Valentine who, despite his National Service, had evidently led a sheltered life.

'You can write it up,' said Miss Dimont, picking up her raffia bag. 'I'm off to Bedlington.'

'Erm . . .' said Valentine, hesitantly, 'can I give you a lift?'

It took two minutes for Judy Dimont to regret her decision to say yes, for there in the car park was Valentine's pride and joy, a Heinkel bubble car. It was red. And very prominent.

'I'm afraid there's no elegant way to step into this,' said Valentine, energetically throwing open the door which comprised the whole of the front of the vehicle. 'You basically have to wish for good fortune and throw yourself in.'

Miss Dimont did as she was told but vowed it was an experiment she would not repeat. As they drove through the town and down Tuppenny Row into adjacent Bedlington-on-Sea, she gave the reporter what he wanted – his intro for the Bickington case.

'We have a place at the end of the newsroom called Curse Corner,' she then added. 'Why d'you think it's called that?'

'No idea. I suppose . . .'

'People sit there cursing and swearing because they can't get started. They know how the story should go, but they can never find the first sentence. You had the same problem last night, but you thought it was stage fright.

'Let me tell you, Valentine, it's a curse which will stay with you the rest of your journalistic career. You can always tell someone else what the intro to their story should be, but you'll almost never be able to think of one for yourself.'

The young man swung the wheel. 'D'you know, I was really looking forward to starting on the *Express*,' he replied slowly. 'I never realised how difficult it would be.'

'Fun though,' said Judy, 'sometimes! You can drop me here.'

While Waterford's fashionable but feeble conveyance struggled its way back up the hill Miss Dimont turned and made for the Seagull Café where her dearest friend Auriol Hedley held sway, dispensing delicious home-made lemonade and oven-warm rock cakes.

'Haven't seen you for a while,' was Auriol's cheery welcome. 'How was your mother's visit?'

'Managed to put it off,' said Judy, who only liked her mother in small doses.

'She sent that letter saying she was coming down on the Pullman.'

'I sent back a telegram.'

'Very naughty. She treasures you.'

Miss Dimont took off her glasses and polished them. 'She's

not *your* mother,' she replied, wearily. 'I get a letter a week and I always feel guilty after I've read them.'

'You might feel less guilty if you bothered to reply,' said Auriol, who knew her friend very well indeed. They'd worked together during the War and knew most things about each other.

'Anyway, she's going back to Belgium for a bit,' said Judy with relief. 'Catching up with the family.'

'Ah yes, the Dimonts of Ellezelles,' said Auriol in mock deference. 'A distinguished lot.'

'Instead, I've got Uncle Arthur coming to stay.'

'Oh, now,' said Auriol, 'that *will be* a treat.' The old boy was the sweetest man in the world, one of life's true gentlemen, but he spent most of his time in South America.

'Now look,' said Judy, 'I want to talk to you about this dead girl.'

'I thought you might,' said Auriol with satisfaction. 'Let me just shut up shop and we can have a nice cup of tea and chat about it. I have a theory.'

Sure to be wrong, thought Judy disloyally, as they went inside.

SIX

It was a surprise, and not altogether a pleasant one, to find Valentine waiting when she emerged an hour later. He was leaning negligently against the red bubble car, head thrown back to catch the sun. The borrowed suit he wore neither fitted nor did it do his rake-thin frame any favours. He looked a bit like an unmade bed.

'Hello,' said Miss Dimont in a not wholly friendly way. She'd done enough nannying for one day.

'Thought you might like a lift back into town,' said the young man with a beguiling smile. 'Hop in.'

'Not sure I want to,' said Judy, disobligingly. '"Hop" being the operative word. What on earth persuaded you to buy this thing?'

'A dear friend misled me.'

Miss Dimont sniffed. 'How long can it possibly have taken you to drive down from London in it?'

'Did my National Service in the cavalry,' he replied. 'No horses any more – well, only sometimes – most of the time it was tanks so I'm used to slow progress.'

He was charming, of that there could be no doubt. Handsome too, though of course a mere child.

'Have you written up the Bickington assault case?'

'When I left you I went straight back to the office. It was wonderful – I used the intro you suggested and guess what – no curses! The story started to flow and I would have finished it in no time but . . .'

'...your typewriter ran out of ribbon.'

'Aha. You have identified a certain disorganisation in the Waterford way of doing things.'

'Far be it from me to point out, Valentine, that one of your shoelaces is undone as well. So what happened, why didn't you finish?'

'The editor told me to stop.'

'Why?'

'Said he didn't want interbreeding stories in the paper – bad for the town's image. Ridiculous, he was only her uncle for heaven's sake! Not as if . . .'

'It happens from time to time,' said Miss Dimont, recalling among others the Vicar's Longboat Party, the Temple Regis Tennis Scandal and the Football Pools Farrago – Rudyard Rhys hated printing the really good stories. 'More often than you might think.'

Later, filched by an underhanded sub-editor, such tales would often turn up in one of the murkier Sunday papers and the residents of Temple Regis would agree, yet again, that the *Riviera Express* was nice enough, but it never really had its finger on the pulse.

'I mean,' said Valentine, firing up the car's tinny engine, 'surely the Bickingtons were a good story?'

'You have the right instincts,' agreed Judy. 'But I must warn you the editor will not always share them. Anything for a quiet life is his motto. Though it wasn't always the case.'

'Oh?' said Valentine, expertly rounding the harbour wall and gauging whether the old bubble had enough puff to get them both up the hill, or whether Judy might have to get out and walk.

'Yes. We worked together during the War.'

'Doing?'

'Well,' said Miss Dimont cagily, 'based in Whitehall. Royal Navy. A bit complicated.'

The young reporter looked sideways at her with interest. He looked a bit too long.

'Look where you're going!' cried Judy. 'The dust cart!'

'Cloak and dagger?' Valentine asked, slowing behind a refuse lorry which was inching at snail's pace up the hill.

'I don't recall anyone ever wearing a cloak.'

'Then you may have known Admiral Godfrey, sort of relation of mine.'

'Ah yes, the Waterfords. Old family, rather a lot of them,' said Judy with only the mildest sprinkle of sarcasm. 'Yes, I knew him quite well. We were in the same quarters.'

'Got you now,' said Valentine, swerving out to overtake the lorry. As a traffic manoeuvre it was brave, but with such a feeble engine, not a great success. Conceding defeat, he slid back into his original position. 'Pretty hairy stuff, I imagine.'

'Actually,' said Judy, 'the lady I've just been to see – Auriol Hedley, at the café – worked in the same unit.'

'Small world.'

'Too small. I came down here because she told me there was an opening on the *Riviera Express*. I'd only been here five minutes when they appointed a new editor. Blow me down if it didn't turn out to be Richard Rhys.'

'I thought his name was Rudyard.'

'Hah!' snapped Miss Dimont. 'That only came later when he tried to become a novelist.'

'So you worked for him in the War Office?'

'Other way round, Valentine.'

'But he's older than you!'

Judy Dimont sighed. The boy was young. He may have served his time in the armed services but he clearly had no idea of what it was like in the days of war, where talent led seniority, and bright young people were put in charge of the nation's defences while their so-called olders and betters pottered obediently along behind.

'Auriol was the boss, I was her deputy. We were a small unit. Richard Rhys – Rusty, we used to call him – was given, ah, certain tasks. He was good at some and . . . *not* good at others. But it's all a long time ago.'

'Yes indeed,' said Valentine, who was still in short trousers when the war ended. He ruffled his blond locks and changed gear.

'I'm going to see a Miss de Mauny,' said Judy, changing the subject. 'Horologist. Know what that is?'

'"Had we but world enough and . . . *time*",' quoted Valentine without hesitation.

'Very clever. Bet you don't know how the rest of it goes, or its meaning.'

'I do, actually.'

Miss Dimont gave him a look, and changed the subject. 'She gave a lecture the other day on the origins of the women's movement and I'm going to talk to her to see how she views the position of women in the West Country today. So if you'll just drop me off at the top of Tuppenny Row . . .'

'No, I'm coming with you.'

'You'll find it awfully dreary.'

'The editor told me to. Said you're a wonderful interviewer and I should pick up some tips.'

'Did he really? Strange he never bothers to say that to me.'

'Anyway, I'm simply nutty about mechanical things. That's why I went in the cavalry, you can spend an awful lot of time there tinkering around with your head under the bonnet. I'd like to see what sort of clocks she's repairing, how they work, sort of thing.'

The red bubble car reached the summit of Bedlington Hill

and they made their way, sedately, past Mudford Cliffs. Women were out walking their dogs, but the warning signs about the cliff fall had been taken away.

Angela de Mauny's pink-painted cottage stood at the end of Tuppenny Row, facing away from its neighbours in an offhand fashion, but occupying a spot where you could see the whole of Nelson's Bay. Miss Dimont had seen the view many times but as she staggered inelegantly out of Valentine's infernal machine its broad sweep caught her gaze once more, and for a moment she stood quite still on the pavement.

'Look,' she said.

It was late in the afternoon and, though the heat had gone out of the day, the sun still shone brilliantly on the water. The piercing blue of the sky was beginning to give way to a more complex colour, purple and grey and yellow, and Athene Madrigale's clouds were starting to put in their appearance – the altostratus, the cumulonimbus, and especially the cirrus which looked like so much candy floss hanging gently in the sky. Wide-eyed guillemots patrolled the air above, while far beneath a pair of gannets flew off the headland, occasionally slicing into the water to collect their dinner.

Valentine came up behind her. 'Fabulous,' he murmured, adding after a moment's pause, 'is it always like this in Temple Regis?'

'My dear boy,' she said over her shoulder. 'You don't know it, but you've arrived in Heaven.'

There was no St Peter, however, to answer Miss de Mauny's green-painted front door, instead an angular lady with steel-grey hair and complexion to match who seemed startled, not to say frightened, to see the two reporters.

'Yes?'

Having shrugged her disapproval after learning their identities, she was on the point of shutting the door again when Valentine stepped forward and said, 'Margaret Plantagenet.' Miss de

Mauny stepped back and looked more closely at the young reporter. 'Yes?' she said again, but her tone was different this time – interested almost.

'Just a guess,' offered Valentine cheerfully. 'She married into your family in the fourteenth century. I'm on the other side. My—'

'—ancient family, lots of them,' interrupted Miss Dimont starchily, but a dubious family connection stretching back five hundred years, if that's what it was, looked as though it might at least get them into the house. First two rules of journalism – (i) knock on the door, (ii) get inside.

What they found, once inside, was breathtaking.

Ancient timepieces glistened as if made of gold. They chattered and clicked and donged, and on a workbench the innards of a large hall clock were laid out in regimented lines as if they were the parts of a firearm.

'...thought they had called to warn you I was coming,' Miss Dimont was saying disingenuously. 'Your speech the other day, you know, attracted a great deal of interest. So sorry if this is an intrusion, we can go if you'd prefer.'

The apology was less than sincere. Miss Dimont had heard that Miss de Mauny was known to be prickly, to say the least, and took the decision not to telephone ahead in the hope she could sweet-talk her way through the door.

As it turned out, it was this very new, very junior cub reporter who'd pulled it off. She'd have to have a word with him later!

'...though we did the article on your lecture on Lady Rhondda – *fascinating*,' she added encouragingly. 'I wanted to do something for the women's interest pages, expanding on the role of women today.'

'I'm no expert,' said Angela de Mauny scratchily, sitting down at her bench and pointedly turning her back to her visitors.

'Well, let's say you know more than most,' said Miss Dimont

soothingly. 'I'd like to write a piece talking about where women are, fourteen years after the War has ended.'

'Why?' said Miss de Mauny, but you could tell she was listening.

'In your speech you made the point that the War was a time when women finally came into their own, were recognised for the skills which had been waiting to be utilised ever since . . . ever since the Vote, ever since they were allowed to take their university degrees, ever since they were accepted as doctors and lawyers and factory workers. The First War broke down some of those barriers, but this one finally gave us true emancipation.'

'Well, yes, yes, yes!' said Miss de Mauny irritably. 'My very point!'

Miss Dimont had used the old journalistic trick of getting a reluctant interviewee to talk by repeating back her own words – words with which she would be forced to agree, and would want to expand on. As a subterfuge, it worked as well on members of the public as it did on politicians.

The clock woman fell for it.

'Come the peace, everything went backwards,' she said. 'It's continuing to go backwards. We women represent half the population, but only have twenty-four Members of Parliament to speak for us – the laws of this country are made by men. And while I am fond of the male of the species, he seems to have taken it upon himself to grab hold of the steering wheel of life on the foolish assumption that women can't drive.'

Judy Dimont nodded vigorously in agreement. Her notebook was in hand, the strange curlicues thought up by Mr Pitman a century before magically spiralling their way across the page. Miss de Mauny looked nervously down at their progress and eyed her interlocutor with caution. 'Who runs your paper, male or female?' she asked sharply.

'Male.'

'Well, we know how this'll end up. "Weepy old woman bewails her wage packet woes", that sort of thing. I think I'd rather not go any further.'

She turned to Valentine, deliberately changing the subject. 'Which family are you? An awful lot of people married into the de Maunys. Most seem to have lost their bloodline while we've managed to hang on to ours.'

'Actually,' said Valentine, 'we also—'

'Let's talk about that *later*,' said Miss Dimont snippily. 'There's no room in the paper to write about family trees. Tell me, Miss de Mauny, how many men are there in your distinguished profession?'

It's what made her such a brilliant interviewer. She had done her homework. Horology was a closed shop to that gender.

'All men, no women,' snapped Miss de Mauny.

'Then how come . . . ?'

'I'm fortunate enough to come from a wealthy family. After university, I wanted to do something no other woman had done, and for a while I seriously considered climbing Mount Everest – I've done a bit of mountaineering – but in the end it came down to this. I paid for my apprenticeship, bought my own tools and premises, and weathered the storm while people got used to having a woman go up the church steeple or the town hall.

'I was helped by the death of old Fred Shallowford, who'd been here forty years. There wasn't anybody else, so gradually I was *granted*—' she used the word quite bitterly '—his work.'

'I wonder what Lady Rhondda would have to say about that.'

'She was a marvellous woman. Without her, without the Six Point Group, women would be in a far worse position than they are now.'

The conversation flowed on like this for some time. Valentine quietly let himself out of the front door and wandered down

Tuppenny Row, drinking in its pink-bricked cottages which were really more like rich men's houses.

He returned a quarter of an hour later to hear Miss de Mauny's voice raised almost to a screech.

'Just so degrading – appalling!' she was saying agitatedly. 'After all we've been through – that women allow this to be done to them, while the public sits by and lets the men take advantage like that!'

'To be fair,' interjected Judy, 'it *is* a passport to another world. Or it can be. There's the money to consider. And the fact they're not qualified for anything else. Yes, they may be exploited and the whole process, frankly, is pretty tawdry, but it's only a fashion. It'll pass.'

'And meantime, meantime . . . it brings women to their lowest common denominator.'

'There's worse,' said Judy, smiling.

'Well, yes,' agreed Miss de Mauny, the hysteria in her voice abating somewhat, 'I suppose that's true. But what *those* women do, they've done since the dawn of time. Beauty parades – pageants—' she spat the word out '—these things are man-made, and man-made now and today.

'Frankly I'm appalled Temple Regis should lower itself in this way. But I don't suppose your *male* editor would agree with that view – probably rubbing his hands at all the photographs he can print of girls in bathing costumes. Hence my reluctance to talk when you came to the door. Nothing will change.'

'Yes, it will,' said Judy, calmly. 'There will come a time, and you mustn't give up hope.'

'You're wrong. The only way any of this will change is if something radical is done.'

'Parliamentary reform?'

'Direct action,' said Angela de Mauny fiercely. 'That's the

only way to get things done. Sometimes men only stop to think when they see blood spilled on the ground.'

*

The journey back to the office was a difficult one. First, Valentine insisted Judy take the controls of the bubble car. Though it was called a car it was more like a motorcycle, but much more difficult to handle than dear Herbert. But it seemed only appropriate, given the tenor of the recent conversation, that a woman should take her turn at the wheel and so the couple made their halting way back to the *Riviera Express*.

They talked over the barely veiled violence in Miss de Mauny's closing remarks.

'Extraordinary woman,' said Valentine. 'I'd say barking mad.'

'I wouldn't say that, but she's certainly unusual. How many more colourful relations have you got up your sleeve? Gilbert Drury, the Admiral, now Miss de Mauny.'

'There are more, many more, believe me. No, I found it quite frightening at one point, actually. When she was talking about blood, it was if she meant it.'

'You see her point.'

'Well, sort of.'

'*I* do,' said Miss Dimont, 'and if you were a woman you might understand things a bit better.'

'I'm a quick learner,' said Valentine, and turned his dazzling smile on her. He meant well, but what did he know? Boys' public school, a stint of National Service, no experience of the world.

'It's a man's world. You're a man.'

'I was brought up by an aunt,' he said, as if by way of exoneration. He started to say something else, but they had reached their destination.

The reporters made their way through the front hall and

trudged up the dusty stairs and along the corridor into the newsroom. People were still hard at work and the place was buzzing with activity. They just walking to their shared desk when . . .

'Miss D-I-I-I-M-M-M-M!'

'Action stations,' said Judy, and pushed Valentine into his chair. 'Yes, Mr Rhys?'

'In my office, Miss Dim! Be quick about it!'

The door slammed shut, but Valentine could still hear above the office kerfuffle the sounds of voices raised in what seemed to be accusation and counter-accusation. It startled him, since he could tell Miss Dimont gave no ground to her employer, rather that she seemed to have the upper hand.

A few moments later, she emerged and returned to her desk, a little tense perhaps, but otherwise perfectly calm. She did not sit down.

'Here's a question to which you should be able to answer yes,' she began, in a tense tone. 'Have you heard of Danny Trouble and The Urge?'

'Well, that sounds rather like . . . I'm not awfully musical, you know.'

'No matter, Mr Ford. They're on stage at the Pavilion Theatre, or just about to be,' said Miss Dimont tersely, 'and there's a riot going on. Get going!'

SEVEN

Geraldine Phipps had seen many West End successes in a long and glittering career, but never anything like this. The chaos and excitement even outweighed anything she'd witnessed at the Coronation – and this was Temple Regis, not The Mall!

Screaming girls with thick sweaters and clumpy shoes had invaded the foyer of the Pavilion Theatre and were raiding the snack counter; the green-eyed pansy in charge had taken one look when they broke through the door and scarpered. Here and there a greasy-haired lout in a leather jacket and jeans ducked between the knots of girls, egging them on by shouting 'Danny! DANNY!!' and the screams would come again and again, thick and fast.

'Stop that immediately, Gavin!' ordered Mrs Phipps severely, for underneath the disreputable disguise she recognised her grandson, once the young man of great promise.

'Danny! DANNY!!' he yodelled, oblivious to the dowager's cry, and the girls took up their screaming once again. 'DANN . . . EEEEEE!!!!'

The singer and his mates felt less enthusiastic about Temple Regis than its inhabitants felt about them. The band's ancient Bedford van had broken down outside Torquay and nobody had the money to pay for repairs. Eventually, they'd been offered a tow down to the town and had arrived long after the fans had settled themselves in. A service road at the back of the theatre had obscured this ignominious arrival and now they were hastily unloading their heavy equipment and hauling it backstage.

'That Gavin,' panted Danny Trouble, whose real name was Derek, 'what a way to start a gig – I'm going to kill 'im.'

'You hold him an' I'll hit 'im,' offered Boots McGuigan, the bass guitarist.

'Crazy, man, crazy' said Taz, who played the drums. 'What's happening to us? We're Number One in the Top Ten and we have to be *towed* here.'

'Well, we aren't going anywhere now. Not for the next six weeks,' said Boots. 'Someone'll fix it.'

'If it don't get ripped apart by the fans.'

'That's another thing,' said Danny, picking up a heavy amplifier. 'Number One, and we're stuck in this dead-and-alive hole for the next six weeks. We should be in London! If anyone's doing the killing it'll be me.'

'Where's Tommy?'

'Where d'you think?'

Britain's No 1 beat group had paused for a quick cigarette in the wings but their guitarist, a red-haired Irishman, was already onstage, guitar plugged in. He was noisily experimenting with various catlike cries he could squeeze from the instrument, fully aware that the racket he was making was filtering through the locked auditorium doors to the fans beyond, driving the girls to even greater ecstasy. He moved his body unnecessarily to the sounds he made, deeply in love with himself.

'Turd,' said Danny. Nobody bothered to respond because the singer had voiced the collective thought.

Boots McGuigan was sorting out the cat's cradle of wires without which the magic and the mystery of their latest hit *Please Me Baby Please* would be inaudible. Each member of the band had a different responsibility beyond their musical role, and Boots' was to make sure the sound equipment worked. Danny made the tea, Taz made sure they got paid. The exception was Tommy – who never did anything except play his guitar and waggle his hips in a most unpleasant fashion.

A curious rumbling, not unlike an earthquake, now gripped the building. The fans were drumming their heels hard on the floorboards, unaware the building was long past its best and a continuation of this heavy-booted tap dance might result in a complete collapse. A safety warning over the loudspeakers would have made no difference because by now delirium had set in.

Meanwhile, the grandmother of popular music's most unpopular manager had scurried into the calm of the manager's office and was lifting her Plymouth gin from the filing cabinet. There was a knock at the door and Judy popped her head round. 'Can we come in? It's terrifying what's going on out there.'

'Quick and shut the door.' Geraldine Phipps knew Miss Dimont well, and liked her. She'd even got out her scrapbook once to show her the snaps from when she was a Gaiety Girl.

'What on earth is going on?' Judy shouted as she introduced Valentine. 'It sounds like the Blitz.'

'Strange how potent cheap music is,' quoted Mrs Phipps, who had entirely ditched her reservations about Danny and the boys now she could see they were box-office gold. 'According to Gavin, when the fans are finally let through the doors they will tear the seats out. Thank the Lord I renewed the insurance.'

'It's a terrible din,' said Valentine.

'You're supposed to like it,' said Judy crisply. 'It's your age group. Myself, I prefer Michael Holliday.'

Mrs Phipps was lighting a cigarette to help the gin down. 'Heaven knows what the town will make of it,' she said happily. 'We had Pearl Carr and Teddy Johnson the year before last. All very sophisticated – and look, they're in the Top Ten now! Why can't these greasy-haired fellows be more like *them*?'

'I think that's the point about them,' said Miss Dimont, and another wave of joyous squealing erupted as the auditorium doors burst open and the Gadarene horde swept in.

'So, Geraldine,' said Miss Dimont, 'I have to write something for the paper. Obviously, we can't ignore this mass hysteria – I mean, Temple Regis can never have seen anything like it. Where have they all come from?'

'St Saviour's Convent, a lot of them.'

'But . . . that's a boarding school. For young ladies!'

'Precisely,' said Geraldine Phipps. 'I sent a nicely worded invitation to Mother Superior – an old friend, don't you know – and here they are. Shocking, isn't it?' But the smile on her lips suggested a remarkable absence of shock, convent girls being what they are.

'So you probably "condemn this unbridled behaviour",' said Miss Dimont, using that old journalist's trick of putting words into the interviewee's mouth (*Mrs Phipps said, I really have to condemn this unbridled behaviour* when in fact all she'd done was answer the question with a simple yes).

'Not a bit, my dear. In fact, I have come to the view that I positively encourage it.'

'Can I say that?'

'But of course. Gavin has assured me that all over the country the floodgates have opened to allow in this rock and roll, as they call it, and they are unlikely to shut any time soon. I want to encourage more of this bad behaviour.'

Miss Dimont was scribbling in her notebook.

'My dear, I first set foot on the stage nearly fifty years ago,' she went on, waving her gin glass gently. 'We wore long dresses and frilly underpinnings. We smiled coyly and threw as many double-entendres as we could at the audience.

'In those days, such things could drive men wild, and when I was a Gaiety Girl they would do the most extraordinary things – one climbed in my dressing-room window. On the third floor! One sent fourteen wedding rings, one each day for a fortnight, in the hope of getting me into bed if not into church. One did a thing far too rude for me to describe. And quite often, too.

'Is *this* so very different? They're noisier, yes. And it's the girls now, not the boys, making the running. But the young have always craved sensation, and this is what we have today.'

Judy's pen sailed across the page. This was supposed to be Valentine's story, but she couldn't resist – Mrs Phipps was priceless!

'Aren't you worried about them wrecking the theatre?'

'My dear, if they do, the publicity will pay for it. These fellows are here for six weeks and we are already in profit.'

'The lads themselves seem so surly,' said Miss Dimont. 'I caught a glimpse of them as I came in.'

'I expect Gavin has got them on short rations. A well-known ploy in our business for keeping your workforce hard at it. They perform much better when they're hungry.'

'Good Lord!' laughed Judy, 'I didn't know you had it in you, Geraldine! You're far better at running this place than old Ray, er, Mr Cattermole.'

'For continuity's sake and for the health of my bank balance, *I* shall be running the Pavilion this season,' purred the miraculous Mrs P. 'Of course I have Gavin here to call on should I need assistance.'

And no Ray Cattermole to dip his hand into the takings, thought Miss Dimont. But any subsequent musings were wiped away by a sudden and frightening cacophony not unlike a bull entering a china shop without bothering to knock. It was Danny

Trouble and The Urge making their debut in summer season at the Pavilion Theatre, Temple Regis, with their latest offering, 'Schoolgirl Crush'.

Mrs Phipps poured herself another of Plymouth's finest and serenely produced some earplugs.

*

Judy and Valentine were reunited in Beryl's café just along the promenade. It was late but both were exhilarated by the day's events.

'Hoped I'd find you here,' said Valentine, his face pink with excitement. 'I went and had a wander backstage but I didn't want to end the day without thanking you for all your help. I already feel as though I've been here for half a lifetime.'

'Well, quite an interesting day,' agreed Judy. 'Heaven knows what Mr Rhys will make of it, but I'd favour writing positively about this beat group thing. No point in denying the future if, indeed, that is what it is.'

'From what you say he may find that hard to accept.'

'He's always had a way of looking backwards rather than forwards. I think it's because of all those old dinosaurs he mixes with in that club of his. They were all grown men long before the War. They cling to the past, want to turn the clock back to the summer of '39.'

'No point in trying to go back,' said Valentine. 'Because in life they're always rolling up the carpet behind you.'

He looked rather sad as he said it, and Judy asked, gently, 'Yes?'

'Look, we hardly know each other. On the other hand, we share a desk and I very much hope I shall be on the *Riviera Express* for a long time to come,' said Valentine. 'I may as well come clean.'

Oh dear, thought Miss Dimont, thinking of Mulligatawny and

her supper, I hope this isn't going to take all night. I shouldn't have inquired.

'I'm grateful to be here,' said Valentine, looking out to sea. 'Very. Life to date has not been entirely kind. I hadn't realised when I applied for the job that this – this journalism, this local newspaper business – is not just a way of life, it *is* a life. I can see that these people, the ones you work with, are your family.

'I have a family – you seem to have met a few already, in conversation anyway – but it's not the same. They're all pretty distant. My father was an alcoholic and died when I was four. All he left me was the title and . . .'

'Title?'

'Lowest of the low. Baronet. I don't use it.'

'*Sir* Valentine Waterford?'

'Bit too much of a mouthful, wouldn't you say? Got me into all kinds of trouble at school and of course in the army, since I never rose above the rank of Trooper. Though, of course, they wanted me to put in for a commission – but I preferred it where I was.'

He lit a cigarette and went on.

'That's not the confession. The confession is, I've been here two days and I absolutely adore it. I couldn't believe that there could be so much . . . humanity out there to be discovered. You went to sea with the fishermen yesterday, I went to the police station. This morning we were in court, we went and saw that positively creepy woman . . .'

'Nothing creepy about her, Valentine. Learn to look below the surface.'

'OK. Bet you half-a-crown there's something wrong about her, remember I've spent most of my life cooped up with odd-bods and I know one when I see one. Anyway, we saw her and then down here to meet the most important beat group in the country.'

'You met them?'

'I went backstage, I told you. More about that in a minute.'

He got up and looked down at Judy. 'I don't want to hang on your coat tails,' he said. 'You've been already more than kind – it's sink or swim, I know that, I have to make my own way.

'What I want to know is, do you think I'll make it?'

Miss Dimont was not quite sure what he meant. 'What was that you were saying about rolling up the carpet?'

He sat down again and pushed back his hair. 'Nothing ever stays the same. I was born in a sort of castle, but when my father died, it went. So that was gone. My uncle paid for me to go to school and I liked him very much but after the war he went to live in France, so he was gone. My mother – well, she was never what you'd call interested in child-rearing and she'd always hankered after a moat. She found the chap with the moat, but the moat didn't want children so I got dumped on an aunt in Eastbourne. Then she died in a car accident – d'you see what I mean about rolling up the carpet?'

'You don't have any brothers and sisters?'

'Alas no. Some cousins but it's not the same. Actually, I get on better with some of the chaps in my troop in the army. Different background, but solid as they come.'

'From the sound of it you didn't inherit any money.'

Valentine laughed sheepishly. 'You see this suit? That's what I inherited. Doesn't fit terribly well either, does it?

'So you see,' he went on, 'this is the first piece of good fortune I've had in quite a while. But before I start to believe in it, I want to know your opinion. D'you think I'll last the course?'

'Yes,' said Judy, after a pause. 'I think you probably will. Just work hard, and don't fall in love with the idea of being a journalist. It's the worst thing you can do.'

The pair walked slowly back to the office. It was brewing day at Gardner's and the precious aroma of hops and yeast still hung heavy in the air, divinely guiding their footsteps towards the *Express*.

'So these Urge are terrible yobs?' asked Miss Dimont.

'Very nice actually, except the one with the guitar. I think they care very much that what they do is good, of its sort, and they were very happy to talk to me about the making of hit records. I made some notes. Thought it might make an article – I was going to mention it to Mr Rhys.'

'Depends. You've got yourself a scoop talking to the most famous beat group in the country,' said Judy, 'but who knows which way Mr Rhys will jump when he hears about the riots – he automatically steers away from what he sees as trouble. I should keep your powder dry for the time being.'

Back in the office car park, Judy was reunited with her beloved Herbert and together they made their way home. All too soon the streets of Temple Regis would be jammed with holidaymakers, but so far only the early birds had come to fill the hotels and B &Bs, and by common consent, they'd decided to make an early night of it. Or maybe it was Eamonn Andrews on the TV compering *What's My Line*.

Mulligatawny was waiting when she got home, threading himself through her legs as she came in the door so that she had to pick him up to avoid falling over. These warm evenings he would often go out mousing, but only when she got home. If she was working, he faithfully kept guard until her return.

'Oh, Mull,' she sighed, 'what a DAY! All that noise, all those people – as if having a mysterious death wasn't enough! And that poor chap who's come to work on the paper. He looks so dashing but he's a very sad figure. Sadder, I think, than even he admits.' Mulligatawny, though, was uninterested in this line of conversation and settled firmly into her lap as, supper having been taken, the pair sat down for an hour with the radio.

This was thinking time for both Miss Dimont and for Mulligatawny, for though cats live independent lives, they like to be sure of certain things. And Mulligatawny liked to be sure of his mistress. He dug his claws in ever so slightly.

Judy had taken up her novel – a moment's bliss at the end of such a busy day! – but her eyes were on the photograph on the silver frame on the mantelpiece.

'That young man,' she said, half aloud, to the photograph. 'Younger than you. But just like you were when you hopped off that last time. Oh, Eric, you fool . . .'

EIGHT

While the rest of the office was feverishly turning out this week's edition, Curse Corner paused to allow history to reinvent itself.

'He kept a Commando dagger in the glovebox of his Alpine,' droned the chief sub John Ross, scratching his back with an em ruler. 'He taught me how to use it. No' many people have had that privilege.'

Betty, relieved to be back from Newton Abbot for the morning but finding herself prisoner of Ross's self-inflated anecdotage, submitted to this old chestnut but wished she hadn't wandered down to ask how her Women's Institute piece was getting along.

Ross was busy revisiting some big-time Fleet Street anecdotes. 'He introduced me to crooks, thugs, gangsters, members of the Sweeney and . . .' here he paused dramatically to take a sip of tea, '. . . *tarts*. In the afternoons we'd drive off to Mayfair or Knightsbridge to take refreshment with the ladies of the night. My dear girrrl, ye have no idea the stories we used to get from *them*!'

'Astonishing, Mr Ross. And all so long ago, too. Now, if you could just tell me about my piece, I'll be off back to Newt—'

The Glaswegian, all convex belly and hook nose to match, had the roar of a lion. 'Stay, lassie, ye'll learrn something here,' he said, and flipped open the Scotch whisky drawer to rest his foot on it. 'He was working on Rachman. The *Mirror* provided him with a bodyguard – they called him Freddie the White Eagle of Poland – a wrestler, ye know, who'd been banned from the canvas for biting off his opponent's ear.'

He looked hard at Betty. 'They always said it was the *ear*, but, lassie, I could tell you a truth or two . . .'

'I'm sure you could, Mr Ross,' quavered Betty, 'but I'll miss my bus.'

'Bus? BUS?' roared Ross. 'In my day it was taxis and chauffeur cars – all expenses paid! Poor Freddie – we were in Churchill's Club and some girl took exception to the way he looked at her. The boyfriend went and found a cricket bat – a cricket bat, lassie, in Mayfair! – and hit him so hard it broke. Freddie just stroked his head and asked what was for dinner!'

More inflated tales were clearly in the pipeline but just then Rudyard Rhys made his way down the newsroom.

'Ah, Betty,' he said heavily. 'My office, please.'

Betty turned to stalk away – she despised the old windbag Ross and under the protective mantle of the editor wanted to show him what a bore she thought him – but unfortunately at that moment one of her ankles gave way as she turned, and her dramatic exit was reduced to a comical limp.

'Trust me, lassie,' bawled Ross after her, 'it was a different worrrld in those days!'

The editor felt on safe ground with Betty. She was not the most instinctive or intuitive of his reporters but she knew when to say yes.

'Want to talk to you about Miss Dimont, Betty.'

'Yes, Mr Rhys.'

'I've got the *Daily Herald* making trouble. The Rejuvenator story.'

'Yes, Mr Rhys, the Rejuvenator? I'm told it does wonders for . . . you know . . .'

The editor sat up fussily. Always between them was that

unmentioned business of when he gave her the lift in his car. 'It's about Ben Larsson, Betty. I want you to go and interview him, and be quick about it. The *Herald* say they've got more evidence against him, and their crime reporter has just called me for help. I want to head them off at the pass.'

'Mr Larsson's always been very nice to me,' mused Betty, recalling a cocktail party on the terrace and a hand proprietorially laid upon her rear quarters.

'Get over there now,' barked the editor, 'and get him to deny all the accusations. You've got the whole of Page 3, top to bottom, I've taken the ads off. Just get him to deny, deny, deny!'

Betty took out her notebook and scribbled something in it.

'With luck your piece will get picked up by the other nationals who're jealous of the *Herald* scoop and want to disprove these ridiculous claims. Could be a few shillings in lineage for you if you sell the story on – I'll give you the name of a chap on the *Daily Sketch*.'

'Well, that sounds sensible, Mr Rhys, but aren't I supposed to be catching the bus back to Newton Abbot? I only came in to take those reels of film over to Photographic. And why aren't you getting Judy to do this, sounds like something right up her street?' Plus, she thought, Miss Dim can write up a full page in an hour – it takes me for ever. AND I've got a date tonight!

'I shouldn't be saying this, but I can't trust her not to cause trouble. When there's a can of worms she's not happy until she's taken the top off, turned it upside down, and sprinkled out every last blasted one.'

'*Is* there a can of worms, Mr Rhys?'

'Certainly not, girl. Just a question of getting things shipshape.'

Betty sighed, but not much: anything was better than going back to that depressing district office. She still didn't know why she'd been sent there, though she supposed it was to make way for the new recruit. Three months out of a young life was a long time. Maybe that splash in the *Daily Sketch* might bring her swiftly back to Temple Regis.

Or maybe . . . if it went well . . . the chance of a job in Fleet Street itself? Betty Featherstone of the *Daily Sketch*, no less! She picked up her notebook and her shoe and limped happily away.

*

Given the goodwill behind this mercy dash, as Fleet Street is apt to describe any well-intentioned act designed to help someone in distress, it was perhaps less than generous for Pernilla Larsson to greet her blonde-haired saviour with such icy disdain. There Betty stood on her doorstep, looking a little chaotic from the sudden shower which caught her as she walked up the drive, but ready and willing to help.

'He won't see you,' said Pernilla curtly.

'But Mr Rhys said he's arranged it. I should come over and . . . and . . . correct what the *Daily Herald* has been saying.'

Mrs Larsson, whose clothes were purchased in Bond Street, did not like Betty's trim waist, however damp she looked: it gave her figure the sort of hour-glass undulation which Mr Larsson had always gone for. Despite the patchwork blonde hairdo and mismatched clothes, there was a certain unsophisticated attraction about Betty which was right up her husband's street. She didn't want them huddled away together cooking up some fiction – not just for that reason, but also because Betty's mercy dash could seriously impede her own strategy.

'I'd come back some other time if I were you,' she said, closing the door.

'Sorry,' said Betty sharply and, looking down, Pernilla Larsson could see the reporter's foot shoved firmly over the threshold. 'Sorry, but Mr Rhys, my editor, has insisted I come back with a full-page story. He's cleared it with Mr Larsson – they spoke on the phone this morning.'

If there's one thing a reporter dreads more than anything else is going back to the office empty-handed. Why, hadn't old John Ross been talking about this very thing before he launched into that boring tale about the Commando knife?

As a cub reporter his news editor had sent him straight back to an armed siege when Ross made the mistake of returning without a quote. 'They wouldnae talk, they wouldnae answer the door, so I came back. The desk just tol' me, "Get back on the bus. Go back there, and kick the door in. Say you smelt gas."'

Betty had no need to kick in the door, her foot was already firmly established across the threshold and Mrs Larsson, seeing that resistance was pointless, stepped back. 'He's on the terrace,' she muttered.

Huh, thought Betty, just where he pinched my bottom. She walked out into the sunshine and, formalities dispensed with, she took out a copy of the *Herald* and placed it before her interviewee.

'They are saying that the Rejuvenator doesn't work.'

'Untrue.'

'And never has.'

'I have a million letters from grateful patients saying otherwise.'

'Patients?' said Betty, stiffening slightly. 'Do they come to consult you, then? Don't they just buy it mail order from the newspapers and magazines where you advertise?'

'Of course they come here,' said Ben Larsson, blinking slightly. 'There must be a hundred come up here to the Retreat every week. I try to see them all, it's very tiring. But I am dedicated to their well-being.'

'The people who come here, surely, they're members of the Lazarus League? The worshippers?' Though their presence in the town was never acknowledged by the *Riviera Express*, the cranks who'd joined Larsson's weird health-and-worship cult at the height of his commercial success still trailed from time to time through the streets of Temple Regis.

'The League *believes*,' said Larsson firmly. 'Everyone has a right to believe in whatever they wish, don't they, Miss Featherstone, in this great country of yours? Freedom of this and that, of which you're so proud?' He paused and eyed her appraisingly up and down. 'Why don't we have a drink?'

'Look,' said Betty, 'please don't take offence – I've been asked to put these points to you. The *Herald* says that people who've used the Rejuvenator have injured themselves with it.'

'They should read the instructions.'

'One man was severely burnt around his . . . oh,' said Betty, flustered, 'you know where.'

'Misapplication of the device. I will get Lamb to bring out the correspondence file to show you just how many people swear by it. Please, if you are writing this, include something from one or two of their letters.'

Betty was coming to the end of her list of questions. She was rather hoping they wouldn't run out before the drinks tray was wheeled over. Sitting on the terrace, looking back down the estuary with the miraculous gardens beneath, was better than the dreary shoebox she'd been occupying in Newton Abbot.

'And it's also said that many have overstretched themselves to buy the Rejuvenator when they can't afford it. And when it doesn't work they ask for their money back, but they get no response.'

Larsson laughed. 'Nobody should buy something they can't afford, that's not *my* fault. And we have a marvellous easy-terms scheme spread over a year or eighteen months if they can't pay the cash.'

'Not being able to return them to you?'

'Miss Featherstone,' said Larsson, leaning forward and turning on the charm, 'the Rejuvenator is a sensitive scientific instrument. Who knows what people do with it once they have it in their own home? I do not have a repair facility at my factory, simple as that.'

'Well, what should they do with them then?'

'Pass them on to a friend,' Larsson said bleakly. 'What would you like? I usually have a glass of Tio Pepe at about this hour.'

*

'That girl,' said Shirley Kerswell for lack of a better topic of conversation. She and Eve Berry were sitting in the Expresso Bongo just off Market Square. 'Miss Dittisham.'

'I never ever saw her before that last heat,' said Eve. 'It's a complete mystery. She just suddenly appeared out of nowhere.' She rattled her cup, trying to make the soap suds which passed for Italian coffee in Temple Regis collect in the bottom of her cup so she could spoon them out.

'Mavis broke her ankle when her high heel collapsed. They had to find someone in a hurry.' Shirley took out a mirror and repainted her lips – the nice young waiter would be along in a minute to freshen their cups – 'I do know she came from London. You could tell by the way she walked.'

'Incomers not allowed,' frowned Eve, a stickler for the rules. 'These are supposed to be local heats.'

'Mr Normandy said it wouldn't matter, she wouldn't get through to the next round anyway. You know, I sometimes wonder if these beauty pageants aren't all a bit of a fix.'

'Maybe you shouldn't be in them,' snapped Eve. Hers was not to reason why and anyway she knew which side her bread was buttered when it came to fat old Normandy.

'Anyway, she didn't show up for the Temple Regis qualifier, maybe she realised she wasn't going anywhere. Probably pushed off back to London.'

'Didn't fancy her perm,' said Eve, 'did you?'

'I always use Twink myself.'

'Looked professional though. Must have cost a bit.'

'Wonder what can have happened to her, though. She told me she had a boyfriend who was coming down here for the summer. Hush-hush though.'

'Probably married.'

'Didn't say. I expect so.'

Only partially drowned by the hiss of the coffee machine, on the jukebox a young man was warbling about the onset of summer and how kissing a girl might make his flat-top curl. Shirley and Eve spent quite some time debating what this might entail.

Soon they were joined by Molly Churchstow, whose triumphant success in Paignton a few weeks ago ensured that, as the bearer of that town's satin sash, she could sit alongside Shirley and Eve. One might be forgiven for thinking the earth had tilted on its axis, for here seated at one table were three of the most glamorous women in Devon – if popular opinion was the judge – Miss Paignton! Miss Salcombe! Miss Exmouth!

There was the usual post-mortem amongst these three on how the latest competition had gone: they were rivals, but they were friends. Or maybe it was the other way round.

'At least there weren't any protests this week,' said Molly, once she'd settled down and checked her make-up in her gold compact. She took out a packet of Kensitas and offered them round.

'Have you ever heard the like?' said Shirley, thinking back to the dust-up in Paignton. 'Who the devil did she think she was?'

'Some daft old bluestocking. They make such fools of themselves. There was another one when we were doing Miss Dartmouth, d'you remember?'

'Not like this one, though. This one was really mad, wasn't she, shouting and screaming? Thank heavens they got her out before the judges arrived.'

Molly lit their cigarettes. 'Needed a bit of *man*handling, I'd say' she said lugubriously, and they all laughed. They found it difficult to understand a woman who claimed that dressing up in nice clothes and parading before a paying audience was in some way demeaning.

'She kept going on about how we were being exploited,' said Shirley. 'Do *you* feel exploited?'

'Only when he doesn't pay our expenses on time. I mean, it's so costly finding the clothes when you start out. Till they begin giving them to you for free.'

Eve nodded. 'But he makes *so* much money. Have you seen that new Jaguar? You'd think he could at least pay us an appearance fee – after all where would he be without us?'

'He knows we can't resist,' said Molly without bitterness. 'I mean, you can win a holiday.'

'Butlins!'

'You go to London. The hotels, the cars, the nice drinks. And sometimes there's a hunk.'

'They only want one thing.'

'So do I, sometimes.'

The jukebox was playing Tommy Steele. The conversation veered back to the protestor ejected from the Paignton eliminator. 'She lives here in Temple Regis, that old bat,' said Molly. 'I seen her the other day. She looked the other way.'

'I know her too,' said Shirley, who used to work at the Town Hall before fame whisked her away. 'She comes to fix the clock in the tower when it goes wrong.'

'Strange job for a woman, maybe that's why she's so peculiar about beauty pageants,' said Eve. She wanted to move the conversation on. 'That Cyril.'

'Creep,' said Shirley.

'Why do we allow him,' said Molly, more a statement than a question, for they all knew the answer. Beauty pageants had lifted them out of the rut, set them apart, offered them luxuriant dreams, and allowed them access to another world. The price was being treated like cattle.

'At least he's not like that other one – Ernie,' said Shirley. 'All hands.'

'And the rest.'

'I don't think Cyril's interested,' said Eve, always surprised when men weren't interested.

'He was past it years ago.'

'Now that's where you're wrong,' said Molly. 'You should have seen him with that replacement girl. You know . . .'

'Dittisham.'

'Yes, what *was* her name? Something very strange.'

'Too posh for round here,' said Shirley.

'Anyway I saw old Cyril with her. There was definitely something going on there, you can always tell.'

The young man brought more coffee. 'That'll be three-and-six, please, Your Majesties.'

'Have you noticed how small boys are always cheekier than the tall ones?' said Shirley drily as she reached for her purse.

'Saw your photo in the paper,' said the brilliantined lad, unchastened. 'You're all beauty queens, aren't you?'

He went to fetch the paper. There they all were, lined up by the swimming pool, the flower of Devon youth challenging the world with their beauty, accomplishments (the organisers always insisted on their being expert in something – macramé, home embroidery, world atlases), and their bosoms. The photograph was taken in full sunlight and they were all squinting slightly, but they had dazzling smiles.

Molly was pleased since the photographer had angled his shot to favour her, so she handed the boy a nice fat tip. 'Can I keep the paper?'

'Sure.' He winked. 'See ya later, alligator.'

The other two had started talking about Cyril Normandy again but Molly continued to leaf through the paper in the hope of finding more shots of her. As she closed it, her eye caught the headline on the front page.

MYSTERY OF WOMAN FOUND ON TODHEMPSTEAD SANDS

The body of a woman has been discovered on the private beach at Todhempstead, police revealed this week.

The woman, in her early twenties, was fully clothed but had no possessions to identify her. Temple Regis police say they have consulted the Missing Persons Register but the body does not fit the description of anybody on their list. They describe the woman as being blonde, in good health, and well nourished. They refuse to say how she died.

'We would urge anybody who was on the Sands on Monday morning to make contact with the police on Temple 1212,' said Sergeant Gull of Temple police.

Todhempstead Sands, a private beach, was in the news recently after its owner Dick Bradford imposed a 1/3d fee on anybody wishing to walk their dogs there.

'Hey,' exclaimed Molly, 'look at this!'

Her friends obliged.

'Good heavens,' said Shirley, 'you don't think . . . ?'

'Can't be,' said Eve.

'It could,' said Molly, firmly. 'Do you think we should telephone in?'

NINE

Inspector Topham sat in the bar of the Grand Hotel and stared into his pint as if somewhere in its depths lay the answer to the dead blonde. There had been other pints and other dead bodies, and if the Portlemouth Ale did not always come up with an answer it could at least soothe away the unease and anxiety which came with upholding law and order for the townsfolk of Temple Regis.

He took a sip, so slow he might almost have been touching his lips with Communion wine, but apart from tickling his palate the beer did little to bring immediate rewards.

The girl wasn't local, no. That much was established after an artist's likeness (they couldn't use a photo, poor thing) had been posted outside police stations all over the county. There'd even been a mention in the SOS segment on the BBC's Home Service – surely, even if she'd come from Liverpool, someone must be missing her?

That it was murder was now beyond doubt – the pathologist had given it to him straight just an hour ago – a detailed account of a brutal blow, followed by another, to the side of her head. Metal object with an edge, delivered by someone slightly taller, right-handed. Topham had been to see the corpse and listened to the pathologist's dispassionate report while he looked down on the remains of this wasted young life. No getting away with passing it off as an accident now; no more evading the ugly truth.

That was why he was sitting in the Grand. There was nothing especially tragic about the death of a man in battle – he'd seen too many – but a fresh young girl like this, it was upsetting. He wondered about her mother and whether she was still imagining her girl was away somewhere having a lovely time with her friends – the promise of the wedding and the grandchildren that were never to be . . .

'Summat wrong with the beer?' inquired Sid the barman, for Inspector Topham wasn't drinking.

'No, Sid, just thoughts. Thoughts.'

A terrible racket was coming from the Cocktail Bar down the corridor. 'What's that all about?' asked the inspector, cross that his sombre thoughts should be disturbed by hilarity.

'That'll be Mr Normandy, the beauty queen man. Spending his ill-gotten gains. You know they 'ad over three thousand people up the Lido for the pageant? That's the way to rake it in!'

Frank Topham was only half listening.

'Those poor girls,' went on Sid, for he'd spent most of the day with nobody to talk to, polishing his glasses and cleaning the beer pipes, 'they come in 'ere the other night – they 'adn't got the price of a gin between them. They made a fortune for that Mr Normandy and they get blummer all for it.'

'Mm.'

'One of 'em told me she 'ad to borrow the train fare off of her mum just so's she could take part in the pageant. They all live in hope, y'see,' said Sid. 'If they win, it's like winning the pools only nicer, what with the sunny holidays and free flimsies. O' course, they never do. Instead they're in here clubbing together to buy a round while their lord and master next door is pouring champagne down his throat like there's no termorrer.'

'Where did the girl – the one who had to borrow her train fare – where did she come from?'

'Only over Tavistock way.'

'Oh,' said Topham and subsided over his pint glass. A flame had flickered alive for a moment, but just as quickly it was extinguished.

Sid looked down from his elevated position behind the bar and saw the hunched figure utterly lost and at sea.

'Drink that up and have one on the 'ouse, Frank,' he said kindly. 'Mebbe a short.'

'Can't get it straight,' came the reply. 'Can't see the reason. Can't see the point. She was very pretty, you see. What was left of her.'

Sid, with a lifetime's experience of hearing the woes of others, knew when to shut up. Pretty soon Frank Topham got up, lifted his hat, and returned his still-full glass to the bar.

'Nothing wrong with the beer,' he said to Sid. 'Something wrong with me.'

He walked out into the hotel and slowed as he came to the entrance to the Cocktail Bar. In there stood suave Cyril Normandy, who had made the place his own and didn't mind who knew it.

'Here's another, here's another!' he shouted commandingly, and the champagne-swillers turned to see Topham's mournful figure standing in the doorway. 'Come in, come in!'

A portly matron with a cottage-loaf hairdo came over and linked her arm through his. 'Come on, handsome, come in and join the party. Cyril's buying!'

If he had one prevailing virtue, Frank Topham liked to know what was going on in his town. In these post-war days, there were right ones and there were wrong ones. The conflict had thrown everything up in the air and society had come down with a bump and you didn't know who was who any more. Now, people seemed to have money for no good reason. What's more they were spending it like there was no tomorrow. Who were they, where had they come from, where would they go when all the money had gone?

The detective sniffed suspiciously, but allowed himself to be dragged in.

'Cyril Normandy,' said the beauty queen king by way of introduction.

'Inspector Topham, Temple Regis CID.'

'Wooooooaaaaah, we could have used YOU on Tuesday!' yodelled Normandy, pinging his braces on his fat belly. 'To hold the crowds back at the Lido. They wanted to eat my girls, Inspector! EAT them!'

'I heard from the uniform branch everyone was very well behaved.'

'Yes but you should see the look in the eyes of some of 'em ! 'ave some shampoo! You see someone like a Lord Mayor, with his chain of office round his neck and his eyes out on stalks – that's what makes Riviera Queen such a smash hit – it brings out the *beast* in a man!' Normandy rolled his eyes and his followers burst into cascades of laughter.

'I think you came down here last year as well, Mr Normandy.'

'And I will do for every year in the foreseeable future.' The entrepreneur splashed champagne into a glass and forced it into the policeman's hand. 'You can say this for Temple Regis, dead-and-alive hole it may be – it provides a wonderful turnout when my girls get into their cozzies! We got a record box office, and it isn't even high season yet.'

Topham masked his distaste and smiled insincerely at Normandy, a man blind to insincerity.

'So tell me,' he said, 'how does it work, this pageant process?'

Normandy was delighted to have someone new to listen to his success story. 'It's a pyramid,' he said, proudly.

'At the top is the title Miss Great British Summer 1959. And above *that*, Miss Great Britain. A beautiful tiara, to keep for ever. At the bottom are a load of shop girls desperate to escape their humdrum lives and crummy lodgings who'll crawl over hot coals to be given a sash to wear.

'Their boyfriends tell them they're beautiful – guess why! – and they believe it. We turn them into royalty. They see the red carpets and the thrones, the fabulous make-up and the hair, and now, the television cameras – it's like a drug. Think of where they come from, Inspector – the gutter!' he guffawed. 'I hose the mud off 'em and make 'em famous!'

Topham put down his glass untouched. 'Well, very interesting, Mr Normandy. And are you staying here for long?'

'They'll beg, borrow, steal and scratch each other's eyes out to win,' chattered the fat man happily, not yet ready to be deflected. There was a wildness about him which had nothing to do with the drink. He seemed, thought Topham, to take a savage glee in manipulating the lives of innocents. And getting rich in the process.

'Each year since 1951 – ever since I created the Miss Festival of Great Britain title – the beauty pageant business has grown. We make so much money we even give some to charity – that brings us in more, because it persuades old fools like your Lord Mayor that it's all innocent fun, it's all above board.

'Which, of course, it is,' added the fat man with a wink. 'No silly nonsense, no hanky-panky, that's my first rule.'

'Relieved to hear it,' said Topham. 'Well, goodnight.'

'Have some more shampoo! 'Ere, you haven't even touched that one!'

'I have a funny taste in my mouth,' said Topham.

*

It was Auriol Hedley who'd sent her reporter friend knocking again on the green-painted door in Tuppenny Row. She had an extraordinary power to see where others cannot; or, more possibly, it was because she was a trained observer, with the right amounts of intuition and suspicion, to look at a problem from the other end of the telescope. Miss Dimont, who prided herself on a swift and deductive brain, did not always agree with Auriol's conclusions – her friend was often too swift to answer a question without considering its wider ramifications – and this had led to occasional disagreements in their wartime service together.

But at their lunchtime chat Auriol had made a statement of the obvious: the dead girl on the sands at Todhempstead had fallen to her death from the Pullman train, or she'd been struck by it, or she had deliberately thrown herself at it. In each of these cases her body would have flown or toppled from the Todhempstead embankment onto the beach below.

'It had to be something else, though,' said Auriol. 'Was the body anywhere near the railway embankment?'

'I see your point. It wasn't too far away, but I don't think, judging from the markers that were left in the sand by the police, that it could be to do with the train. Unless, of course, once she'd been struck, some person or persons dragged the body and left it further out to sea, maybe hoping the tide would wash it away.'

'I wonder how many people would have been on the beach on that morning.'

'Very few, most people can't afford it. You know it's privately owned, by a friend of someone very important. He bought the sands a couple of years ago and now charges people to walk their dogs or put up a deckchair – over a shilling it costs! "One an' three," the old boy at the gate said to me. I had a word in his ear.'

'And?'

'I can use the 1/3d to pay for my tea here.'

'Never in a lifetime of lifetimes, my dear.'

'I know.' The two were the closest of companions, though

their lives were very different. Since she came to Temple Regis Miss Dimont had joined the choir, submitted her best efforts to the annual flower show, and plunged herself deep into the joys and occasional anguishes of life in a seaside town.

Auriol, Judy's senior by a couple of years, had done the opposite. War service, and the loss of her brother Eric, together with the extraordinary discovery that a woman of her gifts could be so valuable in war and so dispensable in peace, had driven her to Devon and to the opening of the Seagull Café in Bedlington-on-Sea. She bore no grudges, she smiled benignly upon her customers and insisted they had another slice of cake, and lived a very private life. Judy sometimes wondered if she were Auriol's only friend.

'So the answer is, she wasn't killed on the beach – her body was planted there. Though why anyone should want to do that, and how, I cannot think.'

The lack of motive was infuriating. That the woman had been unlawfully killed seemed now beyond doubt, but who? As well as why?

According to the police, she wasn't local and must have been a holidaymaker. But Judy had another theory: Valentine had counted the contestants at the Lido and, if his sums were correct, there was one missing. He was sent off to find Cyril Normandy while Miss Dimont sat on a bench in Tuppenny Row and thought about what she was going to do next.

If it *was* a missing beauty queen, and this was only the merest supposition, who would want to kill her? She then recalled Athene talking about the Sisters of Reason, the small group of activists who talked big about emancipation and who'd made such a big fuss at the Paignton eliminator. They'd come close to violence on that occasion – they had tried to storm the stage and pull the girls off – could one of them have gone a step too far this time and actually killed the woman on the beach?

Or was that just too fanciful an idea? Surely nobody would be fanatical enough to kill a girl for taking part in a beauty pageant? Could they?

All this she had discussed with Auriol, who'd urged prompt action. She rose from the bench and walked across the street to knock on the green front door.

'Miss de Mauny,' she said, taking off her gloves as the horologist cautiously answered the door, 'I hope you don't mind.'

'Not a bit,' came the reply. After a sticky start they had got on well, and Miss de Mauny had enjoyed the article on Lady Rhondda and her plan to explode a Post Office letter box in the name of women's equality. 'Come in.'

'I thought you could help me with a related matter,' said Miss Dimont, feeling her way carefully. 'After all we talked about, I imagine you know quite a lot about the Sisters of Reason?'

The atmosphere in the sun-filled cottage changed sharply. 'Why are you asking me that?' snapped Angela de Mauny. 'They're nothing to do with me.'

'Just something I'm following up. We've never written about them in the *Express*, but I've heard quite a bit about them. Very vocal campaigners on behalf of our gender. They succeeded in disrupting the Paignton beauty pageant a couple of weeks ago, and I just thought . . .'

'Well you thought wrong,' snapped Miss de Mauny.

'But from what you were saying only the other day, you agree with their views on beauty pageants.'

'They're a bit of a fringe group,' said Miss de Mauny, dropping her guard slightly. 'Some people think they're rather extreme – not in their views, which are wholly sound, but in their means of action. They're, well . . . disruptive. For myself, I belong to the National Council of Women, a very well-established organisation which seeks the same ends but by democratic means.'

'But you know members of the Sisters of Reason?'

'No.'

'But, Miss de Mauny . . . I don't wish to embarrass you, but you were there with them at Paignton.'

'Who said *that*?' flashed the clockmaker. Her hand dropped to the workbench and her fingers closed on a heavy brass pendulum.

'One of the contestants. She said she recognised you from the work you did on the town hall clock.'

'Complete nonsense.'

'She said she used to bring you tea while you were doing the job.'

Angela de Mauny's hand tightened on the pendulum. 'What are you *saying*?'

'Not saying anything,' said Miss Dimont, suddenly alarmed at the unexpected reaction her questions had triggered and calculating the distance to the front door. 'Just that, you were there. With the Sisters. They seem quite a violent lot. I wondered if any of them could have had anything to do with this missing girl who was in the paper this week.'

'Didn't she fall out of the train?'

'I don't know where you heard that. It's more likely she was killed by somebody.'

'Are you saying she was . . . murdered?' Miss de Mauny's face had gone white beneath its early summer tan.

'Very likely.'

'Why are you asking this? You're not the police.'

'Look,' said Miss Dimont, trying to soothe a woman who suddenly seemed very agitated indeed. 'If she was murdered there has to be a motive. Theft is usually one, the victim being interfered with another, but neither applies in this case. These beauty pageants seem to cause as much offence to a certain sector as they give pleasure to others. I'm just interested in the Sisters of Reason, and clearly you know a lot about them, that's all.'

'Your questions seem to imply the Sisters had a hand in this girl's murder and that in some way I might be involved.' Miss de Mauny's eyes were flashing in the oddest way and she was turning the heavy pendulum over in her hand.

'I said nothing of the kind,' said Miss Dimont sharply. 'Look, please put that thing down and let's talk sensibly.'

Miss de Mauny did not relax her grip.

'The Sisters did their best to disrupt the Paignton heat of Miss Great British Summer. You were among them. One of the contestants, who should have gone on into the Temple Regis round, has disappeared. And now we have a body on the beach. These two facts could be connected.'

Miss de Mauny used her free hand to adjust her glasses. 'Listen,' she said. 'I gave a speech the other day about Lady Rhondda. She died last year. I was a close friend of hers and admired her very much. That's the level of interest I have in this subject.'

'From what you tell me, Lady Rhondda believed in direct action to get what she wanted.'

'Not to the extent of murdering a beauty queen!' shouted Miss de Mauny angrily. 'She was a distinguished suffragette. Her work has inspired generations of women – women who've struggled to get proper recognition for their role in society and their contribution to the wealth of the nation.'

'Do the Sisters believe in Lady Rhondda's more extreme actions? Blowing things up?'

'For heaven's sake!' thundered Miss de Mauny, putting the pendulum down. It was very heavy. 'Can you, a woman, honestly blame them if they become impatient? Look at the state of things in this country, Miss Dimont – a nation of fifty-two million, half of them women. How many of them are cabinet ministers? Company chairmen? Bishops?' She spat out the thought in disgust. 'Honestly, can you blame them?'

'But this girl,' said Miss Dimont quietly, 'I don't see it. Surely if the Sisters wanted to cause damage to Miss Great British Summer, they'd pick on that odious fish who runs it? The man called Normandy?'

A cunning look crept across Miss de Mauny's face. 'I should have thought a woman of your advanced intelligence should be able to work that one out,' she said. 'Were they to wish to do something like that, though it seems pretty far-fetched, wouldn't they allow the police to believe that it was Mr Normandy who did it?

'A criminal trial for murder by the organiser of the nation's so-called number one beauty pageant – wouldn't that put paid to beauty pageants all over Britain, all over the globe?'

Miss Dimont had to confess the clock-mender had a point.

TEN

Valentine Waterford finished his home-made lemonade and chased the last crumbs of rock cake around the plate.

'Delicious,' he smiled.

'Have another,' said Auriol Hedley sweetly, her perennial response to hungry customers.

'I didn't want to bother you earlier because you were busy,' said Valentine, picking up his plate and glass and bringing them over to the counter. 'But you are Miss Dimont's friend. I came and picked her up here the other day. I live just round the corner.'

'Really,' said Auriol, taking off her apron. 'Then welcome, neighbour! You couldn't have picked anywhere lovelier.'

'I've just joined the *Express*. Junior reporter,' he said with undisguised pride.

'She told me about you,' said Auriol. 'You're related to Admiral Godfrey?'

'I gather you both worked with him in the war.'

'*For* him,' corrected Auriol. 'A wonderful man.'

'Miss Dimont's pretty wonderful too,' said Valentine. 'Extraordinary in fact. Could be a leader of men.'

'She'd take that as a compliment,' said Auriol. 'I gather you were in the cavalry.' Clearly Miss Dimont had passed on quite a bit about Devon journalism's newest recruit.

'In the ranks.'

'That's surprising given your family history. The Admiral and so on.'

'Actually, it was Miss Dimont's family history I was interested in.'

'Oh ho! You didn't come here for my lemonade and rock cakes, then!'

'I gather their fame goes well beyond the Devon borders, and of course they're delicious,' parried Valentine. 'No, I'm starting out on what I hope will be a lifetime's career, and I hoped to learn a bit more about the person I share a desk with. I've never met anyone quite like her.'

'Good heavens,' said Auriol, 'you sound like a journalist already. Asking personal questions.'

'Yes and no,' said Valentine, 'the thing is I have a peculiar family myself and my guess is, so does she. I just wondered . . .'

'You want to know what to ask her about her people and what not.'

'That's about it.'

'Well, you know you can't ask about what she used to do before she came here. That's secret.'

'The War seems so very far away now.'

'But the secrets stay secret for eternity – to the grave!' Auriol brought two more glasses of lemonade to the table. She was enjoying this, he seemed a very nice boy. 'Go on, then, ask away.'

'Her name, so unusual, what's her background?'

'Well, she'd tell you in time herself. She's had a very remark-able life.'

'Go on.' The sun was shining brilliantly outside on the dock but the café was empty. People had better things to do on a Saturday morning than sit around with glasses of lemonade going over past history. They were the poorer for it.

'Well, you know her family come from Belgium, very distinguished people.'

'I heard you call her Oog or something when you were saying goodbye the other day. Is that a nickname?'

'No, her real name is Huguette, I call her Hugue for short. You don't say the "h" of course. She escaped with her family from Belgium in the First War and they set up home in Britain. She went to school in Sussex before university, then joined the family business.'

'She has a businesslike brain. You can see that.'

'Her father died and she became quite important running round Europe – Amsterdam one minute, Paris the next. Berlin, Madrid, all over. The diamond trade. It came in handy for her war work.'

'Diamonds? Really?'

'No, you silly boy,' said Auriol. 'The fact that she knew every European capital and could get by in each of their languages. That was a rare and vital asset in 1939.'

'Does she have family still living?'

'Just her mother now. A bit of a battleaxe. No,' corrected Auriol, 'more than a bit. Madame Dimont can't quite believe her daughter has grown up. She knows nothing, obviously, of her war work and so is unable to judge quite how competent a human being she brought into this world. But Madame is the veritable Achille's heel – Hugue can cope with everything in life, apart from a visit from her mother.'

'Which the mother is permanently threatening.'

'You do catch on quickly, Valentine.'

'I rather hoped the one tangible asset I possess might come in useful in journalism.'

Auriol laughed. Underneath that charm, he was pretty sharp.

'And she's never married?' he asked.

'That's enough for one day,' said Auriol firmly. 'She'll tell you if she wants. That's if you stick around long enough. There's a high turnover of young journalists down here – here one day, gone the next. Where do you think you'll be this time next year?'

'D'you know,' said Valentine, getting up and walking over to the window, 'I woke up this morning and decided I might want to stay here for ever.'

'You might not want to,' cautioned Auriol, 'once you've got on the wrong side of that editor of yours. He can be perfect poison. I've known him for years and he gets worse. I don't know why Hugue puts up with it.'

'That's another thing,' said Valentine, turning. 'Why call herself Judy, when her own name is so much more intriguing?'

'Girls can be cruel. For a time she was a bit plump at school and so they called her Huge. No wonder she changed it.'

'Not Judy to close friends, though.'

'No,' agreed Auriol, 'not to close ones.'

'It's strange,' said Valentine. 'I've only been here five minutes and already it seems like home. There's something special about Devon, there's definitely something very special about Temple Regis. Maybe the air perhaps? I don't know.'

'I would have thought a young man like you would prefer to be in London, kicking up your heels.'

'Well, one does get invited to parties – too many parties,' he said, scratching his head.

'Lots of nice girls,' encouraged Auriol.

'Well . . .' said Valentine and looked as though he was going to go on, but then shut up. 'I've been on my own rather a lot. After I came out of the army I decided to go for a walk.'

'Lake District? Scotland?'

'No,' said Valentine, 'something different. I took the train to Dover, hopped on a ferry, and then walked from Calais to Budapest.'

'Good Lord,' said Auriol, who was not easily impressed, 'that must be . . .'

'Nearly a thousand miles, with detours. I hitched a lift some of the way but it still took a long time.'

'Why?'

'I was pretty mixed up. I'm not now.' Valentine wandered over to the door. 'Well, that was lovely, Mrs Hedley.'

'Miss Hedley. Auriol if you like.'

'I'll be in again. I'm just round the corner at Cranmer Cottage.'

'Old Christie's place? I thought he was dead.'

'He is. Last December. He was . . . not quite sure what sort of relation he was, but until they sort out the probate it's on loan. As a quid pro quo I'm supposed to sort out the chaos. Bit untidy at the moment but I hope you and Judy, er, Hu— er . . . will come and say hello once it's straightened out. I really feel at home here.'

'Delighted,' said Auriol spiritedly. 'And if you ever have an afternoon off during the holiday season, young man, I can always use an extra pair of hands.'

*

Miss Dimont was on the point of leaving the Tuppenny Row cottage. Angela de Mauny's mood had veered from friendly to almost threatening during this second conversation, but though she was definitely odd, Miss Dimont could not help admiring her grit – the ambition to conquer Mount Everest a mere handful of years after Edmund Hillary was enviable. To enter horology, a profession as closed to women as the Freemasons themselves, and to prosper, was remarkable too. She was quirky and well read but with a strange urgency about her, her hands often dabbing at her eyes as if trying to rub away non-existent tears.

The matter of the Sisters of Reason remained unexplained, equally Angela de Mauny's presence at the Paignton beauty pageant: Miss Dimont, a gifted interviewer, realised she was talking to a brick wall when it came to these matters. All that could be said was that the clockmaker had helped furnish Miss Dimont's article on the progress of West Country women post-war – the ostensible reason for her return to Tuppenny Row – with some sharp little vignettes. It could be said, therefore, that her work was done.

Just as she picked up her raffia bag ready to depart and pushed the spectacles back up her nose, the front door was pushed open with some urgency and a voice barked: 'Ange! You *promised* . . . !'

'Oh!' exclaimed Miss de Mauny, embarrassed and deflated at the same time.

Miss Dimont felt the hallway suddenly filled with a massive presence. Before her stood a tall, crop-haired eminence, slim and military in bearing, dressed in a sharply cut tweed suit. Though not much taller than the other two, she somehow towered above them. She was little short of magnificent.

'Er,' faltered Miss de Mauny, clearly punctured by the arrival of this newcomer, 'er, my guest is just going. Do, er, do go in and make yourself a cup of tea. Just be a jiffy.'

'Hello,' said Miss Dimont, pleasantly enough, but not wishing to leave without an introduction. 'Judy Dimont.'

'New recruit?' barked the eminence, looking straight past the reporter to Miss de Mauny.

'No, Ursula. She's a reporter from the local newspaper.'

'WHAT!' The stentorian voice crashed against the pastel walls of the cottage and bounced back.

'*Riviera Express*,' said an undiminished Miss Dimont, perfectly at ease. 'May I ask...?'

'Ursula Guedella,' snapped the towering individual, as if everyone should know who she was. Yet the name did not serve to enlighten the reporter. 'We don't want publicity.'

'I don't offer publicity,' said Miss Dimont, sharply, quite undaunted. 'I came to talk to Miss de Mauny about a feature I'm writing about the position of women in the late 1950s.'

'And so you SHOULD!' barked the tweed suit. 'So I should THINK!'

'Perhaps,' rejoined the reporter, 'it is a subject close to your heart as well.'

A strange whinnying noise came from across the hall, one which could loosely be interpreted as laughter.

'My name means nothing to you?' said Ursula, snootily.

'I'm afraid not,' said Miss Dimont. 'I don't believe you're local?'

'LOCAL?' the response came as a bellow. All three of them were standing in Angela de Mauny's hall but suddenly there did not seem enough room to accommodate them. 'We are EVERYWHERE. You're a WOMAN. You surely know THAT!'

Miss Dimont made a gesture of conciliation. Her smile, the dip of her head said that what a fool she must be not to know all these things, including the identity of the rude woman standing so aggressively before her.

The penny finally dropped. 'The Sisters of Reason,' she said, shooting a glance at Angela de Mauny. The clockmaker, who like St Peter had thrice denied all knowledge, had been caught out.

The woman strode past.

'Commandant,' said Angela, chasing after her into the kitchen. 'A cup of tea.' Miss Dimont was left on the doormat; clearly it was expected that she would let herself out. But since she had not directly been invited to leave she took the journalist's view that, perforce, she was allowed to stay. She followed the pair into the back room. 'No milk, no sugar,' she trilled sweetly. 'But if you have a slice of lemon . . .'

*

Betty Featherstone was feeding the customary double-decker sandwich of copy paper and carbon paper into a large Olivetti parked on an unused desk at the back of the newsroom. It had been relegated there because its 'g' had gone missing – very irritating, but every other typewriter was occupied. There were fewer machines than reporters, and when you were in a hurry you had to take whatever there was.

Prominent Temple Re.is resident .athers support a.ainst his critics

She wrote.

A .ar.antuan row over Mr Ben.t Larsson's famous Rejuvenator is buildin. in the national press. But a .roundswell of opinion is also .rowin. in defence of the machine. The Express has .athered a lar.e number of letters from an.ry people who claim to have .ained hu.e benefit from the . . .

'Oh this is hopeless!' exclaimed Betty. 'I can't concentrate.' She had difficulty assembling her thoughts at the best of times, but when there was a hint of a new romance in the air it could scatter her thoughts hither and yon.

'Any su..estion that this life.ivin. .ad.et is a sham is simply outra.eous!' said Mrs .eor..ina Hu..ett, of .ran.e Road, Temple Re.is, this week.

Just then she was rescued by her editor, who ordered her into his office.

'Just writing it up now, Mr Rhys.'

'What did he say?'

'He said what a good friend you had been to him over the years. He said that when you and he . . .'

'Never mind all that. Have you got a significant denial out of him?'

'Well you know, Mr Rhys, I'm no expert but it does look as though what some of these people are saying is right. After I talked to Mr Larsson, his butler gave me some letters to show how much the public adored him, but by mistake the man gave me another file as well which contained . . . well, Mr Rhys, it's shocking! I always thought the Rejuvenator was a good thing – good for people's health, that's what he always claimed. But the letters, Mr Rhys!'

'Rr . . . rrr.'

'These people saying they've been electrocuted, they've been scorched, that it's had a bad effect on the brain when applied to the scalp . . . not just one complaint, Mr Rhys – there must have been hundreds!'

'There was a time, Betty, when Ben Larsson was considered for a knighthood. Just you bear that in mind.'

'He says he's very grateful to you, Mr Rhys. Something about the War, he started talking about it and then stopped. What would that be about? Should I include it?'

'Nothing to do with the present circumstances. You just get on and write that story.' The editor seemed extremely edgy.

'I can't Mr Rhys. The only available typewriter is that broken-down old Remington with the missing "g".'

'Better use mine then,' said the editor with irritation. 'Sit down and get on with it, we haven't got all day.'

Just then his phone rang: 'Sam Southam here,' said a self-important voice.

'Good afternoon, Your Worship.'

'Rhys, I want something in the paper tomorrow about these animals who've invaded our town. These blooming girls and boys ripping the Pavilion to shreds over this skiffle group. I've got hordes of people down here at the Town Hall threatening all sorts of things. There really is no need for a town like ours to bow to . . . *teenagers*.'

'Er, not a skiffle group, Worship. They are in fact the number one beat group in the country,' said Rhys, parroting Judy and Valentine's combined story. 'They will bring glamour and prestige to Temple Regis – the first of the new beat groups to do a summer season, and they choose our town! I'm told we should be grateful, that you should be holding a civic reception for them.'

'Horse manure! They're upsetting the townsfolk, they're making a filthy racket, and there are girls running around our streets in a state of undress, screaming their heads off, getting up to all sorts on the beach. How's that going to make the town rich?'

'Well, I confess I don't know how much they'll boost trade in your butcher's shop, Worship, but it could bring some much-needed national publicity to the town. Especially after the Larsson business.' The editor did not like the Mayor but then it was mutual.

'Just get an article in there telling everybody to calm down. I don't want the Chief Constable drafting in extra police – think of the cost!'

'We never tell the readership what to do,' snapped Rudyard Rhys and abruptly brought the conversation to a halt.

He turned to Betty, whose typewriter had fallen silent.

'Have you finished? That was quick.'

'I can't do it, Mr Rhys. It's lies, honestly. Lies! All these poor people, the damage they've suffered! And if that can't be put right, why doesn't Mr Larsson just pay them back the money? He wouldn't miss it – just look how rich he is!

'Just reading those letters,' she said, quite agitated now, 'most people who bought a Rejuvenator couldn't even afford it, they bought it on the never-never. They just got caught up in the excitement of it and ended up broke.'

Rhys stood bolt upright, almost as if to attention. 'He did some very brave things in the war.'

'Nobody ever said anything about that.'

'It's because it was secret, Betty, a secret! I suppose I'll have to write it myself.'

Betty felt like asking if he knew where the carriage return was, he was so unaccustomed to writing anything.

Rudyard, indeed. No Kipling he!

ELEVEN

Athene Madrigale stood immobile on the shore, watching the ships. Time passed, and their blurred silhouettes slowly blended into each other in the velvet haze of this most beautiful evening. Behind her in the approaching night she could hear a late freight train seething and clanking through the dusk.

Miss Dimont had come down to find her friend, bringing a wrap for the chilly evening breeze coming in off the water.

'Thank you, dear,' said Athene kindly, 'but do you mind if I don't put it on? Wrong colour, you see. Upsets the aura.'

It was nearly dark. The wrap, vaguely beige in colour, could hardly be thought to clash with the confusion of pigments wrapped around the clairvoyant's slight frame, but Judy knew better than to argue.

'I'd so like to talk to you, Athene,' she said, 'but it's getting cold. May we go and sit in the bus shelter?'

Streaks of purple grained the heavy dark clouds. The air smelled of rain but you could still feel the heat rising from the sand. They walked towards the shelter, but then Athene had a better idea.

'Come with me, there's somewhere I'd like you to see,' she said. 'Only a couple of minutes away.'

It was not late, but most of Temple Regis had already tucked itself up for the night. The two women walked through deserted streets towards the fish-and-chip shop whose yellow bulbs were still blazing merrily, throwing pools of sparkling light onto the pavement outside. It was so quiet you could still hear the angry banging as the freight train started up from Regis Junction, making its way towards Newton Abbot.

'Down here,' said Athene suddenly.

Miss Dimont was entranced. She knew Temple Regis well but this little courtyard, Bosun's Alley, was unfamiliar, they passed in front of an antique shop and a tiny second-hand book store then turned a tight corner into what appeared to be a dead end. 'Here we are,' said Athene proudly, and opened a small door.

The lights were low and there was little noise inside, apart from a strange tinkling coming from a back room. 'Sit down,' said Athene, smiling, 'Mr So will come.'

Judy Dimont looked with fascination around a long low room which was lit in part by a string of Coronation lights – red, white, and blue – which most people would have taken down years ago. Strangely they did not seem out of place here. 'Where are we? What is this?' she asked.

Athene smiled at the possession of her special secret. 'The Chinese Singing Teacher,' she said proudly. 'You might call it my spiritual home.'

Two further rooms stretched away from them, but though they appeared to be unoccupied it felt as if a party of happy people had just departed, leaving their good humour behind, hanging in the air.

Mr So brought tea and rice crackers and bowed gracefully away.

'Good Lord,' said Miss Dimont, puzzled, 'how *most* unusual! I didn't know about this place.'

'Nobody does. There are just a few of us . . . souls . . . you might call us. Mr So makes us welcome, dear, he is *sympatico*.

It's very soothing, very good for your aura – look, it's turning green just as we sit here! You feel better, don't you?'

'I always feel better when I see you, Athene. But I've something to discuss.'

Athene looked into her teacup and who knows what she saw there. For most people, the view would be of some faintly coloured liquid with a few stalk-like leaves in the bottom, but to Athene . . .

Miss Dimont gave her a moment to absorb its mysteries before continuing. 'Athene, I want you to think hard about Todhempstead beach. That girl didn't get there by accident. She must have been brought while you were actually there – did you see a car or van, or anything that could have taken a body out there there?'

Athene looked deeper into her cup. 'Don't you think she might have come by sea?' she asked slowly, as if the leaves had spoken to her.

'Her clothes weren't wet.'

'But if somebody had brought her? By boat, for instance?'

'Why would they want to do that, Athene?' But already Miss Dimont was absorbing the idea, recognising the moment for what it was – an abstract notion and not a fact, given to Athene as a gift from the ether. It had happened before.

'She came by boat,' repeated Miss Dimont reflectively. 'Yes.'

'I often wonder about ravens,' said Athene, 'don't you?'

'Well,' said Miss Dimont, who had other things on her mind. 'They . . .'

'When they circle it often signifies a death. I didn't see any at Todhempstead Sands.'

Well, no surprise there, thought Judy, but didn't like to say it so she changed the subject. 'Do you know I'd never even heard of the Chinese Singing Teacher, and I must have walked past Bosun's Alley a million times?'

'Mr So is a very private person,' said Athene, smiling across the room to where the bearded old gentleman stood quite still, attentive to their needs but spiritually in another place.

'Then something else. I came across the most extraordinary woman this afternoon. She was dressed almost like a kind of soldier – tall, military, hair like a brush. Apparently she's quite famous, Ursula Guedella. I'd never heard of her. She seems to be in charge of . . .'

'The Sisters of Reason,' said Athene.

'Well!' said Judy, exasperated. 'How on earth do you know about *them*? You're not secretly a Sister yourself?'

'They came in here one night two or three weeks ago,' said Athene. 'Most unpleasant.'

'What do you mean?'

'Rather manly, some of them. The rest were flibbertigibbets. Mr So is far too kind, but I could tell he did not like having them in here. They made such a commotion, it had a tremendously jarring effect. I had to leave.'

'Wait a moment,' said Miss Dimont, absorbing this, 'how many were there?'

'Six or seven.'

'Did you hear what they were talking about?'

'Oh yes, it was about the Paignton beauty pageant. How they were going to create a fuss and try to embarrass the girls and the organisers.'

Miss Dimont stared evenly across the table at her friend.

'Athene,' she said slowly, 'you never thought to tell me about this?'

'Well, dear,' said Athene sweetly, pouring another cup, 'I ration what I tell you. I receive a lot of information one way and the other, and it would be taking up too much of your time if I were to tell you every little thing.'

'But . . .'

'Very simple,' said Athene, answering the unfinished question, 'what they were going to do was in Paignton. Our newspaper doesn't sell in Paignton, so why weigh you down with useless tittle-tattle? Second, they spent a lot of time talking about "the big one" but gave no clue as to what it was. Why clog up that brilliant brain of yours with puzzles that can't be answered?'

Miss Dimont should have been able to see this point; should have thanked her friend for her courtesy in sparing her additional worries. She did not. With a peppery tone to her voice she barked accusingly, '*Athene!*'

The word echoed across the tranquil room and Judy glimpsed Mr So's look of surprise. He hastened towards their table with an anxious expression on his face but Athene turned and smiled serenely at him, a gesture carrying a message of reassurance, and the old Chinese gentleman slid away again.

'Athene,' said Judy more gently, 'one cannot dismiss the possibility that the Sisters of Reason had something to do with the death of this girl. I was talking to Angela de Mauny and she put forward the very reasonable proposition that whoever killed the girl was trying to destroy this beauty pageant business, once and for all.'

Athene was sketching a picture of a raven on the paper tablecloth.

'In the absence of any other suspects, it's perfectly reasonable to explore the desires and motives of the Sisters. And – Athene – you were here sitting and listening to them! What on earth did they say?'

Athene slowly finished the tail feathers with an elaborate curlicue. 'I got up and left,' she said. 'I was very pained to see how Mr So hated them being there. I made a bit of a nuisance of myself gathering up my things, hoping they could sense my disapproval, they were braying and braggartly, but of course they took no notice of me at all. I said to Mr So, quite loudly, "Good Lord, Mr So, is that the time? Surely it's long past your closing time?" I hoped they would take the hint.

'So in answer to your question, dear, I did *not* take in too much of what they were saying. Anyway, it's bad manners to eavesdrop.'

'You see now what you missed, though, Athene. Vital information. Think of that poor girl.'

'I don't think a woman would kill another woman quite so violently. There are other ways.'

'You saw Ursula Guedella,' said Miss Dimont crisply. 'Are you so sure?'

'Mm . . .'

They said goodnight to Mr So and the Chinese Singing Teacher. The old gentleman did not give singing lessons himself, Judy learned as she paid for the tea, indeed he was sorry he could not help her in that regard, he knew nobody who did. She itched to ask why, then, his establishment was so titled, but Athene, accustomed to her friend's unquenchable thirst for knowledge, bustled her out of the door. There were, apparently, questions which were better left unasked in Bosun's Alley.

As they walked out into the street, Judy turned towards the office in Brewery Street and Athene suddenly disappeared, something she often did – all part of her mystery. But they had already said their goodbyes, and Judy walked on.

It was not yet ten o'clock and from across the street, further down, she could hear great gusts of noise coming through the windows of the Old Jawbones. As she approached, the thin chords of a single squeezebox cut through the heavy sound of a group of men in full voice. Just then the door opened, and as a customer wandered off into the night she could hear the words more clearly:

. . .poor Tom Bowling, the darling of our crew
No more he'll hear the tempest howling, for death has broached him to
His form was of the manliest beauty, his heart was kind and soft
Faithful below, Tom did his duty – and now he's gone aloft
And now he's gone aloft . . .

The poignancy of the message and the sweet simplicity of the harmonies was entrancing, and without a second thought she pushed through the doorway into the crowded bar. Up one end were a dozen red-faced men, burly and muscular, with pint beer glasses in their hands, singing their farewell to poor old Tom. Though their eyes remained dry, Miss Dimont was not sure how longer hers would remain so – seeing strong men sing so delicately, so movingly, about the loss of one of their own plucked at the heart strings.

The air was thrillingly perfumed with beer and pipe tobacco and the heat was intense. The singers, some of whom she recognised from the crew of the *Lass O'Doune*, were bathed in sweat, their faces pinched in concentration as they sought, and found, their harmonies. Miss Dimont realised as she watched they were not really singing about the mythical Bowling but about a friend, a fellow, they had lost to the ocean. She was almost glad when their obituary was done.

There was scarcely time for the men to up their pint glasses before the squeezebox piped the opening chords to 'South Australia' and its noisy chorus of 'Heave away, haul away!' with as much passion and energy as if they were still aboard the *Lass* in that Force Nine gale.

'That be yor poison, baint it?' It was Jacky, in his hand a glass of rum.

'Er, well . . .'

'They'm bright.'

'They certainly are. Bright,' shouted Judy, sipping at the delicious drink. No other word seemed so apt.

Among the shanty men she spotted Cran Conybeer, skipper of the *Lass*, head back and lost in song. He looked like a Viking with his red beard and stocky open-legged stance. Here, as on his ship, he was the leader of these men – urging them on with his swinging pint glass as if they were facing a tempest, willing his crew to give that extra ounce.

Jim Butterleigh, the Jawbones' landlord, had the usual difficulty in making himself heard as he shouted 'Time, gentlemen, *please*!' and even an energetic pull at the ship's bell had little effect beyond telling the singers it was time to stop. The local police were wise enough to know when to leave well alone, and Friday night at the Jawbones usually lasted well into Saturday morning.

Cran Conybeer peeled away from the group and came over.

'Come for a singalong, Miss Dimalong?' he joked. He seemed very pleased to see her.

'What a wonderful sound you make.'

The sea captain casually slung his arm round Judy's shoulder and clinked glasses – she was, after all, an honorary crew member after the way she hauled in those nets – and started telling her something indecipherable about the Azores. She was only half listening, for the men had started a noisy rendition of 'Whisky Johnny'.

'. . . big sou' westerly,' ended Cran, and roared with laughter. Judy laughed too, out of politesse.

'Time to go,' he said, 'we're out again with the tide in the morning.'

'That was lovely – the shanties. I wish I'd known, I would have come earlier.'

'I see you like that rum.'

'When in Rome, Mr Conybeer.'

'What's that? Ha! Ha! You come along a me. I'll make sure you're safe.'

Miss Dimont was confident that the tranquil streets of Temple Regis at 10.30 at night presented no particular threat, but did not say so, anyway she liked Cran's faded blue eyes.

As they left the pub, the skipper's arm still over her shoulder, his men – breaking the rules as these men would always do – burst into one last song:

Eternal Father, strong to save
Whose arm has bound the restless wave . . .

'Ruddy motley crew,' said Cran, leaning his head down so Judy could hear. He smelt of beer and good humour. 'Listen to 'at Bill Chudleigh – missin' the high note like he always do.'

Oh hear us when we cry to Thee
For those in peril on the sea . . .

'You married?' he said. 'You haven't got a ring.'

'No. What about you?'

'Widower.' He drew her closer towards him as they walked. 'You know, every Friday night we go in there and sing about the men we lose at sea, but there aren't any songs about the wives who died.'

'I'm sorry.'

'Kids were only three and four. You get out of the way of talkin' to ladies after that. I'm sorry if I was rude to you the other morning.'

'If you were, I didn't notice,' said Judy and smiled up at him. In the street light he looked like a lion.

They turned the corner into the Market Square and were hit by a sharp cold gust carrying as its passengers the first raindrops of the incoming storm.

'Bumpy in the mornin',' promised Cran. 'Wannoo come for the ride, Judy?' He didn't really mean it.

Suddenly, the reporter stopped so suddenly that the skipper's arm slipped from her shoulder.

'What?' he asked.

'I don't suppose . . .'

'What?'

'I don't suppose when you set sail last Tuesday you happened to notice anything on land as you sailed down the estuary?'

'What sort of thing?'

'Anything unusual on Todhempstead Sands. You sail past there to get out to sea.'

'Would have been too busy navigatin'. That estuary be full of sandbanks.'

'You're sure? That's the day they found the body of that girl. You went out in daylight?'

'We did, but I don't recall anything around T'emstead. What sorta thing?'

'Oh, never mind,' said Judy and they resumed their stroll. The skipper put his arm round her shoulder again.

'Nearly run someone down, though,' he said. 'Some idiot. Bloke with his girlfriend – early to be out, so early in fact she was still asleep by the look of her. Obviously he knew nothing about seamanship, he got right under our bows. Lucky to get away with it, he wor.'

Miss Dimont stopped once more.

'Tell me that again,' she said, all joy drained from her voice.

TWELVE

Valentine's huge old typewriter was surrounded by a jungle of litter, as if someone had upended the contents of a wastepaper basket all over his desk. He sat amidst the debris, his face corrugated with confusion.

'You OK?' Betty was looking particularly attractive this morning in lime-green skirt and royal blue cardigan, the hair not quite so shiningly chrome as when she'd first applied the bleach, and the make-up not quite so patchy today, though her shoes let the side down a bit.

The young man noticed none of this. He appeared to be in turmoil.

Betty sat down in Judy's chair and smiled winningly over the desk at him. 'How's it going?'

'Mm? Oh, very well, Miss Featherstone. Very different from anything I've ever experienced, it's really quite exhausting in fact. I mean, I've driven tanks and been on route marches, all that sort of caper, but nothing like this. It drains you.'

'You look as though you've been here all night.'

'I have. Well, since before dawn. Before that I was over at the Pavilion Theatre.'

'The riots? That beat group? The – what're they called?'

'The Urge.'

Betty snorted with laughter. 'Are they any good? I thought I'd get a free ticket and go and take a look. That Danny whatsisname – he looks quite dangerous really.'

'Derek? Nice enough chap, bit boring really. Spent a lot of time talking to me about how he misses his mother – he's never been away from home for so long before. They usually rehearse in her drawing . . . er, front, room.' He distractedly shuffled among the litter on his desk. Whatever he was looking for, he couldn't find it.

'And that other chap – Boots McGuigan. Sounds so tough, so . . . masculine.' She arched her eyebrows but Valentine didn't notice, he was busy picking up crumpled copy paper from the floor.

'No, no, you've got it wrong,' he said, catching up with Betty's conversational thread. 'No he's not very masculine and he's only called that stupid name because he used to work behind the counter in Boots the Chemist.'

Betty looked so disappointed he wished he hadn't told her. Fame has a way of distorting reality, but it is an ignorant fellow who tampers with people's dreams.

'What's all that rubbish?' asked Betty, though she could see perfectly well what it was – she'd been there herself. He'd gone out on his story without a notebook, and had to beg and borrow anything to write his notes on: paper napkins, a page from a someone's diary, sandwich wrappers and a brown paper bag all covered in a spidery hand bore evidence of his disorganisation.

'You forgot your notebook!'

'Mm.' Valentine was none too pleased at having been rumbled.

'So what's your story? The one you're writing up?'

'Can't quite decide, that's why I've been struggling a bit. Is it, Britain's No 1 beat group terrify Temple Regis – bad? Is it, The Urge draw hordes of new holidaymakers to stuffy old

Temple – good? Or is it, we're No 1 in the Hit Parade but we're broke and living in a van?'

Betty gave him a superior smile. It was such a pleasure to see someone else having to wrestle with an intro.

'I think you should reveal that Danny Trouble is really called Derek and lives with his mum.'

Valentine shot her a glance. 'That would *never* do, Miss Featherstone. Why shoot the fox? Everybody in town is up in arms about this beat group – either they adore the fact they're here bringing publicity and business, or else they're fed up with these teenagers turning up out of nowhere and running amok. Either way they're interested, because The Urge are causing a commotion. The moment you demystify them, there's no story. No fox to chase any more.'

This went slightly over Betty's head. 'Has anyone said anything about their music?'

'Oh, nobody cares about *that*. Actually, they're quite good – in fact, very good. They certainly know how to put on a show. Why, I even saw a wonderful old dowager dancing around at the back of the theatre – she looked deliriously happy. She must be ninety.'

'That'll be old Mrs Phipps. Delirious because the theatre's making money for the first time ever.' Betty harboured bitter feelings about its absent proprietor, Ray Cattermole. There had been an evening when . . . 'She might finally be able to get her pearls out of hock.'

Valentine started rummaging again. 'There's another angle here – you see I'm getting the hang of all this! – and that's your bass player, Boots. Has some connection with that chap you interviewed – Larsson, isn't it? He was telling me last night; I've got a note of it somewhere. To be honest I didn't have a chance to get much on that, though, the boys were going out for their third encore and the screams were deafening. Those girls, Miss Featherstone! Is there anybody you'd ever scream for?'

'You stick to Derek and his mum,' said Betty, shirtily, getting up to go. 'I'm off to Newton Abbot.'

Valentine didn't hear. He was looking under the desk to see whether one of his stray notes had fallen to the floor but the search was in vain.

Time passed. The avalanche of discarded copy paper from his typewriter grew slowly, but gradually he was getting the hang of it – he plumped for 'Temple's Teenage Turmoil' as his entry point and soon the story was writing itself.

'Hello,' said a voice some time later. He looked up to see Miss Dimont dumping her raffia bag on the desk opposite and looking radiant. It was extraordinary how, one minute, she looked almost plain and the next really quite beautiful. She had a glow to her cheeks and, more important, looked as though she had time to talk to him. She was lovely, he thought, but a bit stern too.

'A joyous evening in the company of the Troubled One?'

'No trouble at all, as it turned out. Or only a bit.' He told the story of Danny and his mum. 'How about you?'

This was the joy of working on a local newspaper – you got interested in other reporters' stories, you got the inside information from them, but you didn't have to do anything towards collecting it. You always knew more than appeared in the newspaper and, on the basis that knowledge is power, that made you a powerful figure in the local community. Or, as you stood in the rain at a bus stop on the way back from the Agricultural Show, your feet covered in mud, you could try to convince yourself it did.

'I've made progress on the dead girl,' said Judy seriously. 'I'll tell you later, I have some calls to make just now. How's the story going?'

'Finally under way. Shouldn't take long now.'

Judy Dimont doubted that but was pleased for him – it

looked as though he was getting the hang of it. Though he could do with a shave.

'You could do with a shave, Valentine.'

'Haven't been home. Those Urges drink a lot, y'know. They're living in their van. Quite comfy though – reminded me of my days in tanks.'

'Get it finished soon. You can come and help me.'

Valentine yawned and scratched his tousled hair. 'Be a pleasure. Can I just ask you about – you know the Ben Larsson story? There's a lead here I wanted to ask your advice about.'

'Not now, Valentine, let's talk it over later. I want to go and see your, er, cousin Miss de Mauny.'

'Again? More riveting stuff on the plight of womankind?'

Miss Dimont shot him a glance. 'Don't scoff, Valentine. You should be so lucky as to be one of us.'

The young man laughed and held her gaze. 'You can be awfully stern.'

'When there are idiots around like you, I need to be. It really is a most valuable asset.'

The young man returned so swiftly and so energetically to his keyboard he might have been playing Rachmaninov.

*

If you had to pick a time of day when Ransome's Retreat was at its finest, it had to be late afternoon. By that time the sun had passed over the headland and was backlighting the house and gardens, sending shadows over the sizeable drop on to the rocks far beneath. The energetic squawkings of birdlife, now that beaks had been fed, had given way to a quieter music, heralding, but with no great sense of hurry, the forthcoming dusk.

On the terrace, at an ancient wooden table, sat Pernilla Larsson and her son Gus Wetherby.

'He's asleep?'

'Lamb gave him his usual.'

'Good,' said Gus. 'Let's get on.'

His mother put on her dark glasses. She wanted to hide the sense of betrayal she felt.

'It comes to this,' said Gus, self-importantly. 'The Rejuvenator has had it. The *Daily Herald* has seen to that. Some urgent action now, or you can forget all this.' The merest flick of his hand was enough to tell the tale.

'Ben has spoken to the local newspaper,' said Pernilla. 'That girl Hetty Betty. They're going to print a correction.'

'Mother,' came the irritated response, 'it's the local rag! Who's going to take any notice of that? In a day or two all the other national newspapers will wake up to a story they should have cottoned on to years ago.'

'You know, this could kill your stepfather,' said Pernilla anxiously. The crisis at Ransome's Retreat could not be greater and she was caught between a husband who refused to lift his head out of the sand and a son whose ambition and, yes, greed had robbed him of any sense of loyalty.

'Might be better if he did pop his clogs. He's a busted flush, Mother.'

'Gus! He paid for your fees at Harrow. He's treated you always like a son.'

'And I'm going to save his reputation,' said Gus, who may or may not have meant it. 'If he can't be persuaded to alter course, and quickly, he's dished. We need to get him out of here. You do realise, Mother, that if one person suddenly takes it into their head to sue, there'll be a rush of people to the courts, and we'll be bankrupt.'

Gus stood up and walked over to the terrace wall. 'It needs positive action. Announce the New Rejuvenator. Acknowledge publicly that the old one was based on complicated gadgetry and wishful thinking.'

'You can't say that! It's tantamount to an admission of fraud. Your poor stepfather!'

She's decorative, thought Gus Wetherby, and with a backbone of steel, but she isn't always very quick on the uptake.

'This is how you do it,' he said crisply. 'You simply say what fools people have been to buy this wonderful piece of equipment, and then misuse it. Trials by our company have proved that it was too complicated for most people. Cite all the wonderful letters we've had over the years, and then come out and say that yes, there have been complaints, but it *was the idiots who didn't read the instructions properly*.

'The sooner we do it, the easier it is to nip this thing in the bud. Another week and it'll be too late.'

'Ben won't agree to it. He doesn't see the problem.'

'He's old. I think it's time you took him off to Argentina to visit the ranches, they need looking over. Go for a couple of months and leave things to me. But get him away quick or we're finished.'

Pernilla Larsson lit a cigarette. A butterfly danced by.

'All right,' she said slowly. 'We'll go.'

Just then, the old inventor walked over to join them. His wife looked aghast at this unexpected entrance.

'Oh . . . Ben . . . Ha! Ha!' she laughed awkwardly, patting her hair and smoothing her skirt. 'I thought you were having your nap.'

'No more of those damned sedatives,' said Ben Larsson angrily. 'No more whispering in corners! No more lies and deceit! I know what you've been up to . . .'

'Don't know what you're talking about,' answered Gus guiltily.

Larsson looked at him. 'Don't waste my time! Lamb told me everything. It was that or be sacked, and he never wants to see his native Yorkshire again.'

'Who can blame him?' said Gus sourly. 'It rains a lot in Yorkshire.'

'Just at the moment when I need my family's support, more than at any time in my life,' said Larsson, rising on the balls of his feet, 'they betray me. You want me out of the country so you can renounce my lifetime's work and put in its place some gimcrack piece of gadgetry which you think will save my reputation – and,' he added sourly, 'your inheritance.'

'It's not quite like that,' said Gus, but the bluster was going out of his voice. 'Ben, you have to realise these newspapers will crucify you unless you do something positive, and do it now.'

'Like launch the *Youthenator*?'

'It's a good name,' said Gus defensively. 'Catches the mood of the time. Borrows from your legacy without saying it's the same piece of kit. Modern, up to date. Suited to the needs of the post-war generation. Not those Lazarus League weirdos.'

The inventor walked over to the table, picked up a teacup and suddenly threw it to the ground. He opened his mouth but no words came. Beneath his golden Devon tan he had gone remarkably pale.

'Ben,' said Pernilla urgently, 'come and sit down. Your heart, my dear, your heart . . .'

'My heart,' said Larsson faintly, 'is broken.'

His stepson took no notice. Ben Larsson had not become as rich as he had without using every trick in the book from bullying to blackmail.

'You knew the Rejuvenator didn't work all along,' he said savagely.

'You don't know what you're talking about,' came the contemptuous reply. 'For your tenth birthday I gave you a specially inscribed copy of *A New Electronic Theory of Life*. Did you ever read it?'

'No need,' said Gus airily, 'not while the money was rolling in. But look, Ben, I've learnt the business. And I see where you went wrong in your calculations all those years ago. Those electromagnetic currents you harnessed – it was the right theory but wrong application. If only you'd . . .'

'You know nothing,' retorted Larsson bitterly. 'What's that phrase – a little knowledge is a dangerous thing? – you think you know it all but you know nothing. I am a chemist, a healer, I have studied in depth people's lives and their ailments, I have a real care to make people's lives better,' he paused. 'Lamb showed me your drawings.'

His stepson reacted angrily at the news of this betrayal, jumping forward, looking almost as if he was ready to swing a punch at the old man. He knocked against his mother and her dark glasses fell to the terrace. Sobbing, she knelt to pick them up. Both men ignored her.

'You're a fool, Gus. You don't pay Lamb his wages, I do. You don't look after him, I do. I doubt you even know the names of his children. It might have appeared he was going along with your plan to force me out of my own business, but only to discover what you were up to. I've seen the drawings and the prototype you had made in the workshop – yes, the workforce still know on which side their bread is buttered! – and that contraption you created is just a gimmick.

'It won't work, it'll never work. You're no better than a snake-oil salesman – no care for the people you sell to as long as you can take the money and run. In a matter of months you'll have ruined your reputation, and mine too.'

Pernilla was cradling the broken sunglasses in her hands. 'You're both right,' she sobbed, 'and you're both wrong. You, Ben, have no idea what damage that newspaper article has done. You may as well shut the factory, unless you let Gus have his way.

'But you, Gus,' she said, angrily turning to her son. 'You promised me this thing would work. If, as your stepfather says, it doesn't – then what's the point? Why go to all that effort when you know you're going to be found out?'

Gus Wetherby was unmoved. 'So what if it doesn't work?' he sneered. 'At least it won't do any harm like the Rejuvenator.

'Look, Mum, we live in a new age. People don't cling to the past like they used to. These days, things come and go – look at jukeboxes, they're all the rage now but where will they be in ten years' time? Hula-hoops, coffee bars, permanent waves? Even those Lambretta scooters?

'They're all the fashion now but they'll die a death, as everything does in this day and age. Look at this beat music – that won't last. Early closing day, the Communist Party, shillings and florins and farthings – they're all for the scrap heap. So if the Youthenator has a short life, so what, who cares? Once everybody's bought one and tried it out and got bored with it, it'll just go into the dustbin along with all the other rubbish. Then we just reinvent it for the next generation. Or we sell it on to Africa – those post-colonial nations with all their problems and diseases could do with a dollop of hope. They'd *love* the Youthenator.'

There were tears in old Larsson's eyes, whether real or not it was difficult to see. 'I'll kill you first,' he whispered. 'I'll kill you! Do you think you can just come and ruin my lifetime's reputation, just because you feel like it?'

'Nobody will notice, Ben. I've got a great plan which – sorry, old chap – will make everybody forget the name Ben Larsson. This beat group – Danny Trouble and The Urge – they're on every front page in the land. Radio and TV and magazines can't get enough of them. They're huge, they're massive, and they're the future.

'Even you, Ben, know the headlines they've created since they've been down here playing the Pavilion Theatre.'

The old man looked with steely contempt at his stepson, but there was no stopping him. 'I've talked to their manager Gavin Armstrong – we were at Harrow together – and he's got them to endorse the Youthenator.

'When they do that, every household, every kid, will want my machine. They'll be told it will give them a fillip, give 'em a thrill, just what everybody's looking for these days! Some of these kids take drugs, but this is legal!

'Don't you see, Ben? My God, you're *so* out of touch with what's happening!'

The old man stood up. 'You'll ruin my reputation. Sooner than let you do that, I'd kill you.'

His stepson sneered. 'Not me, Ben. Let's face it, it's *you* who's dead in the water.'

THIRTEEN

The town was filling up nicely. The annual game of musical chairs played by householders had already begun, with the owners of the larger establishments moving to smaller ones while those in more modest properties moved into flats. Short-term discomfort was rewarded by gratifying boosts to the bank balance from these holiday lets, and there was a smell of fresh paint everywhere. The shopkeepers of Temple Regis got out their best smiles and strapped them on.

The Riviera Express – the elegant steam train, not its newspaper namesake – began its sterling work of depositing holidaymakers on the platform of Regis Junction to start their week or fortnight in this heavenly backwater. Even the palm trees, cunningly planted at the platform's edge to make newcomers believe they'd just entered paradise, seemed to have acquired a new sheen. A beguiling breeze tossed their tendrils prettily in the air.

Temple Regis did not have the de luxe air of Torquay, nor the kiss-me-quick jollity of Paignton. It had instead all the assurance of a middle-aged country solicitor – well dressed, efficient, dependable and encouraging – and while its residents were not snobs they instinctively knew their town was a cut above the competition.

Always ready to spot new trends in the competitive business

of selling sunshine, they were not so quick to pick up on the beat boom which was sweeping the country. By accident they'd landed the most famous band in Britain as their guests, but they were mistrustful of the benefits Danny Trouble and The Urge might bring, preferring to put their trust in the old fail-safes – donkeys on the beach, speak-your-weight machines, the Winter Garden dance hall, and the noisy funfair with its dodgem cars and coconut shies. And of course the glittering Grand Hotel.

Outside one of the town's more faded attractions, Mrs Phipps sat in a deckchair with a Plymouth Gin at her elbow. Her grandson wandered out of a side door with a bucket and some rolls of paper looking as though he might make himself busy for once.

'What are you doing, dear?'

'Putting up the Sold Out signs, Granny.'

Mrs Phipps took a sip and raised her still-photogenic face towards the sun. 'Is that wise, darling? I'd say we aren't above 75 per cent.'

'We aren't. But, don't you see, the moment word gets out there are no tickets left, the fans go mad and the price goes up? They'll pay anything to see Danny and the boys.'

'But how do you dispose of tickets when your sign says quite clearly there are no tickets left?'

Gavin looked down at his grandmother pityingly. 'I know a chap, Granny. Black market. He demands three times the cover price and creates the pressure. Nothing more exciting than seeing The Urge with an illegal ticket.'

'Darling, is that strictly ethical?' asked Mrs Phipps, who really didn't care. Business had never been better, and she was enjoying the sensation Danny Trouble was causing in town. Her faded celebrity and rackety life created a distance between her and hard-working Temple Regents, who kept civilised hours and did not drink Plymouth Gin at eleven in the morning.

Gavin splashed glue on the posters which pictured Danny and

the boys looking particularly menacing, then adorned them with his 'Sold Out' signs.

'That looks good,' he said. 'Right across Tommy's face. Lord, he's a snotty one, Granny.'

'We used to have them all the time in the old days. When I recall that Lupe Velez! We were in *Transatlantic Rhythm* together, dear, at the Adelphi, must have been 1936. She hated her costume so much she rehearsed in the nude. She never washed, you know, and had *no* idea what undergarments were for.'

Gavin had heard this one before. 'The boys don't wash much either. But then when you're living in a van, why bother?'

'I thought you were going to get them some rooms.'

'They seem pretty comfortable where they are.'

'In a *van*?' said Mrs Phipps incredulously. In her West End days, she used to slum it at The Ritz between performances.

'Well, maybe I should,' conceded Gavin. 'Anyway, I'd better go and get them their early-morning tea.'

'Not up yet?' The old Gaiety Girl, who was always immaculately presented, started her lengthy beautification process early in the day.

'We were up late. Had that reporter chap from the local rag over, Valentine Ford.'

'*Water*ford, darling, I knew his grandfather. A regular stage-door Johnston.'

'Mm-hmm, ever the siren, Gran. See you later.'

Gavin strolled into the theatre and prepared some mugs of tea. A woeful-looking menagerie, far removed from the demigods on stage last night, started to limp in. Danny Trouble was wearing a duffle coat which doubled as a dressing gown and, as it swung open, it was evident that he'd become a star of the Lupe Velez persuasion.

'Manners, Derek,' said Gavin sternly. His style was to treat the musicians with a mixture of encouragement and restraint, like a housemaster at a minor public school. A cautionary word usually kept them in check, for despite their rebel reputation they were earnest and diligent.

'Oops!' said Danny, and re-established his modesty with a bashful smile.

'Bacon and eggs coming up,' said Gavin, 'then I've got something really wonderful to tell you.'

'We're Number One again next week?' said Boots McGuigan, the bass player, from behind his copy of *Melody Maker*.

'All that and more. One egg or two?'

The others drifted in and Gavin allowed them their breakfast and a fag before calling for their attention.

'I've got some pretty fantastic news, chaps,' he said adopting an important tone. 'Bloke I was at school with lives down here, and has come up with a wheeze to make us a huge dollop of extra money.'

'Speaking of which, when are we getting paid?' said Tommy sourly.

Gavin wished he'd got the glue-pot handy – a nice dollop across Tommy's gob would do him a power of good.

'Not now, Tom. Listen, we're going to endorse a new product called the Youthenator. My old pal Gus Wetherby has invented this machine which makes you feel sexy and at the same time gives you a bit of a jolt, like taking pep pills.'

He went on to explain the deal he'd struck – free advertising for the band and a useful cash payment, as long as they agreed to having their photograph taken with the Youthenator and endorsing it onstage during the act.

'Does it work?' asked Danny.

'No idea,' came the breezy reply. 'Somehow I doubt it. Gus was notorious at school for getting away with it – he always used to come in the first half-dozen when we went out cross-country running. Knew all the corners to cut.'

'If it doesn't work the idea could rebound,' said Danny. 'People complaining. Think of our reputation.'

'What reputation?' snapped Gavin, who'd already signed the contract with Gus on the band's behalf. 'The thing's just a gimmick. It'll work because of auto-suggestion.'

'Auto . . . ?'

'The same phenomenon which put you at the top of the charts,' said Gavin cynically. 'People think you chaps can sing. Well, maybe you can, but not as well as they think you do. Just remember what you sound like when the tapes get played back in the studio before the recording engineer sprinkles his magic dust all over them.

'No,' he went on, 'when you play, you make those girls feel wild and you give 'em an electric shock. You make them want to go on all night, and that's what the Youthenator does. Put the two together – we could make a million!'

'Wait a minute,' said Boots, who had been sitting quietly in the corner with his paper. 'This sounds like something else, something called a Rejuvenator. It killed my mother.'

There was a terrible silence.

'Erm,' said Gavin, 'I'm sure it's not the same thing at all.'

'Box with wires, a couple of tubes connected to them? Uses electricity? Elaborate instructions for use?'

'Well, yes, but . . .'

'This chap, your friend, he's not connected to a man called Ben Larsson, by any chance?'

Gavin was beginning to feel decidedly queasy about having signed the contract. 'Well, yes, as a matter of fact,' he said. 'He's his stepson.'

'How come you got this deal?'

'Gus came to see me, he heard we're in town. He lives in a fabulous house on the top of the cliffs. Honestly,' he urged, 'if we go with this deal, we could ALL end up with a fabulous house on the top of a cliff. Come on, now . . .'

McGuigan's face was like granite. 'Give me the address,' he said commandingly.

His voice sounded ugly.

*

The serene calm of the Chinese Singing Teacher was rarely disrupted – it was almost like being in church, only with a cup of tea, when you sat in its faded rooms. Everyone who dropped in understood how precious this place was in the noisy modern world, and did nothing to disrupt its tranquillity.

That is, apart from the party of six or seven late on Thursday afternoon who occupied a far corner rattling their cups, scraping their chairs, occupying more space than was strictly necessary and acting generally as if they owned the place. Even in the furthermost corner where the ever-solicitous Mr So stood ready to attend to their needs, there could be sensed a jagged disharmony.

'Now to the Big One,' grated a tall and muscular woman who sat, trousered legs spread, at the head of the table. She pointed her chin at a delicate blonde, her eyebrows instructing the poor thing to speak up.

'May I ask, Commandant, whether you feel we're quite ready for this? After all, in Paignton things did not quite go according to plan. There was a certain loss of face, would you not say?'

Ursula Guedella made an angry gesture. 'People who can't keep their heads have no place in the Sisterhood,' she snapped. 'Valerie tripped over and started crying. Then Ann Constable forgot what she was supposed to do. As for Heather, words fail me – heaven knows, we'd rehearsed it often enough beforehand!'

'To be fair, Commandant, Valerie works in the library. She is unused to stress, let alone outright aggression.'

'Then she should not have joined us.' The Commandant planted her elbows on the table and those nearest to her moved slightly aside. She was very intimidating.

'The Sisters of Reason ask much of each and every member,' she said. 'You know that. Everyone is expected to excel, exceed their own expectations, take pride in their achievements. When I joined the Hospital Corps and went to Serbia, I contracted malaria and had to be stretchered off the battlefield. But I came back, I was not to be beaten.' She pushed back a lock of hair with an angular movement.

'I think we are all proud of your Croix de Charité,' said Ann Constable, sweetly, from the far end of the table. She was small and pretty and in love with Ursula.

The Commandant absently fingered the thin red ribbon which passed through the buttonhole of her lapel. 'That is why I founded this Sisterhood,' she said solidly. 'I learnt in the Girl Guides the need for order. I learned from the Hospital Corps the need for discipline. In Serbia I learned the need for exceptional courage. All these things I bring to this movement, and I expect as much from each and every one of you.'

The women around the table studied their teacups. They'd heard it before. Ursula was inspirational, but left unchecked was rather inclined to bang on. On the other hand, who else was there in this country prepared to kick over the table and demand the rights for women which once had been theirs but had been swept away?

'It *was* a bit of a mess, Commandant,' said Angela de Mauny.

'It got the right result.'

'The Mothers' Union are calling us a fascist organisation.'

'They don't know the meaning of the word,' barked Ursula. 'And who are they, anyway? What have *they* done since the war to bring about change?'

Mr So looked unhappily from his perch at the far end of the

room and wondered how much longer they would stay. And, he wondered, would they come again? This was the second time. He could not understand the attraction of his establishment for this clandestine group, but then he did not comprehend the thrill of making and keeping secrets.

'Look,' said Ursula. 'We must prepare ourselves for the day, for the Big One, and constantly remind ourselves why we are doing this. We must risk our liberty and our reputations! We must be bold and brave and big-hearted – and you all know why!

'Equal pay, we don't have it. Women in the clergy, we don't have them. Cabinet ministers? Don't make me laugh! Even when you go to the cinema for every woman in a film there are ten or twenty men.'

Her followers nodded earnestly.

'We fought the war shoulder-to-shoulder with those . . . *men* . . . and they told us we were equal. Are we? Will we ever be, unless the Sisters take direct action?'

These Devon colleagues, she felt, lacked the sense of urgency of their metropolitan cousins. They were slower to show anger and whatever direct action they took was likely to be less effective . . . perhaps, down here, they were all just too nice.

Nonetheless she'd found, and drilled, this small but reasonably effective unit to add to the burgeoning groups around the country, each set the task of pushing forward the march of equality. Here in Temple Regis, a huge protest against beauty pageants. In Canterbury, an embarrassment for the Archbishop at his Easter sermon. In the House of Commons, the showering of confetti from the public gallery onto the heads of Cabinet ministers. At Elstree and Shepperton, broken glass under the tyres of the male stars' limousines.

So far, the national press remained united in its opposition to the actions of the Sisters of Reason. Newspapers sought either to ridicule them, suggesting their number was made up of groups of women who had been unlucky in love, or else exaggerate a sense of alarm at their actions. Not a single newspaper, from *The Times* to the *Daily Sketch*, bothered to examine their arguments or discuss the very issues the Sisters were trying to introduce into public debate. So far their operations had been largely ignored – but not after the Day of Action!

'Shall I order some more tea, Commandant?' asked Ann Constable. She didn't really want it, but hoped to bring the conversation round to more harmonious topics. Politics did not much concern her, but the idea of sisters together did.

'Go ahead,' snapped Ursula without turning her head. Ann blushed and went in search of Mr So.

Angela de Mauny, though still in the shadow of the Commandant, was less in awe. 'Can I just say I had a most sympathetic article from that woman Miss Dimont on my lecture on the Six Point Group. Don't you think we should make more use of the local press?'

'Disliked her intensely,' said Ursula shortly. 'Far too sure of herself. You swept her out of the house and she just turned round and came back and demanded a cup of tea – the cheek of it! These press people – they just push their noses into everything that's going on.'

Angela shook her head. 'They're not always the enemy. Yes, they can be irritating – even when I finally told her to leave the cottage she was in no particular hurry, such bad manners! – but we have to have friends on our side, and she looks like she could be one.'

The Commandant roughly pulled her tweed jacket around her. 'Just another reporter on the snoop.'

'But Ursula, we have to get the message out for the Day of Action. And you know she was in the Royal Navy.'

'Aha! Do I detect a dollop of hero worship?'

'No more, Ursula, than you would expect for yourself,' said Miss de Mauny, nettled.

The discussion wandered back to the matter of equal pay and the shoddy way in which the trades unions – run by men, for men – continued to sidestep this fundamental labour issue. 'They're the worst, of course,' said one of the group, whose husband was a shop steward in the fish-canning factory in Exbridge. 'Always eager to take on the management and have a bit of a scrap, but "Where's my tea?" when he comes home.'

It was a familiar complaint and the conversation appeared to be winding down without the main topic having been fully addressed. That hardly mattered because, when it came to important policy matters, Ursula Guedella took all the decisions and brooked no argument. Some of her followers thought she was a bit touched, what with her military bearing, highly polished brogues and penchant for small cigars. Also, in the evenings, she would drink her whisky neat and boast to her insignificant little dog of her activist friends Dorothy Evans, Monica Whately and Helen Archdale. 'Militant suffragists' were the words which bubbled to her lips most often.

The Day of Action, which they had gathered to debate, would have to wait until next time. It was not only the shop steward's wife who had to go home and make tea for the loved one.

FOURTEEN

Press day was never as much fun as it looked in the movies. It was the only time in the week when the doors between the *Express* office and the cavernous print room next door were opened; and through them came all the sounds of hell – clanking, groaning, and shouting accompanied by a gentle low roar as the presses turned and the newspapers spewed up a fan belt and into the hall where they were tied and hurled into waiting vans ready for their headlong journey through the night to the newsagents.

The heat from the heavy machinery billowed into the newsroom, a welcome bonus in winter but oppressive and almost suffocating at this time of the year. Men came and went, importantly bearing damp proof-sheets, to the editor's office. Later, when Rudyard Rhys had scrutinised every single page, it would be the turn of others to double-check there were no mistakes.

'You don't know the trouble you can cause,' Judy Dimont warned Valentine, 'with a misspelt name or an incorrect address or age. The people in this town are like elephants – they never forget.'

'You mean like the Conservative Ball last winter?' It had been one of Miss Dimont's less glorious moments – in fact what happened that night was still talked about, in the office and in the town.

'No need for cheek,' snapped Miss Dimont, who, despite her many triumphs since, was never allowed to forget that night. 'Anybody can make a mistake.'

'Sounds like a rip-roaring evening. Wish I'd been there.' There was a naughty grin on Valentine's face.

'Oh, do shut up!'

''Ere y'are,' said an ungracious printer, who hated journalists and their lazy life of all-consuming luxury. He plonked an inky sheet on the desk between Judy and Valentine and stalked back to his hellhole.

'Your turn first,' ordered Judy. 'Read every word – the headlines, the dateline at the top of the page, the picture captions, and the stories. Even check the page number. Don't let your concentration waver for a moment, or you'll find yourself down on the front desk tomorrow morning fielding the complaints.'

'I hadn't realised – I thought there was someone who did all this for you. That our job was to find the news and write it up.'

'Wake up, Valentine, that's the easy bit. *This* is what you get paid for – making sure we don't get complaints.'

The young reporter pulled the sheet of paper towards him and started at the top.

BABY'S FOOT IS FREED FROM BENCH

ran the first headline.

'Hmm, interesting,' said Valentine in a funny voice, hoping for a laugh.

'Just *read* it,' ordered his superior, in a very superior tone. He did, aloud.

Firemen came to the rescue of an eight-month old baby after the child's fot became trpped in a public bench.

Mother and child were sitting on the bench on the South Promenade at around 1pm on Wednesday when the child's foot slipped between the slats in the bench.

When the mother was unable to free her child, she called the town's fire brigade who raced to the rescue the few hundred yards from their nearby fire station.

The firemen were able to take out a screw from the bench and move one of the slats so the child could be fred.

'That's a *news story?*' said Valentine, scratching his head and shaking it at the same time.

'Correct the mistakes and move on to the next,' said Miss Dimont primly. 'We haven't got all day.'

'Well, the *mistakes*, it seems to me, are that we don't name the mother. We don't have a photograph of her hapless child with its stupid foot. No questioning of this anonymous idiot to ask why she was unable to release a very small child, the work of a moment I should have thought, or a picture of the triumphant fireman, doughty protector of the town's safety, kissing the baby while standing beside the now-famous bench.'

Miss Dimont had to admit her young colleague was getting the hang of this news business very fast, but he had yet to learn its nuances. Though his criticism of this vapid tale was spot-on, the way it was written suited Temple Regents very well. Quite clearly the mother had panicked – no need to call the fire brigade! Nor was there any necessity for the red fire engine and its jangling bell to be ostentatiously launched when a man could run down the street just as quick. As for the production of a screwdriver and the victorious conclusion, this was what was expected of the town's firemen. Everyone would know who the mother was – word would certainly spread over the coming week – and the way the story was written was sufficient exposure of her maternal ineptitude. No need, by the addition of her name, age and address, to tar and feather her as well.

Miss Dimont tried to explain all this, but the young man had gone back correcting his proof, marking up the spelling mistakes.

WALL BEING REBUILT

went the next headline.

'Oh *Lord*,' wailed Valentine. 'This is news?'

'To those it affects,' said Miss Dimont, crossly. She had written that particular spellbinder.

'Here's a corker,' laughed Valentine, reading on down the proof. Temple Regis Short Mat Bowls Club held the finals of the doubles competition recently, with Pip Membley and Gill Wainwright versus Arthur Stratton and . . .

'You have a lot to learn,' came the unforgiving response. 'These stories allow us to print a list of names – and all those people will buy the paper just to revel in their fame.'

'Oh ho!' said Valentine. 'I see! But, Judy, this is parish magazine stuff! What we need to liven things up is an armed robbery, arson – or what about a nice juicy murder!'

'We have those sometimes,' said Miss Dimont slowly, for though she might secretly agree the paper had to be filled somehow. And anyway it was what the readers wanted and expected. The boy had a lot to learn.

PUPILS' DELIGHT AT NEW CURTAINS

Valentine was now howling with laughter.

'You don't yet understand,' was the stern response. 'People revel in normality – it makes them feel safe. The *Express* holds up a mirror to Temple Regents and offers them the picture of their lives they'd like to see – at least, that's what the editor thinks,' added Miss Dimont, with just the merest sniff. 'And so we do it.'

'And all the bad stuff?'

'That gets in as well – just read the court cases, it's all there – Mr Rhys just doesn't like to rub the town's nose in the fact that not everybody's perfect. And of course, when the holidaymakers come, you don't want them going away with the wrong impression of this lovely place, now do you?'

'Is it time for the pub? Will you come and have a sandwich with me?'

'Dear boy, the most we can snatch is twenty minutes. The canteen is closer. On the other hand, the editor seems to have popped out, so maybe . . .'

'Come on then.'

'If we go to the Jawbones we can get something quick,' she conceded, picking up her raffia bag. 'Have you finished that proof?' She glanced through Rhys's door as they left the office but, sure enough, he'd disappeared. How odd you are, Mr Editor, thought Miss Dimont, to go missing on press day when your baby is about to be delivered.

In the street, Valentine linked his arm through hers. 'I'm so enjoying this,' he said, and his eyes were gleaming. 'I've got a hundred questions to ask.'

He bought the drinks and the sandwiches – *Well, that's taken care of your week's wages, young man!* Judy thought – and the couple sat in the sunlight at the end of the bar where the open door looked out over the harbour. A relentless tooting indicated the fleet were on their way in, warning the fishermen's wives to have the dinner ready.

'You were asking why we print what you call parish magazine stuff.'

'No, no,' said Valentine. 'I'm getting the hang of all that. No,

I wanted to ask about you. You're so brilliant, I want to know why you're here, not in Fleet Street editing one of the nation's more respected organs.'

'Long story. Short lunch-break.'

'Oh, go on. A clue, at least.'

Miss Dimont sipped her ginger beer. 'You don't have to live in London for excitement to come knocking at the door. All the things you were talking about – murder, arson, embezzlement – turn up in Temple Regis sooner or later. This place isn't Toy Town, you know.'

'I'm beginning to register that. But I was asking you about Fleet Street.'

'Not for me. I had another career before this one which gave me enough excitement to last a lifetime.'

Valentine looked at his watch. 'We've got eight minutes left. Two and a half to walk back to the office, that gives us the luxury of five and a half long minutes together before we have to move.' He stretched luxuriantly.

'If I may say so, Mr Ford, you have a curious attitude for one so young. Most people your age would be complaining about how mean a lunch-break is when it lasts only twenty minutes.'

'Depends who you're sharing it with,' said Valentine, looking at her with a shy smile. 'Look, I've got the cottage in Bedlington sorted out now, would you and Miss Hedley like to come to supper tomorrow?'

'Can you cook?'

'What a question!' Valentine snorted, but in his reply she already knew the dread answer.

They walked quickly but companionably back to the *Riviera Express* offices and Miss Dimont wondered for a moment whether this charming young fellow might put his arm through hers again, but he didn't.

It should have been a straightforward afternoon – the same this Thursday as every Thursday for decades past – mounting pressure as the paper's deadline approached, distracted consultations over the rewrite of a sports headline, an apology or correction anxiously inserted at the last minute, and a nervous last look through the pages to make sure that some story had not duplicated itself on another page (a spanner that often threw itself in the works). Final proofs would be OK'd and the papers start to spin off the presses, by which time the responsibility for tomorrow's *Riviera Express* passed from Editorial to Distribution, those anonymous cloth-capped men with cheery smiles and ancient vans. All over for another week!

Instead, on their return, Judy and Valentine were confronted by ashen faces, a silent office, and from the other end the muted bellowing of Rudyard Rhys. His door was shut but from the sound of it he appeared to be berating Betty Featherstone. Outside in the newsroom everything seemed to have come to a standstill, with people looking helplessly about them. Such inaction at such a time and on such a day was disturbing.

'What's going on?' Judy asked John Ross, the chief sub.

'He's been looking for you, girrlie,' came the silky reply. 'Watch your step now.'

Sensing a moment of crisis, Valentine slid behind his desk and hid behind a page proof. Not sharing the same sense of self-preservation, his lunch partner strode purposefully towards the editor's door. She knew a crisis when she smelt one, and it wouldn't be first time she'd had to help Rhys out of a difficulty. For all the massive solidity, the overbearing presence, the ringing tones and the waggling beard, the editor was a bit of a panicker. He always had been.

As she opened the door, the bellowing ceased. Betty was

sitting opposite her editor. She was in tears, which though they came often never suited her, since her mascara had a way of liberally making tracks across her face like the tributaries of the Nile delta. She dabbed at her nose with a handkerchief.

Opposite her stood the editor, hunched and ashen-faced. He glanced up at Miss Dimont and paused momentously.

'Ben Larsson's dead,' he said bleakly. 'Suicide. Or accidental. Don't know at the moment.'

'Oh,' said Judy crisply. She paused for just a second. 'Well, we've still got time to re-plate the front page.' She'd seen the problem and found the solution, all in an instant. 'Betty can come and help me while I write the story – you spoke to him only a day or two ago, didn't you, Betty?'

The blonde on the sofa nodded dumbly.

'Go and kick Valentine out of his desk and get your notes,' she ordered briskly before turning to Rhys. 'Who says it was suicide? Do we have any more facts?'

'Frank Topham called. A rarity for him to be so helpful.' Rhys hesitated then muttered, 'Apparently Ben had hooked himself up to his Rejuvenator and was electrocuted.'

'What?'

The editor started to repeat this simple information but his words were drowned by Miss Dimont's peals of laughter. 'I can't believe it! And after all the denials of the *Daily Herald*'s story! What a delicious irony!'

Rhys ignored this. 'Topham said he couldn't be sure that it wasn't an act of suicide. And, given the pressure Ben was under, that can't be discounted.'

'Pretty theatrical way to go.'

'Just find a way of getting as much in as you can. But remember that Ben Larsson was without question the most important and best-known figure in Temple Regis. Treat him with respect.'

Feeling less respect than might be wished for, Judy returned to her desk. Valentine was over the other side of the newsroom talking energetically to a sub-editor while Betty sat in his chair, leafing distractedly through her notebook.

'Don't like to speak ill of the dead, Judy, but he was a bad lot.'

'I know.'

'The butler or whoever he was gave me a sheaf of letters by mistake. Some of the things that Rejuvenator had done – you know, some people even claimed that it had killed their husband or mother or son. It was shocking to read.'

'I know,' said Judy, feeding copy paper into her Remington Quiet-Riter. 'In many ways Ben Larsson may have been Temple's best-known personality but he will leave the town with a horrible legacy. Now he's dead people will feel free to speak.'

'Why didn't they, when he was alive?'

'They did. They wrote those letters – they even used to write us letters here at the *Express*. Sooner or later the dam would have burst and, if it was suicide, you can see why he did it. He was about to be disgraced after half a lifetime of people saying how wonderful he was, and how brilliant his machine was.'

Betty was perplexed. Unfamiliar with death, she kept it at a distance because she was not really sure how to cope with it. For all her recent disillusion of Ben Larsson, she'd been in the great man's company only a few hours before, and knowing he was dead somehow rendered him innocent of all charges – you can't accuse someone who has lost their life so unexpectedly of the damage and death of others.

'What's your intro, Judy?'

The chief reporter glanced across to Curse Corner, the place where curses are kept specially to be brought out at such moments. But then she started typing. Furiously.

In twenty minutes the new lead story which would adorn the *Riviera Express*'s front page was complete. Miss Dimont had brought it in on time, at the correct length, and with no need of the sub-editor's corrective pen.

I HAVE NO REGRETS – TEMPLE'S BEN LARSSON
Exclusive final interview with the *Riviera Express*
Rejuvenator tycoon found dead at
Ransome's Retreat
by Betty Featherstone and Judy Dimont

There had been some nice words exchanged between the pair as to whose name should go first in the joint byline. Betty wanted hers but didn't like to say. Judy cared not at all whether her name was on the story or not, but in truth every last word on the front page would be written by her. She'd waited for Betty to mention the tricky topic since it was always amusing to see how she pushed herself to the fore – in life, in the paper – whenever she could.

'No, Betty,' Judy said when she finally cranked up the courage to raise the byline issue. 'This is your exclusive – the *Daily Herald* never got a squeak out of him when they printed all that stuff a couple of weeks ago, but you got him to talk. It'll be in all the national newspapers tomorrow.'

Oh, thought Betty, oh . . . maybe, at last, the call from Fleet Street!

'Now Betty, pay attention.' But Miss Fleet Street was looking out of the window, her thoughts many miles away. Already she was making herself at home in the capital city, a seasoned denizen of the Cheshire Cheese and the Old Bell where the thirsty old newshounds hung out.

'Betty!'

'Er . . . Judy?'

'You see this through the subs and the stone – I'm going over to the Retreat. I want to be there before the nationals get to hear about it. I bet there's a lot more to this story – unless *you'd* like to go?'

Betty didn't want to break the spell by leaving the office at such a magical moment – Betty Featherstone of the *Daily Mail*!

Miss Dimont grabbed her raffia bag and strode up the office, notebook flapping from her coat pocket. It was on occasions such as this that the synthesis of her life – all that had happened before, all that happened now, all that was destined for the future – came together.

She took the side door out to the car park, where the ever-faithful Herbert awaited her command, so intent upon her mission that she barely noticed it was raining.

'You're going to get awfully wet,' said a voice behind her. 'Want a lift?'

'In that ghastly death trap?' she said without turning her head, but secretly delighted.

'You can drive if you like,' said Valentine.

Their progress in the red bubble car was sedate, but at least it was dry. 'Shouldn't you be finishing those proofs?' Miss Dimont asked sternly once they were under way. 'The editor won't like you bunking off without saying where you're going.'

'All done. And I told John Ross. He was very disappointed with your headline.'

'He can change it if it doesn't fit. What did he want instead?'

'"Ben Larsson Is Dead".'

'Oh yes. As in, "The Queen Is Dead".'

'Just so.'

'The headline he'll never write.'

'Which?'

'Either.'

With difficulty Valentine's bubble car conquered the steep rise up to Ransome's Retreat. The view from the drive when they came to a halt was particularly beautiful today: the rain had stopped and, as if in deference to the memory of the recently departed, the cloud-base above the estuary had formed itself into tall pillars which stretched high into the azure sky. One might almost picture St Peter and his welcoming committee at the gates between the pillars, until one recalled that Ben Larsson's onward journey might be taking him in a different direction – if all those letters of complaint were to be believed.

Before the reporters lay a familiar sight – a collection of Temple Regis police cars, some in their summer livery of sky blue, others more darkly meaningful in coal black. Uniformed constables stood about the place as if bodysnatchers might come to steal the old inventor away, but the main activity was occurring beyond the massive oak front door.

'Judy Dimont, *Riviera Express*,' she chirped brightly at a particularly stony face sweltering away under a large helmet. 'My colleague Valentine, er, Ford.'

'No press.'

Such was the standard opening gambit on these occasions, a courtly ritual which had to be danced before Miss Dimont got her way, which she usually did.

'Inspector Topham, I think, is expecting me.'

'Di'n' mention it.'

'I think you'll find . . .'

'G'wan, push off. This is a police matter.'

'Come on, Valentine.' Miss Dimont strode away from the door and walked round to the side of the house. The copper let them go.

The corner turned, the reporters stepped through a side door into a long grey hall suffused by the stillness which comes with death. Though people were moving around in a side room, their movements seemed muffled, their conversation deliberately muted.

'D'you really think we should be . . . ?' An innate decency

cautioned Valentine not to step further, but he found himself left behind as Judy launched forward into the centre of activity.

'Faint heart never won fair lady,' she taunted over her shoulder, and barged into Ben Larsson's office.

Frank Topham was going over the train of events with his two henchmen, one of whom was taking notes. On the desk were a handful of Polaroid pictures – a recent addition to the armoury of provincial crime-fighting – but of the body there was no sign.

'What are you doing here?' he snarled. Policeman and reporter had known each other, not entirely cordially, a long time.

'The door was open, so we popped in.' Judy smiled. 'How's everything, Inspector?' Her junior marvelled at this insouciance, not to say barefaced cheek.

'For heaven's sake!' said the Inspector heavily, 'we've had enough press here for one day. Clear out or I'll have you arrested for interfering with police work.'

Miss Dimont turned pale. '*What* press?' she snapped back. Was the *Riviera Express* about to lose its scoop to some enterprising freelancer who'd sneaked in and stolen the story from under their noses? Her competitive instincts gathered force and exploded. '*What press?*'

The Inspector looked hard at her. 'Miss Dimont, this has been a trying day. Your being here is a hindrance to police investigations. I put a constable on the front door and told him, no press. Yet here you are. I won't ask again – clear out!'

'*What* press?'

The Inspector could hear the rising panic in her voice and rather enjoyed the moment. Rarely did he feel he had the advantage over Miss Dimont.

'Well, for heaven's sake,' he chortled, 'you should know, of all people.'

'Come *on*, Inspector!'

The Inspector got out his briar pipe and took some time filling it. Finally, he said, 'You people down at the *Express* ought to get your ducks in a row. If I ran my department like you run your newspaper . . .'

'Who *was* it, Inspector?' Miss Dimont was already calculating how she could grab back the exclusive from the magpie who'd stolen it from her.

'Your bloomin' editor, that's who. Mr Rhys. He was here when we arrived. He called us in.'

Miss Dimont turned briefly to Valentine and he could see the stunned look on her face. Almost to herself, she said, 'Mr Rhys said *you* had telephoned *him*. That you had let him know about the death.'

'That's the press for you, always getting things wrong. Ha!'

'So . . . Mr Rhys was here when you got here?'

'Ask him. I'm surprised he didn't tell you himself.'

What on earth, thought Judy, was her editor – a man who rarely left the office – doing up here at Ransome's Retreat, and on press day too? It didn't make sense.

'Can I speak to Mrs Larsson?'

'No. She's upset, as even you must be able to imagine.'

The reporter inclined her head ever so slightly to her junior who saw the look in her eye; and, as she started on a full-scale interrogation of the policeman, he slipped away.

'Inspector, we've known each other a long time. It would be betraying no confidences to tell you that Mr Rhys is a creature of habit who never leaves his newspaper on the day it's being printed. What on earth was he doing up here?'

'I have no idea. He told me something which I am not permitted to repeat to you.'

'What do you mean, not permitted?'

'Some things are above the law, Miss Dimont, let's leave it at that. You saw war service, as did I – you'll know there's a time to ask questions and a time to keep quiet. This is one of those times.'

Miss Dimont blinked and shoved the spectacles back up her glorious convex nose. She decided to change tack.

'So the death was an accident? Or was it suicide? I gather Mr Larsson had hooked himself up to the Rejuvenator.'

'Take a look for yourself.' He pushed the small pile of Polaroid photographs towards the reporter. They showed the body of the great inventor sprawled backwards in his desk chair, one arm hanging limply down while the other seemed to be attached to his head. In each hand were the electronic tubes whose life-enforcing powers had done so much to so many since the Rejuvenator came on to the market. The old man had a puzzled expression on his face.

'You know,' said Miss Dimont slowly, 'there are some people who claim that the Rejuvenator killed their loved one. We know that from letters we have seen from Mr Larsson's office, and also from letters we received at the *Express*.'

'We had a few of those too,' said Topham blithely.

'Good Lord!' exclaimed the reporter. 'Didn't you ever feel the need to investigate them?'

'We did. Mr Larsson said people who had injured themselves, or worse, had done so because they hadn't read the instructions properly. You can't answer that.'

'So, Inspector. Was it suicide? Or an accident? Or did he,' she went on, barely suppressing a sardonic laugh, '*fail to follow the instructions properly*?'

'You've left out the other possibility,' said the Inspector massively.

'What?'

Topham did not reply.

'You mean that someone tampered with the Rejuvenator?'

'There you go, jumping to conclusions like the press always does. I am saying no more.'

'Well, let's talk about something else then,' said Miss Dimont with more than a dash of pepper in her voice. 'The dead woman on the beach at Todhempstead. What's going on there?'

'What do you mean, what's going on? Police are following up their investigations.'

'We both know what that means, Inspector. It means, I think, that so far you've made no progress.'

'You can think what you like. I've stated the official position.'

'The unofficial position?'

'The Coroner's on holiday. Not back till next Wednesday. Nothing'll happen till then.'

Wonders will never cease, thought Miss Dimont witheringly, as she wandered away. Only the coppers at Temple Regis could make a tea break last nearly two weeks.

FIFTEEN

Valentine was waiting on the terrace when she came out.

'Get hold of the memsahib?'

'With ease,' came the cheery reply. 'Very interesting stuff. Apparently she . . .'

'Tell me later. We're not welcome here and, in any case, I've got some thinking to do.'

'Where to, Captain?'

'My cottage. We can talk there.'

They were walking back across the terrace when suddenly around the side of the house appeared the unmistakable bulk of Rudyard Rhys. He started guiltily at the sight of his two reporters.

'What the devil are *you* doing here?' he snarled.

'I might say the same to you,' replied Miss Dimont coolly, stepping up to him. 'And while there's a bit of asking going on, would you mind telling me why you said that Topham had called to tell you about Larsson's death, when in fact it was you who telephoned him?'

'None of your business.'

'I'm sorry Mr Rhys, I think it is. You can't go around misleading your editorial staff.'

'I didn't tell you to come here – get off! Skedaddle! *I'll* manage this story if you don't mind.'

Valentine sidled smartly away to the car park and started inspecting the tyres on his bubble car. The boy was a born diplomat.

'Look, Richard,' said Miss Dimont – she rarely used his first name, but when she did she addressed him with the one from Royal Navy days. 'This is mighty odd. I never see you anywhere outside the office these days, yet here you are sticking your nose into the biggest story the *Express* has had in many a moon. You aren't a reporter, you're an editor. Your job isn't here, it's in the office, putting the paper to bed.' Away from the newsroom, Miss Dimont did not feel obliged to treat him with the deference his position commanded when the pair were in front of others.

'I just find it extraordinary,' she went on, 'that on press day you find time to come up here to wander round and find a dead body. What were you doing up here? What's going on?'

Rhys had gone deathly pale. 'It really is none of your business,' he said flatly, and turned on his heel to walk away. But his steps were leaden.

'Listen to me, Richard, you could be in serious trouble – I just have the feeling this is not an accident, and nor is it a suicide. I think it could be the other thing – and so, by the way, does Topham.'

The inspector had said nothing of the kind, but Rudyard Rhys didn't know that. 'You discovering the body puts you in a very difficult position. You surely understand that?'

Rhys's big feet crunched on up the drive. He seemed to be trying to escape but was making little headway. 'Can't say anything,' he said. 'All I can tell you is this. I had a call from Ben Larsson this morning, and after the main pages in the paper had been passed, I came up here to talk to him.'

'On press day? What about?'

'None of your business.'

'I saw the Polaroids of Larsson taken by the police. What do you think – accident? Suicide? Murder? He had a lot of enemies, one way and the other.'

'He'd just made one more,' said Rhys bitterly.

'What do you mean by that?'

The editor turned to face his chief reporter. 'Miss Dimont,' he said slowly, 'there was a time, long ago, when I had to answer to you and to Miss Hedley. A lot of water has flowed under the bridge since then, and now you are *my* employee, not the other way round.

'Stop asking these questions and listen to me – I forbid you to continue investigating this story. All information which goes into the newspaper from now on regarding Ben Larsson's death will come through me, and I will get Betty to write it up. I don't want you near it.

'And,' he added angrily, nodding in the direction of the bubble car, 'what's that young man doing up here? He's supposed to be reading the final proofs.'

'Job done. Listen, Richard, if we are to maintain our . . . I was going to say cordial relations, they aren't that, but we seem to have a modus operandi – if we're to go on as before, you're going to have to trust me. You know very well I'm perfectly capable of uncovering whatever terrible secret it is you're clasping to your chest.'

'I doubt that.'

'You also know you could be in serious trouble.'

'I doubt that too.' He was feverishly digging in his pocket for his pipe.

'Inspector Topham said something which suggests to me you were able to stop him questioning you. Some secret or other. Would that be to do with our war work?'

'Mind your own business, Judy, and just go away. There's nothing further to say, except that you will please bear in mind my orders to stay away from this case. What are you doing tomorrow?'

'Wedding reports.'

'That's more like it. Stick to that for a bit. You know, you cause an awful lot of trouble, one way and the other, round the office when you start sticking your nose in.'

It was on the tip of the reporter's tongue to offer a full-scale analysis of Rhys's editorship of the *Riviera Express* – its skirting around controversy, its determination not to rock the boat, its lickspittle approach to certain members of the Bench and the Town Council, and its often tardy response to emergency stories – but what was the point? When she'd arrived as a reporter in Temple Regis, the newspaper had another editor. Only a year or two later did Rhys put his shaggy head around the door to declare that he, now, was master of ceremonies.

She could have quit then. Instead, she chose to soldier on as the servant of her one-time junior officer and if anyone was to blame for conversations like this one, it was her. That much Judy Dimont recognised and so, shrugging her shoulders, she walked over to where Valentine was polishing the windscreen of his Heinkel.

'Take me home. I need a stiff whisky.'

*

Of late, Mulligatawny had seen less of his mistress than he would like. He made his position perfectly clear as Judy let herself into the small stone cottage which had been her home these past ten years, deliberately twining himself through her legs, causing her to trip. Then he redoubled his manoeuvre so that as she caught her balance, she was forced to trip again and land in ungainly fashion against the umbrella stand.

'Oh, *Mull*!' she exclaimed, tired and frustrated. The tortoise-shell cat looked at her with an uncompromising gaze and stood his ground, tail vertical.

'Whisky, d'you say?' asked Valentine, bringing up the rear.

'Over there on the tray. I'll feed the cat and then you can tell me again about Mrs Larsson. To be honest, the way you steer that infernal contraption made it hard to concentrate.'

'Others have likened my driving style to Stirling Moss.'

'Others have no sense. Water, half and half.'

They took their drinks into the garden and sat next to the wicker bower covered in honeysuckle and wild roses. The squalls from earlier in the day had passed, and the evening was hot. Bees from next door's hive wafted inquiringly through the garden and the clear sharp call of a blackbird came from the beech tree.

'Thank heavens,' sighed Miss Dimont, as the whisky went to work dispelling the day's frustrations. For a moment they shared a companionable silence.

'I found the Army a bit of a trial,' said Valentine, apropos of nothing in particular.

'How so?'

'I didn't want to be an officer – there've been an awful lot of them in my family. Didn't want the competition, wanted to do it differently.'

'And?'

'Not a bad experiment. I made some friends for life, I would say. And I kept away from those stinkers in the officers' mess – I don't know why, but the cavalry seems to attract a particular sort of swine – and I survived what turned out to be a pretty rough ride. But, come the end of each day—' he sighed, looking into his whisky glass '—it would be beer, and gallons of it. Not really what I enjoy. This—' he flashed a smile at Miss Dimont '—is what I like. Heaven, in fact.' He stretched his long body and took another sip.

'Come on, the day isn't done yet. No more whisky till you tell me again what happened after you slipped away from the dreaded inspector.'

'First thing, I bumped into their man Lamb. He was carrying a suitcase. I don't know why that struck me as odd, but it did. Also, he'd taken off his manservant manners for the weekend – when I asked where Mrs Larsson was, he just shrugged and pushed off. Couldn't be bothered to reply. You might even suppose he didn't work there.'

'So then what happened?' Mulligatawny, somewhat mollified by the excellent fish supper he'd just consumed, wandered down the lawn to where they were sitting and jumped into Miss Dimont's lap.

'I went into this extraordinary room, full of scientific instruments and blown egg shells and pebbles and oddities, the sort of things you might pick up at a jumble sale . . . and there she was. Seemed pretty calm, which is more than can be said for the stepson – Gus something.'

'Wetherby.'

'Wetherby, yes. Reminded me of someone I was at school with, nasty piece of work. Very, very agitated, I'd say, not able to concentrate on anything. He was pretty rude – "what are you doing here", sort of thing, which of course he was perfectly entitled to ask. But,' said Valentine, smiling, 'I just took a leaf out of your book – "Thought I'd pop in and see how things are." He pushed off pretty soon and I had her to myself.'

'She talked?'

'In a manner of speaking. This business of the editor is a bit rum, though.'

'How, exactly?'

'Well, she told me she came back from shopping in Temple about eleven o'clock to find her husband and the editor having a row. She wasn't quite sure what it was about, but Lamb was nearby just in case there was trouble and so she went out to talk to the gardener.

'When she got back half an hour later, Mr Rhys was racing around the terrace saying he was looking for her because her husband was dead. She went into Larsson's study and there he was – apparently electrocuted by his own device. What *is* this Rejuvenator, by the way? I've never heard of it.'

Trouble with the young, thought Miss Dimont, they've never heard of anything. 'Tell you later.'

'So then, according to Mrs Larsson, the editor called the police and they turned up pretty quickly. He talked to Inspector Whatsisname, and was allowed to push off – then the inspector and those seriously nasty men who hang around him went to work on Mrs L., Gus, and Uncle Tom Cobley and all.'

'Did she hear anything of what was said between Mr Rhys and the inspector?'

'Something to do with a tailcoat – rather odd, don't you think, to be talking about funerals when the body's only just been found?'

'A tailcoat? Are you sure?'

'That's what she said.'

'Decidedly odd. Anything else?'

'She seemed remarkably calm. The stepson was like a cat on a hot tin roof but, though she was obviously shocked, she was completely in control.'

'Hmm. More whisky, please. Let's think about this.'

Valentine kicked off his shoes, trailed back across the lawn, and returned with the whisky decanter on a silver tray. Mulligatawny, disapproving, turned his back.

'Stay for supper.'

'I thought you and Miss Hedley were gracing the Chateau Waterford tomorrow night?'

'Maybe. But I'm going to get Auriol over here tonight so we can talk this thing through. If you drink too much,' eyeing the decanter, 'there's always a spare bed.'

'Lovely. Can I help?'

'It's going to be an omelette. You can make yourself useful

opening the wine. Just wait here while I telephone Auriol. You can talk to Mulligatawny.' The cat did not like the sound of this, hopped off her lap and flashed away.

The eggs had been broken into a bowl, the wine uncorked, the table outside laid with an old oilcloth, and the candles unearthed and trimmed by the time Auriol arrived. She brought with her a cake from her kitchen and an acute and analytical brain.

'How is Madame Dimont, my dear? What news of the invading demoness?'

'Mother? Mercifully still in Ellezelles. But threatening another visit.'

'*Comme d'habitude*. Have you replied to her last letter?'

'I really should, shouldn't I?'

'An apple a day keeps the doctor away. Ditto letters and *mamans*.'

'I'll do it this weekend.'

'Somehow, my dear, I doubt it . . .'

Judy responded by beating the private fury over her mother into the eggs, so that when the omelette was served it was light as a feather.

'Delicious,' said Valentine, pouring the wine.

'Come on,' said Auriol impatiently, 'you'd better tell me what's going on.'

A lengthy reappraisal of all there was to know about the death of Bengt Larsson took place, at the end of which Judy and Valentine turned expectantly to Auriol. She smiled secretly to herself, folded her napkin, looked into her lap and for a moment said nothing.

She could be irritating like that.

'Tell me again about the funeral arrangements,' she said to Valentine.

'Nothing to say. Just that Pernilla Larsson overheard the editor telling Inspector Topham that people would be wearing tails – how would he know that? He's not a member of the family. And anyway, why would Topham want to know? Police uniform, so far as I know, doesn't stretch to tails.'

'Operation Tailcoat,' said Auriol, with just a shade of smugness. 'Those candles, Valentine, please – the sun's gone.'

The young man obligingly brought kindly light to the encircling gloom and sat down expectantly.

'I have to explain this to Hugue, young man, but it involves things you should never hear. Shut your ears.'

'About the War?' said Valentine. 'But that was over before I was born – almost. What can it matter now?' He thought this cloak-and-dagger stuff overdramatic, over-secretive, and largely for the gratification of those who had once played a part in it.

'Pay attention,' said Auriol sharply. 'During the War we had many victories and, I'd say, just as many failures. Official secrets generally stay in place because someone on our side has made a complete mess of things. Where Hugue and I worked in the Admiralty we saved lives, but some were lost. Sometimes, many were lost. Do you understand?'

Valentine nodded.

'You've been in the Army. When someone blows himself up with a grenade because the idiot pulled the pin but forgot to let go, what do you tell his family?'

'Ah,' said Valentine.

'Magnify that incident by a hundred, two hundred, and you'll see why the Official Secrets Act was created. To protect the idiots who made mistakes, yes, but also to ease the burden on those who lost a loved one. How much worse to know that it needn't have happened.'

'I'd never considered it that way,' said Valentine, blushing slightly.

'You're young.' Auriol's throwaway compliment was not

altogether kind. 'So,' she continued, 'what you hear stays here – it goes no further. Even Hugue doesn't know it yet.'

'So,' said Judy, 'go on.'

'Operation Tailcoat. It was while you were dealing with that Belgium business. *That* went off all right, didn't it?'

'Only just.'

'Tailcoat was Rusty Rhys's idea. Have you heard of the British Free Corps, Valentine?'

'Never.'

'They were British servicemen who put on German uniforms and were ready to fight against their own country.'

'I don't believe it.'

'True. Old Rusty's job, like ours but with less clout, was to find traitors. He'd discovered this chap called Railton Freeman, son of a naval officer, who was an out-and-out Nazi long before the War started. Thought Hitler was the bee's knees.

'Of course, Freeman was made to fight for our side but pretty soon he was captured and ended up in a prisoner-of-war camp. Then some bright spark in Berlin thought up the idea of a regiment of British soldiers fighting their own country would be a wonderful propaganda weapon – a buck for the German troops but, more especially, completely demoralising for our boys – and they got Freeman to head it. He was turned into a golden boy, went to Berlin to meet Hitler, all that guff.'

Valentine looked aghast. 'I can't believe . . . people were prepared to fight against their own country?'

'Dear boy,' said Auriol, 'you may have served in the Army but you don't know much about human frailty, do you?'

Miss Dimont poured more wine. The light was ebbing but the blackbird was still singing. Deeper in the dusk another late celebrant joined in the conversation.

'Believe me, this could have become a major propaganda coup for the Nazis and something radical had to be done. Rusty Rhys had done the homework and ordered one of our agents in Berlin to locate Freeman and eliminate him. He wasn't hard to find, it just needed someone to do the job.'

'In Berlin? In the middle of war?'

'You're too young. We used people from neutral countries – women and men – to walk around the streets of Berlin and Frankfurt and Hamburg. They were our eyes and ears, and we learned about Railton Freeman from them. But getting rid of someone requires a different sort of agent.

'We had one of those but something went wrong. Our man went missing, the elimination did not occur, and Railton Freeman just carried on his own sweet way. We lost not one but three people on Tailcoat, and Rusty was pretty much in disgrace.'

'Was that why they sent him to Scotland?' asked Miss Dimont. 'There was so much going on I hardly noticed he'd disappeared.'

'Well, nobody wanted to talk about it anyway. It was a complete failure, black mark all round.'

Valentine jerked forward in his chair. 'Why on earth, then, would Mr Rhys want to mention something like that to the police? Surely you'd do the best you could to bury such an awful failure, carry it to the grave?'

Miss Dimont poured coffee from a vacuum flask. 'The answer to that, dear boy, probably rests with Mrs Larsson, and no doubt she'll be happy to share it with us when we pop in again tomorrow.'

'But I thought Mr Rhys said you weren't to . . .'

Miss Dimont leant over the candlelit table towards her junior reporter and gave him a lingering smile. 'There are times, dear Valentine, when one takes what the editor says with a pinch of salt. What comes first in journalism is finding out the truth.'

'Throwing down the gauntlet?' Valentine smiled back. 'Challenging the Rusty one?'

'You could say that.'

Auriol said it was time for her to go. There was more small talk about Mme Dimont's threatened visit, and then she said goodnight. The tail lights of her car wove off into the night.

'I ought to go too.'

'Well, as I said, there's a bed.'

'No, no, I don't think I will. But thank you. And thank you for a lovely evening. I feel in a curious way as if I've come home.'

'Temple Regis has a way of ensnaring those who . . .' They were walking slowly towards the door.

Valentine suddenly stopped and turned to look down at her. 'No,' he said, 'it's not Temple Regis. It's you.' He paused for a moment, then kissed her.

At that moment the blackbird stopped singing.

SIXTEEN

A new week in Devon's prettiest town and the refugees from less alluring parts of the country were beginning to fill up the houses, hotels and boarding establishments which for a week or two were happy to offer them a pillow in paradise.

The *Riviera Express* – train, not newspaper – did sterling work in bringing them in glamorous style to this place, its chocolate brown and cream Pullman coaches heavily carpeted and generously staffed, gliding luxuriantly to their destination. As the holidaymakers walked or took buses away from Regis Junction the town laid out its best welcome: the funfair at one end of the promenade tooting whistles and blaring hurdy-gurdy music, straw-hatted donkeys patiently awaiting their passengers on the golden beach, and the palm trees waving their welcome.

The cares of the world evaporated as the *Riviera Express* clanked to a halt – but how ruinous would it be to the town's coffers if these joyous visitors were to discover that, only a few days ago, a body had been found on the beach with its head bashed in? And now another unexplained death in the town's smartest quarter. They might be safer in Brixham or Torquay!

It was a glorious day, with no clouds in the sky and only the merest hint of a breeze, and Miss Dimont breathed in the scent of honeysuckle as she rode Herbert up to the gates of Ransome's Retreat. Today her route took her through Primrose Lane and up Cliff Rise, a leisurely climb which gave her a lengthy glimpse of the estuary at its sparkling best.

Dutifully she had followed her editor's instructions, coming in to the office early to dispatch the latest round of wedding reports which, to local readers, were of far more importance than the death of a rich old man.

HONEYMOON AT SECRET DESTINATION

She wrote. This meant that the young couple so recently joined by God's holy law could not afford to take themselves away for their nuptial night, poor lambs, and would be honeymooning on the sofa.

LOVE AT FIRST SIGHT

– the newlyweds had been doing things they shouldn't ever since the fourth form, but now Mother Nature had caught up with them. The bouquet in the accompanying photo was sufficiently generous to cover the bump.

FLORAL JOY AT ST MARGARET'S

– here, a lingering description of the stephanotis, lily of the valley, guipure lace and all the other flapdoodle which every young bride burdens herself with, because Miss Dimont had nothing else to go on – the young couple, eager to get their picture in the paper, had neglected to turn over the green form and fill in any personal details. They'd even forgotten to mention the bride's mother, which was likely to cause ructions. It was a very short report.

Miss Dimont hoped he wouldn't, but it was a certainty that the photographer who took the picture of this priceless pair would be adding it to the Thank Heavens! board down the other end of the office. Long ago someone had instituted this pictorial record of the ugliest people in Temple Regis, the ones with an unerring instinct for finding a matching partner. There seemed to be so many of these romantic lemmings the board was groaning under the weight of their 10 × 8 prints.

Her duties completed, Miss Dimont felt her obligation to the editor had ended. Herbert had brought her up the hill to Ransome's Retreat where she found the front door, only so recently guarded by Temple Regis' finest, abandoned and ajar. The house was silent and apparently empty.

She found Pernilla Larsson in the kitchen staring at a kettle and a bottle of Camp coffee, looking elegant as ever, but evidently suffering from loss of sleep. She did not rise when Miss Dimont put her head round the door.

'Come in. I don't know who you are, but come in anyway.'

'Judy Dimont, *Riviera Express*. I hope you don't mind . . .'

A slight stiffening. 'A colleague of Mr Rhys, I take it?'

'I'm his chief reporter.'

Mrs Larsson turned to inspect the newcomer, then turned back to stare at the kettle. 'I suppose I should kick you out, but there's nobody else here and really, what does it matter now?' She sounded deflated and beaten.

Judy sized up the situation and took control. 'Would you prefer a cup of real coffee? That bottled stuff is pretty foul.'

'I looked round for the tin but I just couldn't see it. Usually Lamb or Mrs Lamb . . .'

'Here it is,' said Judy soothingly. 'I'll just put the kettle on. Have you had anything to eat?'

'I couldn't possibly.'

'Well, maybe later. Is there nobody else around?'

'It's complicated. What do you want?'

'Just a chat, if you feel like talking. Nothing for the newspaper – just a chat really. Sometimes – after things like this – people like to talk. Sometimes they don't.'

'I haven't got anything else to do, so you may as well sit down.' Mrs Larsson ran a hand vaguely through her hair. 'I haven't quite finished dressing. Would you wait while . . .'

'Please,' said Miss Dimont, placing a cup in front of her, 'don't do anything on my account. Just a chat, nothing for the newspaper.'

Gradually, as the coffee warmed her, Pernilla Larsson was able to turn and face her visitor. The women talked about the mechanics of death – the removal of the body, the notifications, the officials, the lawyers, the relatives – until Judy was able to steer the conversation around to what she really wanted to discuss.

'Shall we go and sit on the terrace?' said her hostess, rallying for a moment. 'It's such a lovely day, shame to waste it.' The moment she said it you could sense the bitterness and loss: there was no husband now to share the rest of her day with.

The two women moved slowly out through the long grey drawing room, the ghost of Bengt Larsson walking between them. Just because they are dead does not mean that people go away.

'I know you've talked to the police, but I wonder if you'd mind answering a couple of other questions? When there are official secrets, sometimes it's difficult but . . .'

'Ah,' said Pernilla, turning again, sharpening her focus on her guest, 'I see you know. About all that secrets nonsense.'

'Well, yes,' said Miss Dimont encouragingly, though in fact she didn't really have a clue. But a useful piece of journalistic trickery is to pretend you know more than you do – it can open all sorts of doors. 'I was just wondering why Mr Rhys felt it necessary to come up here yesterday. It was an odd time for him to leave the office, it being our busiest day of the week.'

'He hasn't told you?'

'No.'

'I wonder then,' said Mrs Larsson shrewdly, 'why you want to know. Are you after his job?'

Until that moment the thought had never occurred, but Judy Dimont never missed a trick. 'Well . . . it's a cut-throat business and . . .'

'Thought so!' said Mrs Larsson sharply. 'Well, I can tell you, your Mr Rhys is no longer welcome in this house, no matter what the outcome of the police investigation. Better for him if he did go – he's a thoroughly repellent individual.'

'So why was he here, yesterday morning?'

'The *Daily Herald*.'

'Mm?'

'You know they wrote that terrible article about Ben a week or so ago.'

'Which the *Riviera Express* did its best to correct – my colleague Betty Featherstone . . .'

'Yes, yes. But the day before yesterday the *Herald* rang Ben up again, to say that now they had incontrovertible proof that the Rejuvenator had caused at least half-a-dozen deaths in middle-aged to old people. This wasn't the story they'd run before; this time they were actually naming names. It was shocking to hear.'

'But not surprising.'

'I told Ben, again and again – these complaints still continued to flood in, but he wouldn't listen. He should have done something to refute them. I'll be frank, it's been like living with a time bomb.'

'So Rudyard Rhys . . .'

'*Richard* Rhys, Ben used to call him, yes. They've known each other a very long time.'

'I thought so.'

'He's a terrible man, that Rhys.' The words were bitter, slow. 'Causing my husband's death.'

'Good Lord!' exclaimed Judy. 'Are you saying . . . Are you saying that Mr Rhys killed your husband?'

Pernilla Larsson put down her cup and stood up, her lips working in an anguished way. 'I don't know *what* happened,' she cried. 'Did he kill him? Somebody did. Rhys was here, and it was no accident.'

'You're sure of that?'

'But of course! That foolish policeman, Inspector Thingamum, was trying to suggest that Ben had killed himself with his own machine, either by accident or . . .' The words struggled to come. 'Or because he wanted to. But that's complete nonsense! Ben has worked with that machine for thirty years – for heaven's sake, he invented it! – there was *no accident*. Of that you can be certain.'

'So what was Mr Rhys doing up here yesterday morning?'

'Ben rang him up after he heard from the *Daily Herald*. Asked him what to do. Rhys was his usual hopeless self, couldn't suggest anything useful. So Ben said to him, *I have to go on the defensive. If I'm to stop people ruining me, I must let them know a little bit more about myself, so that they understand I am a good man.*

'He told me all this at breakfast yesterday. He'd decided to tell those Fleet Street fellows that far from being a charlatan and a fraud, he was in fact a war hero. That he did undercover work for Britain in Germany during the War, risked his life, saved the lives of others. So why, with his invention, would he want to put people's lives in jeopardy?

'But Richard Rhys didn't want that. He told him on no account should he talk about work which was still covered by the Official Secrets Act.'

Miss Dimont poured more coffee and nodded encouragingly.

'Ben told Rhys it was too late, he'd made up his mind. He was not going to have his reputation ruined because of some grubby newspaper investigation, digging up the dirt.'

'I think you agree, don't you, that the Rejuvenator probably did cause those deaths?' asked Miss Dimont softly. Digging the dirt, in the circumstances, didn't seem such a terrible thing for the press to be doing.

'That's not the point!' snapped Pernilla. 'My husband has done fine work all his life and now his reputation is to be smashed – of course he was right to tell people what good he had done for Britain during the war!'

'Why do you think Mr Rhys objected so much?'

'Well, as you gathered, they worked together during the war. Ben had been working for others in the Admiralty, but then Rhys came up with this thing called Operation Tailcoat. It was a plan to track down a man called Railton . . .'

'Freeman . . . yes, I know about it.'

Mrs Larsson picked up her cup again, stirring in more sugar. 'It all went badly wrong. People died . . . it wasn't Ben's fault, it may not even have been Rhys's fault, but . . .'

'So Mr Rhys came up here to try to persuade Mr Larsson not to reveal the details of Operation Tailcoat?'

'Bullied him. Shouted about the Official Secrets Act. Of course, Rhys wasn't concerned about Ben breaking the law, but about being exposed himself.'

'So . . . are you saying he might have killed your husband?'

'Yes! No! No . . . I don't really think so . . . I mean – look at him! A dithering old fool – strong enough, yes, but with the capacity to kill? No, no.'

'Do you think, then, that Richard Rhys bullying him like that caused your husband to . . . well, to commit suicide?'

'I . . . just . . . don't . . . know . . .'

The moment she'd asked it Miss Dimont knew the question

was pointless. Ben Larsson was a man who revelled in his image as the bringer of new life to tired souls – how could he smash his own reputation by electrocuting himself with the Rejuvenator? It was absurd to even think he would.

But it wasn't an accident either.

And despite her forlorn appearance, Miss Dimont had caught a glimpse of the steely resolve within this newly-minted widow and wondered, just for a second, whether it was Pernilla who had done the deed. She was, after all, his fourth wife and though the reporter knew little of the married state, she sensed that each new marriage is a paler imitation of the one before, and that a distance can grow quite easily between a couple who had not shared a lifetime together.

'Can you tell me what actually happened?'

'I had come back from shopping, and they were having their row. I went down to talk to the gardener – I must have been gone for nearly an hour – and when I came back there was Rhys running around in a panic saying that Ben was dead.'

'Who else was around in the house?'

'Gus was here doing some business. Then Lamb had let in some of those crackpots – the Lazarus League lot – who'd come to pay homage. There were only five or six, I think.'

'Could one of them . . . ?'

'I doubt it. Haven't you seen them? They're the worst kind of religious nuts – feeble, unfocused, probably vegetarian too. Wouldn't have it in them.'

'Perhaps I could talk to Mr Lamb?'

Pernilla shot her a look. 'That would be difficult. The moment Gus knew his stepfather was dead, he took charge. And the first thing he did was to fire Lamb. Mrs Lamb too.'

'Oh, that's awkward . . . where's Gus now? Where's Lamb?'

An odd look crept into Pernilla's eye. 'Not sure. And anyway, isn't that enough questions? I don't know quite what the form is on such occasions, not having been widowed before,' she added with a dash of sarcasm, 'but I think the wishes of the bereaved are usually respected, and my wish is that you go now.'

Miss Dimont nodded and rose to her feet.

'You know,' added Pernilla finally, 'I always had the feeling it would end like this. Here we are, we live on the edge of the world.' She wretchedly waved her arm out towards the estuary with its golden slick of water and to the slowly circling gulls overhead. 'We have lived in peace and harmony, as if in the land of milk and honey.

'Life isn't like that, though, is it? Life's hard, and each reward we get has to be paid for. We, Ben and I, have been very well rewarded, but I have the feeling that now we are about to pay it all back. He with his life. Me – I don't know . . .'

She pointed vaguely in the direction of her husband's study. 'You should have seen Ben. It was awful. Hooked up to his Rejuvenator, the thing that had made him famous and rich – his unique creation which had given hope to so many people. Now, of course, *you* – the press, I mean – are going to turn it all into a joke. "Inventor killed by his own machine", that sort of thing. No mention *now* of his wartime heroics.'

'No,' agreed Miss Dimont. 'Probably not. It will remain an Official Secret.'

Pernilla walked her towards the door. 'How come you know about these things?'

'I worked with Mr Rhys during the war. I didn't know about Tailcoat though.'

'It was – how do you say it? – a shambles.'

'So I recently learned.'

'I hate that filthy Rhys. I hope they find him guilty of Ben's murder.'

Perhaps, on the present evidence, they will, thought Miss Dimont. And then where will we be?

Friday was the day of rest and recuperation at the *Riviera Express*. Expenses forms were filled in, cups of tea consumed, plans made for the weekend. Usually the editor came in for an hour and then adjourned to the Conservative Club to discuss matters with the town's elders – matters of such importance they would never appear in the newspaper.

It was a day for catching up – there was always an encouraging clatter of typewriters but the effort expended this morning was in pursuit of informing loved ones of the latest goings-on in Temple Regis. Telephone calls were viewed as something of a luxury, wasteful even – and anyway typing a letter made it look as though you were working.

Some of the early pages for next week's paper were already being prepared – women's feature material, village correspondents' notes, and other timeless jumble were collated and dispatched into the system. Athene Madrigale who doubled as Aunty Jill, the children's page editor (though she never admitted it), had just signed off the Birthday of the Week – a celebration of the life of a joyless eight-year-old whose glowering features would dominate the page next week with an account of her recent triumph in the Methodist Church hula-hoop contest.

A couple of the photographers were arguing about the relative merits of their candidates for the Thank Heavens! board. Their comments about these young hopefuls setting out on the path of marital harmony were nothing short of cruel, but then that's photographers for you.

Betty, who by now should be back in the Newton Abbott office, was still clinging on in the hope that the Fleet Street caravanserai would roll into town to wring from her every last drop of that inspired final interview with Ben Larsson. But to justify her continued presence in the newsroom she had purloined the village correspondents' notes and was busy doing a rewrite:

> **Salborough Active Club – three mile Dartmoor walk, level moderate. Meet at Fox Tor Café. St John Ambulance in attendance.**

> **Kempston Silver Alliance – monthly lunch with Madge Monkton giving a talk, 'My Life Prior to Spiritual Awakening'. Bring own thermos as the kettle has not been found.**

Her typewriter clacked on, slow but relentless. John Ross groaned with boredom, reached down and opened his bottom drawer. The whisky bottle was still there, its very presence offering consolation and courage as only the sight of a VAT 69 label can. He stuck his foot on the drawer and pushed it to and fro, the movement bringing small comfort, for he would never taste the glory of the grain again.

Betty finished her nails and had another stab.

> **There is still time for local people to tell the Local Government Boundary Commission for England where they think the new electoral division boundaries should be drawn across Devon . . .**

> **Gara Bay Coastwatch – there have been complaints of a young couple going out nightly into the bay in a small boat and behaving in an undignified fashion. If anyone knows . . .**

Across the desk, in Judy Dimont's chair, Valentine Waterford's body squirmed and twisted in pain.

Chrystanthemums.
Regular incurved: 1 Mrs E. Everett; 2 Edgar Walsh; 3
Miss Hope. Irregular incurved: 1 Mrs E. Everett . . .

'Oh, oh, oh, OH!' he shouted. 'This is impossible! I can't go on!'

Betty raised her eyes slowly from the application of her nail polish; this was her moment. She'd been studying this willowy figure with his ill-fitting suit and perfect manners ever since he'd landed in the office. He was handsome, though his hair could do with a brush, and – she could tell from across the desk – he smelled rather delicious.

'Can I help, Val?'

'Er, it's Valentine . . . sorry. But yes, Miss Featherstone, please. This is driving me mad.'

There followed an intense discussion, the complexity of which required Betty to move round to Valentine's side of the desk, lean over his typewriter, and gently lead him down the byways of typographical folklore. She did not rush to complete her task, for at close quarters the smell was all the more delectable.

Could he possibly be the . . .? Her new date had failed to show up, a not uncommon experience for Betty, and the one thing she had discovered about Newton Abbot in her short acquaintance was that there were few men of marriageable age and none with any looks. 'It's simple, Val. Name of the flower, full point. New par. Species of the flower, colon. Number, name, semi-colon – number, name, semi-colon. Number, name . . .'

'It's a nightmare!' wailed Valentine. 'Like learning how to dance the quickstep. Do this, then do that, then do something else. Too many commas and full stops and numbers and names and – ruddy flowers! For heaven's sake how many flowers are there in the world?'

Betty smiled patronisingly. 'You thought journalism was about big news stories, Val? Murders and such? This is what it's about, my dear – getting people's names right, in the right order, making sure the punctuation is spot on so that there isn't a scene in the print room on press day. Commas and colons – that's what it's about.'

He'd heard all this from Mr Rhys and Miss Dimont – now Betty too?

The new reporter looked imploringly at her. 'Promise this torture does not go on for long. I've never seen so many punctuation marks!'

He wrenched the paper from his typewriter, fed in more, and angrily started beating the keyboard. Across the room, a district reporter wandered in and handed his latest dispatch to John Ross, the sub-editors put the Children's Page to bed, the sports editor promised his deputy it wouldn't be a long lunch, and Friday started to wind down, as it always did, with a steady trickle of people heading for the pub.

SEVENTEEN

Judy and Auriol were closeted in the kitchen of the harbourside café in Bedlington. Outside the gulls screamed as a late fishing boat rode in on the tide, but in here it was deathly quiet.

'So there we have it,' said Judy. 'Ben Larsson was Rhys's place-man in Berlin. Operation Tailcoat was Rhys's idea . . .'

'They called our job Naval Intelligence,' replied Auriol. 'One sometimes wondered whether old Rusty ever had an intelligent thought in his head.'

'Nothing's changed in all these years,' said Judy. It was her turn to make the tea.

'He so wanted to be like Ralph Izzard, but he just wasn't as clever,' recalled Auriol. 'Ralph was just a tiny bit crazy – I mean, floating a fake German bomber in the English Channel with our chaps hiding aboard in the hope of capturing a U-boat? Completely mad!'

'The Admiral was ready to buy it. He said the surprise element meant the chaps could easily take command.'

'Not a chance.'

'Even so.'

'You didn't see so much of Rhys at that time – you had your own fish to fry,' said Auriol, getting down the cups and saucers.

'But he was under my control and was always a terrible nuisance. First, this brilliant idea, then that equally wondrous notion to biff the enemy.

'Of course the Admiral was ready to listen to any idea that sounded half decent – he wanted results – but instead of the half plausible what we got was the half baked – and I always ended up with the job of trying to make a silk purse out of a sow's ear. Tailcoat *should* have worked, but Richard Rhys was never very good on detail and so – disaster.'

'I imagine Ben Larsson was lucky to escape with his life,' said Judy. 'He must have hated Rhys for the foul-up.'

'Curiously it brought them together. I gather he was a frequent visitor to Ransome's Retreat. It was Larsson who alerted him to the job vacancy at the *Riviera Express*.'

Judy was annoyed. 'You never told me that! How do you know?'

Auriol looked out of the window. 'Oh, I kept in touch with Larsson, as one does.'

Judy was annoyed now. 'You never told me that, either!'

'My dear, there are secrets within secrets. Some things are best left in a drawer. It's one's duty to remember where the sleeping dogs lie, but no need to wake them up unless or until it becomes necessary.'

'We know each other so well, and yet we don't,' said Judy thoughtfully.

'That's the nature of friendship,' said Auriol. It was hard for Judy to disagree – she hadn't told Auriol about Valentine's kiss on the doorstep.

'So where does that leave us? Is old Rusty capable of murder? Certainly you can see he had the motive – didn't want Larsson spilling the beans about his failure in Berlin, let alone the collateral loss of life. Our agents in Germany were very precious – we had so few!'

'You know he didn't do it, Hugue – murder, that is. He may have been very angry but he's just not up to it – far too complicated. Anyway, what would Larsson have been doing? Did he just sit there meekly and let Rusty link him up to that contraption so he could be murdered? I don't think so!

'No, it sounds to me more like an act of revenge, a premeditated and coolly planned act, not some spur-of-the-moment thing.'

'You agree it must be murder then,' said Judy.

'Of course. Nothing else makes sense. Larsson had used that particular model for years to give demonstrations to the faithful. In any case the electrical current involved is negligible – the whole caboodle couldn't electrocute a mouse!'

'What about all those deaths? The letters of complaint? The *Daily Herald* investigation?'

Auriol smiled. 'Between you and me, I think Larsson was probably right about some of them. Idiots who didn't read the instructions. Maybe some of the equipment was faulty, who knows. What I do know is that the whole box of tricks was essentially harmless – which is why I'm sure that somebody tampered with it deliberately.'

Miss Dimont thought for a moment. Having these conversations with Auriol could be quite useful – certainly her superior brainpower allowed her to see around corners, or so it seemed – but she was so convinced, when she came to a conclusion, that she was right it dimmed her eyes to other possibilities, whereas Judy's thinking remained flexible.

'Apart from Rusty, who else do you think had a motive?' went on Auriol.

'Well,' said Judy, pouring fresh water into the pot, 'there are several possibilities. First, was it revenge? Or was it for gain?'

'You tell me.'

'Pernilla Larsson would gain from his death, in that her son would inherit the business – she told me as much – and better poor old Ben should die while she was still married to him, rather than wait till he'd found himself a fifth wife.'

'But, Hugue, he was eighty!'

'Still acting pretty lively, Auriol – he pinched Betty Featherstone's bottom, she told me. In addition, without digging too deep you get the picture of a pretty ruthless streak in Pernilla. What was the state of their marriage? Had she had enough of it? She's still in her fifties, time enough to find a younger model for herself, *and* walk away with a sizeable fortune. We don't know she didn't have a *bel ami*.'

Auriol took this in but you could see she was already discounting the possibility. 'Mm . . . maybe. Who else was in the house?'

'Gus Wetherby, Pernilla's son.'

'And?'

'Manservant called Lamb. Interestingly the first thing Gus Wetherby did after discovering his stepfather's death was to fire him – now why would he do such a thing?'

'Anybody else?'

'Well, Mrs Lamb, the housekeeper. Don't know much about her.'

'Any more staff?'

'The gardener. But he was with Pernilla at the bottom of the garden during the period when old Larsson must have died.'

'And that's it?'

'No. Here we come to the difficulty. A small deputation, I'm told five or six, from the Lazarus League – you know, those dotty old people who read Larsson's pre-war book and thought he was the New Messiah. They turn up most weeks and he rather fancied himself as a saviour, and used to give them tea and a talk-to.'

'They sound pretty harmless.'

'Well, I don't know,' said Miss Dimont, seeing that her friend was, as always, dismissing too early the less likely culprits. 'Supposing one of them had lost someone to the dreaded

184

Rejuvenator? Here would be an ideal opportunity to gain access to the chap whose invention had caused the death. We don't know who these people were – they came up for an hour and then wandered away again.'

Auriol waved her hand dismissively. 'No time to set up an elaborate trick to murder the old boy. No time!'

She was right, of course.

'Well, that limits the field then. Pernilla. Her son Gus. The man Lamb. Or Mrs Lamb, of whom we know nothing.'

'I'd like to know more about the relationship between Ben Larsson and his stepson,' said Auriol.

So would I, thought Miss Dimont.

*

'. . . all serene, then?' breathed Athene sweetly, and looked up at Mr So. The old gentleman's expression remained implacable and though he nodded in agreement, the application of her usual graceful calm seemed not to be working.

'Won't you sit down?' The Chinaman gently inclined his head but that was all.

'Well, look, would you like me to speak to them if they come in again? Say something? I don't normally talk to people I don't know but I'm sure it can be done.'

Mr So smiled gently in gratitude, bowed slightly, and faded back into his habitual corner. The Chinese Singing Teacher was empty this morning, its tranquillity almost restored, but it had been an unhappy time. Athene sat at length looking into her teacup in search of some solution to the invasion of the Sisters of Reason, but answer came there none.

She unwrapped her pastel silk scarf ('*so* Isadora Duncan, my dear') from round her neck and got out her battered notebook. Back at the *Riviera Express* the atmosphere had been electric with animosity – not just the usual squabbles in Curse Corner and the point-scoring between rival reporters, but the whole business of Mr Larsson's death and the breach it had opened up between the editor and his staff. Something had gone on at Ransome's Retreat, that was clear, but what was also clear was their grudging acceptance of Mr Rhys's leadership had been temporarily suspended. In effect, the editor and his reporters were not speaking to each other.

Athene rarely wrote her column in the office – except sometimes late at night when everyone had long since disappeared – but this morning she'd walked through the editorial floor and come away unsettled by the angry vibrations swirling about the place.

Here, at the Chinese Singing Teacher, there was sanctuary. Or there should be. Here she should be able to tell her Sagittarian readers of the good fortune which was just around the corner, while Pisceans must prepare themselves for the glorious surprise awaiting them. And yet the words failed to come to her pen and she returned her gaze to the tea leaves, colourless in the bottom of the cup.

The light coming through the windows was grey this morning, rendering the tea room featureless and neutral – just how Mr So wished it. The only splash of colour was from the string of Coronation lights – red, white, and blue – which eerily lit the room in its darker moments. But this morning they remained unlit as the Zen-like atmosphere had gradually reordered itself.

'Wondered if I might find you here,' said Judy, slipping gently into the seat opposite Athene.

'Promise not to tell anyone else. I don't think Mr So wants any new customers.'

'Certainly not. You let me into your precious secret, this wonderful place – I won't share it with a soul,' said Judy, and took off a fetching straw hat which had been keeping her corkscrew curls in order. Freed from their imprisonment, they sprang happily back into their usual disarray.

Mr So brought tea and smiled; he could see Miss Dimont's aura was congenial.

'Dear, the office!' started Athene, 'I have never known such an atmosphere, I had to come away. What on earth is going on?'

'Well, you know,' said Judy, 'it's not good. The editor . . . he seems to have forfeited his authority and everyone feels very uncomfortable.'

'So then I came here,' said Athene, pouring the tea, 'and it was more of the same. Though receding, mercifully. Nowhere, it seems, is safe this morning. I must have missed something when I consulted the stars last night.'

'What is it?' asked Judy encouragingly. She didn't want to talk about Mr Rhys.

'Mr So,' said Athene. 'Those people, you know, the Sisters of Reason, have been back again and seem to think this is their new headquarters.'

'I can see that would disrupt the tranquillity of the place,' said Miss Dimont looking around. Particles of dust floated in the weak light coming from the window, but they did not move: peace at last was slowly returning.

'They were here when I came in,' said Athene in an offended tone. 'Well, two of them – the manly one and the woman who repairs clocks.'

'Ursula Guedella and Angela de Mauny.'

'I saw that you were upset when I didn't tell you about them before, so I shall do now. Is that tea nice?'

'It's . . . lovely,' lied Miss Dimont, who preferred a hot cup of Indian.

'They were talking about the girl who was killed – you know, the beauty queen.'

'Yee . . . ee . . . s?' Miss Dimont said very slowly.

'That Ursula has no sense of decorum, no understanding of atmosphere. She barks like a sergeant-major and cares not who hears what she says.'

Come on, thought Miss Dimont, are we about to get a breakthrough on the dead beauty queen? Do hurry up, Athene!

Aloud, she said, nicely enough, 'Yes, I noticed that when I first met her.'

'Well,' said Athene, pushing the notebook to one side, 'she was complaining about nearly being run down by some oikish fishermen. Rabble, she called them, *and* worse! She had gone out for an early-morning sail and only by her skill did she avoid a collision. I mean to say, Judy, I can't believe any of our people would go out of their way to run over a small boat, I think she was talking through her hat.'

'Wait a moment!' said Miss Dimont a shade too crisply. 'I wonder if you can be more precise, Athene? Did you get any impression of *when* she was talking about?'

Athene blinked uncomprehendingly.

'You see, since I went out deep-sea fishing, I have a new friend who is the skipper of one of the Temple Regis fleet. A very nice man,' she went on, and for a moment it seemed as though she had lost the thread of what she was about to ask her friend. 'He's really . . .'

'Yes?' prompted Athene. 'The body on the beach?' Judy was miles away.

'How could you possibly know I was going to ask about that?' Miss Dimont was evidently put out.

'Your thought processes are quite visible, my dear, does it surprise you?'

Miss Dimont, who did not mind people telling her how brilliant she was, was less pleased that she could appear so transparent.

'Well,' she said, overcoming her slight rise in temperature, 'yes. Yes. Cran Conybeer told me on the morning of the murder he had taken the *Lass O'Doune* out at dawn and there was a man in a small boat which got in his way and nearly went under. He remembers it well because it was an unusual time of day for a pleasure craft to be out and about. Also, he said that the chap had a girlfriend with him who appeared to be asleep. All this happened just off Todhempstead Beach.

'Supposing,' she went on, 'Mr Conybeer had seen, not a man, but Ursula Guedella. At a distance, with the clothes she wears and with that haircut, she could easily be mistaken for a man after all. And could the girlfriend have been not asleep, but dead!'

'I knew his mother,' said Athene, looking out of the window.

'What?' shot back Judy, poised on the brink of a major discovery and not wanting to be sidetracked. 'You know the Sisters of Reason wanted to sabotage the beauty pageants – if it was Miss Guedella who murdered that poor girl, wouldn't that be the most effective way of putting a spanner in the works? All the resultant bad publicity, the criticism of that odious man Normandy and the way he exploits those young women?'

'She belonged to our book club.'

'Mm?' Judy was getting fidgety – her friend could never stick to the point.

'She was very nice, very well read. Her husband had been invalided during the war. A handsome man.'

'Athene!'

'She liked Mrs Gaskell a lot, I remember. Called her son Cranford – could that be the one?'

'I doubt there could be two with such a name,' said Miss Dimont with just a dash of vinegar. 'Look, was this the day of the murder?'

'No idea, dear. They are really quite repellent ladies, I tried awfully hard not to listen. Also, I was most concerned for Mr So – you know it's taken him years to arrive at the level of serenity that prevails here? You know that's an extraordinary achievement.'

Once again, Athene had both given significant information, and had not – infuriating as usual, despite her sweetness and goodness! Miss Dimont disliked Ursula Guedella and did not approve of her methods, and it would be a triumph to bring in this information and secure an arrest while Inspector Topham still waited for the Coroner to wake from his fortnight's siesta.

'Well, look,' said the ever-practical reporter, realising she could be starting up a blind alley, 'did you get the impression they might come back – Guedella and de Mauny?'

'They think it's a secret place. They think they can talk freely here.'

'Just so. So you think they'll be back?'

Athene sighed and drew her notebook towards her. She needed to consult with the heavens, and all this talk of murder really was a terrible distraction.

'Athene, do you think they'll be back?'

'I suppose so.'

'Do you think Mr So could telephone me if they do, and I could come in and listen? Or send Valentine?'

'Mr So rarely talks to anybody, he has no need. His actions speak louder than words, dear.'

Miss Dimont's temperature was rising again. 'Well, he talks to you, Athene. I've seen him.'

'I could ask him to let me know.'

'A spiritualist message through the ether?'

Athene shot her friend a glance. 'That is unworthy of you, Judy. I will ask him to telephone me when they come again and I will let you know.'

The two friends finished their tea. As they chatted, it was interesting to observe the different types of people who came through the door and who gained Mr So's approval. A man who looked like a retired colonel was greeted with a beaming smile, but though dressed rather stuffily in regulation tweed jacket, polished shoes and regimental tie, when he addressed the proprietor in Mandarin – evidently an old Singapore hand – it became clear he too understood the allure of this curious place. A handful of young people, their hair unfashionably long, seemed respectful and well behaved and were rewarded with Mr So's most courteous attention.

Half an hour passed. Miss Dimont finally broached the subject of Rudyard Rhys and the fact that, not only had he lied to his staff about the source of the Larsson story, but that he was also under suspicion of murder.

'Didn't do it,' said Athene.

'I know that. He's too shambolic. But something's up.'

'He didn't do it because I have seen his aura and there's nothing there which could allow him to be a killer. You worked with him during the war.'

'Yes.'

'Would his job have required him to kill the enemy – person-ally, I mean?'

'In certain circumstances, yes.'

'Well, I imagine he can never have been put to the test.'

'This may cost him his job,' said Miss Dimont.

Athene turned her gaze from the window and looked at her friend steadily.

'Time, my dear, that you stopped hiding, and realised that Rudyard Rhys is sitting the chair that was destined for you,' she said, quite firmly.

'It's time you became the editor of our wonderful newspaper.'

EIGHTEEN

It was raining when they emerged into Bosun's Alley, the kind of hard cold rain which reminds the holidaymaker what a treacherous friend the British summer can be. The light was turning darker, menacing clouds had robbed the air of its warmth and comfort.

Opposite the end of the alley stood the off-licence, a dreary sliver of a shop sharing its entrance with the salon of Bob the Barber, a sadistic type who enjoyed executing his tonsorial revenge on the poorer residents of Temple Regis. In the doorway stood a hunched figure, grey-faced and purposeless, in his hand a brown carrier bag which clinked.

'Why, Mr Lamb!' called Judy in lively welcome. The fellow glanced guiltily at her, but immediately his eyes darted away. Bengt Larsson's former manservant was evidently not at home to callers this morning.

'Mr Lamb!' she repeated, reading the signs but blithely ignoring them. 'You look cold standing there. I'm just popping into the Fortescue for a glass of sherry, would you care to join me?' She had grasped in an instant, from the dark rings under his eyes and his lopsided expression, that the man was suffering a dreadful hangover.

'Just getting some tonic wine for the missus,' he said, a shade too quickly. 'She's pretty upset.'

It took very little cajolery to get Lamb out of the rain and into the snug bar of the Fort, and minimal further persuasion to get a large glass of whisky to his lips, though it was barely noon.

'I saw Mrs Larsson.'

''*Er*!' snorted Lamb. This morning, it would appear, his manservant's deference had taken a holiday.

'She said you'd been dismissed by her son. I'm so sorry.'

'Seven years I served that family, ever since his marriage to that one. Mrs Lamb too, she served. But the moment Mr Larsson's dead, we're out. And after all I done for her and her kid . . .'

'Where will you go?' she asked. The Fort's sherry smelt of old wardrobes.

'Dunno. Been told by the police we can't leave Temple Regis. Material witnesses.'

'Have you anywhere to stay?'

'Arst me another.'

'Have another?'

'Johnnie Walker this time.'

Miss Dimont used the time it took to collect the whisky to sum up Lamb's situation. From Pernilla Larsson she'd gathered that her son ruled her – capitalising on her guilt over the divorce, no doubt – and with Larsson dead, she'd given up any ambition to run the business herself. But why the manservant was sacked so peremptorily by Gus Wetherby remained a mystery.

It was as if Lamb was entertaining the same thought. 'After all I did,' he repeated bitterly. 'For them. The ingratitude.'

'Why were you kicked out so abruptly? It does seem odd, I must say.' Miss Dimont put the sherry again to her lips but they rejected it. She took a handkerchief and wiped the taste away.

'You're newspapers, aren't you?' asked Lamb unnecessarily. He knew perfectly well.

'Yes, the *Riviera Express*.'

'D'you pay money for interviews?'

'Never.'

'Might you buy me another of these—' he pinged the glass in front of him with his forefinger '—if I tell you summat?'

'As many as you like, Mr Lamb. It's just that we have a policy of not paying . . .'

'Call me 'arry.'

'Harry.'

'No, Larry.'

'Larry.'

'They was plotting against 'im. Mrs Larsson and that son of hers. Against Mr Larsson.'

'Yes?'

'They realised the game was up. There'd been too many complaints about the Rejuvenator – there'd been letters in the post for years, but suddenly people started telephoning and recently there'd been a couple showed up tryin' to cause trouble. I 'ad to threaten them with the police.

'Things were turning nasty but Mr Larsson, 'e just ignored it all.' Lamb took a stiff swallow of whisky. ''E blinded himself to the truth. In the early days, people would believe anything – that the ruddy Rejuvenator would save their life and cure them of everything.

'Later, after the war, about the time I came to the Retreat, things'd changed. It was as if the whole world had finally woken up to the truth. The Rejuvenator didn't fit any more, didn't even work most people said. And they were always asking for their money back, but old Mr Larsson, he wasn't listening.'

'Was he easy to work for?'

Lamb eyed the thin film in the bottom of his glass. He hadn't shaved and the shirt he was wearing was not exactly fresh.

'Hard taskmaster, but fair. But he stuck his head in the sand – it was always on the cards that someone like that *Daily Herald* article would make him come unstuck.

'O' course that Mr Gus saw it, didn't 'e, and started work on a new formula. 'E wanted to use the workshop, and so after lunch I'd put a sedative into Mr Larsson's coffee and sooner or later he'd toddle off and have a siesta. I never liked to do it, but Mr Gus said it was 'armless and Mrs Larsson backed 'im up.

'So then 'e'd go down and work on the new formula for a couple of hours, and the old boy was none the wiser.'

Miss Dimont waved to the chubby-armed lady behind the bar to bring more whisky. Lamb drank an awful lot, it transpired.

'I don't know whether it would've worked. The boy was always one for cutting corners – basically he don't care about anything or anyone – and if the thing blew up you could guarantee he'd just take the money and sail off into the sunset. Anyway the old man found out somehow, don't know how, and asked me about it. I said I didn't know anything, but he threatened to sack me so I told him the lot – the sedatives too.'

Miss Dimont looked at him with curiosity. 'When Betty Featherstone came to the Retreat, you gave her a file of letters. It looked like you'd made a mistake, because it contained all the complaints from people who'd suffered from using the Rejuvenator – you were supposed to give her all the letters of commendation.'

'I gave her those as well.'

'Why did you give her the complaints file?'

'I was being threatened by Mr Gus. He said it was all over for Ben Larsson, that he'd be taking over the business very soon, and that if I didn't help him out then he'd fire me.' Lamb shook his head and took a swig from his fresh glass. 'Well, he fired me anyway.'

Miss Dimont slowly thought back to the start of their conversation. 'Mr Lamb, was it you who told the *Daily Herald* about the complaints?'

'Might have.'

'And did they pay you?'

'They said they would but they never. Look,' said Lamb, pushing back his chair, 'I didn't do it for the money. It was all part of Mr Gus's plan. There'd been complaints for years and, sooner or later, old Mr Larsson was bound to come unstuck. All Mr Gus did, when he got me to contact the *Herald*, was give the process a helping hand. A push, so to speak.'

'So Mr Wetherby basically stabbed his stepfather in the back.'

'In the front, more like.'

Miss Dimont had taken out her notebook, always a crucial moment in a reporter's routine – bring it out too soon and on confessionals like this your interviewee will shy away or shut up altogether; leave it too long and the mass of detail won't be remembered sufficiently clearly afterwards. But the lugubrious Lamb was too busy looking longingly at the whisky bottles behind the bar to even notice when she laid it on the table.

'Tell me about Ben Larsson's death.'

'It was confusin'. A whole lot of things going on, difficult to keep a grip of it all – my job, first and foremost, was to look after 'im, which I always did. That morning there was the stand-up row with your boss, Mr Rhys. There was Mr Gus snooping around, there were the Lazarus lot, the police, the photographs. I'm seventy, you know.'

'Don't look a day of it.' Miss Dimont smiled absently, but she was thinking about the murder. 'You were familiar with the Rejuvenator?'

'Yes, I used to show visitors who'd never seen one before how it worked. It was all part of the routine before they met Mr Larsson. O' course a lot of them came just to look around the gardens – we've won awards, you know.' Lamb checked himself, realising that everything to do with Ransome's Retreat must now be couched in the past tense.

'What do you think caused Mr Larsson's death?'

'Well—' the manservant looked around furtively and hitched his chair a little closer '—it couldn't have happened by accident, that I do know.'

'How can you be so sure?'

'The thing is, you see, that there machine wasn't hardly giving out any current.'

'But Larsson knew how it worked, of course. Could he have boosted the current and killed himself?'

'Not a chance. Why would he? Hand a victory to all those complainers, prove that the Rejuvenator could kill people? Rubbish! Anyway, he was a fighter was Mr L – he was ready to fight back. No chance he'd bump himself off.'

'Well, then, how could somebody else pull it off?'

'There's an accumulator dial at the back. Turn it up too much and you get the full voltage and – bingo. I reckon that's what done him.'

'Would it be easy to do?'

'You'd have to know the machine. You have to open a small panel on the back and move the calibrator round. But you could do it quickly if you knew what you were doing – wouldn't take a moment.'

The pub was filling up and it was getting harder to hear Lamb's responses. Coupled with that, at the rate he was swallowing whisky, there'd come a point quite soon where it was worthless pursuing the interview. Miss Dimont realised she had to be quick.

'By my reckoning, there are only a small number of people who were near Mr Larsson that morning. There was my Mr Rhys, there was you, and there was Gus and his mother Mrs Larsson.'

Lamb's eyes took a moment to refocus. 'You're not suggesting *I* had anything to do with it?'

'Well,' said Miss Dimont crisply, 'were I a detective I would say you had the means – after all, you knew how the Rejuvenator worked – and you had the opportunity. Motive? You were angry at being kicked around by Mr Larsson and his stepson. Threatened by them both they were going to sack you, when all you were trying to do was your best to save the family fortunes and, I have no doubt, to keep your job. So anger and revenge, prime motives for ending someone's life.'

'After all I done for that ruddy family! But . . . you're not seriously saying I done it?' His ruddy cheeks had gone quite pale.

'If the cap fits, Mr Lamb.' Miss Dimont sounded businesslike and detached, all trace of her bonhomie suddenly gone. 'There are four other suspects and I can tell you now that Mr Rhys can be discounted. It has to be one of you.'

'How so – Rhys, I mean?'

'Too bumbling to pull off a murder, if you want to know. Now look, you can see you're in a very difficult position and the best way out is to help me. I need to know everything, and I need you sober.'

Lamb instinctively reached for the carrier bag under his seat. The contents clanked.

'You can have some of that when I've finished with you,' said Miss Dimont, crisply. 'Come on, we're going to Lovely Mary's and she'll fill you up with a proper lunch. With,' she added forcefully, 'a nice cup of tea to help it down.'

Lamb seemed reluctant to move. He felt safe in the half-light of the Fortescue, did not want to face daylight and the reality that came with it. 'I'm stayin' here,' he said purposefully.

'No you're not,' said Miss Dimont, and with an elegant curve of her arm whisked away the carrier bag from his feeble grasp. She stalked off towards the door without a backward glance.

The manservant followed like, well, a lamb.

*

'He was a sweetheart, darling,' said Mrs Phipps, tumbling an overlong cigarette ash into her tea. 'The perfect gentleman.'

'I never met him,' said Valentine.

'Sir Jefrye Waterford,' sighed the old lady, 'such a *euphonious* name, don't you think? I loved just saying it. Of course he was a terror if he got you on your own – "NSIT" we used to say, not safe in taxis! – but in every other respect, the perfect gentleman. He would call at the stage door, always a gardenia for one's ball gown, then it would be the Embassy Club, we always used to go there. The Prince of Wales would be in a corner with Mrs Dudley Ward, and sometimes that sweet Prince George too.'

'I don't think he worked much,' said Valentine. 'Bit of a rascal, really. Ran through the money like wildfire.'

'Mustn't speak ill of your grandfather, dear, he made me very happy – for a while. But he had a roving eye. There was a girl who used to come in with Prince George, Alice Gwynne was her name – a bad lot. Something to do with the Vanderbilts but no money. In the end the King had her run out of the country, she was very wayward. When she left, forcefully escorted to Dover I heard, poor Georgie was in a terrible way what with drink and . . . other things.' She lit another Player's Navy Cut and smiled mysteriously, the smoke occluding other, more private, memories. 'Sir Jefrye was very interested in her.'

'It must have been a wonderful time between the wars.'

'I never left Mayfair. Well, of course, except to go to work, the West End isn't exactly the same thing at all. They do things differently there.'

Valentine was lapping this up. The old boy had always been looked on as the black sheep, the one who bankrupted the family. He had never heard him recalled quite so exotically.

'Did you come up to Lovelocke?'

'That was your place, was it? I don't think so. Cliveden, Longleat, I was a friend of Eric Dudley so I went to Himley.

Reggie Pembroke took a fancy to me as well – you know my friends among the Gaiety Girls all seemed to end up marrying earls, but somehow all mine were already married.'

'That must have been disappointing.'

'Not always, dear,' said Geraldine Phipps, looking fondly at the heavy diamond ring weighing down one finger.

'This is lovely,' said Valentine, finishing his tea, 'but you know I came here to see Gavin. See how the riots were getting on. The editor seems very keen for us to write something other than about that chap Larsson.'

'Married four times,' said Geraldine, wistfully. 'Ben wasn't that attractive but he certainly got the women all right.'

'How come?'

'Fur coats, darling. He would always buy them the coat first before knocking on the bedroom door with his . . . you know.'

'Another world,' marvelled Valentine, running his hand through his wavy blond locks.

'And now here we all are, in Temple Regis,' said Mrs Phipps with a sigh. 'What a fall from grace!'

Valentine looked up sharply. 'I've been here a short time only, Mrs Phipps, but to me it seems like paradise.'

'Hang around as long as I have,' said Geraldine drily, reaching for the Plymouth gin, 'you'll see things differently.'

'Miss Dimont says . . .'

'Miss Dimont again! You've mentioned her quite a lot. Are you soft on her?'

Valentine coloured slightly.

'She's old enough to be your . . .' said the old trouper, sensing a secret.

'I think I'll go and find Gavin now, Mrs Phipps,' said Valentine quickly, and wandered off. The Gaiety Girl smiled, and nodded privately to herself – just like Sir Jefrye!

Inside the Pavilion Theatre, Danny and The Urge were rehearsing their new number. He may not have had much feel for music but Gavin Armstrong had a mill-owner's work ethic and constantly warned the boys they must not rest on their laurels. A new record once every six or eight weeks until the bubble burst, he said, and was keeping them to it.

The noise was unbearable. Valentine tapped Gavin on the shoulder and the two escaped through a side door on to the boardwalk of the pier. A few people were pushing penny coins into the What The Butler Saw machines but a chilly wind had kept most of the crowds away.

'Been asked to do a follow-up on Danny and the boys.'

'Great story you did last week,' said Gavin enthusiastically. 'We're sold out. Completely! Trouble is, the boys have never played night after night like this before and they're exhausted. The atmosphere in the van is getting a bit out of hand.'

'Can't they afford a bed and breakfast?'

'Not a question of that. In the van, I can keep an eye on 'em, stop 'em from wandering off everywhere. I lost Boots – he just disappeared – couldn't be sure he hadn't quit the group to go looking for his girlfriend.'

'Oh?' said Valentine. A primeval yet so far untapped instinct urged him on, telling him that maybe there was a story here. 'Is she missing?'

'Yes. I mean, it was an on–off relationship anyway, she was rather attached to one of The Shadows. She only got interested in Bootsie because suddenly The Urge were getting more Number One hits. And then she had her own career to follow as well, so they only saw each other from time to time. She promised she'd be down here when the boys were playing and that she had a big surprise for him, but she never showed up.'

'Hmm, that could make a story for the *Express*.'

'Don't think so,' said Gavin with finality. '*Very* bad for business. In fact, I'd say fatal.'

'Oh?'

'The boys aren't supposed to have girlfriends. We want to leave the fans free to dream that one day, one day . . .'

'OK,' said Valentine obligingly, and with secret pride drew out his notebook and a pen. His notebook! A pen! He had them both! 'What else then?'

'You can reveal they're writing new hits in Temple Regis. That this dreary old dump will finally get put on the map because of the musical legacy the boys'll leave behind.'

'It's quite famous already,' retorted Valentine. First Mrs Phipps, now Gavin – what had they got against this wonderful town?

'Huh. Look at this broken-down old theatre – is that the best you can do? It could use the urgent attention of a bulldozer.'

'Hardly needs that,' riposted Valentine, 'when it's already getting a pretty thorough demolition job from your fans. Have you seen what they're doing to the place?'

'Insurance will cover it,' said Gavin airily, patting his pockets and preparing to depart. 'Be the best thing that ever happened to it. Look, why don't you go and talk to the boys, they can give you all the guff on their latest – *platter*.' He laced the word, a favourite of disc jockeys of the moment, with heavy irony; and in that moment Valentine realised that Gavin Armstrong was well on the way to becoming an extremely successful entrepreneur. With not a friend in the world.

He stood on the boardwalk for a moment and looked at the sea. He was facing, for the first time, the dilemma which confronts all reporters – whether information given in confidence should be used to the greater good, or whether it should be dutifully forgotten as its donor would wish. Writing about a beat group making a new record was, well, like writing about a bricklayer laying another brick. Whereas the story of the missing girlfriend of the bass player sounded different, fresh. If she were found as a result of his writing the story, it would be a real coup.

'Human interest,' said Valentine, rather pleased that he'd discovered what this overworked justification for intruding into people's private lives actually meant. 'Human interest!'

He was about to plunge back into the theatre when the man in question came out, nodded, and walked over to the rail. Boots McGuigan – the dark, handsome, secret and dangerous dream of a thousand schoolgirls! About to give voice to the world's press!

The guitarist stared moodily out to sea and fished in his pockets for a cigarette,

'Have one of these,' said Valentine. 'Though they're a bit rough – not good for the vocal cords.'

'I don't know if you've noticed,' came the surly reply, 'that when I sing in the choruses, no sound comes out of my microphone. That's because it's switched off. They don't like the way I sound.'

Good Lord, thought Valentine, now *that's* a story! Britain's No 1 beat group gags its bass guitarist!

'Don't write that,' ordered Boots McGuigan, 'or I'll thump you.'

'OK,' said Valentine, unmoved, 'tell me about your girlfriend then.'

He was amazed by the change which overcame the irritable musician. 'Can you do something about it? Write about it, I mean?'

'I'd have to know more about it.' He was getting the hang of squeezing information out of people without appearing to ask questions.

'She's called Faye Addams, she's twenty-two and very beautiful. She said she was coming down here to see me and was bringing a big surprise with her. That was a week ago but I haven't heard from her since. I telephoned her mum and she hasn't heard from her either. I'm really worried.'

'Does she have any other friends?' Valentine was thinking of the chap in The Shadows – was he a bass player too? – had she gone back to him?

'I've tried,' said McGuigan. 'Nothing. Look, could you write something about her in the paper? I've got a photograph you can have. Only you can't say she's my girlfriend – Gavin won't allow it.'

'Not much of a story without that,' said Valentine with finality. It was extraordinary how the words sprang to his lips, words which pushed the interviewee on, possibly against their will, to give more of themselves than they would like.

'Look,' he explained, 'your girlfriend – Faye – she could be anywhere. She could still be in London, she could be in Timbuctoo. That's *not* a local newspaper story. You, on the other hand, *are* a local newspaper story all the time you remain in Temple Regis, and a girl that's associated with Britain's No 1 beat group gone missing, now that's a story!'

The musician tossed his cigarette end into the waves beneath him. 'OK,' he said. 'To be frank, I'm getting pretty fed up with Gavin. Do this, don't do that – all he cares about is money. I'm sick of it. I'm a musician.'

'I know what you mean,' said Valentine, though he didn't really. 'What does she do, Faye?'

'A beautician. She was working in the West End – Selfridges – but gave it up to concentrate on her hobby. Reckoned she could make a living out of it.'

Here the future star reporter fumbled it. He should have asked a certain question but failed to do so, instead turned his attention to getting a full description of the missing Miss Addams. The two young men stepped inside the theatre to find the photograph of her when they bumped into Gavin again.

'Ah, Boots,' he said proprietorially. 'Is the song finished?'

'They don't need me,' came the sour reply. 'They told me, give us another hour and we'll have a Number One. But they don't want me to have a hand in it, they don't want to share the royalties.'

'Well, don't you go buggering off again like yesterday,' ordered Gavin. 'He just pushed off in the middle of rehearsal,' he said, turning to Valentine. 'So unprofessional. What did you think you were doing, Boots?'

'None of your business,' snapped the bass player and headed for his dressing room.

'You know,' said Gavin, who liked talking about himself, 'I nearly made a million this week. Well, not a *million*, but a nice wedge. Then that old geezer had to go and electrocute himself and all bets are off. That's showbiz, Val.'

'Valentine.'

'Mm.'

'You're talking about old Mr Larsson? What happened?'

The manager wheeled into his office and sat behind the desk. He told the story of Gus Wetherby and the Youthenator and how much money the pair were going to make, but how Gus had telephoned to say they'd have to forget about it for the time being.

But as he rattled on, Valentine's thoughts drifted back to the band and to a conversation he'd had previously with Boots, about his interest in Ransome's Retreat. Though part of his brain was taken up with his scoop on the missing girl, another part was wondering why Boots McGuigan was interested in Ben Larsson. Had he gone up to the Retreat? Did his visit coincide with Larsson's death?

He realised he'd failed to ask the right question.

Dammit!

NINETEEN

However crowded the Grand Hotel got, there was always room for Fleet Street's emissaries. They had expensive tastes, prodigious thirsts and lordly ways, but such were the benefits of a timely mention in their pages they were always treated like royalty.

Recently they'd descended *en masse* after the tragic loss of Gerald Hennessy, the country's best-loved actor who ended up dead in the first-class carriage of his Pullman train at Regis Junction. Now here they were again, lounging with their feet splayed out all over the Palm Court, ordering drinks as if they'd just returned from the desert. Individually, they were genial and amusing, but in a pack they were far less attractive: shards of malice spiked their comradely badinage, and you could see that every single one of them would sell his mother's soul in return for a Page One splash.

The death of Bengt Larsson coincided with one of those lulls when there is no news, but these men, lolling comfortably in the Palm Court, running poor Peter Potts off his feet, were supreme alchemists, gifted in turning nothing into something. They were past masters at filling their pages with hot air.

At their centre sat Guy Brace, a red-cheeked Mephistopheles whose self-ordained job, wherever the pack went, was to conduct the orchestra. On complicated stories he would assign other members of the group specific tasks so that no lead should be missed; all would then retire to a convenient hostelry to pool their findings while keeping back a morsel so they could claim an 'exclusive' to their rapacious news editors. There were probably more efficient ways of obtaining the news but nobody had yet taken the trouble to discover them.

'So, Sinclair, you'll go up to the Retreat and get Mrs Larsson's side of things. Wilson, you'll track down the son. Who's covering the Lazarus League?'

'Me, Guy,' offered an eager newcomer to this piratical crew. 'Can I get you another drink?'

'Now, Spraggs,' said Brace to the *Daily Herald*'s chief reporter, displaying just the merest hint of irritation, 'how much are you holding back? After all, you've already had two bites out of this cherry, there must be something left for the rest of us to share.'

'We put all we knew into those two splashes, Guy. The cupboard's bare.' This meant the *Herald* had more, but weren't prepared to share.

'Come off it, Spraggs,' said the token woman reporter, from the *Daily Mirror*, 'remember the time we helped you out on the Acid Bath murders – you mucked that up, big time. Time to pay back.'

'That was a lifetime ago, Marje,' retorted the *Herald* man. So long ago, he implied, that time had expunged the debt. 'You were still in pigtails, sweetie.'

'A Campari for the lady,' yodelled Brace to Peter, and the waiter scuttled off in pursuit. Pretty soon, all avenues and eventualities covered, the talk among the group turned to absent friends and to long-ago scoops. The day's work was over, the prospect of a fine dinner lay ahead, and then a comfortable night's sleep in the Grand's sumptuous four-posters to bring them fresh to the bright new morrow.

*

Round the corner in the bar a very different kind of journalism was at work. Frank Topham sat motionless, clutching his pint of Portlemouth, while before him Miss Dimont smiled and coaxed and dissembled.

'I understand your concern, Inspector. Temple Regis is going to hit the headlines, but there's nothing you can do to stop it. And, frankly, in a situation where that pack of Fleet Street reporters next door is likely to tear the place apart, wouldn't it be better to give an official version to me, which will help – shall we say guide? – their thinking. Keeping the nastiness out of it?'

Topham was inclined to agree but didn't want to show it. Behind his reluctance was the fact that, on the Larsson murder – and on the dead blonde, come to that – he hadn't a clue, and he didn't like people knowing it.

Both knew Miss Dimont had the upper hand. Topham's first concern, always, was the reputation of Temple Regis – he was a loyal man, a good man – and if she could be trusted to filter out certain inconsistencies in the Larsson case (the Fleet Street boys hadn't caught wind of the blonde; he hoped they never would), part of his role as defender of the town's reputation would have been discharged.

'Off the record, then,' said Miss Dimont, helpfully, 'it's murder.'

'What else,' said Topham gloomily and took a sip of Portlemouth. It tasted sour but that was him, not the beer.

'Suspects are—' began Miss Dimont before the Inspector cut her off.

'I'm not going to idly speculate.'

'You must have *some* idea,' said the reporter, goading him on.

'Of course I have, but I don't want to . . .'

'The stepson. The wife. The manservant. The manservant's wife. Somebody from that ragtag-and-bobtail lot, the Lazarus League. Have I left anybody out?' Miss Dimont was crisp, focused, alert.

Topham looked into his beer and pondered what his answer might be.

You could still hear raised voices floating down the corridor from the Palm Court, but slowly they were drowned out by the ancient string trio who were getting stuck into a regrettable Viennese medley. While Topham procrastinated the threat remained that tomorrow he would be filleted by Fleet Street's finest, and having grilled him, they would pick over the carcase till the bones were clean.

'All right, all right,' he said finally. 'I've talked to Mr Wetherby, and I think we may very well arrest him – just waiting to see what his next moves are.'

'Don't think it's him,' said Judy firmly, pushing up her spectacles and giving him a beautiful smile. She was recalling her lunch with Lamb in the Signal Box Café.

'I hope you'll forgive me,' said Topham, wearily, 'but *I* am the policeman around here, Miss Dimont. Mr Wetherby wanted to get his stepfather out of the country – sending him with his mother to their estate in Argentina – and then he was going to stage a coup. He'd developed a rival product, which he was going to announce while Mr Larsson was away – his aim being to get over the embarrassing publicity which was going to kill the business stone dead unless something was done.'

'I don't think . . .'

'The trouble was that Larsson found him out and kicked the lad out of the house. Told him never to come back. Remember he's only the stepson, no guarantee he would inherit Larsson's millions, and all he had was a small salary from his mother for helping in the business plus his board and lodging. There's motive enough there.'

'You don't think it could be Mrs Larsson?'

The inspector blinked. 'Say that again?'

'You've talked to her. She's a steely one. If her husband

threatened to kick her son out of the house, that would weaken her own position in the family. Remember, he'd been married three times before and could easily go out and find a newer model.'

'He was eighty,' said Topham, uncomprehending.

'Nonsense – life in the old dog and all that,' responded Miss Dimont in parrot-like fashion. She couldn't believe what passions these ancients were capable of.

'You can see how tough she is. Larsson discovers she's been plotting with her son against him, she's out on her ear as well. There's a precision about her, a Scandinavian coldness however beautiful she may be – don't you think she's more likely to do the job efficiently than that useless son of hers? He had the motive and the means, yes, but did he have the capability?'

'Of course he did!' said Topham. 'He knew the Rejuvenator inside out, he'd been working on a replacement for months. It would be easy for him to alter its settings and give the old man a fatal shock, though we're still not sure how it was done.'

'Hmm,' said Miss Dimont, who was sure but wasn't ready to share. 'Another pint?'

Surprisingly. her company had eased the constriction in the policeman's throat. His glass was now nearly empty.

'Go on then.'

'The problem for me is that there are so many suspects,' Judy went on. 'Mrs Larsson could easily have slipped away from the gardener during that hour she was down in the potting shed, so she had the opportunity.'

'Well, if you want to look at it that way,' said Topham, 'it could equally have been the manservant Lamb. He's the only person who was in the background for the whole time when the murder could have occurred. Everybody else came and went. Plus, he knew how the Rejuvenator worked – he used to demonstrate it to the visitors.'

'What about those loopy people from the Lazarus League? Has anybody spoken to them?'

'Oh, come on! You've seen enough of them in town over the years – these are people who wouldn't even swat a fly, let alone murder someone in cold blood. And do you honestly think there'd be one amongst them who was sophisticated enough to be able to fiddle with the machine so that it became lethal?'

'I can quite easily see one of them with a grudge,' said Miss Dimont. 'Maybe a family member had been injured – died even – because of the Rejuvenator. Think how much worse that would be for a devoted follower – a double betrayal, you might say. I can see them being very angry and, of course, because he used to have open house for the Lazarus League, they'd have no problem with access to the machine and its inventor.'

Topham did not like this, because though what he said about the League was incontestable, he'd been perhaps less rigorous in following up this particular line of inquiry. 'My men are on it,' he said vaguely, but the words had a hollow ring.

A pink face poked its nose around the door of the bar – a poor little lamb who had lost his way. Soberer, he might have recognised the undeniable figure of a plain clothes policeman and the urgent body language of a reporter debriefing him, but his eyes only vaguely took in the room before fixing on Sid, the barman.

'The gentleman . . . schroom?' he inquired mildly, if a little slowly.

'Next on the left,' said Sid. The man from the *News Chronicle* waddled away.

*

Every local newspaper has its prize bore and Ray Bennett, the *Riviera Express*'s arts reporter, had long ago won every prize going when it came to talking the hind leg off the proverbial.

Fresh sacrificial lambs were hard to come by, so the fat old man in his floppy bow tie gleamed with joy as he stepped into the newsroom to discover Valentine's slender figure crouched over his typewriter. He wandered over, sat down noisily, and, without the bother of an introduction, launched forth.

'Schism in the choir!' he announced with grandeur.

Valentine glanced up distractedly, then went back to work.

'The most extraordinary thing. They're at each other's throats. Temple Regis has never seen anything like it! Really – you know – the *most* important story!'

It being relatively easy to spot a bore, especially at such close quarters, Valentine adopted a defensive body posture but the fat old man droned on – and whatever his drawbacks, when Ray Bennett got hold of a story he knew its value. The schism in the choir, he declared, went to the very heart of Temple Regis' inner life. The town might put on a special face to welcome visitors during the summer months, but that didn't mean the ebb and flow of rancour and disorder which veins all small communities was not alive and well!

Valentine found it hard to concentrate. The sad tale of missing Faye Addams and her distraught admirer, Boots McGuigan, had all the makings of a follow-up in the national newspapers, and this could be his first big scoop.

'So the point is, they're not speaking,' wheezed on old Ray. 'It's all to do with the piano accompaniment – half the choir come down on the side of the Schubertian dotted crotchet, the other have plumped for Brahmsian polyrhythms. D'you see? D'you understand? The Stabat Mater only three weeks away and rehearsals have stopped. Stone dead!'

Valentine wanted to be polite but was too absorbed to pay proper attention. In addition, though burdened with few prejudices, he found the sight of a bow tie worn during the day rather hard to swallow.

'Tricky,' he replied, while modulating his tone towards the end of the second syllable to indicate how busy he was.

Bennett maundered on. 'I tried this out on the editor but he was really quite dismissive. The man is uncultured and knows nothing of music – I mean for heaven's sake, he's completely missing the point!'

'Which is?' said Valentine without lifting his head.

'Schism in the choir means schism in the community. There's Bardel the greengrocer and Retson his next-door neighbour in the boot repair shop, they're not speaking. Multiply that by sixty, which is the number of the choir, add in their wives and families who are bound to take sides, and half of Temple Regis isn't speaking to the other half! The Schubertian dotted crotchet, my boy!'

Valentine looked up from his notebook and started to pay attention for the first time.

'Lord,' he said, 'that does sound quite interesting.'

The fat man looked replete. 'Won't be in the paper though,' he said smugly, gratified his scoop had been acknowledged, 'the editor is too busy even to discuss it.'

'If I may say so,' said Valentine, feeling his way, 'surely the story is not about the technical detail, the dotted whatnot, but that such a paltry matter has caused this town to stop speaking to its neighbour?'

'That's what I said,' said Bennett stoutly.

No you didn't, thought Valentine. You were so busy showing off your musical knowledge the poor fellow was unable to see the wood for the trees – no wonder he turned the story down.

'Well I think it's brilliant,' said Valentine, feeding copy paper into his typewriter – an act of body language in newspaper offices which says, go away now, I am composing my thoughts and entering that torture chamber where I have to discover what the intro to my story will be.

But Bennett, as well as being fat and old, was deaf as well: 'Well, you tell him then!' he blundered on. 'Go and tell him what a good story it is!'

'I don't think he's receiving visitors at this hour,' said Valentine, glancing at the editor's closed door.

'Well, all I can say is that choir rehearsal was a waste of an evening when I could have been at home with my novel.'

The way Ray said 'novel' it sounded important – though whether he was writing one or reading one passed Valentine by. 'It was all very tiresome, and I kept being pestered by some young flibbertigibbet who wouldn't leave me alone. Is there some young girl missing, or something?'

Valentine's head rose slowly once again from his typewriter and he fixed the arts reporter with a steady gaze. 'As a matter of fact there is, Mr Bennett,' he said slowly. 'A girl is, indeed, missing.'

Don't you read your own newspaper? he thought. For heaven's sake! 'What did the young lady have to say?'

'Apparently she's a beauty queen or whatever you call it.'

'Which, the dead girl? Or your flibbertigibbet?'

'Both. Is she dead? Oh dear.'

'Er, Mr Bennett,' said Valentine evenly, 'this might be quite important. Do you recall the name of the fli—the young lady?'

'No idea,' said Ray, whose idea of journalism, learned long ago, was that a correspondent of his stature talked only to the important people. 'You could try the choir secretary, Mrs Southpool – though of course if the woman is on the wrong side of the Schubertian–Brahmsian divide you probably won't get very far.'

*

It took Valentine an hour to track down the secretary, and a further thirty minutes to find himself seated opposite Molly

Churchstow in the Expresso Bongo coffee bar. 'Blinkin' wonderful newspaper yours turns out to be,' she said, coldly.

'Sorry?'

'Call yourselves reporters?'

'Sorry, not quite with you Miss, er, Churchstow.'

'Molly.'

'Molly.'

'I rang you up and said, it's Faye Addams that's missing. Did you do anything about it? Not a proverbial sausage!'

'Erm, who did you speak to?' Molly was attractive in an artificial sort of way, but hard. She smelt of cigarettes and face powder.

'I ask for the editor. He said he'd make a note of it.'

'When was this, Molly?'

'Three, four days ago. Nothing happened, I waited for someone to phone me back but nobody did. Then I saw that old fool at choir practice and let 'im 'ave it.'

As she lit another Woodbine, Valentine regarded the beauty queen with curiosity. On the jukebox Danny Trouble and The Urge's ballad 'A Beautiful Summer Place' – not Temple Regis, obviously, given the manager's contempt for the town – was playing and she was humming along to it.

'I must say,' he said after a moment, 'most unusual for you to be in the beauty business and to love pop music like this, and then to sing in a classical music choir as well.'

'My dad was a verger. I went to church so many times a week I lost count. I used to sit in the verger's pew, but it was easier to see the boys from the choir stalls so I joined the choir. Stayed with it.'

'So, anyway, you saw our Mr Bennett and . . .'

'Pompous old git, couldn't even be bothered to listen. Though I s'pose he must of done or you wouldn't be here.'

'Quite,' said Valentine, too polite to reveal that Bennett

wouldn't know a story if he tripped over it on the promenade. No, that wasn't fair – but not reading your own newspaper!

'Please, then, go back to the beginning and tell me everything. D'you know Boots McGuigan?'

'What? From The Urge? The dishy one?'

'He was Faye's boyfriend.'

'Never! Lucky girl – he's gorgeous! She kept that pretty quiet!'

'He's been looking for her. He doesn't know she's dead – in fact, Molly, half the world seems to know she's missing while the other half has been worrying about a dead body on the beach over at Todhempstead. Nobody seems to have put two and two together.'

'One and one, *actually*.' Molly looked at him. She was older but she liked what she saw – his blond curls were particularly attractive. 'Anyway, *I* did,' she simpered, and smiled a certain sort of smile.

This was lost on Valentine, who was not used to certain smiles. 'How well did you know her?'

'Hardly at all. She turned up out of the blue for one of the heats for Queen of the English Riviera. She'd been working as a beautician in one of the London stores and decided to chuck it in and get on the pageant scene. She thought she was going to become Miss Great Britain. Don't we *all*,' added Molly, wearily.

'Yes?'

'Told me she'd got a new boyfriend and she was coming down here to do the Riviera heats because he had a summer job in Temple Regis so she could be near him. So that was Boots McGuigan?'

'Yes.'

'Well I never. Wonderfully hunky sort of name – Boots – so manly!'

Valentine didn't mention the chemist. He couldn't see the point.

Just then the door swung open and a vision in yellow clacked in on perilous high heels – the glorious Eve Berry, currently riding the crest of the wave as Miss Exmouth. She carried about her the air of detachment she'd picked up from once seeing Diana Dors in the street. Her look said 'Fame!' and set her apart from Molly and the others who hadn't learned this secret trick, but it made her no more successful on the beauty pageant circuit. The interview always let her down.

'Thought I'd find you here,' she breathed, talking to Molly but eyeing up Valentine. 'Who's this?'

The reporter rose from his seat. 'Valentine, er, Ford . . . from the *Riviera Express*. May I get you a cup of coffee?'

'Cappuccino,' said Eve, in her Diana Dors voice. 'Put a wizzle in it and make it extra *frothy* . . .'

The boy had no idea what she was talking about.

When he returned, the beauty queens were discussing the late Faye Addams in suitably hushed tones.

'Stuck-up bitch,' said Eve.

'Broad in the beam as well. Wrong shape to win the title,' added Molly.

They both eyed Valentine in a mildly carnivorous sort of way. 'So what are you doin' about it, handsome?' barked Molly. 'Not much, eh? Call yourself a reporter?' She found an aggressive approach to fit young men sometimes could provoke, well, a thrillingly muscular response.

Valentine was more interested in his notebook. 'D'you mind if we go over this methodically? I'll be asked about it when I get back to the office and I want to make sure I've got this straight.

'As I understand it, Miss Addams was not part of your usual beauty pageant circuit, sort of came out of nowhere?'

'She wasn't even local,' said Eve, 'though that's not against the rules. She come from London, been working at a beauty counter.'

'All you lady contestants down here know each other, but nobody had seen Miss Addams before?'

'That's right. She was brought in by Cyril Normandy. In fact,

I thought she was his bit of stuff,' said Eve, whose lips were now coated in coffee froth.

'Nah,' said Molly. 'Cyril never touches the goods, far too fly.'

'That's where you're wrong,' retorted Eve. 'The Brixham eliminator, I caught them havin' a go at each other.'

'Er,' said Valentine, 'what exactly do you mean when you say "having a go"?'

The two queens looked at each other and burst out laughing. 'Not what you're thinking, sonny,' said Eve, who'd switched off her headlights now – she could see he wasn't interested.

'They were havin' a ding-dong, a spat. A row. But to me it looked like a lovers' tiff. And I reckoned that he'd picked her up in London and told her he'd make her the Riviera Queen. All she had to was turn up and he'd rig the voting. Like 'e always does,' she added bitterly.

'He uses us like cattle,' said Molly. 'Puts us on parade, takes the money. He's cruel, that's what he is.'

'So they could have been boyfriend and girlfriend, Faye and Mr Normandy?'

'You *hev* been brought up proper,' mocked Eve, affecting a posh tone. 'That devil is old enough to be her grandfather.'

'Not quite,' cut in Molly, who'd once tried it on with Normandy in the hope of advancing her cause. 'He *is* older, but not that old.'

'Those nasty pudgy hands.'

'That dandruff.'

'Those nasty niffs . . .'

'Weeeeeurgh!'

Valentine felt they were straying from the point. 'So Miss Addams may have been having a fling with Mr Normandy. But at the same time she was the girlfriend of Boots McGuigan? And this chap in The Shadows *as well*?'

'How old are you?' asked Molly witheringly.

Valentine didn't respond. 'So one might assume, if one was

in the detecting sort of lark, that if Boots or Normandy got to hear of the other, they might take out their, er, disappointment on Miss Addams?'

'You mean *murder* her?' asked Eve, fascinated.

'Well, since you put it that way. I think we can take it that her wounds were not self-inflicted,' said Valentine drily. 'There has to be some explanation for her being found on the beach with her head caved in.'

'D'you think he would have made her queen?' said Molly to Eve, a plaintive note in her voice. This was more important than their rival's bloody end, for the what-if governed their every thought and action. What if she'd won, what if they'd lost?

'It's always a fix,' replied Eve vigorously. 'I tell you, one day I'm going to do that Normandy in, I swear I will!'

TWENTY

Miss Dimont and Valentine met in the front hall of the *Riviera Express*.

'Haven't seen you for a while,' said Judy shyly, looking at him sideways. 'Been busy?'

'Just a bit. There's lots going on.'

'Let's go outside,' she said, leading the way through the back office into the car park. She sat down on a low wall, turned her face up to the sun and shook out her curls. 'Far too lovely to be cooped up in the office.'

Valentine remained standing. He felt the need to report. 'Rusty, as you call him, has gone to ground. People go into his office, they come out. The door's permanently closed. I'm beginning to wonder what's up.'

'He hates it when the Fleet Street pack come into town. Pretty soon they'll be in the office parking themselves at people's desks, commandeering the phones and the telex, the photographers elbowing their way around the darkroom.'

'I don't think it's about Fleet Street.'

'I think it is.'

The two looked at each other afresh and their glances lingered. They had not seen each other since the night at Judy's cottage.

'Rudyard Rhys knew about the identity of the dead girl, and he didn't do anything about it. Couple that with his extraordinary behaviour over Ben Larsson and . . .'

'Wait a minute,' said Miss Dimont sharply, 'wait a minute . . . the dead girl? Go back – I don't know about this!'

'Name of Faye Addams, contestant in the Riviera Queen pageant. Girlfriend of the bass guitarist in The Urge and, come to that, probably of that creep Cyril Normandy. And possibly somebody else as well.'

Miss Dimont sat up straight. 'Where did you get *that* from?'

'Oh, just been doing a bit of digging,' said Valentine casually.

'You seem to be catching on quite quick,' she said after a pause, and smiled. Valentine came over and settled beside her.

Just then Betty poked her head out of an upstairs window. 'Byeeee,' she called down in a fed-up voice. 'Back to Newton Abbot.'

'Bad luck,' cried Judy. 'Can't be for too much longer.'

'Another two months. I don't think I can bear it.'

'Good luck,' answered Valentine. Betty had run out of time to meet the Fleet Street boys and catapult herself into their ranks, and he felt sorry for her, but at least it meant she wouldn't be swarming round his desk any more. He waved to her then turned his face to the sun as well.

'There's a lot to talk about,' he said. 'Should we . . .'

'Not here,' declared Miss Dimont with finality. 'I've got some ginger beer in the pannier,' pointing towards ever-ready Herbert, 'want to come up to Mudford Cliffs? It's on your way home, you can take your devilish machine and I'll see you up there.'

Valentine grinned. 'Ha!' he said, 'sure you wouldn't prefer a ride in the Heinkel?'

'Are you joking?'

They made their way separately.

*

From where they sat on the green above the cliffs, it was as if they could see the whole world. Spread below them were the pink sand, the ivory blue water, the red rocks – and now the tide was at low water, they could see the remains of old ships, spines intact but bodies long gone, sticking up out of the waves like broken teeth. The sun's rays, sharper now as the day drew out, pinpointed the harbour beneath with its ships and trawlers and small boats bobbing gently on the water. The air was still, the gulls were silent, and for a moment the world appeared to stop turning.

They were sipping ginger beer from tin cups but Miss Dimont's eyes were focused on the prospect below.

'"*Verweile doch, du bist so schon*",' she said, almost to herself.

'What's that?' asked Valentine. 'The old German's a bit rusty.'

'Faust. He discovers what for him is the most beautiful moment in life and he wants to stay in it for ever . He says, "Stay awhile, you are so beautiful."'

There was a pause.

Then Valentine replied, 'No words I might write in a lifetime in journalism could express it better.'

Miss Dimont turned to see the young reporter suddenly delving in his notebook; he hadn't necessarily been talking about the beauty of the seascape below. 'Better bring me up to date,' she said briskly, pouring more ginger beer.

'I don't know what to make of Mr Rhys's behaviour,' began Valentine. He described Molly Churchstow's call to the *Express*, and that she had been put through, after a lot of fuss, to the editor's office, that she had said that she believed the dead body on Todhempstead Beach could be that of missing Faye Addams, and that the editor said something would be done about it.

'Why didn't she call the police?'

'No idea. Maybe she thought there'd be some personal publicity in it for her – you know, Judy, those beauty pageant girls live a desperate life. They exist on cigarettes and I know not what, they save all their money for make-up and nylons in the hope their beauty will carry them through to a better life. They're exploited appallingly.'

Judy thought about this. 'You could also say they do it of their own free will, nobody asks them to parade around in swimming costumes with a cardboard number taped to their wrist.'

'I'd say they can't help it,' said Valentine. 'All they have is their beauty.'

'Do *you* think they're beautiful?' asked Miss Dimont, curious.

'Not really. In fact, not at all.' He lifted his head and looked away.

'So then . . .'

'So then Mr Rhys sat on the information, didn't tell a soul. Why would he do that? Do you think that in some way these two deaths are linked?'

'I doubt it. In any case, far too early to say.'

'Well, I'm no detective but I think it strange that he should hide in his office like that.'

'Fleet Street, I told you.'

'No, it's something else,' he insisted.

'Anyway,' said Miss Dimont, who felt this was going round the houses, 'we've established the identity of the murder victim. You talked to her friends – did you discover who might want to kill her? And why?'

Valentine turned a page in his notebook. 'She was having a love affair with Boots, the guitarist. Molly thinks she may have been involved as well with Normandy, the beauty pageant man. And then there was this chap in The Shadows. Each one might have wanted to kill her simply on the grounds of jealousy.'

'Aren't you forgetting the Sisters of Reason?' asked Miss Dimont, for these were her preferred candidates.

'Women killing each other in order to make a point about exploitation? I don't see it.'

'You haven't met Ursula Guedella, she's positively frightening. And more than a bit mad. Athene heard the Sisters talking about the murder when they were in the Chinese Singing Teacher.'

'What's that?' asked Valentine, baffled by this abstract notion – a Chinaman teaching singing? An Englishman teaching you how to sing in Chinese? Neither of these?

'Tell you later. There's definitely something about to happen with the Sisters of Reason – they were talking about an Action Day. Athene got the impression it was a series of events likely to happen all over the country.'

'Well,' said Valentine practically. 'Clearly, Action Day is not yet upon us. The murder of this girl happened days ago. If they *are* planning something, they're not very co-ordinated about it.'

'That sounds like your Army training coming out,' laughed Miss Dimont. 'With women it's different, it doesn't all have to be straight lines and precision timing. We do things the way we think is best, when we think is best, not by ticking off a list on a clipboard.'

'Well,' said the young man, 'if the Sisters of Reason killed Faye Addams simply to make a point, they made a pretty poor job of it. Nobody knew who she was until just now so there's been no publicity, which surely must have been the point of the exercise. I think if you're going to kill someone to make a point, then the point should be made.'

'It's chilling to think they could kill in cold blood like that,' agreed Miss Dimont, 'but, to be fair, behind all this extremist talk is a very potent argument about women and the way they're treated. For heaven's sake, we're very nearly in the 1960s, but for all the progress that's been made since the War we may as well be in the 1860s.'

'Huh!' snorted Valentine. 'There are more efficient ways of going about achieving your aims.'

'Men!' huffed Judy.

'Women!' riposted Valentine.

It had come to this.

What looked like blowing up into a heated debate was punctured by the arrival of a brace of dog-walkers with a selection of adorable companions. Normally during the day, the green up on Mudford Cliffs was the province of the She-Club, the group of enthusiastic dog owners whose knowledge of this quarter of Temple Regis was second to none – they would have provided a wonderful intelligence-gathering unit during the war so rigorous was their interview technique, so sharp their observation of each other. But now, at the day's end, it was the turn of the men.

'Oh look,' said Judy. 'That's Captain Hulton! And his dog, Bruce!' She gave them both a wave and the ancient soldier gently fluttered a hand in reply.

'I wanted to ask you about the Larsson business,' said Valentine. The evening sun was hot and he took off his tie and undid the top button of his shirt.

'Not so fast. The girl – Faye whatshername. You think it's jealousy, and that the murderer could be one of three men she was involved with. I think it's more likely it was the Sisters, and though the most likely candidate there is Ursula Guedella, it could equally be that de Mauny woman – she seems to be very much under Ursula's thumb. The Commandant, she calls her – such nonsense!'

'That about sums it up. By the way, are you thinking of sharing any of this with the venerable inspector?'

'But of course – at the right moment. I had a most useful conversation with him last night in the Grand, as a matter of fact.'

'Oh?'

'We were going over the Larsson case. The problem here is that there are so many suspects – the stepson Gus Wetherby being the most obvious, so one can almost certainly discount him straight away.

'Then there's Mrs Larsson – my preferred candidate if it's not the Lazarus League – fearing the loss of her position as chatelaine of Ransome's Retreat. She'd betrayed her husband and had everything to lose.

'There's the manservant Lamb, about to lose his job. I had lunch with him at Lovely Mary's and I'll tell you more about that separately. It could be him – he had the motive and the opportunity – but he's a pretty sad figure with a drink problem, so I think probably not.'

'May I kiss you?' said Valentine.

'You may not. Pay attention.'

The young man rolled over onto his back and stared up at the sky.

'Then there's that group of oddball followers who Larsson encouraged – no way of knowing if one of them had lost someone and planned an act of revenge. Anonymous people with easy access – we have no idea of their names or where they came from – and if it was one of them, they've performed the perfect murder.'

'We're never going to find them,' said Valentine.

'That's where you're wrong. If you are scrupulous in your examination of the *other* suspects, it may be that you're able to identify one of them as the culprit. If you can't do that, then – and only then – it could be the Lazarus lot.'

'Or not.'

'Yes. Or not.'

'There's one more you can add to the tally,' said Valentine. 'And that's Boots McGuigan.'

'The beat group chap, boyfriend of Faye?'

'How does he come into the picture?'

'Well,' said Valentine, 'apparently at about the same time Mr Larsson was rejuvenating himelf to death, Boots disappeared from a rehearsal. He came back later in a foul temper and shut himself in the van.'

'That's not much to go on. How do you make a connection out of that?'

'He'd been asking the manager, Gavin, about Ben Larsson and Ransome's Retreat. He was really agitated. And it was just after that he bunked off the rehearsal. Derek told me.'

'Derek? Who's Derek?'

'One of the biggest stars in our pantheon – you know him as Danny Trouble.'

'Huh!' said Miss Dimont, who if not interested in Danny was certainly interested in what he had to say. 'No evidence, though, is there that this Boots actually went up to the Retreat? Why would he want to?'

'No evidence he went up there, none at all, but if he did he could easily have joined in with the Lazarus lot and gained access to the great man that way.'

'Why would he?'

'I've been chewing that over. Can't think of an answer. But it links the two murders, doesn't it?'

'It most certainly does,' said Miss Dimont, briskly packing up the cups. You could tell she didn't think so at all.

*

The editor's door was tight shut, just as it had been the past couple of days. Essential work was conducted through intermediaries while everyone tried to pretend it was business as usual.

Athene sat at a far desk with the deputy editor Peter Pomeroy, whose wife loved the astrologer's predictions so much she read all twelve star signs each week, just for the sheer pleasure. Athene had made Peter a cup of her special tea while they discussed the contents of this week's page, but soon their conversation strayed – as it often did – from matters temporal to those of a higher plane.

Pomeroy was ready to spend the rest of the morning in private debate with Devon's most gifted astrologer but found his attention distracted by the arrival in the newsroom of a well-dressed, perfectly groomed woman of a certain age carrying a battered leather portfolio. Though her forward progress appeared determined, it was clear she was not sure where to go.

'Can I help?' asked ever-courteous Peter.

'Looking for the editor's office. I don't have an appointment but I expect he will see me.'

'He's very busy, what with the . . . Perhaps I can help?'

'Please kindly mention my name to him. He'll see me.' She seemed very sure.

'And the name is . . . ?'

'Auriol Hedley.'

At that moment the office door opened and the bewhiskered face of Rudyard Rhys appeared. 'Auriol,' he said, his voice conveying a mix of disbelief and fear.

'If I may have a minute, Richard.'

Rhys looked at her, then at Pomeroy. Though he said nothing his eyes conveyed a beseeching plea for help.

'Anything I can do, er, Rudyard?' Peter was confused by Auriol's choice of first name.

'Nothing,' said Rhys blankly. Turning to Auriol he said with distaste, 'You'd better come in.'

The door had barely shut and Rhys was still lumbering back to take shelter behind his desk when Auriol started in.

'Not a social call, Richard. Official business. As your former senior officer I've been asked to come in and enlighten you as to a few matters.'

Rhys knew the routine all right. He'd done a bit of enlightening himself in his time, and he knew this was not going to be pleasant.

'What authority?'

'Room 39.'

'Get on with it, then.'

'For the duration of this conversation, Richard, you will bear in mind our respective ranks,' said Auriol commandingly. 'Please address me properly, and with respect.'

The editor reached for his pipe. 'The War's over, Auriol. Fourteen years. Half a lifetime.'

'The Official Secrets Act lasts several lifetimes. You are bound by it. And please don't light that thing.'

Rhys scratched his beard and looked out of the window. 'All right,' he muttered in surly tones. 'Go ahead.'

Auriol opened her portfolio and took out a sheaf of papers. 'Operation Tailcoat, obviously. Bengt Larsson.'

'Well, *obviously*.'

'I won't go over the mess you left behind back in Berlin. Three agents dead, the failure to find and fix that traitor Railton Freeman. Larsson – *our* man, Richard, not your man – left high and dry in Berlin with the Gestapo surrounding him. If it hadn't been for some great good fortune, Richard, Larsson would never have got away.'

'You don't know anything, Auriol. I never heard a word of criticism from him about what went wrong, and quite right too. Once he'd got over the initial shock, of course.'

'I must say I marvel at human nature's ability to heal its wounds,' replied Auriol scornfully. 'What a mess it was. But let's not dwell on it – what I want to know is what on earth you were doing up at the Retreat when Ben Larsson was killed. The Office wants to know too.'

'He told me he was going to the newspapers to prove he wasn't a fraudster as they claimed, but a war hero. I told him he couldn't, reminded him of Official Secrets.'

'I know all that. Hugue – Judy – told me. Did you kill him?'

'Certainly not. Why would I? The threat of prosecution was enough to make him see sense.'

'You *threatened* the man whose life you so nearly lost? With prosecution?'

Rhys turned to look at his inquisitor. 'Yes,' he said unblushingly. 'He had no right to reveal what went on during the War, he knew that.'

'If he had, of course, your reputation would be in ruins. I'd say that was motive enough to consider murdering him.'

'I didn't do it,' said Rhys, the authority draining out of his voice.

'No, Richard,' said Auriol, after a pause, 'with your general level of competence I think it's most unlikely that you did. But is Tailcoat going to make headlines in the next few days?'

'I can't say,' said the editor, shaking his head. 'I got Mrs Larsson to promise that she wouldn't mention it.'

'Oh yes? She went and told Judy all about it straight after.'

Rudyard Rhys looked alarmed.

'I'll take care of *that*,' he said after it had sunk in. 'I *am* her editor, you know. She can just forget all about it. Anyway, I ordered her to stay away from the Retreat.'

'Just so she didn't learn any more about Tailcoat, Richard? About how incompetent you were?'

'Accidents happen. In war, in peacetime.'

'Tailcoat was no accident, Richard. You were lucky to get away without an official inquiry. And when I think how we tried to salvage your reputation after your failure to arrest Lord Sempill.'

Rhys levered himself out his chair. 'Don't start that up again!' he roared.

'There he was, running round the Admiralty – a Japanese spy.'

'And, if I may remind you, a member of the House of Lords. He had powerful friends – for heaven's sake his father was a chum of the King!'

'He was selling secrets to the Japanese and, because of your failure, the best we got was his resignation from the Royal Navy when he should have been court-martialled and executed!'

'I really don't see what this has to do with anything,' said Rhys. He looked angry and cowed.

'The Office want to be sure that Tailcoat does not come out into the open.'

'I can't guarantee that.' Rhys's voice was shrill. 'We've got half of Fleet Street buzzing round Temple Regis, determined to get a scoop on Ben Larsson. Even if Mrs Larsson stays quiet, there's still the stepson, Wetherby. Who, by the way, killed his stepfather in my opinion.'

'I'll let the Office know your thoughts on the matter,' said Auriol crisply. 'Meantime your job is to stifle any mention of Tailcoat by whatever means you have at your disposal.'

Rhys grunted into his beard and reached for his pipe again.

'One last thing,' said Auriol. She rose from her chair, the picture of authority in her twinset, pearls and perfectly set grey hair. 'And that is Miss Dimont.'

Rhys affected disinterest.

'It's been brought to my attention that you refer to her as Miss Dim, which is a pretty poor joke considering the conversation we've just had. Please remember that when we were all together in naval intelligence, she was senior in rank to you and should be treated with respect.'

'The War's over,' repeated Rhys, reasserting himself. 'She is now my employee and how I address Miss Dimont is a matter between herself and her editor.'

'You won't like it when I talk to the Admiralty pensions people,' said Auriol. 'You got off lightly when you left the service. Were I to write to them listing the botched jobs you masterminded – Lord Sempill, Tailcoat and the rest – you do know there's an annual review board, don't you?'

'All so long ago.'

'You bury your head in the sand if you like,' said Auriol witheringly, 'but your rear end is still sticking up in the air. Time somebody kicked it.'

And with that she strode magnificently out of the office.

TWENTY-ONE

'. . . and then, son, you sabotage the phone.'

'What? Why? How?'

'In my day, you'd just nip the diaphragm out from the mouthpiece. That way your opposition could feed as much money into the coin box as they liked – they could hear the switchboard at the other end asking "who is it?" – but *nevairrrr a worrrd* would that switchboard hear from them because you'd fixed the phone.'

Valentine looked at John Ross. 'The purpose being?' he asked in bewilderment.

'Look, sonny, ye're bright I'll grant you, but ye have a lot to learrn. You get to the phone first. You file your story to your newspaper from the phone box. Then you scupper the opposition by destroying their line of communication. Rip the wires out if need be! You learned about that in the Army, didn't ye, destroying lines of communication?'

'Not in quite that way, Mr Ross. And surely wrecking a GPO telephone box is a criminal offence?'

John Ross pulled out his bottom drawer and stamped his foot down hard on its edge. The whisky bottle clanked its disapproval.

'Ye don' get it, do ye?' he asked in exasperation. 'In journalism, laddie, it's not sufficient that you succeed, *others must fail*. Ye ken

I thought you had promise as a reporter, but if you can't grasp the fundamentals of competition, then you may as well give up.'

'They're not competition.'

'Wha'?'

'Today is Tuesday, Mr Ross. The inquests will be held this morning. The boys from the Fleet Street papers will file their copy and it'll be on everybody's breakfast table tomorrow morning. The *Riviera Express* doesn't come out till Friday when the story of Ben Larsson and Faye Addams will be as appetising as old cold fried potatoes.'

'No' ruddy competitive these days,' grumbled Ross and turned his attention back to a wet page proof on his desk.

Having extricated himself from the Scotsman's top tips for young reporters, Valentine made his way out of the building and walked towards the Coroner's court. Only slowly was he making the acquaintance of the many rituals which small towns across the land replicate daily without variance – the council meetings, the voluntary bodies, the churches – and the Coroner's court. This morning Miss Dimont had promised she would unlock its mysteries while they witnessed the inquests into the deaths of Bengt Larsson and Faye Addams.

The grey room at the back of the main courthouse had the antiseptic air of a pathologist's chamber, a wooden-benched expanse kept specially to investigate uncommon death in the fervent hope it was an accident, rather than deliberate. If the Coroner, Dr Rudkin, had one thing to be said for him it was his ability to rob a promising death of all possible drama.

This minimalist approach puzzled visiting journalists whose job it was to feed sensation to their readers, but came as a balm to the relatives of the dead who, in general, wanted to see the formalities over with as little fuss as possible. And Dr Rudkin always wore a flower in his buttonhole, which was nice.

When Valentine Waterford arrived he discovered a party going on in the lobby. He'd chosen a sombre necktie suitable to the occasion, but found the gesture was futile – the Fleet Street gang were in high spirits, making jokes and comparing train times back to London. They'd sewn up the Larsson story and just needed the Coroner to say something noteworthy before they hit the telephones, then on to commandeer the refreshment bar on the 2.30 back to Paddington.

In one corner, the red-cheeked Guy Brace, resplendent in a necktie worthy of Picasso, was conducting his orchestra: Sinclair and Wilson and the others had been given their schedule for note-taking so that no two reporters expended unnecessary energy writing at the same time – they would meet up afterwards in the pub to share out the morning's gleanings. All of them were used to Coroner's courts, and perhaps less sensitive to the delicacy of the occasion than they might have been; certainly the jokes which tumbled from their lips paid little heed to the poor bereaved who gathered almost apologetically down the other end of the hall.

The Coroner's Officer, a grey-faced police constable of many years' service, wandered over to the reporters and handed them a sheet of paper. 'Larsson, you've come for?' he asked with studied indifference. 'There's another one first – open-and-adjourn.'

'You know,' said Brace, a shade too loudly, 'that really is inconvenient, Officer, most inconvenient. You can see all these representatives of the national press here, all with deadlines to meet – can't you ask the Coroner to swap the two hearings round, put the other one second?'

'You don't know Dr Rudkin,' said the man with a tinge of bitterness. 'This is his court.'

'Don't worry,' said Inkpen, the eager-beaver new reporter whose job it was to keep Brace's glass full, 'I'll sit in. Open-and-adjourn, shouldn't take long. I'll let you know.'

'Come on then,' said Brace, huffily, and led his troops out of the lobby to the Admiral Benbow next door.

Forty minutes later, Keith Inkpen returned to their number with the news that Dr Rudkin had taken a twenty-minute break before the Larsson inquest commenced.

'Anything in it?' said Brace boredly, referring to Inkpen's keen activities in court.

'Actually rather good,' said the young man. 'Beauty queen murdered. Blonde found dead on beach.'

The grizzled heads of the press pack looked up sharply. They hadn't expected this. And suddenly the marginalist Inkpen, lowly drinks waiter and general factotum, was the centre of attention. Nothing to grab the readers' attention like a dead blonde – and murdered, too!

'Have you got a full note?' quizzed Brace.

'Are there pictures?' chipped in Wilson.

'How was the dread deed done?' salivated Sinclair. 'Interfered with?'

'*Boyfriend???*' chorused the assembled scriveners. They may have been sitting around like a bunch of idlers two minutes ago, but these were Fleet Street's finest – now they were on their feet, pork pies pushed aside, ready for the chase.

As was the custom, Guy Brace rose regally to dish out orders, instructions, gathering points and general words of wisdom – and, in the twinkling of an eye, the sad tale of poor Ben Larsson was chucked into journalism's wastepaper basket. The luckless Inkpen was instructed to stay behind to cover Dr Rudkin's inquest, but everyone knew his labours would never see the light of day – the *Daily Herald* had taken two bites of the Larsson cherry and there wasn't much nourishment left on the stalk now.

On the other hand, a dead beauty queen!

Thus it was that when his court reassembled a few minutes later, the desiccated Rudkin, who'd steeled himself to face the jackals of the Fourth Estate, found only three figures on the press bench – Inkpen, and the two representatives of the local rag, Miss

Dimont and the new chap. He took off his pince-nez and polished them furiously to cover his disappointment. To be prevented from venting one's anger at the press and their impertinent nosiness made one, well, *very* angry.

The legal procedure which followed would not bear scrutiny at a Home Office inquiry, for to say the details Dr Rudkin allowed in evidence were sparse would be an understatement. A ferocious defender of the town's reputation, he jumped on any fact offered by the pathologist and by Inspector Topham. No member of Larsson's family or staff was allowed to take the stand, and within a short space of time the inquest had skidded to a halt, the Coroner's conclusion being that he was minded to record an open verdict.

'Gosh,' whispered Valentine, 'I thought we were in for a day of it.'

'You don't know Rudkin,' said Miss Dimont, who did. 'He's an absolute shocker. But coroners are coroners, they hold the law in their own hands and they can do whatever they like. He would say that he is sparing the family unnecessary grief, but in fact his aim is to spare Temple Regis unnecessary headlines.'

'Lunchtime,' said Valentine cheerily, looking at his watch. 'What's the Benbow like?'

'It'll do.'

A curious sight greeted the pair as they walked in to the sun-filled front bar. At a corner table sat a bulky figure in tweed suit, sporting full beard and sunglasses.

'Mr Rhys!' called Valentine in a friendly way, 'can I get you something?'

'Sssh! Come and sit down!' The man looked hunted. 'What's happened to that pack of rats?'

'Chased off after the Pied Piper,' said Judy, not in a sympathetic way. Valentine ambled over to the bar to order drinks while she took a chair opposite her boss.

'Where are they?' repeated Rhys anxiously. The light in the bar, despite the sunshine outside, wasn't that bright and he looked comical in his dark glasses.

'You can take those off, Richard,' said Judy tartly. 'The Larsson story's a dead duck – they're off after Faye Addams now.'

'What do you mean?'

'You know, Richard, you've been in journalism longer than I have but you don't seem to have learned much. The wind changed direction. When they arrived here yesterday, those reporters would have set fire to Temple Regis if necessary so they could get a story on Ben Larsson. As of 11.30 this morning, they couldn't care less about him – they've found bigger fish to fry.'

'But,' said Rhys, scratching his head and removing his glasses, 'Ben was *murdered* – we know that now.'

'We do but *they* don't. Or if they do, they don't care. Larsson's inquest was never going to make a Page One story – unless it was discovered his Rejuvenator had accidentally electrocuted the Queen! – but, Richard, a dead blonde will always make the front page.'

'Thank God . . .' said Rhys in a broken sort of way.

'Thank God we don't have such seedy values on the *Riviera Express*? Or thank God that Operation Tailcoat will be given the go-by?'

'Don't even mention it,' the editor said bitterly. 'I've had the Office on, threatening me with all sorts if it gets out.'

'Yes,' said Miss Dimont wickedly. 'Auriol told me she was coming to see you, how was she?' She knew the answer.

'Perfectly bloody, if you want to know. A bully, if you want to know. She has no right.'

Miss Dimont sighed. 'Your trouble is you see her as a lady with a tea shop in Bedlington. I see her as a fine naval officer who made an important contribution to the War effort. It's significant that the Office didn't get in touch with you direct but asked her to have a word.'

'Rr . . . rrrr' growled Rhys.

Valentine sauntered over with drinks and a sandwich, relieved to see his editor preparing to leave.

'You're writing the Addams inquest?' Rhys asked him.

'Yes, sir.'

'No fancy stuff, just do it straight.'

'I've got a lot of background which didn't come out at the inquest. She was the girlfriend of the bass player with Danny Trouble and The Urge, but she may also have been entangled with Cyril Normandy, the beauty queen man.'

'Put in the first bit, leave out the second.'

Valentine looked at his editor with interest. 'Really?' He paused. 'May I ask a question?'

'What is it?' said Rhys, edging towards the door.

'One of the other beauty queens, Molly Churchstow, told me that a few days ago she rang up the office and spoke to you. She told you that she believed she knew the identity of the dead woman on Todhempstead Beach. At the time nobody knew who the woman was, and this was the first clue. A crucial one. But, sir, you didn't pass that on to Miss Dimont or me, who were both working on the story. Can you say why?'

'No.'

'Oh,' said Valentine, deflated, and looked into his glass.

'Why not, Richard?' Miss Dimont's voice was stronger, more insistent.

'Nothing to do with anything,' said Rhys in a confused sort of way, 'and anyway mind your own business.' He straightened up and lumbered out of the pub.

The two reporters sat opposite each other in silence sharing a cheese and pickle sandwich. Valentine sipped his beer. He has green eyes, thought Miss Dimont, so unusual, and really very beautiful.

'You don't know what hell I'm going through,' he said suddenly, those eyes looking straight back at hers.

'What do you mean?'

He was talking about something else. 'When I arrived at the *Riviera Express* I thought, just another training course like the ones I went on in the Army. Learn the stuff up and then you're qualified. I had no idea it would be like this.'

'Like what, exactly?'

'Well, for a start, thanks to you—' he smiled '—it's a two-part course. The first bit is learning how to be a journalist. Second, is learning how to be a sleuth. You have a mind that goes thisaway and thataway and it seems you never take anything at its face value.'

'Good for sleuthing *and* for journalism. Just because people say something doesn't mean it's true. It often means it isn't.'

'My old aunt would call you a cynic.'

'I'm not. I'm a realist. And an optimist. There's something about Temple Regis that makes you want to believe the best in people, something in the air, something in the people – I don't know. You asked the other day why I wasn't in Fleet Street – well, now you've had a chance to meet the seasoned practitioners of the dark arts, what do you think? Is London a better place to be than here?'

'Betty thinks so. She's desperate to get away.'

'Oh, Betty!' said Miss Dimont, laughing. 'For her the grass is always greener anywhere else. If she's dancing with a man, she's always looking over his shoulder to see if there's a handsomer specimen across the floor. She's got a good job here, and she's pretty competent, but nothing will do for her until she's got to Fleet Street. Where, by the way, she wouldn't be taken seriously and would find herself being used for stunt stories which would usually involve her lifting her skirt. Or writing about her private life.'

'Nothing terribly private about that,' laughed Valentine.

'Agreed, but would *you* want to share your innermost feelings with two million souls every morning?'

'Just the one,' said Valentine, smiling steadily at her.

'Anyway, you seem to have learned a few things since you've been here,' said Judy, brushing this aside. 'Donning your sleuth's hat, where have we got to with these two deaths?'

'I can't believe the Coroner didn't declare Larsson's death a murder!'

'Believe it, dear boy – this is Temple Regis!'

'Didn't you just say this town is perfection?'

'Almost,' said Judy, with a wry smile, 'but not quite. Now, where are we with Faye Addams?'

Valentine took a sip of beer. 'I'm confused, I have to admit,' he said. 'To start with, as I said, it looked like it had something to do with the Sisters of Reason. They wanted to make a point about female exploitation so, paradoxically, they killed a woman.

'But then you recall I talked to Danny, or Derek, whatever you want to call him – and he thought that Boots could have slipped away up to Ransome's Retreat. You remember he said Boots went deathly white when he heard Larsson's name mentioned by Gavin Armstrong, then asked where he lived. Soon after that he pushed off and was missing for some time.'

'Now concentrate, Valentine,' chided Judy. 'We're talking about Faye Addams at the moment.'

'Yes, yes, I *am* talking about her. Don't you see, that if Boots McGuigan is capable of killing one person, isn't he capable of killing two? She was supposed to be his girlfriend but wasn't she having an affair with Cyril Normandy? Or maybe she'd gone back to that chap in The Shadows?'

'Two very different motives, Valentine. Boots kills Larsson, let's say, because his mother dies at the hand of the Rejuvenator – then goes off and kills his girlfriend in a fit of jealousy? According to my grasp of the way murderers work, that would be unique. It takes really quite a lot to work your way up to killing a human being, unless you're a hired assassin which, from how you describe him, Mr Boots most definitely is not.'

'No, he doesn't strike me as the homicidal type – too obsessed with his hairstyle. But you know, the way those boys are cooped up inside that van, like animals in a cage, might trigger all sorts of behaviour. I had a few drinks with them and they're a thirsty bunch, also I imagine they have other means to keep themselves lively when on stage.'

'You really are quite worldly for one so young,' remarked Miss Dimont, 'knowing all about drugs.'

'Well, yes and no – we used a variety of pills to keep on top of the game when we were out on army manoeuvres. Black mark if you fell asleep, you see. But there were some nasty side effects, people used to turn quite unpleasant. Take that into account and there you have Boots, chief suspect for both murders.'

'You believe that?'

'Well, no, not really. That's where I'm confused.'

'Well,' said Judy, 'you could just go and ask him. That might set your mind at rest. He wasn't in court for the girl's inquest, was he?'

'Curiously no. Dr Rudkin did that open-and-adjourn business so no witnesses had to be called.'

'You'd think, though, if he was so very much in love with her, he'd be there anyway.'

'Yes, but on the other hand he wouldn't want to be anywhere near the Larsson inquest, if indeed he did kill him. It's all very perplexing.'

The Benbow was filling up with the lunchtime trade, though the landlord clearly believed in keeping the crew on hard-tack rations – the choice was cheese sandwich, or cheese sandwich with pickle. For an extra twopence you could have it toasted: a short menu, but at least the beer was drinkable.

'Let's sit outside,' said Valentine, 'unless you'd rather be somewhere else?'

Miss Dimont smiled. 'Another half of bitter?'

'Lovely.'

When she returned, Valentine was riffling through his notebook with a worried look on his face.

'Can't read my notes back,' he said, running his hand desperately through his wavy blond hair. 'There's a page here which is complete gobbledegook.'

'Have you started shorthand lessons yet?'

'I got a book. It's like Chinese. A language in signs.'

'Better a language you can learn than gobbledegook you can't read back.'

'I suppose so,' he sighed. 'Look, are you and Auriol coming to supper at Chateau Waterford? You promised you would. Or if she can't come,' he added hopefully, 'just you?'

'Don't change the subject. We were talking about Faye Addams, and I wanted to say that while your thinking is sound, it's wide of the mark. You can't discount the Sisters, and Mr Boots is a definite possibility – we need to do further work on them. But since you discovered Miss Addams was having an affair with Cyril Normandy we really need to focus on Normandy – getting involved with the contestants is a risky business, and if he was exposed it'd put paid to his reputation. So he may have had grounds for getting rid of her if she'd suddenly turned difficult.'

'More likely than the Sisters.'

'Really, Valentine, if Ursula Guedella isn't locked up for murder soon it'll be something just as bad. I'd say she's seriously unbalanced, what with that man's hairdo and her tweed suits and demanding to be called Commandant.'

'Why,' said Valentine, smiling in worldly fashion, 'I believe there's a word for all that.'

'If you mean, is she a lesbian,' huffed Miss Dimont, 'I have no doubt that if she had any interest at all it may lie in that direction. Certainly some of those women hanging around her probably hope so. But that's not it – it's what's beneath those outer layers of manliness. She has a power complex, she wants to lead, she wants to rule, and she wants people to see the world as she sees it – and doesn't mind whatever needs to be done to achieve that. It's not about being, or not being, lesbian.'

'Put in my place.'

'Don't talk about things you know nothing about.'

'What about that dinner?'

'You really are persistent, aren't you,' laughed Miss Dimont. 'I thought we'd talked it all out the other night at my house.'

'Well, not quite,' said Valentine, though he couldn't be sure they were talking about the same thing. 'I've been very fortunate to get this cottage for the time I'm here but at present it feels as if I'm in a bedsitter, just me and my radio-oh-ho . . . You can only make a place like that a home if you have guests.'

'Good point. I'll talk to Auriol.'

'She says tomorrow night, I already checked.'

'Oh well, yes, then,' said Miss Dimont, cornered. She was not entirely pleased.

'What you can do meanwhile,' she added, 'is once you've written up the inquests go back and see this Mr Boots. You know what you have to get out of him.'

'Hardly likely to confess to me if he's just done a double murder. Or even a single one, come to that.'

'Look, Valentine,' said Miss Dimont quite sternly, 'I am encouraging your interest in these unusual goings-on because I can see you have an above-average intelligence and an aptitude for getting to the bottom of things. If you feel you can't worm something out of this Mr Boots, then give up and go home. And cancel that supper.'

'Boots,' said Valentine gruffly. 'He's called Boots.'

Miss Dimont picked up her raffia handbag and pushed her glasses up her convex nose. She looked down at the young man.

And smiled. Beautifully.

TWENTY-TWO

Dr Rudkin's blasé verdict on the death of Ben Larsson may have papered nicely over a looming scandal, but Inspector Topham's conscience could not allow matters to rest. Each morning in the CID room he and his faceless assistants waded their way once more through the leads and clues, debating where next to tread.

'The latest on the stepson?' he asked his henchmen.

'Not much,' said one. 'I went down to the factory and he's still pursuing this spin-off of the Rejuvenator machine.'

'The Youthenator.' The way Topham spat it out he'd already got the confession out of Gus Wetherby.

'Apparently he thinks Ben's death puts him in the clear regarding the Rejuvenator. With that open verdict from Rudkin, I shouldn't be surprised if he puts it about that Larsson killed himself because of all the adverse publicity. Or out of remorse for the deaths he caused.'

'He's got a nerve,' said Topham.

'He certainly has. He's taken charge of the house and, according to the staff, is spending all his time liquidating his stepfather's worldwide assets.'

'He isn't the beneficiary of the will. That's the first place we looked for a motive.'

'No,' agreed the faceless one. 'Mrs Larsson cops the lot apart from a few bequests, but he's acting like it's all his.'

Topham groaned. 'She's putty in his hands. They back each other up, you can't get a cigarette paper between their stories. I can't see she had a hand in killing Larsson because of the way she reacted when it happened, and her behaviour since. She's profoundly affected by it, though I'll admit she's a tough one.

'But she'd do anything for that son of hers. And if she believed he'd done it, she'd cover up for him – no matter how much she loved Larsson.'

The faceless ones shuffled their papers and looked out of the window, waiting for further instructions. They did not share their senior officer's inner turmoil.

'I'll go up to talk to her again,' decided the Inspector resignedly. 'You two carry on.'

*

His arrival at Ransome's Retreat was unannounced and unwelcome. 'Please, Inspector,' said Pernilla Larsson sharply, 'do me the courtesy! A telephone call first, if you please!'

Topham eyed her evenly. 'Many apologies,' he said, but they were just words – he didn't mean them and she knew it. 'Just a few more questions.'

'I should have thought there had been quite enough already.' She was looking particularly dazzling in the morning sunshine, a loose cotton cardigan around her shoulders and a large turquoise stone glittering on her cream silk shirt. Her hair, as always, looked as if she'd just stepped from a Mayfair salon.

'It won't take long,' said Topham and, without invitation, sat down on a sofa. It was an act calculated to be rude.

'Look,' said Pernilla in exasperation, 'the inquest decision . . . it effectively means that Ben wasn't murdered – that's the *official* verdict. It's all over – why carry on with your questions? It's very distressing!'

'Because an open verdict means nobody could make up their mind at the time. But if new evidence comes forward, that verdict can be set aside.'

'So you're still pursuing the idea that Ben's death was murder?' She seemed genuinely shocked.

'Of course it was!' snapped Topham. 'Mrs Larsson, you're a clever woman, and a woman of the world – I offer you that as a courtesy. But in return I expect to be viewed similarly. Don't treat me like the village bobby!'

'Have a drink, Inspector, and calm down.'

'No thanks.' He drew out his notebook, a gesture which seemed almost threatening. 'Your son is liquidating the late Mr Larsson's assets.'

'I wouldn't know about that.'

'I imagine you do, madam. Official papers usually require the signature of the parties involved, or don't they do things that way in Sweden?'

'Don't sneer at me, Inspector. If I say I don't know what Gus is getting up to it's because he rarely tells me. I've given him carte blanche to do what he feels is right – I'm no businesswoman, you know – it's better he handles it.'

'I'm keen to know if this liquidation means you, and he, are planning to leave the country.'

Pernilla Larsson lit a cigarette, her hands shaking slightly. 'We have properties abroad,' she said, exhaling slowly, 'in France, Argentina. Are you saying we can't leave England to visit them?'

'My question,' said Topham, 'is whether you're planning to leave for good. That's rather different.'

'Why should we? Gus plans to launch his Youthenator after a decent interval has elapsed. That's enough to keep him here.'

'Not really,' said Topham. 'The prototype is complete, tested, and ready to go into production, according to my officers who visited your factory. Once he's pressed the start button on the production line, no need to hang around here.'

Pernilla eyed the policeman with disdain. 'We don't "hang around" here, Inspector – this place is my home. Look about you – why would I want to leave?'

'My question is more about your son, Mrs Larsson. What does *he* want to do, and if he goes, will you follow him?'

'Why don't you ask *him*?'

'I will, I will. But first I must go over again some of the questions I put to you after your husband's death.'

'I hope it won't take long. I have rather a lot on today and I'm going to see a friend in Salcombe later.'

As Topham probed, it seemed that Mrs Larsson was retreating ever further into an invisible shell.

'You are the beneficiary of your husband's very considerable estate. He is worth several millions, I understand.'

'I believe so, I never asked him.'

'In the rules of policing, when there's a murder the first question always is – who stands to gain? In this case, Mrs Larsson, it's you. So you had the motive. On the day in question you were in the garden when your husband met his death. Yet although we checked with the gardener who confirmed you and he spent some time together discussing next year's planting, you were not with him for the whole of the time you claimed. It would have been easy to come back to the house. That gives you the opportunity.'

'Nonsense. That man Rhys came looking for me – he'd discovered Ben's body and he was desperately trying to find me. He told you so himself.'

'He also told me, Mrs Larsson, that when he found you, you were walking *away* from the house, not *towards* it, which you would have been had you just come up from the garden. Remember, Mr Rhys was not with your husband at the time of his death, they'd had that row and he'd walked off.'

Pernilla was looking out on to the terrace and down the shaved lawns to where a robin was hopping languidly about. She was pushing away the conversation with all her might, but Topham was having none of it.

'Mrs Larsson, you had the motive and the opportunity. As to the means – nobody knew the Rejuvenator better than you. It was your husband's passion, his life. He must have showed you a thousand times what it was capable of doing, and how its intricate mechanisms worked. You would have known about the panel at the back and the rheostat which . . .'

'My dear Inspector, you pay me a compliment in saying that I am clever. Maybe I am, but I can tell you now my knowledge does not extend as far as you think. I have no earthly idea what a rheostat is.'

Topham stood up suddenly. 'Nonsense!' he thundered. 'Call it what you like, but you know perfectly well what it is – a little dial hidden behind a panel which you have to unscrew. When you turn up the dial, the voltage mounts. Turn it up to its fullest extent and you have a fatal charge of electricity – the fatal charge which killed your husband!'

Pernilla eyed him coldly. 'Do tell me, if you know so much, how I put those tubes into his hands without giving myself a fatal shock.'

'You didn't. He was about to receive the Lazarus League, and one of the things he always did when they came was to sit with the Rejuvenator and give them a little demonstration of its powers. They had the habit, I gather, of taking photographs of the great man using his invention. So, he switched it on and . . .'

'How do you know? There were no witnesses to his death.'

'There is no other possibility, Mrs Larsson. Unless, that is, he chose to commit suicide – are you saying he killed himself?'

'Certainly not! Why would he?'

'Those deaths the Rejuvenator undoubtedly caused. The fact that he had not only been exposed in the *Daily Herald* but that the newspaper was about to return to the attack. The thought of having to face all those admirers of his, the Lazarus lot, knowing that their belief in him was about to be shattered – that the Rejuvenator had not saved lives, but ended them. That, I should have thought, would be enough for any sane man to want to put an end to it all.'

Pernilla Larsson got up and walked over to the drinks tray. She uncorked a bottle and poured something, but did not offer a glass to the inspector.

'You have it so entirely wrong,' she said and, though her back was to him, Topham could see she was crying.

'I loved my husband, I loved him dearly. He was kind and generous. When my marriage to Gus's father failed, I was on the floor, finished. I had no money, no house, no position, and a son who was about to lose his education because his father rejected him and refused to pay.

'All I had,' she said, turning towards the Inspector, 'were my looks, and the fact that I was Swedish, like Ben. He was soft and he was kind and he took us both in. He said I was the only woman he had ever truly loved and I believed him – his previous marriages were all based on aspiration, Inspector, not love. He gave Gus his education at Harrow, and he gave us his home. He was a great man, no matter what you say.'

'But misguided, I think we must agree.'

'Maybe, I couldn't possibly comment on that. What I will say, Inspector, is that you may be a fine policeman but you do not know women. If you've found me less than helpful with your inquiries it's because of your line of attack – when you walked through the door I knew you believed I killed Ben. That is the most terrible thing a man could suggest to a woman who has lost her life's partner.

'Why should I show you my hurt, though? Why give you the pleasure of seeing how you doubled the agony of losing my husband?' She clutched the cardigan around her shoulders as if it could provide much-needed warmth.

'Unexplained death – murder – *is* a terrible business,' agreed Topham. 'But don't you see, it's my job to find out who killed your husband, that's why I have to ask these questions.'

'It doesn't matter, he's dead,' she sobbed. 'I don't care who killed him.'

Despite the tears, and they seemed genuine, Topham was not ready to let go. 'Let's talk about your son, then.'

'If you must.'

'What were his relations with his stepfather?'

'Extremely cordial.'

'Loving?'

'When you have two men in the house, when they are not related by blood . . .'

'So Mr Larsson and Mr Wetherby had, you might say, a polite relationship.'

'Better than that.'

'Even though Mr Wetherby was plotting behind Mr Larsson's back to steal his idea and make it his own.'

'No!'

'Yes, Mrs Larsson, yes! We have the testimony of your man-servant Lamb, who told us how – on Mr Wetherby's instructions – he would slip a sedative into his coffee after lunch so that Mr Larsson would sleep long into the afternoon and he could work on his new Rejuvenator without fear of discovery.'

'My husband was an old man. Old men do sleep in the afternoon.'

'Come now, Mrs Larsson, Lamb *told* us what he did!'

'The man's an alcoholic. And, what's more, he betrayed my husband. It was he who gave the information to the *Daily Herald* which prompted this terrible crisis. How can you trust a man like that?'

'Who told him to telephone the newspapers? Was it you?'

Pernilla angrily got up to pour herself another glass of sherry. 'Don't you listen to a word I say?' she snorted. 'I loved my husband, I would never betray him.'

'That leaves only your son then. Lamb was clear that he was under instructions to pass that information on to Fleet Street.'

'I have no idea about any of that.'

Topham was taking notes steadily, one eye on his notebook and the other on his quarry. 'Let me be perfectly frank,' he said, 'from what you have told me, and what I already know, a clear picture emerges.

'To start with, yes, I thought you had a hand in this. You were almost the sole beneficiary of his vast fortune and had the most to gain by his death, so of course you were top of my list.'

'Thank you,' came the bitter response.

'On the other hand, do you have the know-how to tinker with the Rejuvenator, and in any case, if you *had*, would you have had enough time to get down to the bottom of the garden again? Probably not. But if not you, then who?' He turned the pages of his notebook back.

'Clearly someone else with something to gain – or in this case, preserve – was Rudyard Rhys, the editor. He was here, he was angry, he had the opportunity and he had the motive – he didn't want the fiasco of that wartime operation coming out into the open.

'The only thing about Mr Rhys,' went on Topham resignedly, 'is that he is clearly not up to the job of murder.'

'He was a spy. All spies know about death.'

Topham smiled. 'Spies come in all shapes and sizes, and levels of competence too. I don't think Mr Rhys was all that competent.'

He went on, 'Then there are the Lazarus League, but they

scattered to the four winds in the panic after your husband's body was found, and we have no way of knowing who they were, or where they are now. Eventually, we'll track them down but looking at who they are, and their dotty nature, they don't figure highly on my list. Any more than does Lamb, too broken-down an old carthorse. Or Mrs Lamb, who it appears never left the kitchen. Nor again the gardener who was with you – he was given a stern interrogation and it's clear he stayed down at the bottom of the garden, a ten-minute walk from here. That leaves one person.'

Permilla Larsson sat bolt upright, her face pale underneath its golden tan.

'Your son, Gus Wetherby.'

'No!'

'Yes, Mrs Larsson, yes. Motive, means and opportunity. An ambitious young man in a big hurry to prove himself – maybe to his real father, maybe to you, maybe to himself, who knows – but not one to waste time climbing to the top of the mountain when he can parachute in.

'He knew the Rejuvenator business was holed below the waterline. He reckoned he could pull a cheap trick by admitting its failings publicly – thus, as you describe it, betraying the man who had brought him up as his own – and by jumping on the publicity bandwagon by coming up with the Youthenator. I repeat, Mrs Larsson, he is *very* ambitious – do you understand what I'm saying?'

Pernilla put her head down and stared at her lap. 'All right,' she said after a long pause, 'all right. I will confess that my son and my husband did not get on well. Ben was forever pushing Gus as he was growing up, whereas a child like that needs to be pulled. When Gus had finished his National Service, which was not a great success, Ben took him into the business, but pretty soon Gus saw the flaws and weaknesses in the Rejuvenator – well, Gus called it "a big con"! I don't know what that means but he did not believe, as Ben believed, in the ability of the Rejuvenator to restore good health.

'And,' she added, sighing, 'Gus was always the kind of child who'd take a clock down from the mantelpiece, pull it apart, and then not bother find out how to put it back together again. There's a lot of that in what he attempted to do with the Rejuvenator. To be honest, I don't believe that his version would be any more effective than Ben's.'

'His stepfather found him out. His plotting. His big plan.'

'Yes. Inspector, I can't tell you how agonising it is to see the two people you love most in the world at each other's throat. Ben did not become so successful by being a patient or forgiving man, and he threw Gus out of the house. I pleaded with him to give the boy another chance, but he was beside himself with rage – his stepson destroying his business the same way he did those dratted clocks!'

'Mr Wetherby wasn't in the house at the time of your husband's death.'

'It's a large house, Inspector, I can't say.'

'Your husband surrounded him with wealth but gave him no money, is that correct?'

'His expenses were paid – tailor, dentist, and so on – but he was expected to work voluntarily until he was made a partner in the business. I have an income of my own, and I used to give him a weekly allowance.'

'Mr Wetherby would have resented that, living in a house like this.'

'He had everything he needed, Inspector.'

'Except independence. He must have hated that.'

'I really couldn't say.'

'So, not only ambitious and – I think we can deduce from the betrayal to Fleet Street – malicious, but resentful and devious. Ready to drug his stepfather and, you might say, rifle the till.'

'That's my son you are talking about!'

'In the matter of murder,' said Topham sadly, 'certain niceties go by the board. And I'm afraid that all you tell me has borne out the deduction I made soon after your husband's murder – that the person who committed the crime was your son.'

'Complete rubbish,' said Pernilla, avoiding his eye and looking nervously out on to the terrace, 'I don't believe you. But if you want to find out the truth, here's your opportunity.

'There's my son. Out there. Go and arrest him – if you dare!'

TWENTY-THREE

'Suki Raffray.'

'I told you never to mention that tart's name!' snapped Geraldine Phipps.

'Sukisuki*sukee*,' warbled her grandson in a falsetto voice. He started to make a calypso of it.

'Oh, Gavin, stop, please stop!' cried the old Gaiety Girl, looking imploringly first at Gavin and then the Plymouth Gin.

'Well, you wanted to know,' said Gavin Armstrong with barely hidden malice. 'And I went and found out for you. Mrs Raff and your Mr Cattermole are holed up in her flat in Chelsea, and she's threatening to make an honest man out of him.'

'At *his* age?' gurgled Mrs Phipps. 'Too late to become honest now. What an absolute stinker!'

'Told you so,' said Gavin happily. 'Time to cut him out of your life, Gran. And while you're at it, isn't it time you made things a little bit easier for yourself? Get out a bit and smell the roses? When did you last have a holiday?'

Mrs Phipps was unused to such solicitude in a man. 'What are you up to, Gavin?'

Her grandson picked up a bottle of beer and forcefully wrenched off its cap. 'This dump,' he said, looking grimly round the theatre's office, 'it's no place for you, Gran. Dirty and depressing.'

'It's home.'

'You can't be serious. It's a run-down old ruin that would benefit from a can of petrol and a box of matches, that's what it is.

'You might say the same about your grandmother.'

'Hah, I might, Granny, I might! But look, you shouldn't be stuck in a hole like this – your glory days were in the West End with stage-door johnnies waiting to take you to Ciro's and the Café Royal. Compare all that to this place – not exactly Berkeley Square, now, is it?'

'What are you saying, Gavin? That I should give up the theatre here, just when we're beginning to make a nice profit?'

'Only because of me, that profit, Gran. Only because I brought Danny and the boys here – against your better judgement – and started to show you how to fill a theatre.' Gavin gulped greedily at his beer, and for the first time Mrs Phipps realised she disliked her grandson, and quite a lot at that.

'Well,' she said firmly, 'if you think I'm giving up the Pavilion you can think again.'

'Time to retire,' said Gavin smoothly, but with an iron edge to his voice. 'You've had your share of the box-office take, but from now on it's all mine. I'm taking the place over – old Ray is never coming back, and the lease is in his name.'

Mrs Phipps put down her gin. At moments of crisis she could do perfectly well without its support, she was remarkable that way. 'No, Gavin, no, this is mine! I've supported Raymond for the past fifteen years and I know every inch of this place. It is *I* who is taking over, not you!'

'Darling, how old are you?' The endearment was not kindly spoken.

'That's neither here nor there. And anyway, I thought you had a – how d'you say – a Number One beat group on your hands – isn't that enough to be going on with?'

'They'll only last a few more records then that'll be it. People are saying the beat craze will be over by Christmas. As entertainers they're not really very talented, y'know.'

'That's where you're wrong. I've watched them, and they know how to galvanise an audience, and whether I like or hate their music, that's what show business is all about – generating excitement. They certainly do that all right. And one of them is remarkably good-looking,' she added.

'They're a rotten bunch. Anyway, come Christmas I plan to be down here full-time.'

Mrs Phipps viewed him with distaste. 'Doing what, precisely? What on earth do you know about entertaining the traditional type of audience we normally attract here in Temple Regis?'

Gavin finished his beer and tossed the bottle aside. 'Oh, for heaven's sake, Granny, don't you get it? Rickety old place like this, an accidentally dropped cigarette, a nice stiff south-westerly to fan the flames – the whole place'd be gone in no time at all. I pick up the insurance and move on. I promise to get out of your hair, and keep out, after that.'

Mrs Phipps looked at him in horror.

'You're just like your father.'

'I take that as a compliment.'

'Before he went to jail, he had everything going for him. Good school, good regiment – well,' she corrected herself, 'it *was* the Life Guards, and they're such a bunch of stinkers I should have known how things would turn out. But the one thing that can be said for him was he socked enough cash away before he was arrested so you could still go to Harrow.'

'Do you ever hear from the old chap?'

'That question rather implies that you don't, Gavin. He's your *father*, for heaven's sake!'

'In Tangier last time I heard. Best place for him, I'd say.'

Mrs Phipps stood up. The crumpled, gin-doused figure had disappeared and in its place there was a straight-backed, clear-eyed, commanding presence. If there was more than a hint of Lady Bracknell about her, well, hadn't she played opposite old Raymond in that production of *The Importance of Being Earnest* where Gerry Hennessy had broken Ray's arm and stolen his part? 'Terrifying' had read the reviews, and they weren't talking about Ray or Gerry.

'Gavin, I can't disinherit you because you never figured in my will. Until very recently I'd seen very little of you – rather like your father,' she added imperiously. 'I was happy to give you a roof and, I will confess, delighted when you brought that band of brigands to fill the empty space left by Raymond.

'This theatre, Gavin, has been part of my life for a long time now and it will continue to be a part of my life. Your idea of setting fire to such a . . .' she searched for a suitable word '. . . *wonderful* and *ancient* landmark simply appals me, and really what I should be doing is telephoning the police to warn them.'

Gavin said he didn't care if she did.

'What I am going to do, though, is something else. I am going to close the theatre as from today and you can take your brigands back to London. Let them make another record and go and bother the good people of some other seaside town.'

'You can't do that, Gran. I've just . . .'

'I can and I will. In fact, I just have.'

'But . . . I've just got Jack Good to agree to come down here! The boys missed out on his TV show, *Oh Boy!*, but he's got a new one starting in the autumn and they could get a residency on it.'

'When this improbably named Mr Good shows up he will find the theatre dark. With you and your cocksure chums stuck outside in that van, because, Gavin, I'm afraid I can no longer offer you a roof.'

You could see the young man swiftly recalibrating. 'OK,' he conceded, 'OK. We'll go back to the arrangement we had before – you get your cut and I get mine. Fifty–fifty.'

'It'll be sixty–forty now. I need to increase the insurance. Just in case.'

Before Gavin could agree, Valentine Waterford poked his head round the door. 'Hello,' he said, not sensing murder in the air, 'just popped in to see how things are going? Thought I'd write something new about the boys. Our readers don't seem to be able to get enough of them!'

This was actually a lie – the residents of Temple Regis were hot under the collar about Danny and the noisemongers, and sincerely wished the boys' van in the sea off the end of the pier. It was the holidaymakers who were mad for the No 1 group – but since they rarely bought the local paper there wasn't much point in writing about beat groups in the *Express*.

But Valentine had been instructed by Rudyard Rhys to find something to draw his readers' attention away from the thing they were far more interested in – the deaths of a beauty queen and a famous magnate – and was determined to find a new angle.

'Hello, Mrs Phipps,' he added solicitously, 'hope you're well?'

'All the better for seeing you, dear boy,' she twinkled happily at this reminder of profligate old Sir Jefrye. How much nicer was this young man than the grandson she'd been burdened with!

'Come outside,' said Gavin curtly, 'there's something I can give you.'

They went out leaving the old trouper to her Player's Navy Cut and her Plymouth Gin, safe in the knowledge she'd seen off an enforced retirement. Slowly, they wandered together down to the theatre auditorium where Danny and the brethren were fiddling with their equipment.

'Here's your story,' said Gavin, 'we're turning the Pavilion into a permanent Pop Palace. Temple Regis will be the first venue in the country to have a rolling rocking menu, seven days a week, twelve months of the year. Beat groups from all over the country will come down here and their fans will come flocking after them– just like Danny and the boys.'

'Heavens,' said Valentine, 'what an extraordinary idea, when everyone is saying beat music is already dead on its feet, it's jazz that's the coming thing! And what will the townsfolk say, d'you think? They seem to have done a good job tolerating the mayhem Danny and the boys have created, but twelve months of the year? How long have you had this up your sleeve?'

'Been working on it for ages,' said Gavin, who'd only just thought it up.

'And what will Mrs Phipps do? She's used to more, er, traditional entertainment I'd say. How's she going to fit in to this new plan?'

'Oh,' said Gavin, 'she's retiring. She'll be gone in the next few weeks.'

'Really?'

'Oh yes, only don't write that just yet. Give her a chance to find the words to make the announcement herself. It'll be an emotional moment for her.'

'I can see that,' said Valentine drily. He liked Mrs Phipps and was slowly getting the gist of what was going on.

'Give me a minute or two, I'm just going to sort something out, then I'll tell you all about the Pop Palace,' said Gavin, who needed to do some quick thinking. 'By the way, which school were you at?'

'Ah, well, one doesn't often talk of schooldays. Rather a long time ago.'

'I was at Harrow,' said Gavin, pugnaciously.

'Since you put it like that, then, I spent a bit of time at the other place.'

'Thought so,' said Gavin triumphantly. 'Can smell you lot a mile away. But you can't have been called Valentine there, it's so effeminate!'

'How perceptive of you,' said Valentine, not in the least moved by the manager's patronising tone. 'Actually, I was called Bart.'

'Eh?' Gavin frowned. 'Why Bart?'

'I haven't the slightest idea.'

Valentine went to sit in the back stalls and watched the band setting up their instruments for the evening performance. He caught the eye of Boots McGuigan – the most photogenic of the lot, even if he had a voice like a foghorn – and signalled to him.

'We're doing a warm-up in ten minutes,' said the bassist, ambling over. 'What do you want?'

'Bengt Larsson.'

'What about him?' The musician looked angry at the mention of the old man's name, but not defensive.

'Why don't you tell me all about it?' This vaguely worded invitation, Valentine had discovered, was a useful journalistic trick when you had absolutely no idea what question you should be putting.

'About my mum?'

Bingo, thought Valentine, this works!

'Yes, your mother,' he said encouragingly. The canary was about to sing, but his notebook was stuck in his pocket and he didn't dare drag it out in case the yellow bird took fright and flew away.

'That bloody machine of his killed her,' said Boots without further encouragement. 'We weren't close, Mum and me, but why the hell should Larsson get away with it? Living in that castle, telling those lies, making money hand over fist while people were dying?'

'Go on,' said Valentine, hoping he would be able to remember all this so he could write it down later.

'There were ten of us in our council house in Hackney. Too many,' said Boots. 'I was moved out when I was twelve to live with my Nan and I didn't see much of them after that. But bringing up all those kids was more than she could manage. She bought one of those Rejuvenators on the never-never. I s'pose she thought it could give her back some life – she was exhausted from the moment she got up to the moment she went to bed – anyway, it killed her. Don't know how, she wasn't electrocuted, it was something to do with her nerves, but it was the Rejuvenator what done it.'

'I'm sorry to hear it,' said Valentine, genuinely.

'We come down here, we're playing to the crowds, hoping to make some money, when Gavin announces he's struck a gold-plated deal with this man Larsson's son.'

'Stepson, I think.'

'I don't care who the hell he is. Apparently they were at school together and the son is making a new version of this machine and selling it to teenagers. We were going to help promote it. Well,' said Boots, 'I was never going to agree to that, was I? What's more, I had no idea that this – what's the word – this *murderer* lived down here in Temple Regis. So I decided to go and sort him out.'

'You went up to the Retreat? How did you manage to get in? Did you hide yourself among those dotty old folk from the Lazarus League?'

'I had to queue outside with them – they're crazy. They truly believed in Larsson, talked of him like he was a god. I started to tell them about my mum but it was as if they were on another planet. Anyway I didn't want to draw attention to myself because I wanted to get inside the house, so I shut up and waited for someone to open the door.'

'You actually got to see Mr Larsson?' Valentine couldn't believe he was about to hear a killer's confession; he agonised over the fact the notebook was still in his pocket.

'Well, no.'

'You *didn't* see Larsson?' Meaning, *you didn't murder him?*

'No. While I was standing in the queue up came Gavin, our manager, and he hoicked me out and told me to push off. He gave me a long lecture about how the Youthenator was going to make a fortune for us all and that I had no business sticking my nose in. He was really angry, angrier than I've ever seen him, so I thought, I can always come another day. I was determined to confront that murderer, face to face.'

'What were you going to do when you did? Kill him?'

'*Kill* him?' said the bassist, looking alarmed. 'What are you talking about? I was going to show him a photograph of my dead mother with the so-called bloody Rejuvenator by her bedside. I wanted him to see what he'd done with his so-called invention, to say sorry. To say sorry, and to mean it. That's all.' His face was ashen and he was near to tears.

It seemed convincing, but it had the effect of destroying Valentine's carefully constructed double-murder theory. He couldn't let it go just yet – what would Miss Dimont say if he did?

'So . . .' he said, choosing his words carefully, 'Faye Addams . . .'

'I thought we were talking about Larsson.'

'When did you last see Faye?'

'Before we all came down here. Faye and me went to the Hackney Empire to see them making *Oh Boy!* because The Urge hoped to get on the show. Marty Wilde, Cliff Richard, the Dallas Boys . . . It's hot stuff, the future of television I can tell you!'

'Did you know Faye was going out with one of The Shadows?'

'Had been. She was out with me now.'

'Do you know someone called Cyril Normandy?'

'Never heard of him. Why?'

'He was the man organising the beauty pageants down here, the ones that Faye went in for.'

'I didn't know his name, but she did tell me what he was doing. She said she'd been promised a win if she quit her job at Selfridges and got on the beauty pageant circuit.'

'Promised a win?'

'It's all a fix, didn't you know?'

This offended Valentine's sense of fair play, but it was hardly the time to be pondering the ethics of making money out of semi-clad women.

'Did you know she was entering Queen of the English Riviera?'

'She didn't say, but then the band was on the road playing gigs here, there and the other place. Quite often we wouldn't see each other for two-three weeks at a time.'

'Was she the kind of girl who . . . ?' Valentine faltered. He was too new at the journalism game to know how to phrase a fundamentally offensive question about a dead person.

'Faye and this man Normandy?' Boots McGuigan was more worldly than Valentine had given him credit for. 'Nah. She said he tried it on but she told him to go fly a kite.'

'Look,' said Valentine, 'I've something terrible to tell you. Will you sit down for a moment?'

Boots narrowed his eyes, as if Valentine was threatening to stab him with a knife. 'What is it?' he said. 'What . . . ?'

'A girl, a beautiful girl, was found dead on a beach five miles away from here. She had been killed. Nobody knew who she was, we're not sure even yet, but almost certainly it was Miss Addams.'

'I knew it!' cried Boots, throwing his arms around his chest and clutching himself tight.

'You knew it? *How did you know?*'

'I knew she'd leave me. She only stayed because I asked her to marry me – she didn't care who she married, as long as he was rich! I knew she wouldn't stay in my life! Dead? Oh my God!'

This was not the confession of a killer. Or was it? The Urge put on a tremendous show when performing – none of them was like his stage persona in real life – was Boots putting on a huge act now? Valentine tested the water gently, telling the guitarist about how Faye was found, the story in the newspaper, the missing persons broadcast on the radio. The hopeless inquest.

'I only listen to music on the radio. The only newspaper I

get is *Melody Maker*. And the only inquest I heard about was Larsson's.'

'You see,' said Valentine, still trying to gauge Boots' reaction, 'you appear to be the link between two dead people – Ben Larsson and Faye Addams. You were up at the Retreat at the time Larsson died and Faye . . . er—' here his logic started to falter '—Faye was your fiancée.'

Boots' eyes looked wide with grief. 'How much do they pay you on this local rag of yours?'

'Not very much.'

'Pay peanuts, you get monkeys,' Boots said in a voice packed with emotion. 'Are you honestly trying to tell me these two deaths are connected, and that somehow *I'm* the link? Are you saying somehow *I* killed them both?' His voice started to climb as he rose out of his seat. The other members of the band down at the stage end of the auditorium stopped what they were doing and stared.

'Well, not exactly,' said Valentine, fumbling for words and the thoughts to support them. 'But you see the link,' he ended lamely.

'Look,' said Boots, 'Faye and me was an item. Solid. She was the best-looking girl I'd ever had, but I wasn't allowed to have girlfriends, it would kill the sex appeal of the group stone dead.

'OK, I'd asked her to marry me – you can't print that! – but the last few months we only saw each other from time to time because I was on the road with The Urge. But I'd got worried because I hadn't heard from her like she promised, and so I telephoned her mum. She told me Faye had come down to do this English Riviera circuit so she could be with me during the summer season.

'And so she did,' he said soulfully, 'so she did. Maybe she wanted to marry me more than I thought.'

'I'm sure she did,' said Valentine soothingly.

'But it would never have worked with her down here. Gavin has us cooped up in that van day and night – he wouldn't let her near the place. He warned us all with the sack if any of us got hooked up with a girl. "Look at Marty Wilde," he used to say. "Britain's top pop idol. Marries his girlfriend, career's killed stone dead. Overnight." Gavin threatens us all the time like that.'

'You could have rented a cottage. There are plenty down here in out-of-the-way places.'

'He's got all our money. It's in a special account, we'll get it when we get back to London.'

I wonder if you will, thought Valentine. He went on, without much hope, 'So you last saw Faye when?'

'End of May.'

'You planned to meet up again when?'

'She told me she'd send me a telegram when she knew where she was going to be. It never came.'

Well, bang goes my theory, thought Valentine. 'Let's just go back to your visit to the Retreat.'

'Look, we're going round the houses now. I've got a new number to rehearse.' Valentine could see he wanted to get away and put the hurt from him with music and noise and distraction.

'Just one last thing,' called the reporter desperately. 'Gavin Armstrong sent you back to the Pavilion after he winkled you out of the queue with the Lazarus lot.'

'I already said that.'

'Did he come back with you?'

'No.'

'What did he do then?'

'Went in with the Lazarus lot, as you call them.'

Good heavens, thought Valentine. Never thought of *that* as a possibility.

TWENTY-FOUR

His years in the desert had strengthened and shaped Frank Topham, and if perhaps he'd once been a better soldier than he was now a policeman, that did not take away from his integrity and his determination that things which were wrong in the world should be put right.

'Sit down,' he said, coldly.

A supercilious Gus Wetherby looked down from where he stood on the terrace steps. 'No thanks.'

'I'd like you to sit down so that we can talk. This is official business, not a social cup of tea.'

Gus stuck his hands deep into the pockets of his white cricket flannels and looked down his nose at the policeman.

'This is my house,' he drawled, 'I'll do what I like.'

Topham's instinct was to get up and shout in Wetherby's face. He knew the words to cower supercilious brats, had learned them on the parade ground, but his police training taught him that bellowing at suspects does not always bring the most useful result.

'Then *I* shall stand,' he said, and did so, very slowly. He was a good head and shoulders taller, and the two men eyed each other warily – the younger, believing himself to be of officer class, attempting to pull rank. The other, with the law on his side, impervious to this innate snobbery, was nettled by it all the same.

'Oh, stop behaving like dogs waiting to attack each other,' said Pernilla crossly. 'Come and sit down, both of you!'

Reluctantly, they obliged. Topham picked up his notebook, more for show than anything else, and started his questioning.

'You disliked your stepfather and you plotted against him.'

'No.'

'You were to benefit by his death on two counts – one, because you could distance yourself from his invention, while the publicity caused by his death after all that press criticism would bring the spotlight favourably on to your Youthenator. Two, because you were the ultimate beneficiary of his very considerable estate.

'There's the motive,' said Topham emphatically, 'plain and simple. And then you had the means so readily to hand – you knew the inner workings of the Rejuvenator, you knew how to alter the rheostat so that when it switched on it would spark a fatal electric charge.'

'Complete rubbish,' said Gus easily, crossing his legs and reaching for a table lighter.

'You had the opportunity,' Topham soldiered on, 'you were in the house when there were a lot of other people milling around. There was Mr Rhys from the local paper having a row with your stepfather, there was Mrs Larsson popping her head round the door, there was the manservant Lamb fussing about the place – plenty of time to get into the study and alter the machine.'

'You're talking through your hat, Inspector. I wasn't even there.'

'Motive, means and opportunity. Of all the people who might wish to see an end to your stepfather's life, name me one other who . . .'

Gus Wetherby smiled. 'Lamb. He'd been caught out selling stories about Ben to the newspapers, plus he'd been discovered putting something in Ben's coffee.'

He raised his hand and counted off his fingers. 'Then there's my mother. She and Ben weren't getting on particularly well. This *Daily Herald* business – she challenged him, told him he must stop selling the Rejuvenator before it killed any more . . .'

'GUS!' shrieked Pernilla. 'Are you trying to imply *I* killed Ben?'

'Could have done,' came the insouciant reply.

'Gus, I am your *mother*!'

'Married to a murderer, Mum. Maybe you felt he'd done enough and it was time to stop him. You knew as well as I did how that Rejuvenator worked. How difficult would it be for you to recalibrate it? All done in a matter of moments.'

Pernilla Larsson burst into tears. They washed down her face, irrigating its perfect make-up, but her son remained unmoved by the sight. 'You helped me,' he went on ruthlessly, 'and if there was a plot, you were part of it – you'd told me you couldn't bear to hear any more about the Rejuvenator deaths, you wanted my Youthenator to take over and save the family reputation. You colluded in putting sedatives in his coffee to give me the breathing space to be able to perfect the Youthenator. And then you said you'd take Ben off to Argentina so I had a clear field to issue a statement which would say the Rejuvenator had been withdrawn, and a new and radically better model was taking its place.'

Wetherby seemed settled and in his element. 'You knew Ben wouldn't buy that. You knew he had to be stopped somehow. And, Mum, you're soft on your one-and-only Gus, aren't you? You'd do anything for him, now wouldn't you, darling?'

Mrs Larsson was beside herself. 'After all I've done for you,' she sobbed. 'Protecting you from your stepfather, giving you money when he wouldn't. Getting you into the family business so that you could eventually take over. And then . . . and then . . . you say *I killed Ben*! He may not have been particularly kind to you, but then why should he? You were never particularly kind to him, were you?'

She dabbed at her tears with a flimsy handkerchief. 'He was

lovely to me, kindness always. I adored your stepfather, I looked up to him. If I encouraged you with your invention it was because I wanted to save his reputation before it was shattered by those animals in Fleet Street.'

She turned to Topham, eyes wide. 'There was no plot, Inspector. Just a wife who wanted to protect her husband. And,' she added bitterly, 'a son who, it turns out, hated his stepfather far more than his mother had cause to know or understand.'

Topham looked at them both. Experience told him that, left to their own devices, those closest to the seat of a crime will often squabble among themselves to the point where a shaft of light emerges, pointing directly at the true culprit. He felt they were reaching that important moment.

He turned to Wetherby, who looked not the slightest bit unsettled by his mother's outburst.

'We seem to have run through the suspects,' Topham said slowly, 'and despite what you say you're still the one who . . .'

'All right, all right!' snapped Wetherby. 'If we're getting serious about this, what about that man Rudyard Rhys? You know perfectly well he had a violent row with my stepfather just before his death.'

'Wouldn't hurt a fly. Would have forgotten where he'd parked the fly-swatter.'

'Lamb.'

'Too drunk to think in a straight line.'

'That Lazarus lot.'

'Oh, come ON!' barked Topham. 'That's enough of this silly nonsense. I've been patient long enough! This is a very grave matter, and I have the responsibility of finding and arresting the person who murdered Bengt Larsson. I've given you every opportunity to clear yourself, but – really – the circumstantial evidence points to one person, and one person only.

'As a result,' he said, standing up, 'Augustus Wetherby, I am arresting you for the murder of Bengt Larsson. Anything you say will be . . .'

'Just a minute, just a minute,' said Gus, lolling back on the sofa cushions, eyes flicking. 'You failed to ask me one very important question, Inspector.'

'What's that?' said Topham suspiciously.

'Where was I at the moment my stepfather died? *Where . . . was . . . I?*'

Topham waited impatiently. 'Well?' he barked.

'I wasn't here, Inspector, I wasn't here,' crowed Wetherby, 'and what's more, I can prove it!'

*

The seagulls were gossiping on the roof, no doubt exchanging vital information about where the best day's fishing was to be had or, more likely, who'd left their dustbin lid off down the street. Out in the kitchen, Valentine was wrestling with the rudiments of supper while his chief reporter wandered about with a gin and tonic in hand.

'So how did you come by this place, Valentine?'

'I told you, relation of mine.'

'As yes, the Waterfords. Large family.'

'Just so. Erm, look, you couldn't help me with this casserole, Judy? I don't quite seem to have got the hang . . .'

Miss Dimont smiled serenely at her junior. 'Just carry on, Valentine, I'm sure it'll be delicious.' She had no intention of sharing the blame for the culinary disaster which lay ahead.

'It's just not my line of country. In the Army they did the cooking for you.'

'Then what you need is lots more practice.'

She continued her inspection of the cottage; it was clear that Valentine's idea of making it into a home was to stuff the mantelpiece with photographs and a surprisingly large number of engraved invitation cards, but little more.

'You seem to be enormously popular.'

There was a muffled noise coming from the kitchen. He put his head round the door, blond hair in disarray. 'The invitations? Mostly from people I don't know, I think it's because they like writing my title.' Indeed, the heavy pieces of pasteboard summoning him to drinks and dances and dinners all carried his full due: 'Sir Valentine Waterford, Bart.' as if he were some ancient tweed-suited grandee instead of an ill-clad junior reporter making a dog's breakfast of a supper in the cramped kitchen of a borrowed cottage.

'Most impressive,' said Judy, though he couldn't be sure she meant it. 'And these photographs? This is your mother?' An elegant fowl with diamonds aplenty stared out of the picture with a chilly expression on her beautiful face.

Valentine had obviously given up the struggle in the kitchen and came to join her with a glass in his hand. 'Merely a reminder,' he said distantly, 'I haven't seen her for years.'

'And this?' A not dissimilar face, wreathed in smiles, animated and interested.

'My Aunt Baxter. She brought me up.'

'And this?' A crenellated edifice looking as though its better days had been many centuries ago.

'Lovelocke. The old place. We don't own it any more – it went at about the same time as my short trousers did.'

'How's the supper coming along?'

'I think you'll be quite thrilled by my culinary skills.'

'Will I?' said Judy, and smiled at him. He really was very handsome.

'Are we going to talk about this murder tomfoolery, or are we awaiting Miss Hedley before we get stuck in?' asked Valentine. He suddenly seemed a trifle nervous.

'She'll be along in a quarter of an hour; I looked in on my way here. She had to wait for a delivery.'

'Good. Have another?'

'No thank you, Valentine.'

'Well, I will, there's something I wanted to tell you.' He disappeared into the kitchen and came back with an over-full glass.

'Look,' he said, 'I don't know quite how to say this but . . .'

Miss Dimont caught the look in his eye. 'Then, Valentine, don't say it.'

'I will, I will.' He took a slug of whisky and she wondered for a moment if it was neat. 'What I'm trying to say . . .'

'I know what you're trying to say,' said Judy. 'And it is very flattering, *Sir* Valentine. But please don't.'

'Let me put it in the abstract then,' he went on determinedly. 'Young chap grows up, lonely life, not much love about the place, if any. Wonderful aunt takes him in and makes life fun, but still, because of the unusual circs perhaps, he still feels very lonely. Chap tries to counteract it by going into the Army and being amongst the jolly chaps. It works, up to a point, but not really – the moment he comes out, it's the same as before. Something terribly missing.

'Then he goes somewhere – somewhere a bit like this, actually.' He looked at her with his grey eyes and smiled. 'And then everything's suddenly all right. In fact, not all right, but amazing.'

'The sea air down here does wonders.'

'It certainly does. But not only that – not *even* that. Chap suddenly finds the most remarkable person he has ever encountered – someone so dazzlingly gifted, and brave, and clever. And beautiful.'

'Valentine.'

'No, I will say it. Judy – Huguette – I've fallen in love with you.'

'No you haven't.'

'I really have. *Really* I have. I can't begin to tell you . . .'

'Then don't. Let's talk about something else. The detection of murder. Assisting aged police officers across the street. That's what we should be concentrating on.'

'May I kiss you?'

'You may not.'

'I must.'

'No, Valentine, no! And if you want to carry on working with me, don't ask again. Now what are we going to discuss with Auriol?'

'Let me tell you about Boots McGuigan.' He was not in the slightest dismayed. 'Darling . . .'

They were talking about McGuigan's links to both Larsson and Faye Addams when Auriol slipped in: 'Door was open, hello, Valentine!'

'Wasn't the Boots man,' said Judy to Auriol, over Valentine's shoulder.

'Whoever thought it was?' Auriol was irritating like that, she always seemed to imply in retrospect that she was right, even if she hadn't ever voiced aloud her thoughts. Clearly, only an idiot could ever have entertained the idea that McGuigan was a murderer.

All three agreed to draw a veil over the supper which followed but then such occasions are not only about food; the wine and conversation anchored them to the small pine table long after the memory of Valentine's *Spag Bol à la Waterford*, an emergency replacement for the abandoned casserole, had evaporated. As Judy made the coffee Auriol interested herself in the host's social life.

'All these invitations on your mantelpiece – they're from London and the Home Counties. Do they expect you to drive up there every other day of the week?'

'They just like to have my name on the invitation list.'

'I expect they'd probably like you to pop along and propose marriage to one of their daughters,' said Auriol shrewdly.

'I expect so,' sighed Valentine. 'That's why I don't go. Though I'm tagging along to one tomorrow, it's only up the road in Gloucestershire. One of my cousins is . . .'

'Ah yes,' sang Judy, bearing in the coffee pot and a collection of cracked china. 'The Waterfords. Big family.'

'In that tiny little bubble car?' asked Auriol.

'Only two or three hours if you put your foot down.'

The talk, which had circled around the two murders, turned to the future of Rudyard Rhys.

'Can't see how he can go on at the *Express*,' said Auriol. 'Honestly, Hugue, he is *so* incompetent. And dictatorial. And the decisions he takes – when he takes them, that is – always the wrong ones!'

'I don't know,' said Miss Dimont, kindly, 'I've got used to it.'

'You'd make a much better editor,' said Valentine. 'Clear-sighted is what you are. I had a captain in the Army just like that – always knew which way to jump in an emergency – one learns so much by example.'

'Have you been learning, by example, from Hugue?' asked Auriol, teasingly.

'A great deal,' said the young man, his gaze lingering a little too long on his chief reporter. It was not lost on the other guest.

Just then the telephone rang and Valentine went off to answer it.

'Hugue, I do believe that boy's in love with you.'

'Yes,' sighed Miss Dimont, 'he certainly thinks he is.'

'Same thing then.'

'Not quite sure what to do about it,' said Judy. 'Going to be difficult in the office if he keeps up this sort of thing.'

'Banish him to the backwoods, then, if you're not going to take him home. The air in Newton Abbot is magnificent at this time of year, I believe.'

'What a cruel thought. Anyway it's not a decision I can take. That's up to Mr Rhys.'

'He *is* awfully sweet.'

'He's a child, Auriol. I'm nearly fifty and he's still talking about short trousers.'

'And very handsome.'

'Look,' said Judy, lowering her voice. 'Of course he is. Of *course!* But, Auriol, doesn't he remind you of someone? Doesn't he remind you of Eric?'

'My brother didn't have hair like that.'

'For heaven's sake! Look at him – he's got the same questing spirit, the same untamed intelligence, the same sort of courage and devil-may-care that Eric had . . . When I sat at home the other night with Mulligatawny, I was looking up at Eric's photo on the mantelpiece, and just for a moment I saw the face of this young man.'

'Ah,' said Auriol, and wrinkled her eyes at her friend.

'No, Auriol, no! I have the power to resist – besides, think how foolish the whole thing would be. Furthermore,' she added, not quite sure how far to go in sharing her secrets with dead Eric's sister, 'I've rather taken a shine to someone.'

'Really?'

'The captain of a trawler. I know,' she added hastily, 'not what you might expect, but he *is* rather magnificent in his way.'

Auriol was far more intrigued by the boy and his unusual love, though, and the conversation passed quickly on.

TWENTY-FIVE

The vestry of St Margaret's looked particularly dreary with the sun shining through its lattice windows, casting shadows on the unswept floor and highlighting the choir's threadbare surplices. Next door, the chancel was alive with colour, its brass and silver and oak shining transcendently, but the back room was a place of gloom scented by old peppermints and floor wax.

The people gathered around the small oak table looked as dingy as their surroundings yet, if you were to believe the newspapers, they were the flower of Devon's youth, the most beauteous creatures God's own county had ever created. They hunched moodily over their cups of tea and sucked biscuits.

'So just remember,' ordered Cyril Normandy, lighting up a fat cigar which somehow seemed sacrilegious in the present surroundings, 'no more talking to the press. And if the police come sniffing around, you refer them to me. This is just an isolated incident of no real importance and . . .'

'Go on, Cyril, you'll be saying that Adolf Hitler was a lovely fellow next,' chipped in Molly Churchstow. 'For heaven's sake! She may not have been one of us, but that girl Faye was a human being after all. She deserves a bit more respect than that.'

Normandy didn't even look at her but addressed the small group with his arms held wide. 'What do we care about?' he asked genially, 'what do we *really* care about? Do we want to become queen of this jolly old Riviera with a chance to move on to the semi-finals of Miss Great Britain? Or do we want to sit around here moping about a poor girl who met with an unfortunate accident? Telling tales and causing trouble – really! The show must go on!'

'Not exactly an accident, was it, Mr Normandy?' said Eve Berry, who normally watched her ps and qs. 'She was *murdered*. Who's to say one of us here won't be next? You read all the time about these men with a yen for dead blondes.'

'Well, *you* should be safe then,' mocked Normandy, pointing at the dark roots emerging from Eve's scalp. 'Not quite the flaxen filly today, Eve!'

The reigning Miss Exmouth blushed angrily but said no more.

'Look,' said Normandy, 'we have no idea who killed Faye or why. It was just a . . .' he struggled to find the word '. . . a random attack. Some nutcase! She was probably taking a stroll on the beach when . . .'

'Expensive girl like that only strolls down Bond Street,' snapped Molly, who might know Paignton Beach well but would need a map to find her way round Mayfair. 'Strolling? On that beach? In a dress? I don't think so!'

Cyril Normandy didn't like his girls to think, they were there to ease a sore eye or two and to make him bundles of cash, nothing more. 'Shut up, Molly,' he barked. 'You don't know what you're talking about. You hardly knew the girl.'

'Ah, but *you* did, didn't you, Mr Normandy?'

'What's that supposed to mean?'

'I saw you and her. I saw you when you—'

'Shut up!' snapped Normandy. 'You saw nothing of the kind. You say anything more like that and I'll kick you out of the pageant – there are a million girls, you know, ready and willing to take your place.'

'Not a million girls with ones like *these*.' She gave a sardonic smile and stuck out her chest. 'That's why you always put me at the front in the publicity pictures, isn't it, Mr Normandy?'

The other girls looked sour and stared into their teacups. They weren't being paid to be here, why were they wasting their time?

'I've called you here because I've decided there's going to be an extra heat in the competition,' announced Cyril. 'We need to budge people's imaginations away from Faye Addams. I'm going to call it the Goddess of the Riviera, and you can all be here next Saturday.'

'Expenses?' came the chorus.

'Double expenses,' said Cyril magnificently, and re-lit his fat cigar. 'Let's just remind everybody how beautiful Devon girls can be.'

'And forget about how Faye was fixed up to win the next round,' whispered Molly.

The girls were getting restless. Their attention span was short and Normandy had made his point – keep your traps shut, keep smiling. He got up from the table, brushing cigar ash from his shirt front, and the queens, there being no servants or footmen around to do it for them, picked up the cups and took them over to the sink.

'I'll have a word with you, Molly,' said Normandy menacingly. She knew he wanted to talk about her seeing him pawing Faye Addams.

'I'm off now,' she said, skipping towards the vestry door. 'Got to get the bus back to work.'

As she reached for the heavy iron handle it turned, and the door opened.

'Ah,' said a commanding voice from outside, 'just in time. Would you all mind resuming your seats?'

''Oo the ell are you?' demanded Normandy.

'I think we've met, Mr Normandy, the name's Judy Dimont, chief reporter of the *Riviera Express*.'

The impresario eyed the new arrival up and down. She was clearly not his kind of woman: wrong age, wrong hair colour, haphazardly dressed and buzzing with a visible intelligence. He disliked her on sight.

'This is a private meeting. Would you mind making an appointment with my secretary? We're here to discuss strategy and that is not a matter for the public prints.'

'Come off it, Mr Normandy,' said Judy in jollying fashion, 'it's just you and this group of nice young ladies having a cup of tea. Don't you want me to write anything nice about Miss English Riviera?'

'All publicity is most welcome,' said Normandy quickly, for though he was rattled by the interruption he knew on which side his bread was buttered. The *Express* had been lavish in its spreads and layouts and hadn't the editor been ever so accommodating in agreeing not to mention Faye Addams' name in connection with the pageant? Though, of course, thanks to these stupid girls it had got out anyway.

'I know Mr Rhys,' said Normandy in patronising tones, 'your *editor*.' Meaning, *Push off or I'll telephone him*.

'So do I,' Judy replied, smiling sweetly – meaning, *That won't save you from what's coming next*.

'What d'you want?'

'I'm glad to find you all here because I'm writing a big feature about the future of beauty pageants, in the light of the attack in Paignton and the murder of one of your contestants.'

This caught the attention of the gathered beauty queens – anything that was written about them was of interest, especially if accompanied by a photograph they could cut out and keep.

'These girls are all pretty shy, they don't like talking to the press. They're busy people, they've all got appointments, so shortly I shall be letting them get along. You can get all you need from me.' Normandy smelt danger in a newspaper feature about dead beauty queens.

'Ladies, are you in a hurry?' asked Judy sweetly. She was gratified by their happy demur.

'I'd like to ask you some questions, Mr Normandy, but let the girls speak first.' Their combined majesties nodded approval and the fat man sat down in disgust. Showing a united front was good for business and he couldn't be seen publicly to be bullying his girls, no matter what happened in private.

'Ladies, tell me first, do any of you know Boots McGuigan, one of the beat group playing at the Pavilion?'

'Of course we do,' said Eve. 'By reputation anyway. Faye's boyfriend.'

'Did any of you ever see him? Did he come to any of the heats?'

Like a wheat field being tossed by a sou'westerly there was a gentle shaking of blonde tresses. With only a few more questions, Miss Dimont had established what she needed to know: that the musician had never been seen in Faye's company, and his claim that he did not know his sweetheart had arrived in Temple Regis seemed to stand up. Faye had spent all her time since her arrival in town in the company of the other girls and, as Molly did not hesitate to point out, Cyril Normandy.

'Was she a special friend, Mr Normandy?'

The fat man did not like having his impartiality questioned. 'She was a contestant like all these girls,' he huffed.

'Not quite,' said Molly defiantly. The other girls' eyes widened.

'What do you mean?'

'My dad's a greengrocer,' said Molly. 'He don't stand in the shop pawing the fruit.'

'Shuddup,' snapped Normandy.

'But Mr Normandy doesn't mind 'elpin' himself to a peach when he wants one,' continued Molly. 'He don't bother with us girls, but this fancy piece he brought down from London, that was different.'

The queens were appalled by their friend's candour. Molly was rapidly talking her way out of any further participation in the pageant – there would be plenty of candidates ready to take her place. That was always the threat, that was why they did all this for no money and for pitiful expenses – they were on the very brink of fame, and they were paying the price by making Normandy rich and themselves even poorer.

'Yes,' said Molly, her bridges burning magnificently, 'he had a bite or two of that peach, believe you me! And I shouldn't wonder that he told her she'd win the Riviera crown and go on to Miss Great Britain. Yes, maybe Miss World, who knows? He's a nasty one, that!'

Normandy, so powerful when left in sole charge of his hen coop, suddenly seemed completely deflated. Even if only temporarily, his girls had shifted their allegiance to this dumpy-looking reporter in her trench coat and glasses, and the game was up: there were too many secrets the girls knew. He could only hope they'd remember in time on which side their bread was buttered.

'I think you have just resigned your title of Miss Paignton, have you not, Molly?' he hissed, but the queen of that ancient place of pleasure wasn't listening.

'I saw them in the changing room,' she went on to Miss Dimont. 'They'd obviously had a row, don't know what about. But she told him – I heard her say it – "You wait till I get back to London, I've got a friend who's a reporter."'

'Did she say that?' said Miss Dimont sharply to Normandy.

'What if she did? That's private,' huffed the fat man.

'He was really mad and he was threatening her,' went on Molly resolutely, 'like the bully he is.' The other girls couldn't believe how foolhardy she'd suddenly become. 'And I'll say this now – when I heard she was dead I thought, well old Normandy won't mind. Whatever trouble she was going to bring 'im ain't going to happen now.'

'What are you saying?' asked Miss Dimont, pushing her glasses up her nose.

'Look at 'im! 'E's not a very nice man! 'E's a cheat and a fraud and these pageants are all a fix. 'E drinks champagne and drives round in a huge car and 'e doesn't give a damn about us. If Faye Addams was going to the newspapers to say that he'd make her the Riviera Queen in return for a little what-ya-ma-call-it, I wouldn't put it past 'im to get rid of 'er. I wouldn't! There!'

Flushed with triumph she stared at Cyril Normandy. 'You're evil, you, you're a user. Look at us all here! We're practically starving and you're drinking champagne!'

'I've promised you double expenses, what more do you want?'

'A kind heart!' cried Molly with passion and the others, still bewildered, murmured their assent. Eve Berry burst into tears.

'You killed her?' said Miss Dimont, turning to face the accused. Normally, her questions would be less direct, more forensic, more detailed, but a sixth sense told her when to pounce.

Normandy looked as if the air had been pushed out of him. His strength lay in his being on top – once he became the underdog, he was weak and confused. The girls knew too much and he'd only bought their silence by the promise of fame; now they were turning against him, he was stripped of his armour and there was nothing left to save him.

'Of . . . course . . . I . . . didn't . . . kill . . . her,' he wheezed. 'Look at me. Do I look like the kind of person to kill anything?'

'Anybody can kill,' said Miss Dimont, unrelenting, 'if the circumstances demand it. If they're desperate enough, if there are enough secrets there, if enough bad deeds have been done – yes, they can kill. Did you? Did you kill Faye Addams?'

Normandy took out a handkerchief and wiped his eyes. He senses, thought Miss Dimont, that this is the end – that his beauty pageant business is over, that his money-making machine has churned out its final pound note.

'How could I? I'm not a strong man, I have a weak heart. I heard from the police that someone put her in a boat and took the body round to that beach – I've never been in a boat in my life. Lifting a body and dumping it in the sand? Look at me!'

And with that he limped out – the girls knew where. He always kept a flask of brandy in the glove compartment for moments when he, or his lady companion, was in need of a restorative.

The queens, sensing she knew more than they, gathered round Miss Dimont. Eve Berry spoke for them all when she said: 'So, do you know who killed Faye?'

'I think I do,' said Miss Dimont. 'But I need to be clearer about some other things before I finally make up my mind. And you can help.'

This was more exciting even than being told they could have double expenses and a free pair of nylons.

'When there was that fracas at Paignton,' she started, 'what actually happened?'

'Those Sisters of Treason?' asked Molly brightly. 'What a hopeless bunch! Honestly, they couldn't organise a . . .'

'Did any of them look violent? Try to remember, this is important.'

Eve Berry thought about it. 'It was like they were back at school being forced to cheer on the hockey team,' she said. 'They came in, looked around, then started chanting away, but you could tell their heart wasn't in it. There was a mannish-looking woman at the back pushing them forward to get between us contestants and the crowd sitting by the pool, but they didn't want to do it. Weedy-looking lot.'

'Yes,' said Molly gathering together her memories of the day which were still surprisingly clear. 'There was one of them called Valerie who tripped over and started crying. The others forgot they were supposed to be protesting and gathered round to help her. Then there was a woman called Ann something who raced over to where Mr Normandy was standing and I thought she was going to grab the microphone, but when she got there, it looked like she'd forgotten what she was supposed to do. It was pretty comical really.'

'And it got the crowd on our side,' agreed Eve. 'There were a few boos and catcalls, and some men said some very nasty things about the protestors preferring women, y'know. Just what they *would* say,' she added.

'That one at the back, though,' said Molly, and raised her eyebrows. The others nodded.

'I think you must be talking about Ursula Guedella,' said Miss Dimont. 'She's rather famous, you know.'

'Has she been to jail? She'd like that!' asked one of the queens pointedly, and the others laughed.

'Seriously,' said Miss Dimont, 'did any of you get a close look at how she was behaving?'

'I did,' said one of the young women. 'I was late getting onto the stand and got caught behind them and I was standing right next to her. It looked to me like she was goading them on, like you do at school when two people start a fight – but she stood well back, she didn't want to be part of the pushing and shoving, More a sort of "do as I say" rather than "do as I do" type. Shouted a lot but kept well back herself.'

'Mm,' said Miss Dimont. 'You know these people have a good cause – they don't want ladies like you being exploited by people like Normandy.'

'Yeah, but they don't want us to have fun, either,' said Molly.

'That's as maybe. But none of you was frightened by the protest, you didn't sense they wanted to do you any harm?'

'When they burst in it was frightening,' said Eve, 'but I think they were so surprised they'd managed to get that far they didn't know what to do next.'

'Mm,' said Judy again. 'So we can pretty well discount Ursula and the Sisters from Faye's murder – none of them had the guts to do it. I think your Mr Normandy has talked himself out of the list of suspects. And Boots McGuigan apparently didn't even know Faye was down here.

'There are no other suspects,' she said, as she viewed the assembled pulchritude before her.

'It looks as if Faye Addams must have been killed by a ghost.'

TWENTY-SIX

The two faceless men who never seemed to be far from Frank Topham's side were standing very close to Gus Wetherby as the Inspector enumerated the reasons why the young man should be detained while further investigations continued. Wetherby smirked and started to light a cigarette before both cigarette and lighter were brusquely whipped away.

'I think you'll find where you're going is not quite so comfortable as here,' said Topham unkindly. It wasn't part of accepted police procedure to describe the privations of being detained, but he hadn't liked Wetherby's supercilious tone.

'*This is the army, Mr Jones,*' he half-sang the old song, '*no private rooms or telephones. You've had your breakfast in bed before, but you won't have it there any more.*'

Wetherby looked grim. 'A big mistake you're making,' he said stonily. 'I've given you my alibi. My lawyer...'

'I've already told you,' said Topham, 'I don't believe you, and I'm not going to give you the chance to skip the country.'

'Wrongful arrest,' snapped Wetherby. 'It's shameful! This is my stepfather we're talking about! Me? *Kill* him?'

'Precisely,' said Topham crisply. 'Take him away.'

Pernilla Larsson was sitting on a sofa underneath a small painting by Degas, her husband's prize possession; the blue of the dancers' dresses almost matched that of her eyes. 'I don't know what to do,' she said inconsolably as her son was led away. 'My husband gone, and now you're taking my son.'

'It's a well-worn old saying, but justice has to be done,' said Topham. 'However painful.' He looked down, not unkindly. 'If what he says is true, he'll be back later today. I'm not a cruel man, Mrs Larsson.'

She did not reply immediately. Then: 'I suppose I should tell you, Inspector. It can't go on like this.'

Topham sat down. 'Yes, madam,' he said gently.

'We had reached a crisis, Ben and I. The problem with the Rejuvenator was far worse than I told you – we'd started to get legal letters, and from some quite prominent people. It would be fair to say that in a week or two – certainly before too long – the whole thing would have blown wide open. Writs, court cases, accusations of murder.'

'Murder?' prompted Topham.

'That piece in the *Daily Herald* started the avalanche. People suddenly realised that the Rejuvenator, which may have had some virtues, was not what they thought. My husband had got carried away by it – he was just a chemist, you know, when he invented it, no great future ahead of him. Then suddenly, this huge crest of a wave just before the war, everybody wanting relief from their ills, both physical and imagined.

'The book he wrote – *A New Electronic Theory of Life* – just seemed to add to the momentum. And it made him very rich. But he was a prickly man and could not bear any criticism – so when people complained he shut it out.'

'I see.'

'Now, finally, in those last few days, he woke up to what was coming. That's when he received a call from that man Rhys – the editor chap – and Ben told Rhys he was going to make public his part in Operation Tailcoat. A kind of plea-bargain, do you see, to try to win some public support before the guillotine dropped.'

'I gather Mr Rhys was forced to remind him of the Official Secrets Act.'

'He did more than that, Inspector. Ben told me Rhys blackmailed him out of going public because he'd be arrested if he did. What he didn't tell me – but Rhys explained after Ben died – was that my husband wasn't quite such a war hero after all. That actually it was Ben's handling of the agents in Berlin that went wrong and lost them their lives, not Rhys's.

'Rhys covered for him then, and took the blame on himself. Very gallant he seems to have been – I have no idea why. He wasn't trying to cover his own back when he shut Ben up, he was trying to stop Tailcoat from being re-examined because it could only bring more anger and criticism on my husband. Rhys liked Ben, rather admired him, and all was forgiven when the war ended. He used to come up here quite often for a drink and was quite friendly. I honestly think he was trying to help, but it ended up in a terrible fight between them – I think because Ben wouldn't see reason.'

'What are you saying, Mrs Larsson?' asked Topham slowly.

'I think Ben killed himself.'

'Do you?'

'Yes, I do. He was proud, defiant, king of the hill. He had made his name and made his fortune, and left his mark on the landscape. His proudest day was when he was included in *Who's Who*. And so, Inspector, like all self-made men, he saw himself as being perhaps bigger than he was. All this—' she waved her arm elegantly '—he couldn't quite believe he'd acquired all this from a little box he invented in his bedroom in Hull.

'But having climbed to the top of the hill, he was not about to be pushed down. He was too proud, Inspector, too proud. I think in the end he couldn't bear the shame of it all so he killed himself.'

'You're not saying all this because we have your son in custody?' Topham was no fool.

'Of course not! It's what I truly believe!'

'I wonder if you do. You loved two men who sadly did not love each other. You've lost one, you don't want to lose the other. That's understandable.'

Pernilla Larsson looked away.

'Your son killed your husband, Mrs Larsson. I know that to be true.'

The blue eyes filled with tears. 'Don't take him away from me, please,' she whispered. 'Take anything, but don't take him . . .'

'His alibi may stand up, though I doubt it. If it does, like I say, he'll be home this afternoon. But I think you must prepare yourself for the alternative. Do you have someone who can come in and be with you?'

There was a blank look on Mrs Larsson's face. 'I don't really have a lot of . . . you know I lived only for Ben . . . and of course Gus . . . perhaps Mrs Lamb would come in.'

'I thought you'd fired the Lambs.'

'Oh, yes,' she said. She'd forgotten. 'Gus did. But if Gus is to . . . then maybe she'll be kind and come back, just for a little while . . .'

*

Miss Dimont and Auriol Hedley sat on a bench watching two motorboats chase each other, churning up white foam from the indigo water. The promenade was quite busy, it being Saturday morning, with children wafting by on their scooters and the occasional cyclist weaving their way slowly towards the bandstand. The two women had fixed expressions on their faces.

'I must say it would've been helpful if Valentine was here,' said Auriol discontentedly. 'After all, he knows these people.'

'Not his fault,' said Judy. 'He wasn't to know we'd make the breakthrough. He's on his way to Gloucestershire now for that party.'

'Well it's not *helpful*,' said the former spy boss, who liked her troops around her when the action was about to happen. 'He'll never get anywhere if he takes his eye off the ball.'

'Auriol, he's a reporter, and a very junior one at that. He's bright but he's too inexperienced in investigations like this to be of real use.'

'He likes to think he is.'

'Well, I suppose you're right. He *has* been a great help. If he hadn't left that note, we shouldn't be where we are now.'

Auriol was keen to get the business over and done with. 'Well, never mind about him,' she said. 'I'll come along.'

'I should have told Topham.'

'Oh,' said Auriol dismissively, 'he'd be no use. I mean, look at him – old and clapped out – and that's just his brain I'm talking about.'

'Sometimes,' said Judy, 'you can be so critical, Auriol. He's a decent chap. In many ways just what the police force needs. Not like those two horrors who trail around after him.'

As if in agreement, the two women rose as one and walked towards the Pavilion Theatre. The doors to the foyer were open and the cleaners were swabbing down the floor. Judy smiled at them and, stepping around their work, made for the management office halfway down the left-hand aisle.

'Geraldine!' she greeted the old soubrette warmly but with an unaccustomed formality. 'Just come to have a word.'

'Not more nonsense about Danny and his Trouble?' chirped Mrs Phipps. 'I never met such a mummy's boy, he's wretched being away from home. I had to give him his lunch yesterday.

He's never had to fend for himself and the way Gavin keeps them locked up in that van, I really think it's too bad. As for that poor boy Boots – heartbroken, he is.'

'No, this isn't about the group. Well, in a manner of speaking it is. Is Gavin around?'

'Cooking up something or another no doubt. I've made him take up residence in one of the dressing rooms, he made such a nuisance of himself in my office.'

'Which one?'

'The one with the star on the door, dear, of course.'

Judy and Auriol followed a cramped corridor down towards the backstage area and the No 1 dressing room. Inside, Gavin Armstrong was thumping away on an old portable typewriter.

'Can you spare a minute, Mr Armstrong? Judy Dimont, *Riviera Express*. This is Miss Hedley.'

'You do me an honour,' said Gavin lazily without looking up from his work. 'But I had your chap Val Whatsit in yesterday. He's got all the latest guff. I'm just writing up a press release now for the national newspapers, but he's got the scoop.'

'I think,' said Judy, sidling round the desk so that he was forced to look up at her, 'that it is I who have the scoop.'

Gavin carried on typing.

'I wonder if you'd mind paying attention for a moment,' said Judy, her tone coming not from the newsroom now but from the quarterdeck, 'I have a few questions to ask.'

The fledgling impresario looked up, startled. He'd become used to being the one issuing the orders. Now he was being told what to do, and by a woman?

'I'm rather busy as you see,' he snapped, but Miss Dimont took no notice.

'Danny and The Urge,' she said. 'How successful are they?'

'If you don't mind me saying so, that's a pretty stupid question.

They're the nation's No 1 beat group. They've had five hit records and they are about to break it big on television. I've got Jack Good, the producer of *Oh Boy!*, coming down here next week with a view to having them as his resident band on his new show starting in the autumn.

'That means they will be beamed into millions and millions of homes every Saturday night, and will become the most famous musicians since, since . . .'

'Are they millionaires yet? The boys?'

Gavin finally wrested his eyes away from the typewriter and focused on the reporter. It was as if he'd only just woken up.

'Millionaires? Whadd'you mean?'

'Have you made them all sufficient money so that when the bubble bursts, they can retire at the age of twenty-one with a nice little nest egg?'

'You obviously don't know this business,' said Gavin patronisingly. 'It takes time and investment to reap the rewards from this caper. Everybody thinks these chaps are driving around in brand-new Rolls-Royces whereas . . .'

'Whereas they're living in a broken-down van in a car park,' said Judy. 'I wouldn't describe that as success.'

'As I say, it takes time and investment . . .'

'Would some of your investment include buying airtime for your group?'

Gavin looked startled. 'I have no idea what you're talking about,' he said slowly. There was a nasty edge to his voice.

'I think the technical term is "payola". You pay disc jockeys to play the records and talk favourably about them, and then you buy the records in bulk from the stores which you know supply their sales figures to the people who compile the best-selling charts.'

'I . . .'

'In other words, you create a climate in which the public feel they've helped create a new star or stars, whereas the truth is they've been manipulated. Hoodwinked. Duped.'

'This is nonsense!' snapped Gavin. 'Those boys are hugely talented. They're hard-working and dedicated. Their records are good and people buy them because they admire them! And now they're going to be household names to people who don't even *listen* to beat music because they'll be on TV on Saturday nights when everybody's watching!'

'You know,' said Miss Dimont, 'I have the feeling that may turn out to be not the case.'

'Jack Good! He's coming down to see them!'

'I wonder how he'll feel about them when he learns you ramped their records into the charts.'

'Who told you this?' Gavin had gone quite white, and rose from his desk. It was only then that he noticed Auriol sitting quietly by the door.

'Valentine *Whatsit*, as you call him, had a chat with Mr Boots after he talked to you yesterday.'

'McGuigan?'

'The very one. You were a little too generous in the way you boasted of your manipulative skills to the boys. Whatever you think of them, they're not complete idiots.'

'That's where you're wrong. Who other than a complete idiot would agree to live in the back of a van for a whole summer? Do their hearing permanent damage by standing next to those deafening amplifiers? Injure their health, probably permanently, with all those pills they take? All so they can be screamed at by a bunch of schoolgirls?'

'I see you have their interests very much at heart,' said Auriol sarcastically.

'They'd be nothing without me – nothing!'

'Where did you get the money to pay off those people? To get the records to the top of the hit parade?' asked Judy.

'I didn't, I keep telling you.'

'Five thousand pounds, I think it was. If I am right you are not rich. Where did it come from?'

The young man looked baffled and frightened at the same time. He reached into a crate on the floor and brought out a beer bottle which he proceeded to wrench open with his bare hands.

'Let me put it like this,' said Judy. 'You and Gus Wetherby were at school together, were you not?'

'What of it?'

'Harrow?'

'That doesn't mean . . .'

'I spent a long time talking to Pernilla Larsson, Gus's mother, the other day. She told me Gus had asked her many weeks ago for a loan of £5,000. She assumed it had something to do with his new invention and handed it over. But that money never went into the Youthenator – after Gus was arrested, she had a look through his papers and saw that when it came into his account it went straight out again. And you, Mr Armstrong, were the beneficiary.'

She went on: 'When Valentine *Whatsit* talked to Mr Boots yesterday, he told him you'd boasted about buying the boys their place in the hit parade. You said that was why they couldn't have any money and had to live in a van – you'd bought them their fame, but at a high price, and they had to earn it out. One more hit record, you kept saying to them, and they'd be in clover.'

'McGuigan's lying. He was about to be fired from the band.'

'Really? Your biggest draw? The one all the girls swoon over? Why would you get rid of him, Mr Armstrong? Because he'd proposed marriage to Faye Addams? Because a married member of the band would destroy its allure in the eyes of the fans? Is *that* why he was about to be fired?'

'I warned him, I warned them all.' Gavin's eyes were flicking from side to side.

'I'll tell you what I think happened. You struck a deal with Gus Wetherby that in return for that loan to buy your way into the hit parade, you'd let your newly famous teen stars endorse his Youthenator. All the fans would want to buy an exciting new piece of machinery which they thought would give them a thrill and at the same time keep them young for ever.'

'You're wrong. You . . .'

'The whole plan came unstuck when Ben Larsson found out Gus was plotting against him and threw him out of the house. Suddenly, he had no money and, just as important, he didn't have access to the workshop. He was high and dry.

'That's when Gus suggested you kill his stepfather, wasn't it? The publicity of his death, particularly in the way he devised it – being killed by his own machine – would draw attention to Gus and his new invention. Your musicians would still endorse it, according to the original plan, and everything would go on as before.

'You'd bamboozled your grandmother Mrs Phipps into giving the band a summer season here at the Pavilion, and you made a fortune out of it – enough to pay back Gus, and to plan a future for yourself once the band lost their popular appeal. Am I right so far?'

'I'm not sticking around here to listen to this complete madness. Where do you get these ideas? You're crazy, both of you – just look at you, a couple of old spinsters with nothing better to do than make up fairy tales. Go out and get yourselves a man! That'd give you something to think about!'

'Don't think about leaving,' said Auriol quietly and commandingly. 'I telephoned Inspector Topham. He's on his way.'

Miss Dimont was relieved to hear it.

'You went up to the Retreat and, while Ben Larsson was having an argument with my editor, you slipped in to the room where Mr Larsson greeted those oddball guests he used to have, where the

Rejuvenator lay on the table. You'd been told by Gavin he always gave a little talk and demonstration to those loopy visitors of his.'

'No.'

'Such are the depths of your cynicism, your plan was that old Larsson would pick up the Rejuvenator and fatally electrocute himself in front of the Lazarus League. At a stroke, you'd have killed Larsson, destroyed the League's faith in him, placed the suspicion of murder on the League themselves, and allowed the *Daily Herald* to crow that finally Ben Larsson had got his just desserts.'

'You're just making this up. You . . .'

Miss Dimont dismissed his denial with a powerful sweep of her hand. 'You got into the Retreat by pretending to be a member of the League and while Lamb was giving them a cup of tea you stole into the reception room and fixed the calibrator on Larsson's machine. You'd be out of the building and back at the Pavilion before he was dead.

'What you couldn't know, but Lamb confirmed to me, is that sometimes Mr Larsson would test out the machine before he admitted his visitors to the room. On this occasion, that's exactly what he did, and so he died alone. How furious you must be that your hideous plan went awry – you may have killed Mr Larsson, but you failed to throw suspicion on the Lazarus League. They never entered the room, as Lamb confirms.'

'I was never there. I . . .'

'You *were* there, Mr Armstrong. Your handsome Mr Boots was standing in the queue and you sent him away with a flea in his ear. If you'd been a bit cleverer, you could have pinned the murder on him when your first plan failed. As it was, your perfect alibi was blown. Meanwhile, Gus Wetherby had established *his* alibi by going into town and buying some aspirins from the chemist. You planned the murder between you, but it was you who committed it.'

Gavin gulped at his beer and said nothing.

'And so we come to Faye Addams.'

'Oh yeah, I suppose I'm to blame for that as well.'

'You are, Mr Wetherby, you are,' said Miss Dimont. 'Your biggest worry was that the magic bubble created by Danny and The Urge would burst if it emerged that Boots McGuigan was engaged to be married. You could fire him, certainly, but the contagion was certain to spread anyway – if he'd secretly got himself hitched, what about all the other members of the band? Did they have secret wives and children? You could see the end was near even though with just a little adjustment, the loss of a single life, this particular golden goose could go on laying a few more golden eggs for a while yet.'

'Rubbish. Complete rubbish!'

'It might well be, but for one thing – the Larssons have a boathouse at the foot of the cliff, do they not? In it they keep the motor tender which used to take old Mr Larsson out to his big yacht in the estuary. My guess is that when you visited Gus in the school holidays, you both used to take it out to race round.

'All such boats have a unique registration number, registered to the nearest port. Mr Larsson's tender is TR536. And when you took the body of poor Faye Addams from wherever you killed her out to the beach at Todhempstead, you borrowed that tender and dumped her on the sand.

'You hoped she'd be washed away by the incoming tide and that the current would sweep her round the headland so nobody would know where she'd come from. If it hadn't been for the eagle eye that morning of a very distinguished fishing captain—' she allowed herself a private smile '—you probably would have got away with it. He didn't recognise you, or your "sleeping" girlfriend, but he did recollect the number of the tender.'

Gavin Armstrong looked numb.

'You killed them both,' said Miss Dimont. 'You did it for

money, but I think you also did it because it gave you a thrill. You like manipulating people, you like manipulating situations. And you . . .'

The door opened.

'OK,' said Inspector Topham stolidly. 'Stand back, please. I'll take it over now.'

TWENTY-SEVEN

The newsroom was almost deserted. The paper had been put to bed and now only the diehards remained, gathered around Miss Dimont's desk. Athene had put in a surprise appearance and was administering, not her special tea, but a divine summer cordial of mint and lemon.

'Just for a change—' she smiled as she handed glasses around '—so cool, so soothing.'

It had indeed been a hot day, and the sun still burned fiercely through the upper-storey windows. The musty smell of old copies of the paper lying on a sun-splashed shelf filled the room with an aroma which was reassuring though not altogether pleasant.

'You're so good, Athene,' said Judy, looking up. 'Always here when we need you. Always such a help.'

'Not always, dear,' said Athene.

'What do you mean?'

'I knew it was him. Gavin whatever his name is. When I stood on the beach that morning he took shape before my eyes – I just didn't know who he was at the time. Now I've seen his photograph, of course . . . but even then I *knew* it was him.'

'We might have been grateful for that insight a little earlier,' said Auriol Hedley, with just a drop of acid.

'Now, now,' Judy warned, 'the way Athene sees things is not

the way the rest of us do. And you *did* help, darling, didn't you, with the business about coming by boat?'

You could tell though that Athene was mortified by what Auriol had said. She didn't answer but went away to refresh the cordial jug while Judy shot her friend a cautionary glance.

'Who we really have to thank,' she began, for her small audience was anxious to hear every detail of the story, 'is dear Valentine.'

'Shame he isn't here,' said Betty Featherstone comfortably, but you could tell she didn't mean it, she was thrilled to be occupying her old desk.

'I must say,' said Judy in a not entirely friendly fashion, 'you managed to get back quick-smart from Newton Abbot.' Instead of the untroubled features of her blond-haired baronet, she would now have to put up with the sight of Betty applying nail polish to the runs in her stockings.

'When duty calls,' replied Betty airily. 'Meanwhile, you'd better have this.' She passed across the desk an unsealed envelope. 'He left it in the drawer.'

'Last will and testament,' joked someone, but nobody laughed.

Truth to tell, they were all shocked by Valentine's sudden disappearance.

'He'll be back, won't he?' asked Auriol.

'I don't think so,' said Judy slowly, as if discovering the truth only as she spoke. 'I think he got in that bubble car of his and decided to disappear out of our lives. I saw something in his eye just as he was leaving. He didn't really want to look at me, just told me he'd left a note.'

'Which brought the whole story together,' said Auriol.

'Yes. It did.' The others were listening and she felt she owed them some explanation.

'Valentine is a clever young man,' she began. 'He's been here only a short time and seems to have learnt so much – I don't mean about journalism, I mean about the real art of getting to the bottom of a story. When he went off to see Gavin Armstrong he had no idea he'd end up getting the key piece of information to both murders in a chance aside from that bass player, Boots McGuigan.'

'Boots,' said Athene, her ethereal voice lifting as she poured more cordial. 'Such an unusual name! Conjuring up a lifetime of tramping up, up, up a long hard road, striving to reach the end of his journey, soldiering on to . . .'

'The chemist,' chimed Judy and Auriol in unison. Athene eyed them both uncomprehendingly, and then the penny dropped. She looked crestfallen.

'Mr Boots told Valentine he'd gone up to Ransome's Retreat to wreak some kind of revenge on Ben Larsson for the death of his mother. Gavin caught him up there when he should have been rehearsing with the rest of the band and sent him back down to the Pavilion with a flea in his ear. Gavin then slid into Ransome's Retreat along with those Lazarus League lot – but Valentine rightly sensed there was something more to it than that.

'Valentine's note to me of that meeting put everything else into place – Gavin had said to Boots that he had been at school with Gus, and so assumed he was going up to the Retreat to see his old chum – they were supposed to be doing some deal on the Youthenator together.'

Athene had curled her legs round the office chair and was hugging her teacup. She loved these explanations, even if she couldn't quite follow every detail.

'But at the time Gus wasn't up at the Retreat – he'd gone to town to the chemist to buy some aspirin. Made a bit of a fuss, not too much, about having severe headache – the perfect alibi.'

'So how come Topham arrested him anyway?' asked Peter Pomeroy.

'It took time for Gus's alibi to stand up. When Topham's men went down the town to check it out they found the pharmacist had taken a few days off for a walking holiday. It was the devil's own job to track him down and confirm it – but by then I'd pieced together the rest of the story, and Gavin's connection to Gus was established beyond doubt.'

'Astonishing,' said Peter.

'But we couldn't have done it without Valentine. He recalled that Boots had told him the only way he could hang on to Faye was to propose marriage, but also that Gavin would stick at nothing to make sure the band's bachelor status remained intact.'

'Despicable, both of them,' said Auriol. 'But then that's Harrow for you.'

'Yes. Gus was arrogant, and thought he could do even better than his stepfather at bamboozling money out of a gullible public. But it's Gavin who's the evil one – when I mentioned Faye's murder to him his attitude was, "what's the fuss, she's only a piece of fluff". He seemed to enjoy the fact that I was shocked.'

'So both of them are charged with murder?' asked Peter Pomeroy.

'They would have to be – doesn't matter who did it. They both conspired to kill Larsson, even though it was only Gavin who killed Faye.'

'How?' It took Athene to ask the really important questions.

'Gavin sent a telegram to Faye, though apparently from Boots, suggesting they meet in the boathouse at Ransome's Retreat. That wouldn't have struck her as unusual because they had to keep their engagement secret. Once she got there, he killed her with a heavy spanner. No question, he's got the taste for killing.'

'Just appalling,' said Peter, shaking his head.

'At least the veil of suspicion has been lifted from your revered editor,' said Auriol, nodding towards the far end of the newsroom.

'He's such an idiot,' said Judy. 'Got himself into a complete tangle over nothing. Made himself into a murder suspect the moment we bumped into him up at the Retreat – all that obsessive secrecy and his pathological hatred of sharing confidences! Then he compounded it all by withholding Faye Addams' identity when he should have told his reporters the moment he learnt her name.'

'But what a decent sort he turns out to be!' said Auriol. 'And very interesting what Mrs Larsson had to say about her husband's part in Operation Tailcoat – "Your Mr Rhys took the blame for those dead agents and has lived with the shame of it all these years – when all along he knew it was Larsson who lost those lives, not him."'

'He knew, and the Admiral knew. That was enough for him.'

'Ah, the Admiral,' laughed Auriol. 'That distant cousin of the well-connected Sir Waterford!'

'Why did he resign?' asked Betty, who was not altogether following the thread of this conversation, '…that sweet boy?'

'Personal reasons,' said Judy.

'Care to share?' said Auriol.

'Tell you later.'

'All the good ones leave,' said John Ross, who'd strolled over from Curse Corner. 'Too talented for this place.'

'Valentine? That's not what you said to him the other day.'

'Aye, well.'

Betty was busy now inspecting her split ends. 'What was in that envelope I gave you?'

'Valentine's obituary,' said Judy sombrely.

'Aye,' said John Ross, nodding appreciatively. 'His first assignment. Any good?'

'Read it if you want,' said Judy, and took off her glasses. Athene shot her a glance and saw her friend was close to tears.

'*The death has occurred of Valentine Ford, junior reporter on the* Riviera Express,' he read. '*He was twenty-three. After National Service in the Army he joined the* Express *in June this year and . . .*'

Athene stood very still, the cordial jug poised in her hand. Her face had gone white and the jug trembled slightly. Whatever it was she had seen, and it was clear she'd seen something, Miss Dimont did not want to hear it.

'Come on, Auriol, let's go,' she said very quietly. 'And quick about it.'

*

The stillness and calm which greeted the two women as they walked into the Chinese Singing Teacher made Miss Dimont feel stronger. Mr So greeted them gravely and bowed them to a table.

'I never knew about this place,' said Auriol. 'How strange it is!'

'It was Athene who introduced me,' said Judy, 'and at times of stress and upset it is the best place in Temple Regis to be. Your own establishment notwithstanding,' she added hastily.

Auriol peered round her but seemed unimpressed. It was not a place that suited everybody.

'So glad to have you to myself,' said Judy. 'I am feeling less than my usual robust self, as you can see.'

'Valentine?'

'Yes.'

'You're worried about him in that death trap of a car.'

'Don't say that!'

'When they started reading out that obituary and Athene looked as though she was going to faint . . . you don't think, do you, that . . . ?'

'I have no idea,' said Miss Dimont wearily. 'Having him around was like having a puppy – you're constantly on the alert that they're going to do something fatal.'

'He survived two years of National Service.'

'Real life is different.'

They looked around the room. It was quite full for a change. 'Why did he go?'

'In his letter, the one he left on my typewriter, he not only wrote a brilliant resumé of the Larsson and Addams cases, but also pointed the way to their solution. Of course he isn't sufficiently experienced to see his way to the whole story but, Auriol, he's a natural. Quick, sharp, doesn't take no for an answer, and – he *thinks*.'

'Well,' said Auriol, 'not such a pest after all.'

'No,' sighed Judy, 'not such a pest. A worry but not a pest.'

'He loves you.'

'Just a phase he's going through. I could have loved him too, but not the way he would like.'

'The sea captain.'

'Perhaps, perhaps not. In his note Valentine did tell me he loved me, and that was the reason for his resignation. He said he couldn't sit and look at me all day and not do something about it. So he went to see Richard Rhys and told him he'd inherited a sizeable estate and had to go off and look after it.'

'Has he?'

'Doubt it. The Waterfords may be many but they're no longer rich. My guess is he'll try to make it in Fleet Street – he has, naturally enough for a Waterford, a distant relation who might be able to help.'

'That was a short apprenticeship.'

'Some don't need anything more than being shown the ropes. He didn't have to hang around here and I'm relieved for his sake he's gone. You know, more than anything he reminded me of Eric – brave, headstrong, ready to set off on a mission with no regard for personal safety. It made me love him in a special way, a way really very difficult to define.'

'I see your point,' said Auriol, 'and yes, he reminded me of Eric as well. You couldn't say foolhardy, you couldn't say headstrong, but something like that. He was rather beautiful though, wasn't he?'

'It's what's inside, Auriol, though I must admit my eyes did not ache when I sat opposite him.'

'But that bubble car. The three-hour race up to Gloucestershire for a party . . . he's reckless!'

'Who knows?' said Judy. 'I hope he goes on for ever, but I have the feeling he won't last long.'

'Like Eric.'

'Yes.' Both stopped speaking for a moment.

Just then Mr So approached their table and gently laid the tea things before them.

'So what about our Rusty Rhys?' asked Auriol, swift to change the subject. 'Is it time for him to go? I think this business has rattled him, and he's never really been comfortable in that editor's chair. Don't you think you should have a go – as editor, I mean?'

'Not while he's still there. Apart from anything else, I'm still having too much fun as a reporter. Just think, Auriol, when I get into the office tomorrow, I'm going to be writing a story about a manhole cover that's gone missing in Fore Street!'

'That's the sort of thing Rusty likes.'

'He'll make it Page One! No, Auriol, I love it. Those Sisters of Reason – we haven't got to the bottom of them yet, I have the feeling they'll be back causing more trouble. Just think of the fun biffing old Ursula Guedella and that soppy handmaiden of hers Angela de Mauny!'

'Since we're on the topic of frightening women, have you written to your mother yet?' Auriol could be like a scolding older sister sometimes.

'Oh . . . do *stop* it!'

'You know what'll happen if you don't.'

'She keeps threatening. Meantime, I've got Uncle Arthur coming to stay.'

'What a treat! I adore him!'

And so the two friends companionably ended the day.

Or would have done, if the door to the Chinese Singing Teacher had not urgently clanged open to reveal a panting figure with a camera slung around his neck.

'Good Lord!' said Miss Dimont, starting out of her chair. 'Terry!'

The photographer looked at her, his eyes trying to focus in the sombre half-light.

'Trouble, Judy,' he panted. 'Big trouble!

'You'd better come . . .'

THE END...

(... until next time!)

Missing Temple Regis already?
Turn the page for an exclusive extract from

THE RIVIERA EXPRESS
Out now

And look out for the next in the series

A QUARTER PAST DEAD
Murder can strike at any hour...

Coming November 2018

ONE

When Miss Dimont smiled, which she did a lot, she was beautiful. There was something mystical about the arrangement of her face-furniture – the grey eyes, the broad forehead, the thin lips wide spread, her dainty perfect teeth. In that smile was a *joie de vivre* which encouraged people to believe that good must be just around the corner.

But there were two faces to Miss Dimont. When hunched over her typewriter, rattling out the latest episode of life in Temple Regis, she seemed not so sunny. Her corkscrew hair fell out of its makeshift pinnings, her glasses slipped down the convex nose, those self-same lips pinched themselves into a tight little knot and a general air of mild chaos and discontent emanated like puffs of smoke from her desk.

Life on the *Riviera Express* was no party. The newspaper's offices, situated at the bottom of the hill next door to the brewery, maintained their dreary pre-war combination of uprightness and formality. The front hall, the only area of access permitted to townsfolk, spoke with its oak panelling and heavy desks of decorum, gentility, continuity.

But the most momentous events in Temple Regis in 1958 – its births, marriages and deaths, its council ordinances, its police court and its occasional encounters with celebrity – were channelled through a less august set of rooms, inadequately lit and peopled by journalism's flotsam and jetsam, up a back corridor and far from the public gaze.

Lately there'd been a number of black-and-white 'B' features at the Picturedrome, but these always portrayed the heady excitements of Fleet Street. Behind the green baize door, beyond the stout oak panelling, the making of this particular local journal was decidedly less ritzy.

Far from Miss Dimont lifting an ivory telephone to her ear while partaking of a genteel breakfast in her silk-sheeted bed, the real-life reporter started her day with an apple and 'The Calls' – humdrum visits to Temple's police station, its council offices, fire station, and sundry other sources of bread-and-butter material whose everyday occurrences would, next Friday, fill the heart of the *Express*.

Like a laden beachcomber she would return mid-morning to her desk to write up her gleanings before leaving for the Magistrates' Court, where the bulk of her work, from that bottomless well of human misdeeds and misfortunes, daily bubbled up.

After luncheon, usually taken alone with her crossword in the Signal Box Café, she would return briefly to court before preparing for an evening meeting of the Town Council, the Townswomen's Guild, or – light relief – a performance by the Temple Regis Amateur Operatic Society.

Then it would be home on her moped, corkscrew hair blowing in the wind, to Mulligatawny, whose sleek head would be staring out of the mullioned window awaiting his supper and her pithy account of the day's events.

Miss Dimont, now unaccountably beyond the age of forty, had the fastest shorthand note in the West Country. In addition, she could charm the birds out of the trees when she chose – her capacity to get people to talk about themselves, it was said, could make even the dead speak. She was shy but she was shrewd; and if perhaps she was comfortably proportioned she was, everyone agreed, quite lovely.

Why Betty Featherstone, her so-called friend, got the front-page stories and Miss Dimont did not was lost in the mists of time. Suffice to say that on press day, when everyone's temper shortened, it was Judy who got it in the neck from her editor. Betty wrote what he wanted, while Judy wrote the truth – and it did not always make comfortable reading. She didn't mind the fusillades aimed in her direction for having overturned a civic reputation or two, for ever since she had known him, and it had been a long time, Rudyard Rhys had lacked consistency. Furthermore, his ancient socks smelt. Miss Dimont rose above.

Unquestionably Devon's prettiest town, Temple Regis took itself very seriously. Its beaches, giving out on to the turquoise and indigo waters which inspired some wily publicist to coin the phrase 'England's Riviera', were white and pristine. Broad lawns encircling the bandstand and flowing down towards the pier were scrupulously shaved, immaculately edged. Out in the estuary, the water was an impossible shade of aquamarine, its colour a magical invention of the gods – and since everyone in Temple agreed their little town was the sunniest spot in England, it really was very beautiful.

It was far too nice a place to be murdered.

*

Confusingly, the *Riviera Express* was both newspaper and railway train. Which came first was occasionally the cause for heated debate down in the snug of the Cap'n Fortescue, but the laws of copyright had not yet been invented when the two rivals were born; and an ambitious rail company serving the dreams of holidaymakers heading for the South West was certainly not giving way to a tinpot local rag when it came to claiming the title. Similarly, with a rock-solid local readership and a justifiable claim to both 'Riviera' and 'Express' – a popular newspaper title – the weekly journal snootily tolerated its more famous namesake. If neither would admit it, each benefited from the other's existence.

Before the war successive editors lived in constant turmoil, sometimes printing glowing lists of the visitors from another world who spilled from the brown and cream liveried railway carriages ('The Hon. Mrs Gerald Legge and her mother, the novelist Barbara Cartland, are here for the week'). At other times, Princess Margaret Rose herself could have puffed into town and the old codgers would have ignored it. Rudyard Rhys saw both points of view so there was no telling what he would think one week to the next – to greet the afternoon arrival? Or not to bother?

'Mr Rhys, we could go to meet the 4.30,' warned his chief reporter on this particular Tuesday. 'But – also – there's a cycling-without-lights case in court which could turn nasty. The curate from St Margaret's. He told me he's going to challenge his prosecution on the grounds that British Summer Time has no substantive legal basis. It could be very interesting.'

'Rrrr.'

'Don't you see? The Chairman of the Bench is one of his parishioners! Sure to be an almighty dust-up!'

'Rrrr . . . rrr.'

'A clash between the Church and the Law, Mr Rhys! We haven't had one of those for a while!'

Rudyard Rhys lit his pipe. An unpleasant smell filled the room. Miss Dimont stepped back but otherwise held her ground. She was all too familiar with this fence-sitting by her editor.

'Bit of a waste going to meet the 4.30,' she persisted. 'There's only Gerald Hennessy on board . . .' (and an encounter with a garrulous, prosy, self-obsessed matinée idol might make me late for my choir practice, she might have added).

'Hennessy?' The editor put down his pipe with a clunk. 'Now *that's* news!'

'Oh?' snipped Miss Dimont. 'You said you hated *The Conqueror and the Conquered*. "Not very manly for a VC", I think were your words. You objected to the length of his hair.'

'Rrrr.'

'Even though he had been lost in the Burmese jungle for three years.'

Mr Rhys performed his usual backflip. 'Hennessy,' he ordered.

It was enough. Miss Dimont noted that, once again, the editor had deserted his journalistic principles in favour of celebrity worship. Rhys enjoyed the perquisite accorded him by the Picturedrome of two back stalls seats each week. He had actually enjoyed *The Conqueror and the Conquered* so much he sat through it twice.

Miss Dimont did not know this, but anyone who had played as many square-jawed warriors as Gerald Hennessy was always likely to find space in the pages of the *Riviera Express*. Something about heroism by association, she had noted in the past, was at the root of her editor's lofty decisions. That all went back to the War, of course.

'Four-thirty it is, then,' she said a trifle bitterly. 'But *Church* v. *Law* – now there's a story that might have been followed up by the nationals,' and with that she swept out, notebook flapping from her raffia bag.

This parting shot was a reference to the long-standing feud between the editor and his senior reporter. After all, Rudyard Rhys had made the wrong call on not only the Hamilton Biscuit Case, but the Vicar's Longboat Party, the Temple Regis Tennis Scandal and the Football Pools Farrago. Each of these exclusives from the pen of Judy Dimont had been picked up by the repulsive

Arthur Shrimsley, an out-to-grass former Fleet Street type who made a killing by selling them on to the national papers, at the same time showing up the *Riviera Express* for the newspaper it was – hesitant, and slow to spot its own scoops when it had them.

On each occasion the editor's decision had been final – and wrong. But Judy was no saint either, and the cat's cradle of complaint triggered by her coverage of the Regis Conservative Ball last winter still made for a chuckle or two in the sub-editors' room on wet Thursday afternoons.

With her raffia bag swinging furiously, she stalked out to the car park, for Judy Dimont was resolute in almost everything she did, and her walk was merely the outer manifestation of that doughty inner being – a purposeful march which sent out radar-like warnings to flag-day sellers, tin-can rattlers, and other such supplicants and cleared her path as if by miracle. It was not manly, for Miss Dimont was nothing if not feminine, but it was no-nonsense.

She took no nonsense, either, from Herbert, her trusty moped, who sat expectantly, awaiting her arrival. With one cough, Herbert was kicked into life and the magnificent Miss Dimont flew away towards Temple Regis railway station, corkscrew hair flapping in the wind, a happy smile upon her lips. For there was nothing she liked more than to go in search of new adventures – whether they were to be found in the Magistrates' Court, the Horticultural Society, or the railway station.

Her favourite route took in Tuppenny Row, the elegant terrace of Regency cottages whose brickwork had turned a pale pink with the passage of time, bleached by Temple Regis sun and washed by its soft rains. She turned into Cable Street, then came down the long run to the station, whose yellow-and-chocolate bargeboard frontage you could glimpse from the top of the hill, and Miss Dimont, with practice born of long experience, started her descent just as the sooty, steamy clouds of vapour from the

Riviera Express slowed in preparation for its arrival at Regis Junction.

She had done her homework on Gerald Hennessy and, despite her misgivings about missing the choir practice, she was looking forward to their encounter, for Miss Dimont was far from immune to the charms of the opposite sex. Since the War, Hennessy had become the perfect English hero in the nation's collective imagination – square-jawed, crinkle-eyed, wavy-haired and fair. He spoke so nicely when asked to deliver his lines, and there was always about him an air of amused self-deprecation which made the nation's mothers wish him for their daughters, if not secretly for themselves.

Miss Dimont brought Herbert to a halt, his final splutter of complaint lost in the clanking, wheezing riot of sooty chaos which signals the arrival of every self-regarding Pullman Express. Across the station courtyard she spotted Terry Eagleton, the *Express*'s photographer, and made towards him as she pulled the purple gloves from her hands.

'Anyone apart from Hennessy?'

'Just 'im, Miss Dim.'

'I've told you before, call me Judy,' she said stuffily. The dreaded nickname had been born out of an angry tussle with Rudyard Rhys, long ago, over a front-page story which had gone wrong. Somehow it stuck, and the editor took a fiendish delight in roaring it out in times of stress. Bad enough having to put up with it from him – though invariably she rose above – but no need to be cheeked by this impertinent snapper. She had mixed feelings about Terry Eagleton.

'Call me Judy,' she repeated sternly, and got out her notebook.

'Ain't your handle, anyways,' parried Terry swiftly, and he was right – for Miss Dimont had a far more euphonious name, one she kept very quiet and for a number of good reasons.

Terry busily shifted his camera bag from one shoulder to the other. Employed by his newspaper as a trained observer, he could see before him a bespectacled woman of a certain age – heading towards fifty, surely – raffia bag slung over one shoulder, notebook flapping out of its top, with a distinctly harassed air and a permanently peppery riposte. Though she was much loved by all who knew her, Terry sometimes found it difficult to see why. It made him sigh for Doreen, the sweet young blonde newly employed on the front desk, who had difficulty remembering people's names but was indeed an adornment to life.

Miss Dimont led the way on to Platform 1.

'Pics first,' said Terry.

'No, Terry,' countered Miss Dim. 'You take so long there's never time left for the interview.'

'Picture's worth a thousand words, they always say. How many words are you goin' to write – *two hundred*?'

The same old story. In Fleet Street, always the old battle between monkeys and blunts, and even here in sweetest Devon the same old manoeuvring based on jealousy, rivalry and the belief that pictures counted more than words or, conversely, words enhanced pictures and gave them the meaning and substance they otherwise lacked.

And so this warring pair went to work, arriving on the platform just as the doors started to swing open and the holidaymakers began to alight. It was always a joyous moment, thought Miss Dimont, this happy release from confinement into sunshine, the promise of uncountable pleasures ahead. A small girl raced past, her face a picture of joy, pigtails given an extra bounce by the skip in her step.

The routine on these occasions was always the same – if a single celebrity was to be interviewed, he or she would be ushered into the first-class waiting room in order to be relieved of their innermost secrets. If more than one, the likeliest candidate would be pushed in by Terry, while Judy quickly handed the others her card, enquiring discreetly where they were staying and arranging a suitable time for their interrogation.

This manoeuvring took some skill and required a deftness of touch in which Miss Dimont excelled. On a day like today, no such juggling was required – just an invitation to old Gerald to step inside for a moment and explain away his presence in Devon's prettiest town.

The late holiday crowds swiftly dispersed, the guard completed the task of unloading from his van the precious goods entrusted to his care – a basket of somnolent homing pigeons, another of chicks tweeting furiously, the usual assortment of brown paper parcels. Then the engine driver climbed aboard to prepare for his next destination, Exbridge.

A moment of stillness descended. A blackbird sang. Dust settled in gentle folds and the reporter and photographer looked at each other.

'No ruddy Hennessy,' said Terry Eagleton.

Miss Dimont screwed up her pretty features into a scowl. In her mind was the lost scoop of *Church* v. *Law*, the clerical challenge to the authority of the redoubtable Mrs Marchbank. The uncomfortable explanation to Rudyard Rhys of how she had missed not one, but two stories in an afternoon – and with press day only two days away.

Mr Rhys was unforgiving about such things.

Just then, a shout was heard from the other end of Platform 1 up by the first-class carriages. A porter was waving his hands. Inarticulate shouts spewed forth from his shaking face. He appeared, for a moment, to be running on the spot. It was as if a small tornado had descended and hit the platform where he stood.

Terry had it in an instant. Without a word he launched himself down the platform, past the bewildered guard, racing towards the porter. The urgency with which he took off sprang in Miss

Dimont an inner terror and the certain knowledge that she must run too – run like the wind . . .

By the time she reached the other end of the platform Terry was already on board. She could see him racing through the first-class corridor, checking each compartment, moving swiftly on. As fast as she could, she followed alongside him on the platform.

They reached the last compartment almost simultaneously, but Terry was a pace or two ahead of Judy. There, perfectly composed, immaculately clad in country tweeds, his oxblood brogues twinkling in the sunlight, sat their interviewee, Gerald Hennessy.

You did not have to be an expert to know he was dead.

ONE PLACE. MANY STORIES

Bold, innovative and
empowering publishing.

FOLLOW US ON:

@HQStories